PRAISE FOR KELLEY ARMSTRONG

"Armstrong is a talented and evocative writer who knows well how to balance the elements of good, suspenseful fiction, and her stories evoke poignancy, action, humor and suspense."
The Globe and Mail

"[A] master of crime thrillers."
Kirkus

"Kelley Armstrong is one of the purest storytellers Canada has produced in a long while."
National Post

"Armstrong is a talented and original writer whose inventiveness and sense of the bizarre is arresting."
London Free Press

"Kelley Armstrong has long been a favorite of mine."
Charlaine Harris

"Armstrong's name is synonymous with great storytelling."
Suspense Magazine

"Like Stephen King, who manages an under-the-covers, flashlight-in-face kind of storytelling without sounding ridiculous, Armstrong not only writes interesting page-turners, she has also achieved that unlikely goal, what all writers strive for: a genre of her own."
The Walrus

ALSO BY KELLEY ARMSTRONG

Rockton thriller series
City of the Lost
A Darkness Absolute
This Fallen Prey
Watcher in the Woods
Alone in the Wild
A Stranger in Town

Standalone Thrillers
Wherever She Goes
Every Step She Takes

Past Series
Cainsville paranormal mystery series
Otherworld urban fantasy series
Nadia Stafford mystery trilogy

Young Adult
Aftermath
Missing
The Masked Truth
Darkest Powers paranormal trilogy
Darkness Rising paranormal trilogy
Age of Legends fantasy trilogy

Middle-Grade
A Royal Guide to Monster Slaying fantasy series
The Blackwell Pages trilogy (with Melissa Marr)

A STITCH IN TIME

KELLEY ARMSTRONG

Cover Design by Cover Couture www.bookcovercouture.com

Photo (c) Shutterstock/ASC Photography
Photo (c) Shutterstock/Irina Alexandrovna
Photo (c) Depositphotos/romansl
Photo (c) Depositphotos/tolokonov
Photo (c) Depositphotos/Avella2011

ISBN-13 (print): 978-1-989046-21-0
ISBN-13 (ebook): 978-1-989046-20-3

ACKNOWLEDGMENTS

A Stitch in Time is a departure from my usual fare, which means I have a host of people I need to thank, both for encouraging me to write it and for helping get it into shape.

In 2018, I sat in on Jennifer Barnes's *Writing for Your ID* workshop. I've known Jen for years, and I love how she delves into the psychology of fiction. This particular workshop encouraged authors to embrace the story they most want to write. That got me thinking of an idea that had been at the back of my mind for years.

After Jen's workshop, I half-jokingly mentioned on Twitter that I'd like to write a time-travel-Victorian-haunted-house-mystery-romance. I expected nothing more than a few laughs from followers. Instead, the response was huge and overwhelmingly encouraging.

So, thank you to Jennifer Barnes, for giving me the first nudge with her workshop, and thank you to my online followers for turning that nudge into a shove.

With something this different, I knew I needed editorial help. Lots of it. Here my thanks goes to Melissa Marr, who read multiple drafts as I endlessly tinkered with the plot. Thanks, too, to my daughter Julia, who listened to all my revision ideas and helped me work them through.

Thanks to Yanni Kuznia and everyone at Subterranean Press for publishing the hardcover version. We've worked together for years, but this is the first time I've come to you with an original (non-series) project, and I appreciate how open you were to a new direction.

Finally, thanks to my freelance copyeditor, Margaret Morris. You've been working with me for years, Maggie, on projects where I didn't do acknowledgements pages so I never properly thanked you. You always do amazing work, but you went above and beyond with this book, and I am so grateful for your help.

If you're a reader picking this one up, thanks to you too, for giving it a try.

Six months ago, I inherited a haunted house. I also inherited the ghosts that go with it. Or that's what Aunt Judith said to me in her final letter, smelling of her tea-rose hand cream, the scent uncorking a fresh spate of ugly crying. But I understand what she meant. Not that the house is haunted, but that it haunts *me*. If I can wave burning sage and tell myself I've put the spirits to rest, then I should. What happened there twenty-three years ago does indeed haunt me.

It's time for me to face that, and so I'm heading to Yorkshire, where I'll spend the summer ostensibly on sabbatical in my great-aunt's country house while I decide what to do with it. What I really want, though, is answers.

☙❧

As my taxi rolls through the Yorkshire countryside, I tick off the landmarks, as if I'm a child again, plastered to the window of our rental car as we make our way to Thorne Manor. Outside Leeds, I saw changes—houses where I remembered fields, shopping centers where there'd been forest—but as we roll into the moors, we seem to slip back in time to my childhood, every tiny church and stone sheepfold and crumbling barn exactly as I remember it.

The last time I came this way, I'd been fifteen, a girl just starting her life. Now, I return at thirty-eight, a history professor at the University of Toronto. A widow, too, my husband—Michael—gone eight years.

We drive through High Thornesbury itself, a picture-perfect village nestled in a dale. As we start up the one-lane road, the cabbie has to stop to let sheep pass. Then he begins the treacherous climb up the steep hill. At the top stands Thorne Manor, and my heart trips as I roll down the window to see it better.

The house appears abandoned. It is, in its way. Aunt Judith rarely visited after Uncle Stan died here all those years ago. Yet from the foot of the hill, Thorne Manor has always looked abandoned. A foreboding stone slab of a house, isolated and desolate, surrounded by an endless expanse of empty moor.

As the taxi crunches up the hill, the house comes into focus, dark windows staring like empty eyes. No light shines from windows or illuminates the long lane or even peeps from the old stone stables. I push back a niggle of disappointment. The caretaker knows I'm coming, and yes, I'd hoped to see the house ablaze in welcoming light, but this is more fitting—Thorne Manor as a starkly beautiful shadow, backlit by an achingly gorgeous inky purple sunset.

The driver pulls into the lane and surveys the lawn, a veritable weed garden of clover and speedwell.

"Are you sure this is t' place, lass?" he asks, his rural Yorkshire accent thick as porridge.

"I am, thank you."

The frown-line between his bushy brows deepens to a fissure. He grips the seat back with a gnarled hand as he twists to look at me. "You didn't rent it from one of those online things, did you? I fear you've been played a nasty trick."

"I inherited it recently from my great-aunt, and there's a caretaker who knows I'm coming."

I hand him the fare with a heftier tip than I can afford. He scowls, as if I'm offering blood money for his participation in a heinous act against innocent female tourists.

"That caretaker should be here to greet you properly."

"I already texted," I say. "She'll be here soon."

"Then, I'll wait."

He turns off the diesel engine, takes exactly the fare from my hand and settles in with a set of his jaw that warns against argument. When I say that I'm stepping out to stretch my legs, he mutters, "Don't go far. Nowt out here but sheep and serial killers." And then he peers around, as if one of each hides behind every jutting rock.

I close the car door and drink in the smell of wild bluebells. As I walk toward the house, I catch a sound on the breeze. A rhythmic *squeak-squeak*, each iteration shivering up my spine.

A figure labors up the hill on an ancient bicycle, the chain protesting. Atop it sits a black-clad figure, long coat snapping in the wind, the hood pulled up, face dark except for a glowing red circle where the mouth should be.

Squeak-squeak.

Squeak-squeak.

The figure turns into the laneway, and the cab driver gets out, slamming the door hard enough that I jump.

"I thought you said the caretaker was a woman," he says.

I see now that the bicycle rider is a man with a lit pipe clamped between his teeth. He wears a macintosh draped over the back of the bike, the hem dancing precariously close to the rear wheel. Under his hood is a round, deeply lined clean-shaven face and bristle-short gray hair.

"Miss Dale?" The rider's voice . . . is not the voice of a *he*. I look again, and in that second glance, I'm far less certain of gender.

"Ms. Crossley?" I say, sloshing my pronunciation of the title, in hopes it could go either way.

"Aye." She eyes me with a sharp gaze. "You were expectin' someone else?"

"No. Just making sure. We've never met."

As I say that, moonlight illuminates her face, and I hesitate.

"*Have* we met?" I say. "You look . . . familiar."

"I've been takin' care of t' place twenty years now. Never seen you visit, though."

There's accusation in those words. I say, evenly, "Yes, I used to come out as a child, but after my uncle's death, I only visited Aunt Judith in London." I turn to the driver. "Thank you very much for staying with me. It wasn't necessary, but I appreciated the company."

Delores Crossley looks at him, her arms folded. When he doesn't move fast enough, she shoos him with one leathery hand. "That was the lass bein' polite. Get gone. She's not askin' you in t' tea. Or owt else you might'a been hoping for."

He straightens, affronted. "I was keeping an eye on her—"

"I'm sure you were. And now you can keep your eyes t' yourself. Go on. Git."

The driver stalks back to the car as I call another sincere thank-you. He ignores it, and the taxi peels out in a spray of gravel.

I say nothing. Translating Delores's North Yorkshire accent is taking all my brain energy right now. At least she isn't using "thees" and "thous" as you sometimes find with locals her age. Dad says, when I was four, I came back from our summer trip talking like an eighty-year-old North Yorkshire native, and my junior kindergarten teacher feared I'd suffered a brain injury, my speech garbled beyond comprehension.

The more Delores talks, though, the faster my internal translator works, and soon my brain is making the appropriate substitutions and smoothing out her accent.

After the taxi leaves, she turns to me. "So, you're staying."

"For the summer, yes. As I said in my e-mail."

"I hope you didn't buy a return ticket just yet, 'cos I have a feeling you'll be needing it sooner than you expect."

I meet her gaze. She only locks it and says nothing.

"I'll be fine," I say firmly.

With two brisk taps of her pipe against an ivy-laced urn, she sets the pipe on the edge and stalks inside.

I drag my suitcase through. The smell of tea wafts past, the distinctive Yorkshire blend I haven't drunk in so many years. I pause, and I swear I hear my father's "Hullo!" echo through the hallway and Aunt Judith calling from the kitchen, where she'll emerge with a tea tray, pot steaming, having calculated our arrival to the minute.

Grief seizes me, and I have to push myself past the grand entranceway. To my right, footsteps echo, and lights flick on, and I follow the trail of illumination into the sitting room. The sweet scent of tea roses wafts over me, as if it's engrained in the wood itself. The last time I saw this room, it was mid-century modern. Now, it's cottage chic, in cream and beige with pink accents. A striped couch begs me to sink into its deep cushions, as does a massive wooden armchair buried under pillows and blankets. Books are artlessly strewn over a rough wooden coffee table.

Aunt Judith also painted the woodwork, and I try not to cringe at that. When Michael and I married fresh out of college, we'd rented a house for which the term *fixer-upper* would be a compliment. A crash course in home renovation turned into a shared passion I haven't indulged since his death. Now, I imagine stripping that paint and refinishing scratched wooden floors, and a long-buried thrill runs through me.

"Miss Dale," Delores calls from the next room.

"Bronwyn, please," I say as I follow her voice into the kitchen.

At one time, cooking would have been done outside the house —in a courtyard kitchen. The modern version would have been more of a service area. It's compact but pretty with painted wood cupboards and a smaller refrigerator than I have in my condo. A good quarter of the space is dedicated to the AGA stove, already lit, warming the tiny room enough that I peel off my sweater. The faint smell of oil wafts from the stove, the scent as familiar as the

Yorkshire tea I smell here, too, an open box on the counter, as if Delores drank it while preparing the house.

"Got a few groceries in the cupboard. Fresh scones and a loaf of bread, too. My wife baked them." Her gaze lifts to mine, defiant now, waiting for a reaction.

"Please thank her for me."

A grunt, and she waves at the AGA stove. "You know how to work that?"

"I do."

"You'll need to do a proper shopping. Don't know how you'll manage ba'ht a car."

Ba'ht. It takes me a moment to access my rusty North Yorkshire dictionary, substitute "without" for "ba'ht" and realize she's commenting on my lack of a vehicle.

"My aunt's will said my uncle's car was still in the garage?"

A bark of a laugh. "You couldn't get that mouse motel running down a steep hill, lass. You'll need to get sowt else. I can't be running you around. You saw my mode of transportation. I'm not giving you a croggy."

I smile. "I don't think I'd fit on the handlebars anymore. I'll be fine. I won't need anything more now that I'm here."

"Nah, now that you're here, I can fix that mullock of a yard. Been wanting to for years, but your aunt insisted it wasn't worth the effort. Her will pays me five years of wages, so I'll be fixing up the property."

She circles through the dining room, a small office and then the formal parlor. The last stands empty.

"Your aunt had me sell the furniture. She asked me to put it in the town shop and use the dosh for the upkeep. I have her letter, if you want to see it."

"I don't need that. Thank you."

While I hate the thought of Aunt Judith selling furniture, I'm not surprised. Thorne Manor had been her one luxury, passed down from her grandfather, whose first wife had been a Thorne. The fact that she passed it on to me is both an honor and a responsibility, one that makes my heart ache and tremble at the same time.

I follow Delores up the wide, grand staircase. My hand slides over the wood railing, worn gray and silk-smooth with age, and at the feel of it, I remember all the times I stepped through the front door, dropped my bag and raced straight upstairs as my dad laughed below.

"Uh, Bronwyn? Your aunt and uncle are down here."

True, and I adored them, but first I had to see . . .

"Your room," Delores says, as if finishing my sentence.

I smile. "I know the way," I say, and I turn left at the top of the steps.

She shakes her head. "I made up the master suite. That old room is small and dark, and the bed's ready to collapse. No reason for you to use it."

No reason except that it's mine, and I spent some of my happiest days there. My perfect, wonderful room, with its perfect, wonderful secret.

Secret? No. Delusion.

I swallow, tear my gaze away and hurry after Delores to the master suite.

"Linens are all new and laundered," she says.

I cross the large, airy room to the king-sized bed and make a show of smoothing the linens. I'm ready to gush politely, but they're five-star hotel quality, and I sigh with pleasure as I rub them between my fingers. Then I notice the thick quilted comforter. It's clearly handmade . . . by someone who knows what they're doing. It's a star pattern, diamonds of jade and wine against a black backdrop.

"Oh, wow," I say as I stroke the comforter. "This is amazing."

Delores harrumphs, but she's clearly pleased. "The wife made it for your auntie and never got a chance to give it to her."

I turn to face her. "Thank you. For everything. This is far more than I expected."

Delores waves a gnarled hand. "I told her she was making too much fuss. You'd think Queen Liz herself was coming." She tromps from the room. "I'd best be getting home."

I walk her down to the front door, and then say a heartfelt, "Thank you, Ms. Crossley."

"It's *Mr.*" She doesn't give me time to respond, just meets my gaze with that challenging stare. "I prefer *Mr.*"

"And *he*? Or *they*? *Ze*?"

His eyes narrow, as if I'm mocking him.

I hurry on. "I'm a university professor, Mr. Crossley. I use proper pronouns."

A slow, thoughtful nod. "I prefer *he.*" A pause. "If you forget and use *she*, though, I won't hold it against you."

"I won't forget, Mr. Crossley."

"Del's fine, too."

That's right. He'd signed his e-mails "Del." The only time I'd seen "Delores" was in the introduction from the lawyer handling the estate.

He heads for the door. "You have any trouble, call. Or come on down't. We're at the bottom of the hill, first cottage on the left. Easy enough run for a strong lass like you."

"I'll be fine, but thank you."

"I'll be back come morning. Take a look at that old car. See if there's any life left in her."

I thank him again, and then walk out and watch him leave, a shadowy figure on a bicycle, newly lit pipe gritted between his teeth.

D el leaves, and I'm alone, which is nothing new, and hardly bothers me, even in this isolated old house. I plan to snuggle in with tea and biscuits and a book. I get as far as donning my nightshirt—one of Michael's old tees—before the bed upstairs seems a lot more inviting than tea or biscuits or even a book. I've spent the last day crammed into a seat of some sort: plane, train, taxi. I desperately need to stretch out and sleep.

When I flip on the stairway light, it flashes once and sputters out. I flick it a few times before fetching a candlestick from the kitchen.

Being this isolated means the house is subject to power outages, and the utility company is never in a rush to fix them. Granted, I don't actually need to light a candle. It's one burnt-out bulb. I could get to my bedroom by leaving on the foyer light. Which would be no fun at all. I'm climbing a darkened staircase, alone in an eighteenth-century haunted house in the English moors. Anyone with a speck of imagination would want to ascend with a lit candlestick, white nightgown—or oversized white T-shirt—billowing around her.

I do exactly that, and I hear not a single ominous creak of a floorboard, catch not one unearthly flicker in the corner of my eye. Terribly disappointing.

I step into the bedroom and—

Something moves across the room. I jump and spin, nearly dropping my candle, only to see myself reflected in a mirror. It's Aunt Judith's antique vanity with three-way mirrors. I see it, and I can't help but smile, that spark of fear snuffed out. As a child, I'd sit at that vanity for hours, silently opening jars of cream and pots of makeup, sighing over the exotic scents and jewel colors. Aunt Judith would always "catch" me, and I loved to be caught because it meant a little girl makeover, creams rubbed on my face, stain on my lips and my hair stroked to gleaming with her silver brush. Then out came the cold cream, as chilly as its name, wiping off Aunt Judith's work before my mother saw.

I walk over and lower myself into the seat. The top is still covered in pots and boxes, their cut glass and silver tops gleaming as if Aunt Judith were here only moments ago. I open one jar of night cream, and the smell that rushes out is so familiar my eyes fill with tears. I sit there a moment, remember. Then I rise and pinch out the candle.

With moonlight flooding through the drapery-free window, I crawl into bed, and oh my God, I was not exaggerating about the linens, sheets so soft I want to roll in them like a kitten in catnip.

My eyes barely close before I'm asleep.

ॐ

I WAKE TO A TICKLE ON MY CHEEK, LIKE A STRAY HAIR DANCING IN the night breeze. Michael used to say it had to be twenty below before I'd sleep with the windows shut. I crack open my eyes and—

A face hovers over mine.

I jump up with a shriek and crouch there, fists clenched as my gaze swings around the room. The *empty* room.

When I spot something big and pale to my left, I twist to find myself gazing out the huge bay window. A nearly full moon blazes through . . . a pale circle hovering above me.

I exhale and shake my head. In the bleary confusion of waking, I mistook the moon for a face, the shadowy craters for features. And I'd woken because a stray hair tickled my cheek, caught in the breeze coming through that window, which I . . .

I look over. Which I did *not* open last night—the window is shut tight.

Well, then, it was a draft. It's an old house.

I flip onto my side, away from the window. No sooner does my head touch the pillow than someone whispers in my ear.

I jump, flailing as the sheets tangle. I fight my way free and scramble from the bed with a "Who's there?" so tremulous that shame snakes through me.

A memory flickers, from my last night in this house, twenty-three years ago. I woke to a figure looming over me. A figure whose face I can never remember, who said words I can never recall. Who sent me screaming from my sleep and then—

I swallow hard and rub my eyes. There is no ghost here. There never was. A hair tickled my cheek. I opened my eyes to see the moon, and then I imagined the whisper. I'm tense and stressed, overwhelmed by memory and emotion, in a place I once loved above all others, a place I haven't set foot in for two decades when that love twisted to heartbreak and grief and fear.

There's nothing here except memories, and so many of them are wonderful. Focus on those. Remember those. Exorcise the ghosts and reclaim Thorne Manor as that place of magic and mystery.

I cross the room and open the window. The night breeze rushes in, and I gulp it down, lowering my face to the screen. As I do, I see my beloved moors, paths winding through it, familiar trails that make my feet and my heart ache with wanting. A cow lows somewhere, and a dog barks, as if in answer. My gaze moves to the narrow road down the hill, and the glow of houses below. A reminder that I'm not truly alone.

I'm crawling back into bed when something thuds deep within the house. I go still, my head swiveling. Another thud, coming from the direction of my old room.

I push to my feet, but a yowl sends me tumbling back onto the bed. I grab the nearest thing at hand, wielding it like a shield, taking sanctuary behind a . . . pillow? I stifle a choked laugh, cut short by another yowl, weak and quavering, a drawn-out cry of despair.

Still clutching the pillow, I creep to the door. The sound comes again, prickling the hair on my neck. My fingers graze the doorknob.

What? You're going out there?

That only makes me square my shoulders. Yes, I'm going out there. I'm not fifteen anymore. I won't huddle in my bed, a frightened mouse of a girl.

Except I hadn't huddled in my bed that night. I'd run, which is when everything went so horribly wrong.

Well, I'm not running now. I'm acting clearly and decisively, armed with my . . . I look down at the pillow, toss it aside and snatch the umbrella from my open luggage. I take my cell phone, too, before I slide into the hall.

The creature keeps yowling. Pitiable sounds that come from behind the closed door to my old bedroom.

I turn the knob. Then I knee the door hard enough that it slaps against the wall.

A cry. A skitter of claws on wood. A streak of orange hurtles under the bed.

Orange?

Well, it's not a ghost.

I play back a mental video of that streak. Too big for a mouse. Too *orange* for a rat.

Huh.

As I step into the room, the stink of still air and mildew washes over me. Dust cyclones in my wake. Ahead, my old bed is indeed broken, the box spring sagging, mattress gone.

Propping my umbrella against the wall, I turn on my phone's flashlight and lower myself to the floor. When I shine the light under my bed, teeth flash. Razor-sharp teeth half the length of my pinky nail. Tiny black lips curl in a hiss, and orange fur puffs, little ears flattened in the most adorably fierce snarl ever.

It's a kitten. One barely big enough to be away from its mother.

It hisses again. *She* hisses. I know enough about felines to realize that *calico* means female.

When I move the light aside, the kitten spots me. Or she seems to, her tiny head bobbing, her eyes likely still struggling to focus.

How young is she?

And what is she doing in my old bedroom?

The kitten lets out the tiniest mew.

"Where's your momma?" I ask.

Another mew. I reach under the bed, and she skitters away, claws scrabbling over the hardwood.

I eye her. Then I back out and look around. There's clearly no mother cat in here. My gaze trips around the moonlit space as my heart swells with love for this room, and I have to remind myself I'm looking for a mother cat . . . or some way a kitten could get in. Even then, of course, I notice everything, the disrepair hidden by shadow. Two large windows, one overlooking the moors, the other the old stables. My narrow bed and double dressers, and something I'd almost forgotten—a small vanity with a padded stool and mirror, a surprise from Aunt Judith and Uncle Stan when I'd returned at fifteen. My gaze slides over my own collection of makeup and creams, and my eyes mist until the room swims.

I blink hard. This isn't solving the kitten mystery. I circle the room, studying the walls. They're in perfect repair without a baseboard gap big enough to let in a mouse. I look behind the dresser and vanity and bed. No holes there.

I walk to the windows. They're shut tight, the smell in here guaranteeing this room wasn't aired out with the rest of the house.

I turn to look around again, and I spot the kitten peeking from under the bed. I lower myself to the floor. When she mews, I stay where I am and dangle my fingers. A pause. Then she takes one tentative step. Another. She makes her way across the floor until she's sniffing my fingers. Then she rubs against my hand. When I go to stroke her head, she hops right onto my lap and purrs up at me.

I chuckle under my breath. "Not a stray, are you?"

She is adorable, a puff of long, soft fur, her back and head abstract stripes of black and orange, her belly and paws snow white. As I pet her, she rubs against my hand. A house cat, then, raised with people and a mother who trusted those people to handle her babies.

I lift the kitten as she motorboat purrs. She really is tiny with an oversized head and huge blue eyes. I know kittens are born with blue eyes, so does that mean she isn't old enough to be weaned? Either way, I'm sure she's not old enough to be exploring on her own. So, where did she come from?

As I pet her, I lift my phone in my free hand and thumb to the browser to see how old kittens are when their eyes change color. When I get a message that I'm not connected to the internet, I glance at the signal strength icon. It's flat. I had a signal on the drive here, but I haven't checked my phone since I arrived at Thorne Manor.

I push to my feet. I hold the kitten just tight enough that she can't jump to her doom. I needn't have bothered. She isn't going anywhere, and when I tuck her into the crook of my arm, she snuggles onto the convenient boob perch.

I take the kitten downstairs and give her a plate of water. There's a cold chicken in the fridge, and I tear off tiny bits, which she ignores. When the grandfather clock chimes, I expect it to be three or four in the morning. Instead, it gongs twelve.

Only midnight? How early did I go to bed?

Maybe I didn't fall asleep at all. Or not as deeply as I thought. That might explain that phantom touch. One explanation for ghosts is hypnogogic and hypnopompic hallucinations, where you think you see something while you're falling asleep or waking up, but you're actually asleep and dreaming without realizing it.

Overtired and unsettled by a long day of travel, I'd fallen into a restless sleep and thought I woke to someone leaning over my bed . . . but it was the dream-hallucination that actually woke me. And the dream itself was precipitated by the eerie sound of a trapped kitten.

Even with the explanation, I'm not eager to return to the master suite. Also, it makes a fine excuse to reclaim my former bedroom. I find the old mattress wrapped in storage and drag it in while the kitten watches in fascination. I put the oversized master suite sheets and comforter on my narrow bed. One corner sags, but I can fix that tomorrow. For now, I settle the kitten into a blanket-filled cardboard box, and by two a.m., I'm drifting off to the music of tiny kitten snores.

I WAKE TO THE CALL OF A MOTHER CAT. AS I SURFACE, I CATCH scents that don't belong in my bedroom—the perfume of sandalwood, and the musk of horse and the tantalizing aroma of a smoldering fire. Which means I haven't woken at all. I've tumbled into a dream where the kitten's mother anxiously searches for her lost baby.

In the dream, someone sleeps beside me, and when I shift, a hand slides onto my hip. A broad, masculine hand tugs me closer, and I ease into the heat radiating from the other side of the bed. My legs bump his, and his reach forward, inviting me in, our feet and calves entwining.

It isn't Michael. Not his scent or his touch or even his still familiar breathing. That doesn't make me pull back in alarm. It's been eight years. I no longer suffer pangs of guilt on the rare occasion that other men invade my dreams. Michael still visits them often enough.

The man's fingers splay over my hip, pulling me closer. A nuzzle, then lips parting against my forehead in a whispered, "Bronwyn."

I hesitate.

I know that voice.

No, I know that inflection to my name. I do *not* know the voice. The man's scent, equally familiar and yet not familiar, smelling of sweat and horse and sandalwood, teases me with hints of familiarity.

I touch his hand on my hip and slide my fingers over the hard muscles of his forearm, making him shiver against me. He exhales through his teeth as my fingers trace up his biceps to his shoulder. That shoulder shifts under my hand as his mouth drops to the crook of my neck, kissing there, whispering words I can't catch, just the sound of a British accent, again both familiar and not, a voice in my head, insisting I know him yet refusing to fill in the missing piece with a name.

I crack open my eyes to see jet-black hair curling over pale skin. He's still kissing my throat, tickling kisses as he murmurs my name.

One hand still rests on my hip. The other slides underneath, gripping and pulling me closer, until I feel the hard urgency of him against my stomach. I ease up, breaking his kiss to adjust my position to a more satisfying one. He chuckles and shifts to accommodate me.

I arch my hips into his, and he lets out a low groan, the sound ending in my name. I try to see his face, but it's buried in my hair. He's tall, then. Tall, dark and possibly handsome, but I'm not terribly concerned about the last. This is quite enough, a well-built man groaning my name, his body hot and hard against mine, perfect fodder for a midnight fantasy.

Our legs entwine further, and I realize he's naked. I'm still wearing my nightshirt and panties, and he seems to be in no rush to relieve me of those. I'm in no hurry, either, enjoying the journey, the destination inevitable. He presses against me, and I part my legs, and he groans again, his hands gripping my hips.

Then the cat yowls.

His eyes fly open. The room's too dark for me to catch more than a flash of light eyes, blue or green. Before I can get a better look, he shoves me away with, "What the bloody hell?"

That voice . . .

No, not the voice. The accent. A proper upper-crust London accent, one that isn't actually heard in London anymore, a relic of a bygone era.

He scrambles out of bed, realizes he's naked, and yanks the coverlet with him, imperfectly draped over his front.

"Who are you, and what the devil are you doing in my bed?"

I don't answer. I'm waiting to wake up. That's what will happen next, obviously. Two dreams overlapped—the anxious momma cat and the lovely sexual fantasy—the former inexcusably interrupting the latter.

Or perhaps the dream will restart. Yes, I'd like option two, please. Silence the cat, and return this shadowy cursing figure to his proper place in bed.

"Are you deaf?" the man snaps. "Dumb? I'm asking you a question!"

Any time now, Morpheus. Rewind ten minutes please, and hold the cat.

The man stands there, half-lost in shadow but presenting a very fine figure, broad shouldered and naked except for the unfortunate coverlet.

"I asked you a question," he says.

"Two."

His shadowed face scrunches. "What?"

"You asked me two questions. Who am I, and what am I doing here."

When I speak, he goes still, head tilted, face slackening. He blinks, those light eyes vanishing for a second.

"Speak again," he says.

"Is that an order, m'lord?"

"Yes, it is, girl."

"Well, not having been a girl for many years, I decline to comply." I pause. "Though I suppose I just did, didn't I?"

"Who are you?" he asks, his voice lower now, tense, as if fearing the answer.

"Just a woman who was enjoying a very fine dream before the cat yowled. Please stop yelling at me. You were so much more appealing half-asleep."

He stares at me. Just stares. I'm about to speak again when he lunges and grabs me by the arm. I'm still in bed, kneeling, and his sudden yank topples me before I can object. Next thing I know, I'm on my feet, being dragged into a patch of moonlight. My nightshirt tears, but he doesn't seem to notice. Fingers roughly grip my chin and wrest my face upward.

Then he stops. Goes completely still again and breathes, "Bronwyn."

I look up into a face as familiar as his smell and his voice. I know them by heart, and yet do not know them at all. A broad face, hard edged and beard shadowed, with a knife-cut line between thick brows. A face that I remember as soft edges and smooth cheeks. Yet under that hard maturity, I see the boy I knew. I see his sky-blue eyes. I see the curve of his jaw. I see the dark hair curling over a wide forehead. I look at the man and instead gaze upon a boy I haven't seen in twenty-three years.

"William," I whisper, and he releases me, recoiling.

I fall backward, thumping to the floor, and when I look up, the man is gone.

I sit on my bedroom floor, blinking. A cat mews, and I jump, but it's only the kitten, crawling onto my lap, as if wondering how I got on the floor.

Good question, kitten.

Obviously, I'd fallen out of bed after dreaming I'd been yanked from it by . . .

William.

Twenty-three years ago, I fled this house, screaming about a ghost. One episode, however, was not enough to land me in a psychiatric ward. That came when, in my grief and shock, I began babbling about other people I'd seen in Thorne Manor. About a boy who shared my room hundreds of years ago. A boy who'd been my friend . . . and then more than a friend.

William Thorne.

I don't remember the first time we met. For me, William has always been as much a part of this house as the grandfather clock. My earliest memory of Thorne Manor is of being in a room that is mine and yet not mine. In William's bedroom, the two of us, little more than toddlers, playing marbles as if we've known each other forever. In that memory, I sense that I've already been there many times, seen him many times, played this game many times.

I'd been too young to think anything odd about that. William was my friend at Auntie Judith's summer house. If I closed my eyes and thought about him in my bedroom, I would open them to find myself in *his* room.

When we got older, we roamed farther afield. To the stables, to the hay barn, to the moors, to the attic, and the secret passage and every corner of this house. We avoided his family and staff. I was William's secret, and he was mine.

Then came my parents' divorce, and it was ten years before I returned. At fifteen I came back, and I had only to think of him while in my bedroom, and I stepped through, and there he was, my age again and as awkwardly sweet as any fifteen-year-old girl could want.

I fell in love that summer, and it was the most perfect first romance imaginable. We walked hand in hand through the moors. We kissed under a canopy of stars. We talked, endlessly talked, and wanted nothing more than to be together even if I was curled up in the stable with a book while he groomed his horses.

As for *how* I traveled back to William's time, we didn't need an explanation. The answer was obvious. He was real, and I was real, and therefore, what happened must be equally real—real magic. A shared room, a shared life. A reasonable explanation for a fifteen-year-old girl, madly in love with a boy who lived two centuries before her.

The truth was much harsher. After my uncle died and I babbled my confession about William, the doctors explained that stress had twisted memories of an imaginary childhood friend into vivid hallucinations of a teenage boy.

My father is a historian, and I caught the bug from him, and so, the doctors explained, I imagined a Thorne boy who once lived in my Thorne Manor bedroom. An imaginary playmate for an only child who spent her summers in an isolated country house. At fifteen, I'd been reuniting with Dad against my mother's wishes. The stress of that proved too much, and my mind conjured William anew, shaping him into the friend and the first love I desperately needed.

Tonight, I visited William again to find him a grown man, still my own age. Yet this was clearly a dream, and somehow that makes it worse, the flame of loss igniting another, never quite snuffed out. Michael is eight years dead. And William Thorne never lived at all.

It's a long time before I fall back to sleep, and when I do, my pillow is soaked with tears for a husband I lost and a boy I never truly had.

༺❀༻

I WAKE THE NEXT MORNING IN A FAR BETTER MOOD. THERE IS A KITTEN curled up at my side, as if drawn there by my silent crying, and it's hard to laze in bed with a tiny creature who needs you to fix her breakfast.

Midmorning, I tuck the kitten into my newly kitten-proof room. Then I pop into the detached garage—formerly the stables —in case Del was exaggerating about the condition of the car. When I tug off the tarp, dust motes fly, and a few mice scatter, but the chrome and cherry-red paint still gleams.

Uncle Stan's baby, Aunt Judith had called it. At the time, I hadn't seen the appeal of such an old car. Now, I realize my mistake. It's an Austin-Healey convertible. I have no idea what year or model, but she's a beauty, and my fingers itch to wrap around the leather-bound steering wheel. That, however, is where Del was telling the truth. While the keys are in the ignition, the motor doesn't turn. I'm no mechanic, but my dad taught me enough to confirm the problem isn't a dead battery or empty gas tank. Still, I fold the tarp aside and leave the garage door open to air the car out.

Tucked behind the convertible, I find two ancient bicycles. I take Aunt Judith's, with its huge front basket. A few drops of oil on the chain, a bit of air in the tires, a backpack for extra storage, and I'm off to town.

At around a thousand people, High Thornesbury is just big enough that I can blend in with the June holiday crowds. I'll socialize when I'm less jet-lagged and better able to put names to faces twenty-three years older than I last saw them.

After a visit to the hardware shop and the grocer, my backpack is full, but my bicycle basket holds only a small bag of kibble and a bottle of red wine, cushioned by a pair of thick woolen socks. Then I smell fresh bread wafting from the tiny village bakery, and since I have extra room . . .

By the time I leave town, my bicycle basket is full to overflowing. I blame Mrs. Del's scones. Sure, one might think that since I already have a box of them at the house, I shouldn't need more, but having *some* only makes me worry about the morning when I'll have none. Also, as lovely as tinned biscuits are, they're no match for fresh shortbread. Or gingersnaps. Or butter buns.

If I don't get the convertible running, I'll be doing a lot of riding on this old bicycle. The seat feels as if it were cast in cement —I need all the extra padding I can get.

The ride back to Thorne Manor is straight up a twelve percent grade, and I'm spurring myself on with the promise of chocolate-dipped flapjacks when I see Del heading my way on his bicycle. He looks even more bizarre in daylight, his macintosh thrashing, clunky work boots pumping the pedals, the pipe clamped between his teeth. On a fishing boat, he'd be right at home. A bicycle? Not so much.

His face is set in a way that defies anyone to stop him. So I'm about to lift a hand in greeting as we pass, but he pulls to a halt, and I realize that's just his normal expression. Impatience and annoyance, set in the stone of his weathered skin.

"Won't be up today," he says. "Got a call in town. Urgent business." A roll of his eyes doubts it's urgent, and if he's right, I wouldn't want to be the person who summoned him. "I was going to come by and see if you needed owt. You've found the grocer." He peers into the basket, and his face darkens. "Frey's scones not to your liking?"

I smile. "They're too much to my liking, which means they'll be gone by tomorrow morning."

"I'll bring you more, then. Saints knows, she baked enough of them. Said she remembers you eating a whole basket by yourself when you were a sprog. I said you had probably learned restraint. Guess not."

"Frey?" I say. "Is that short for Freya?"

"Aye-uh."

"She used to teach in town, didn't she? She played whist and bridge with my aunt."

Freya was living in Liverpool when I returned at fifteen, so it's been over thirty years since I've seen her. I pull up a mental collection of a soft lap and a softer voice, a laugh too hearty to come from that voice. A pile of dog-eared books. A basket of fresh scones. The smell of chalk and sage and browned butter.

"I'd love to see her," I say.

"She doesn't get out much these days. Waiting for a hip replacement. She's off to the city today for a doctor's visit. She'd love to have you for tea tomorrow, though."

"I'll enjoy seeing her whenever it's convenient. Oh, and I found a kitten upstairs."

"Upstairs?" His gray eyebrows soar into his hairline.

"Locked in my old bedroom."

He frowns. "I was there all last week, cleaning. No kittens inside or out. They'd have a feast in that garage, but I've never seen any even in there."

"This one's very young." I show him the picture on my phone.

"Huh." He eases back on his bicycle seat. "Doesn't seem big enough to be away from her ma."

"I know. Last night, I tried looking up what to feed her, but I don't have a cell phone signal."

"Aye, we're in a bit of a dead zone here. It's fine down't the road, but at the house, you need to be in the sitting room. Or the front yard. Unless the wind picks up. Or the fog rolls in. Or it rains. But I don't need the internet to tell you that's a very young kitten who can't eat that." He points to the dry kibble in my basket. "You'll need to mix it into a slush." His gaze lifts to mine. "You keeping her?"

"I'd like to find her family if I can."

"Kitten that young? She hasn't wandered away from town. Someone dumped her. If you want her, she's yours."

I should say that I'm only here for the summer, and I know nothing about caring for pets. Mom was allergic, and Michael and I had been preparing to buy our first house—which would have meant our first pet—when he got his diagnosis. After that, I just didn't get around to it. Like I "didn't get around" to dating again, "didn't get around" to having kids, "didn't get around" to buying a house . . .

All that was on The List. After three doctors declared Michael's tumor terminal, he made a list of everything he wanted me to do when he was gone. Buy a house. Fall madly in love. Get married and have children. Well, no, actually, I was supposed to have a few flings first. Forget long-term relationships, and just have sex with hot guys. Yes, that was actually on The List.

Somewhere on it was this, too. Adopt a cat. And so, while I'm sure I'm not the ideal pet-parent for a barely weaned kitten, when Del asks whether I'm keeping her, I find myself saying, "Yes."

He nods and says he'll talk to the local vet and then come by tomorrow morning.

۞

WHILE I PROMISED MYSELF CHOCOLATE FLAPJACKS AS MY HILL-climbing reward, in reality . . . Let's just say it's probably a good thing Michael and I never had kids, because I display a strong risk for becoming my mother, who'd promise me treats for an accomplishment only to bait-and-switch later.

No, I wouldn't actually do that to my child, not when I know what it was like. I do, however, do it to myself. I postpone the flapjacks and boil a couple of farm-fresh eggs instead. Then, for added masochism, I do twenty minutes of ballet exercise.

Mom had been a professional ballerina, who'd hoped her only child would follow in her slippers. Unfortunately, I inherited Dad's body shape. I'm five-foot-ten and not thin. Never been thin. I was a "big-boned" kid, who became a "voluptuous" adult, both being polite euphemisms for a figure that will never grace the princess—or even the queen mother—in *Swan Lake*.

When I was little, my mother held out hope that I would shed my baby fat even when my bone structure scoffed at the notion. That probably explains a childhood of "You can have ice cream if you clean your room," which turned into "Here's a nice yogurt parfait."

I went to ballet lessons twice a week and adored it. By the time I turned nine, though, Mom realized I'd never follow in her professional footsteps and declared the lessons a waste of money, claiming her child support wouldn't cover them. That last part was a lie. As I later discovered, Dad always added extra for my lessons.

I don't remember my parents ever getting along. They were like colleagues forced to work together on a shared project, and that project was me. When I was five, they finally split. As Mom put it, Dad "ran off with some girl." The truth is that he reunited with his childhood sweetheart and asked Mom for an amicable split with joint custody.

In leaving for another woman, Dad stole Mom's dignity, and she retaliated by stealing me. She claimed Dad was abusive, and he lost all visitation rights. I hated her for that—I hated her for a lot of things—but there *was* love in our relationship. Taking me out of ballet lessons wasn't spite or greed. I clearly would never be a ballerina, and she didn't want to set me up for disappointment. The idea that I'd have been happy dancing as a hobby likely never occurred to her because she wouldn't have been.

My mother has been gone two years. Lung cancer from a lifetime of cigarettes to keep her ballerina thin. Dad lives in Toronto, and I see him at least once a week. He's still with his second wife, who is as lovely and non-evil a stepmom as anyone could want.

As for ballet, when Dad discovered I'd stopped, he insisted I take it up again. I still dance with a troupe every week—the ballet equivalent of community theatre—and I love it even if you couldn't pay me to wear a tutu.

So I might grumble about masochism, doing those ballet exercises, but spinning my way through Thorne Manor sends my already kite-high mood into the stratosphere. In the daylight, the house is pure magic. Its shadows become pockets of cool shade among the rectangles of sunlight stretching across the rich wood floors. A heather-perfumed breeze blows through every open window. I dance between sun and shade, drinking in the scent of the moors and feeling the wind kiss my skin. If there's anything dark in this house, it's not here now. In the daylight, I can't imagine it was ever here at all.

After my dance exercises, I explore the house, poking around its nooks and crannies. What surprises me most is the smell: a mix of moor and wet wool and old wood and the faint whiff of camphor. It shouldn't be a pleasant odor, but it is because it's the smell of Thorne Manor, sparking memories of endless days curled up in one of these nooks or crannies with an old blanket and a book.

I kneel beside a storage hole under the stairs. I open the tiny crooked door, and I'm not sure I can still fit inside, but I want to try, grab a blanket and a pillow and a novel and a cup of milky tea and pretend I'm five again, fifteen again, half-dozing in the lantern light as I listen to the clomp of Uncle Stan's boots, and Aunt Judith's shout for him to take those bloody things off and Dad's laugh at this daily routine of theirs. My eyes prickle at the memory, but it's a good one, and maybe someday this summer, I will indeed crawl in here and read. For now, the kitten explores the space, and I watch, smiling like an indulgent parent.

When she tires of that, I find Aunt Judith's sewing kit and

fetch my shirt from last night. I noticed a small rip in the seam this morning.

A rip . . . after William yanked it?

I shake my head. No, a rip because the shirt is ten years old, and I've stitched it more than once. It's one of Michael's, from my collection, three of which made their way into my suitcase. This particular one is a Toronto Maple Leafs tee. Born in Cairo, educated in England, Michael had never seen a hockey game until he came to Canada for his graduate studies. That didn't stop him from becoming a bigger Leafs fan than my father, who still drags me to games. Michael had never strapped on skates before, but by his second year, he was on a varsity team. He joked they let him play to inject a little color in the team, but that wouldn't explain the MVP trophy still proudly displayed in my condo. Michael did nothing by halves. People presumed he learned hockey to assimilate into Canadian culture, but that never crossed his mind. He'd watched a few games, thought, *That looks interesting*, and threw himself into learning it.

Michael threw himself into *life*. Every driving trip we took, I knew to double the travel time because he'd constantly detour to "see what's over there." He spoke four languages and started learning Japanese "for fun" after the diagnosis. When that diagnosis came—a glioblastoma brain tumor—the joke was that he'd worn out his brain from overuse.

I have a stack of his old T-shirts and jerseys, my only sleepwear for the past eight years. I treat them like antique lace, washing them on delicate, mending every hint of a separating seam. And now this one needs repair, which has nothing to do with a dream from last night and everything to do with the fact that, perhaps after eight years, I should stop wearing my dead husband's shirts to bed.

Perhaps someday. Not today, though. Today, I grab the shirt and the sewing kit and settle in with my kitten and a cup of tea and stitch the torn hem as if the shirt's owner will return at any moment and expect it back.

By late afternoon, Enigma is ready for a nap. The name seems fitting, given the mysterious circumstances of her arrival. I take her upstairs and settle her into her box. Then, I glance at the bed and realize perhaps it's not the kitten who's in need of a nap. I barely got five hours of slumber after a sleepless night of overseas travel.

I kick off my slippers and slide under that wonderfully thick quilt. As my cheek touches the cool pillow, I remember my dream from last night, the one of waking in William's bed. I smile and snuggle down in hopes of recapturing it. But as soon as my eyes close, I realize what I'm truly hoping for—not a dream of William, but the reality of him. And it's more than hope. It's a wild soul-deep plea that William be real, that I can cross time and reach him.

Dreams like that are false fantasies guaranteed to twist into nightmare. For years, I'd dream of waking to find Michael beside me, alive and whole and safe. Then I'd truly wake up, shaking with grief and longing, terrified of falling back asleep. Terrified of wanting to fall back asleep and *stay* there, of eyeing the sleeping pills on my nightstand and wondering what would happen if I took the whole bottle . . .

I shiver and climb from bed. Hoping to drift off into fantasies of William smacks of those Michael nightmares. A dream that could drain my soul with wanting.

I peer into the dresser mirror, checking the baggage under my eyes. Definitely not carry-on size. Time to brew a pot of strong coffee.

As I'm turning away, I catch a flicker in the mirror. It disappears in a blink, and I tense, imagining a ghostly visage, but that isn't what I saw. A face, yes. But firm and real, severe and masculine, with a tumble of black curls over the broad forehead and eyes blue as the summer sky.

"William," I whisper, and the word barely escapes before my dresser disappears and I'm gazing into another mirror, my reflection slightly warped, the glass imperfect. Behind me, William turns toward the bedroom door.

He's dressed in a cutaway morning coat over a white linen shirt with a high collar, wide necktie fastened with a sapphire pin. A dashing figure, his dark hair slicked, curls tamed. He's already turning away, and I catch only a glimpse of his profile, and then his back is to me, his shoes clicking as he strides from the room.

"Lord Thorne?" a voice calls from the hallway. "Your solicitor is here."

"Put him in the parlor."

"Not the pantry?" the voice asks with a teasing lilt.

William grumbles, but there's no rancor in it.

I know the other voice. It's older than I remember, but I heard it many times as a child, a voice that would set us scrambling for a hiding place before she spotted me. Mrs. Shaw, the Thornes' housekeeper.

As soon as I think her name, I picture her face, and then I see another one, weathered with short-cropped steel gray hair and a pipe in his mouth.

Have we met? You look . . . familiar.

William's footsteps clomp down the steps, Mrs. Shaw's click-clacking after him as she asks about tea, and William mutters that refreshments might induce his solicitor to linger, so, no, they can skip tea.

I smile at that, and my gaze turns to the bed. It's not the narrow child's bed I remember, but a four-poster mahogany one, still no larger than a modern double. There should be curtains, but they've been removed.

Seeing the folded-back sheets, I remember how they felt against me last night, cool and featherlight and coarse. The perfect counterpoint to the fingers on my hip, warm and strong and smooth until they slid up to my waist, the callused skin of William's fingertips tickling across my—

I yank my thoughts from that precipice and shiver with something between delight and dread. I told myself I wasn't going to dream of William, and yet, I am. I curled up in bed thinking of him, and then I must have dreamed that I rose and saw him in the mirror.

This very room proves it's a dream. It's a child's bedchamber, for one who is no longer a child. William would be Lord Thorne now, as Mrs. Shaw called him. His father died when he was ten, and his mother had been ill when I saw him at fifteen. His only sibling was Cordelia, five years his junior. As the lord of the manor, William would have the master bedroom, yet in my dream, I nonsensically see him in his old room.

I look back at the bed. If I crawl into it, will the dream end? Or will I then dream of being in it with *him*? Another shiver, delight mingled with dread again. That way lies madness. Best to keep this dream in the light of day. It will end soon enough.

I glance down at the dresser, the wood smooth under my hands. It's more dressing table than modern dresser, with a wardrobe to one side and a washstand to the other, all in gorgeous gleaming mahogany. In less affluent families, furniture in a Victorian bedroom was recycled from lower rooms as it began to show wear, but the Thornes had the money to furnish their bedrooms new, and while this one is small, it's well-appointed. Overdone, with more square footage allotted to furniture than is my taste, but that, too, was the Victorian way.

With no closets, most of the furniture is for storage, primarily clothing, and that includes the dressing table, topped with a horsehair brush, a pair of brown gloves, a pocket watch and several stickpins in an enamel tray.

I touch the washbasin pitcher. Without thinking, my fingers move to a crack in the handle, a rough spot under my fingertips. In my mind, I see my chubby five-year-old self demonstrating my ballet positions, and then executing a clumsy pirouette, hitting the pitcher and sending it tumbling to the floor. I wail in dismay as the handle snaps free and bounces over the hardwood, and I manage to clamp a hand over my mouth before anyone comes running. Tears stream from my eyes as I stare at the broken pitcher.

"I—I'm so—"

William catches me in a hug before I can get the apology out. "I'll tell them I did it. Papa's away, and Mama's busy with the baby coming. I'll hardly get in any trouble."

"You shouldn't get in any trouble at all. It's my fault." I pick up the handle and turn it over in my hands before spinning on him. "Do you have Super Glue?"

"Super glue . . . ?" His brow furrows in a way I know well. It's the same expression I must make when he talks about an abacus or a Punch and Judy show.

"I'll get some," I say. "Uncle Stan keeps it in the cupboard."

I brought a tube of Super Glue and fixed his pitcher, and it's still here, with that barely noticeable repair. I run my fingers over the handle again and then look down, seeing my reflection in the water. When I touch the surface, it ripples.

The old pitcher is no family heirloom, just a cheap water jug, perfect for a child who might knock it over in the night. It's out of place now among the lavish furnishings. As out of place as . . .

My gaze snags on what looks like a scrap of yarn tied to a post on William's washbasin. It's a bracelet. A braided one made of Chinese knotting cord.

Behind me, I imagine an echo of my voice saying, "I'll be leaving soon."

In my mind, I see myself at fifteen. I'm outside, perched on the pasture fence with William, watching his horse, his gaze moving between the horses and me. His eyes light up a little extra when they land on me, and that's the secret reason I always suggest we hang out here. I know how much William loves his horses, and if his gaze brightens even more when it moves to me, that means something. It really does.

We're sitting hip to hip, our hands clasped on my thigh. He's been talking about horses—not surprisingly. He has his eye on a young stallion, and his mother says he should stick to geldings, but he's trying to convince her the stallion would make good breeding stock.

When I say I'll be leaving soon, his hand tightens on mine.

"You'll be going soon, too," I remind him. "Back to London."

A grumble, one that sounds remarkably like the man who just stalked down the stairs.

I lean against his shoulder. "I'll be back next summer. Mom can't keep me away anymore. Dad won't let her."

A pause. A long one, and I smile as William's new colt kicks up his heels and tears across the pasture to nudge a filly. William has been breeding horses since he was twelve, and he already has buyers for this colt and filly. They'll go to their new homes before he leaves for London.

I'm about to ask whether it's hard, parting with them, when he says, "I want to ask you to stay, but I know that's wrong. You don't belong here, so I shouldn't ask . . ." His voice trails off. When I don't reply, he straightens and says, "I wouldn't. Ask, I mean. You have a life and a family there. I understand that. I'll miss you, but I'll see you next summer."

"You will."

He turns, face over mine. "In the meantime, perhaps I can

have a little something to remember you by?" His lips twitch, eyes dancing.

"Of course, my lord." I lift my mouth toward his. Then I tug off my braided bracelet and hold it out. "How about this?"

He laughs, plucks it from my hand and tucks it into a pocket. "I'll take that, but I was hoping for something a little more like . . ." His fingers tuck under my chin, lifting it. The barest brush of his lips. "This?"

"Mmm, yes. I believe I can part with a few of those."

"I may need more than a few. They have to keep me until you return." His eyes turn serious for a second. "You *will* return, won't you?"

"Always," I say, as I lean over to kiss him.

The memory fades, and I'm back in his bedroom, staring at the bracelet hanging on his washstand.

You will return, won't you?

Always.

I swallow.

A corner of my mind whispers that this is all a dream, but the reminder drifts past unheeded. Then a sound from the hallway has my head jerking up.

A cat's meow, like the one that interrupted my night.

I push aside all other thoughts and follow the sound from the room.

I stand in the hall, listening. The cat has gone silent.

As I take another step, a reedy voice from downstairs says, "If you don't intend to return to London, my lord, perhaps you should consider selling the townhouse."

"Why? Do I need the money?" William replies. "Have the coffers mysteriously emptied since your last unnecessary visit, Phelps?"

"Of course not, sir. Your estate is in excellent financial health. I simply meant—"

"You meant to scold me into returning to London. Remind me

of my responsibilities there. Responsibilities that I pay you very well to tend."

"He isn't scolding you, William," says another man. "Phelps is suggesting, politely, that you are overdue for a return. Five years overdue. I won't be nearly so polite about it. Get yourself home, old boy, and stop moping in the hinterlands."

"Moping?" A short laugh. "Is that your plan, August? Insult me until, in proud indignation, I stride from my manor house, ordering my footman to prepare the coach for London."

"That would work so much better if you had a coach," August says dryly. "Or a footman."

August. I remember the name. I'd never met him, of course, but he'd been a good friend of William's, whose family's estate was nearby.

August continues, "You don't even allow your housekeeper to live in."

"No, I *permit* Mrs. Shaw to live out where she can enjoy her grandchildren. In future, August, please announce your intentions to visit and do not sneak in with my solicitor like a stray cat slipping through an open door. If I'd known you were coming, I'd have had Mrs. Shaw prepare a room."

"No, you'd have told me to stay in London."

"Only because, lately, your visits transform you into a fishwife, haranguing me to return to a society that no longer cares to have me. And before you accuse me of sulking, let me clarify that I am perfectly happy for the excuse. Being a social pariah only gives me justification to live as I wish."

"You are not a social pariah. Yes, there are the blasted rumors, but no one of good breeding believes those."

Silence.

August comes back, his voice strained. "All right, yes, not as many invitations may land on your doorstep as once did, but it's been years. Whatever tar they brushed on your reputation, it's faded to an intriguing lacquer of mystery and scandal. The well-born ladies will fight like gaming dogs to get you to their balls."

"Yes, that's what I long to be: a scandalous addition to their party list. *My word, Lady Grayson, did you say Lord Thorne is coming Tuesday night? Lord* William *Thorne? How delightfully wicked of you to invite him.*"

August sighs. "Forget balls and dinners. Come to town for some fun. How long has it been since you visited a gaming hall? A brothel?"

"When did I ever visit a brothel?"

August chuckles. "True, you never needed to. The ladies do love a mysterious lord, particularly one with a past as dark and danger—" He clears his throat. "I'm sorry, William. That went too far. You know I pay no heed to those ridiculous rumors. No one who knows you does." A sound, as if August is shifting in his seat. "No brothels, then. Why don't we get you a wife. You're well overdue for that."

"Too overdue, sadly. I'm past my prime, and so with deep regret, I have removed myself from the pool of eligible bachelors."

August snorts. "Nice try, old boy. You are prime marriage material. Wealthy as an earl. In as fine a physical condition as you were at twenty, the one advantage to locking yourself up here with the fresh country air. And you're not *un*attractive."

"Thank you," William says dryly.

"There's a little too much of the dark and brooding about you, but the young ladies today have all read *Wuthering Heights*. They'll positively devour a mysterious lord who lives in the moors, pining for—"

"Dear God, yes, that is exactly what I want. A silly chit who mistakes me for a sadistic, obsessive fictional lout. Please, send a dozen on the next train."

I choke on a laugh. It echoes through the stairwell, and I slap a hand over my mouth as the parlor goes silent below.

"Don't tell me you still have that bloody feline," August says. "Blasted thing nearly ripped my arm off last time I visited."

"Pandora is an excellent watch cat. Perhaps I can send you

home with a kitten or four?" William pauses. "No, it'd be three, I'm afraid. She seems to have mislaid one."

August makes some retort, but I don't hear it.

She seems to have mislaid one.

I look behind me. The meow I'd heard came from there. I tiptoe and peer along the hall. There's only one open door. The master bedroom.

I creep to it. The door's only open a crack. I push as gently as I can, braced for the screech of hinges. The door swings open soundlessly, and a calico cat pops her head up from her box. Green eyes fix on mine, and she rises, fur bristling.

A peep. Then a tiny meow. Three sleepy kittens' heads rise to see what's the fuss.

Three kittens, two black and one orange, all of them the same size as Enigma.

She seems to have mislaid one.

Pandora stands with her back arched, tail bristled.

"It's okay," I whisper. "I'm not going to—"

She zooms from the box, a blur of orange fur, yowling as if her tail's on fire.

In the distance, I hear August say, "Your cat doesn't appreciate you offering up her babes, William."

I frantically wave the cat to silence. She yowls and hisses louder.

"Excuse me," William says. "I believe Pandora has found her missing kitten, trapped in a hole or some such predicament. The bloody thing is always getting into trouble, wandering off and needing rescue."

Footsteps sound below.

August calls, "I think it's perfectly charming that you're so devoted to your kitties, William, but might I suggest young ladies may not feel the same? Get yourself a big hound dog or something far more befitting your status as a mysterious man of the moors."

William calls back, "Draw me up a list of everything you're

certain eligible society ladies would not find suitably attractive in a man's home, and I shall fill mine with them forthwith."

I smile at that. Then I realize William is coming up the stairs, and I'm standing in the hall. The nearest door is shut. It's the bath. I ease it open as quickly as I can, but when I push, it squeals, and I barely get through before William's footsteps crest the stairs.

I'm inside the bathroom, but the door's open, exposing me, and I don't dare shut it. I press myself against the wall, and he walks past, his gaze on the hissing cat.

"Please tell me you found that damnable kitten of yours, Pan. Your little doppelgänger, that one, no end of trouble."

Pandora keeps hissing, her gaze firmly fixed on me. I wave, as if I can distract her.

"What's—?" William says as he turns. Then he sees me.

"I—I'm sorry," I say. "I didn't mean to disturb her. I think one of her kittens came through . . ." I trail off.

He's staring at me. Not staring in shock. Certainly not in delight. After a moment of surprise, his jaw sets, face darkening, blue eyes icing over. Then he turns on his heel, abruptly putting his back to me.

"William. Please." I grasp his upper arm as he walks away. "I just want to—"

He wheels sharply, jerking his arm away. The moment we break contact, the hall stutters, and I stumble back, landing on the floor, looking up at . . .

Nothing.

William is gone, and I'm sitting on the floor of my own bathroom.

5

I pick myself up off the bathroom floor as Enigma yowls from my bedroom, furious that I tricked her into thinking I was napping alongside her, and then, boom, I snuck out and closed the door, trapping her in there like a toddler at nap time.

As for how I got on *this* side of the closed door, the obvious answer is sleepwalking. I'm not known for doing that, but it's certainly more plausible than "I stepped through a time portal into Victorian Thorne Manor." And if part of me longs to jump to that implausible conclusion, well, I can't allow it. This one makes perfect sense. I lay down for a nap, dreamed of William and walked from my room, waking when I stumbled and fell.

I release Enigma to cuddles and promises of supper, and then I stride downstairs, putting the dream from my head . . . as much as I can.

❧

I TAKE MY EVENING TEA AND NOVEL AND KITTEN INTO THE SITTING room, where I open the front window, snuggle onto the sofa and tuck a wool blanket around me. I don't read right away, though— I just relax and inhale the perfume of dew-laden heather as I cuddle under the warm blanket, nibble my chocolate biscuits and sip my tea.

Does it remind me of summers I curled up in a chair in this very room, munching biscuits and sipping milky tea with Aunt Judith? Or days wandering the moor with Uncle Stan? Of course it does. It also makes me think of Michael, how I wish I'd brought him to this house, shared it with him.

I let the memories and regrets float into consciousness. Like lifting necklaces from my mother's jewelry box, running them through my fingers. I allow myself time to feel the grief and pain, hard as diamonds and just as bright. Then I put them into their box, safely stowed in a treasured spot in my subconscious.

Don't dwell on what isn't here. Dwell on what *is*. A perfumed breeze, hot tea, rich biscuits, a warm blanket, a purring kitten. And me. That last is the hardest. Focus on being in the moment with myself, comfortable in my own company.

Even as I'm luxuriating in the break, my mind compiles a to-do list from what I see around me. Strip the wood trim. Sew curtains. Buy a comfy chair for the front porch so I can curl up in the moonlight. Repaint the walls. They'd look lovely in a soft rose, a counterpoint to the cottage-chic. Of course, if I'm planning to sell the place, pink walls won't help.

Am I planning to sell it?

I have no idea, and that's yet another thought to tuck into a box for now.

I sit, and I think, and then I refill my cup, and my cookie plate and curl up with my kitten and my book. I read as the clock chimes eight and then nine. When it strikes ten, I declare it's late enough to call it a night.

I take Enigma upstairs and tuck her into her box. Then I step into the hall, heading for the bathroom and . . .

A shape flits past the doorway to the master bedroom.

I go still. In my mind's eye, I see it again, a dark human figure sliding past.

I swallow and squeeze my eyes shut. Then I glance back at

Enigma. She's curled up in her box. When she sees me watching, she only lifts her head with a drowsy meow. Nothing has set off her internal alarms. So whatever I saw exists only in my imagination.

It only ever existed in your imagination, Bronwyn. It's time you accepted that.

I square my shoulders and stride down the hall into the master bedroom and—

A woman stands at the open bay window. A woman wearing what looks like a long dress of black lace with a veil over her face.

She turns to me, and I stagger back and knock something behind my foot, and thank God I still have the mental awareness not to step down because it's Enigma. The kitten stares at the figure, her eyes wide, fur on end, tiny tail bristled like a bottle brush. Then she leaps in front of me, hissing and spitting.

The figure steps toward me. She doesn't float like a horror movie spook. She walks, one soundless step at a time, her face hidden behind the veil. As she grows closer, I'm not sure it's a lace dress at all. It seems more like a swirling layer of black, obscuring her from view.

Enigma shoots forward, hissing. The figure slows, veiled face lowering to look at the kitten.

I dart forward to scoop Enigma up. The figure lifts her head, watching me, and I'm close enough to see through the veil, and yet I can't. There is only that fluttering black, by turns solid and semi-translucent, pale skin shimmering behind it.

The woman lifts a hand swathed in black. Glimmers of moonlight shine through her body. I see that moonlight gleam, and I swallow hard.

I'm looking at a ghost.

Not a hallucination. Not a prankster. Enigma sees the figure, and so it exists. Yet light shines through it, and so it's not real, not solid.

That hand reaches toward me, and I shrink back. Enigma growls, her eyes huge as they follow the hand. When I flinch, it pauses there, a finger outstretched toward me. Then the hand drops, and the figure steps forward.

One step. Another. Closing the gap between us.

I wheel. Something flickers by the linen closet door, a shimmer of light and shadow. I don't pause to look—I race past, careering down the hall, Enigma clutched against me.

I spot the stairs. I could turn that way. I should. Instead, I barrel toward my room. At the last second, I realize I'm running deeper into the house. But the last time I fled a ghost, I ran outside and—

The black-veiled figure rounds the corner, and that settles the matter. I race into my room and slam the door, the whole house shaking with it. I back up until I hit the bed, and then I half-sit, half-fall onto it, my gaze fixed on the door, expecting the woman to walk right through.

She doesn't.

I sit there, Enigma's tiny heart tripping under my fingers, my own heart pounding so hard I can barely breathe. When I finally wrest my gaze from the door, I scan the room, my muscles tensed.

It's empty.

Enigma relaxes into my arms. Her purrs come jagged, like someone laughing in a carnival spook house, trying to convince themselves they're okay. After a moment, though, those purrs smooth out, and she lifts her head in a miniature lion's roar of a yawn, her needle-teeth flashing.

Still clutching her, I scuttle up the bed until my back is firmly against the headboard. When I listen, I hear only the kitten's purrs and the ticktock of the grandfather clock.

I've seen enough horror movies to know that the moment I relax, the woman will pop up from the foot of the bed. It soon becomes apparent, though, that the ghost has never seen a horror movie. She doesn't pop up. She doesn't moan at the door. She doesn't appear floating outside my windows.

I'm safe here. She can't follow me into my room.

Or that's what she wants you to think!

I have to laugh at that even if it's as rough as Enigma's forced purrs. I do relax a little, though, and still nothing bursts through the plasterwork.

The clock downstairs strikes two before I finally fall asleep, still braced against the headboard, kitten in my arms.

☙❧

AFTER BREAKFAST, DEL COMES BY WITH RONNIE, A KID FROM THE local garage. And when I say *kid* I mean the guy is twenty-five. God, I'm getting old fast. So damn fast it leaves me with an ache in my heart and a panic in my gut. My life is a train rushing past, and I'm just standing there, acting as if I have no choice but to watch and grieve its passing.

Ten years ago, I had the kind of life that made my friends tell me to shut up if I dared raise a complaint. They were joking, and not joking. I'd lament a night spent marking freshman papers, and to them, it was like hearing someone complain about the property tax on her summer home.

Oh, you poor baby. Did Michael sit up with you? Bring you ice cream? Rub your shoulders?

Er, yes, actually, he did.

At twenty-eight, I had my PhD and my dream job—assistant professor at one of Canada's top universities. I was married to my college sweetheart, who also had a PhD—in economics—and a job at a Toronto think tank. We'd spent the last two years living rent-free as we renovated our landlord's house, and we were about to move into a house of our own after which we'd buy a dog and have a baby . . . in that order.

We were *that* couple. Madly in love, financially stable, and ready to embark on the "children and a white picket fence" stage of our nauseatingly perfect lives.

Then came Michael's diagnosis.

Canada has a wonderful health system, but that didn't keep me from spending our new home down payment on experimental treatments. I knew they were a waste of money. I didn't care. I couldn't live my life without knowing I'd done everything I could to save his.

By thirty, I was a widow. A broke widow, barely clinging to her job because she'd spent every spare minute with her dying husband.

After that, my life paused. Or, more accurately, I paused. I stood at the tracks, watching the train whip past. At first, I didn't care. When I finally did, I couldn't figure out what to do about it. My dreams and my future and part of my soul died with Michael, but now, deep inside, a voice has begun to scream that I'm letting the best years of my life slip past.

I'm sure someone like Del would laugh at me. At thirty-eight, I'm as much a kid to him as Ronnie is to me. Yet when I look in the mirror and see the first deepening lines, the first strands of silver, I imagine a wrinkled face and gray hair and a woman who has not taken a single step forward since her husband died half a lifetime ago.

This may explain why I don't run screaming from Thorne Manor after my ghostly encounter. Granted, I'm not the sort who'd do that anyway, which isn't an excess of courage so much as an excess of self-consciousness and ego. I've been in *that* place before, the distraught fifteen-year-old ranting about ghosts only to be told it was my brain rebelling against me. That had been humiliating beyond measure. So I'd never run and pound on Del's door at midnight, sobbing about ghostly figures in black.

Come morning, however, I could have calmly decided I no longer wished to stay at Thorne Manor. Too isolated. Too many memories. I'd sell it and let someone else return the old dame to her former glory.

Instead, I tell Ronnie I'd like the car fixed if that's possible with my budget. Once I'd crawled from under the debt of Michael's treatments, my mother borrowed money from me for her own hospice care, insisting it'd be covered by my inheritance. The only thing I inherited was her collection of pointe shoes. So I can afford to spend no more fixing the car than I would renting a vehicle for the summer.

I also invest a hundred pounds in drapery material, paint stripper and varnish. Which means I'm staying for the summer. This is my house, the only one I've ever owned, possibly the only one I ever will. Along with the adopted cat, it's forward motion. Another milestone to be ticked off the long-neglected List.

It's not just a home, either, but a summer home abroad. It makes me feel as if I've drawn a special card in the board game of life, fast-forwarding me to where I could have been if Michael lived. I might not have the husband or kids or suburban home, but I have a summer house in England, as an overachieving middle-aged professional should.

Thorne Manor is a start. A huge one for me, terrifying in its way. Like watching that passing train, realizing it's not going to stop for me, and taking a running leap onto it. I *am* taking that leap, starting with renovating the house. First, though, I'm having a guest over for afternoon tea.

el brings Freya by at exactly four. Ronnie's younger
brother, Archie, drove them. He waves as I step outside
but stays in the car while Del helps his wife to her
walker. The moment I see Freya, I recognize her. She's smaller
than I remember her, my mind's eye being that of a child. She's a
good six inches shorter than me, plump and pretty, with the kind
of smile that makes you smile in return.

I hurry to help them, but Del only hands me a basket with
"More scones, apparently. And pastries. And sourdough bread.
And choccy biscuits. At least you won't starve."

Freya embraces me in a cloud of sweet sage and browned
butter as the car backs out with a friendly honk. "He's just grumbling because I'm baking more for you than I do for him." She
turns to Del. "You, my dear, are supposed to be retired. You have
plenty of time to bake for yourself. Miss Bronwyn is a university
professor on sabbatical, which means she has a paper to write."
She glances at me. "Yes?"

"Allegedly, though my real work this summer is fixing up the
house and relaxing."

"Not doing much of the latter, I'll bet." She pats my arm. "You will, once you're settled, and I'll keep sending you scones and biscuits and bringing them up when I have the excuse."

"That's her real goal," Del says. "Forget this nonsense about giving you time to do your paper. She's angling for visits to her favorite house. Seeing if the ghosts will finally spark her gran's second sight."

I give a start at that, but they don't notice.

Freya chuckles. "I don't want the Sight, but I'll take the visits. I do love this marvelous house. Now, get on with you, old man. You have work to do on that car. Give the lass back her mobility."

Del stays until she's in the house, and then tromps out to do whatever first aid Ronnie prescribed for my car.

Freya and I chat as I bring out tea, and I relax, partly because I realize I won't need my rusty dialect deciphering skills. I suppose that has something to do with Freya being a former teacher—if she uses the dialect at home, she code-switches with me.

When we're settled, Freya glances toward the door and then says, her voice lower, "Thank you, dear. For being understanding with him."

"Of course. Like I told Del, I'm a university prof. For a lot of young people, college is the one place they feel comfortable being themselves." I start to pour tea. "I suppose it's not easy being here. I know kids from rural areas have a much tougher time of it."

"Actually, we're blessed that way, and it's one reason Del decided to retire in High Thornesbury. He says it was because he met me"—her gray eyes twinkle—"but really, he found a place where he's comfortable. Our village has always had a soft spot for outsiders. They have the Thornes to thank for that. Hard for a town to be judgmental when its most esteemed family had its share of eccentrics. Let's just say it isn't the first time this house has seen someone like Del."

I smile. "I have heard the Thornes were an unusual lot."

"They were, indeed. Whatever their eccentricities, though, they were kind, and they were generous, and it had an impact on those around them. I'm no monarchist—and I despise the lingering class system—but the Thornes led by example, and the village is the better for it. Plus, they left a lot of stories. Strange and wonderful stories."

She watches me, expectant. Yet what flies to the tip of my tongue isn't a laughing request for a fun tale, but a very specific one.

Do you know the history well? Was there a Lord Thorne named William? Silly question—I'm sure there was when it's such a common name. But was there one named William with a sister named Cordelia?

Even if Freya doesn't know, I could look this up online. There's a reason I haven't done that. A simple reason. Fear.

Fear of what, exactly?

Everything.

So I just chuckle and murmur, "Yes, I've heard there are stories." And then I spread clotted cream on a scone and change the subject.

Soon we're talking about teaching, something we have in common. When I discover Freya has a combined degree in English and folklore, I'm overcome with envy.

"I desperately wanted my undergrad in history and folklore, but my mother was horrified enough by the history major. A completely unmarketable field of study."

"Wasn't your dad a historian?"

"Yep, still is. So, as much as I wanted to minor in folklore, I agreed to economics instead. Hated it. Only one good thing came of that . . ." I think of Michael and then hurry on with, "Anyway, my dream is to someday go back for a degree in folklore. A couple of Canadian universities offer them."

"You like folklore, then?" she asks.

I chuckle. "That's an understatement. My historical era of expertise is Victorian with a particular slant toward women's roles. Women have always found power in the realm of folklore. Folk magic, charms, witchcraft . . . With the rise of spiritualism, men shouldered them aside, but they were still active participants, equal participants with real power in the movement. It was a way to engage in scientific study and be taken seriously even if it was pseudoscience." I pause and sigh. "I just switched into Professor Dale mode, didn't I?"

Freya smiles. "You have a willing pupil here. Lecture away." She lifts her teacup and says, far too casually, "So you believe spiritualism is a pseudoscience?"

"Er . . . misjudged my audience, did I? Sorry."

Her smile softens. "That's quite all right. I'm very fond of lively debate. I just thought it was unusual"—she sips her tea —"coming from one with the Sight."

I wince. "Aunt Judith told you about the ghosts. It was only one, actually, and even then, it wasn't real. I had a hypnopompic hallucination. That's—" I pause, not wanting to presume she doesn't know what that is.

She nods. "Thinking you wake to see a ghost by your bed, when really, you aren't awake yet. I'm well aware of the phenomenon, but that doesn't explain your experience, Bronwyn. You fled from the ghost. You saw it while clearly awake. And Stan . . ." She sips her tea. Then she says, "So you haven't seen anything since you've returned, I presume?"

In my mind, I say no and make some silly quip. What I hear myself say, though, is nothing. Dead and damning silence.

"You *have* seen something?" Freya presses.

I set down my cup. I want to answer. I want to talk about this to someone exactly like Freya. Kind and open-minded and educated in the subject.

When I still don't reply, she says, "Whatever you tell me doesn't go outside this room, Bronwyn. Not even to Del. I might believe in ghosts, but I'm not going to hare off to an online forum and share your story. I don't think the world needs proof. Either people believe, or they don't. Trouble only arises when those who see things are convinced they don't by well-meaning loved ones who persuade them they've had a mental breakdown."

I tense. I can just imagine what passes over my face, as she leans forward, saying, "I'm sorry, lass. I shouldn't have said that."

"No, it's okay."

"It isn't. It's none of my business. I'm the only person your aunt told, and just because she knows I can keep a confidence. She needed to speak to someone about it. She was so angry with your mother, but she couldn't tell *you* that and risk your relationship when you'd only just reunited. If it's any consolation, I talked Judith down when she was in a right fury over it. Your mother didn't mean any harm. In her world, that explanation made sense."

"I don't . . . I don't normally see ghosts. I never have outside this house." I force a smile. "God knows, since Michael—my husband—died . . ." I inhale. "I've never even seen an eye speck that I could pretend was him."

I try to say it lightly, but my eyes still fill, and Freya moves beside me, taking my hand.

After a moment, she says softly, "When he passed, were things settled between you?"

"Settled?"

"Was he ready to go? I know it was a brain tumor. I'm presuming you had time. Not enough time, of course. It's never enough."

"With the tumor, we knew Michael's mental capacity could become impaired, so we got our affairs in order, financially and emotionally. I miss him terribly, but there were no loose ends, and I'm grateful for that."

Freya squeezes my hand, and I relax into my grief, the kind that no longer feels like a stiletto through the heart. It's a wound that can lie quiet even if it still never fully heals. A wound that I don't want to heal. Even if I ever fall in love and marry again, I hope that thoughts of Michael will always bring a pang of loss and regret. He deserves that much.

"This is why you won't see Michael," Freya says after a few minutes. "He's at peace. He said what needed to be said. Did what needed to be done. That let him cross over as he should. No matter how much a spirit might want to linger with loved ones, it isn't healthy for them or us."

"I . . . I'm not sure that's the entire answer for me. I really haven't ever seen anything outside this house. There was the night Uncle Stan—" I swallow. "The night he died. Even that was the only one I ever saw until"—I force the words out—"last night."

As I tell her about the black-veiled ghost, her eyes widen.

"My gods, lass, I'd have fled, bad hip and all. Why didn't you come to our house?"

I shrug. "I was fine. It—she—didn't follow me into my old room."

"Do you think it was the same ghost you saw the first time? When Stan—"

"I don't know. I can never remember that ghost. Apparently, I said it was a woman, though, and I think . . . Well, I've been trying *not* to think about it, but yes, it must be the same ghost. Did Aunt Judith ever see anything?"

"She had minor experiences here. Fleeting glimpses. Whispers. A flicker caught in the corner of the eye. A tickle that sets your hairs on end. The smattering of sixth sense we all share, as animals do." She looks around. "Which reminds me, Del mentioned a kitten?"

"She's sleeping in the kitchen."

"Was she there last night? Did she detect anything?"

When I describe Enigma's response, Freya's brows lift and she says, "Well, then, I hope you aren't doubting you saw a ghost."

"I'm not."

We munch our way through two biscuits before she says, "May I ask you about the boy? The one you used to see here?"

I sit up so abruptly my chair squeaks, and I'm still collecting myself when Enigma toddles from the kitchen, having woken and realized there's a party to which she wasn't invited. Her timing is perfect. I pick her up, and Freya *oohs* and *aahs* over her, and Enigma revels in the attention.

"Should I not ask about your imaginary friend?" Freya says as I pass Enigma onto her lap.

I swallow the automatic denial and say carefully, "Yes, I did have an imaginary friend here when I was young, but I never told anyone about him."

She chuckles and leans back, scratching Enigma's ears. "Not once you were old enough to know better, but as a little girl, you chattered about him all the time to your aunt. It was a secret between you. Then, when you were about four, you stopped mentioning him. When Judith asked, you pretended not to know what she was talking about. She said you were adorable. Like a tiny MI6 agent protecting top-secret data. All shifty-eyed and 'I don't know what you mean, Auntie.'"

My cheeks heat. "I don't remember any of that."

"Well, clearly, by that age, you'd realized you were experiencing something you shouldn't discuss with grownups." Freya slants me a knowing look. "Lest they try to convince you that your boy wasn't real."

My cheeks burn now. I don't speak, though. I'm afraid if I do, it'll be a denial, and I don't want to deny this. It's as if I really am four years old again, hoping someone will drag a secret from me so I can share it guilt-free.

"There were several Williams in the Thorne family," she says.

I look over sharply.

"Yes, your aunt had a name for your friend. Not that it does much good. The original house was built by a William Thorne, who passed it to his oldest, also named William, who then passed it, yes, to William the third, who passed it on to his oldest . . ."

"William the fourth?" I say with a forced smile.

"No, that Lord Willie attempted to buck tradition. Only his son wrested it back and named *his* firstborn William. Then it passed to a cousin, who rechristened his heir William to properly reclaim the family tradition."

"So, lots of Williams. I must have read the name somewhere and used it for my imaginary friend."

"Read it at the age of *two*?"

I say nothing.

Freya pets Enigma. "Have you seen him since you've been here?"

"I . . . I've dreamed of him."

"Ah. So, in your 'dreams,' is he still a little boy?"

My cheeks heat, and she chuckles. "Obviously not."

"My age. He's always my age. When I dream about him, I mean."

"Have you considered it's not a dream, Bronwyn?"

"It is. I dreamed I woke up in his old room, which wouldn't be his room now if he were real. He'd be the lord."

"That hardly sounds like damning proof. What else did you see? Hear?"

I tell her everything about the second visit. His bedroom, what I overheard downstairs, the cat, Mrs. Shaw . . .

"Mrs. Shaw?" Freya says.

I nod. "That's another thing that proves it's a dream. Mrs. Shaw reminds me of Del."

"You saw Mrs. Shaw this time?"

"No, but I've seen her before. When I was a child."

"Before you *met* Del. His mother was a Shaw. She left High Thornesbury when she married, but her brother used to be the caretaker here. His family has worked at this house for generations."

"Then that explains it. I must have known Del's uncle, whose face I used for Mrs. Shaw."

Freya's lips twitch. "Only if Mrs. Shaw is six feet tall with red hair and a beard. You're reaching, Bronwyn. Stretching as far as you can to explain this away. You're afraid of considering the possibility that William exists, only to be told you've lost your mind again."

Enigma hops over onto my lap, and I stroke her head.

"So what's your explanation?" I say. "I'm not sure time portals fall under the umbrella of folklore."

"Ah, but they do. Think of every fairy story where a person disappears into another world, another time, and returns to tell the tale. Or consider the Moberly-Jourdain Incident at Versailles. Or the three cadets who stumbled over a deserted medieval English village. The list goes on. Not time travel so much as time slips."

"Is that what you think this is? A time slip."

"More like a stitch in time."

"Saves nine?" I manage a smile. "Fix something today, while the problem is small, to avoid a larger fix later. That proverb has nothing to do with time travel, though."

Freya picks up two decorative cushions. "Imagine this pillow is Thorne Manor right now, and this other one is the house in your William's time." She holds his pillow under ours, separated by a few inches. Then she catches a fold in the fabric, tugs it down and pinches them together. "This is your room. A stitch between the two timelines. A spot where they intersect."

"But time doesn't run like that." I take the pillows and lay them on the floor with a third between them. "This is time. A straight line."

"If you really want theories on the nature of temporal reality, I can give them to you as both a folklorist and the wife of a retired scientist."

My brows must fly up because she laughs. "Del doesn't strike you as a fellow academic? He's a physicist. He just takes his retirement very seriously. But this isn't about proving time isn't linear. It's about proving that, in this particular house, you have a stitch that connects you to another era, a very specific one with a very specific person."

"How would I prove that?"

"The next time you 'dream' about William, ask him to hide something. If you find it now, and it dates back to his time, that proves he exists."

"I don't think I can ask him anything. He's pretending not to hear me." My cheeks heat. "I, uh, I mean that in my, uh, dream, he seems to be angry with me."

Freya bursts into such a ringing laugh that I give a start. "Sorry, lass." Her eyes twinkle. "Is he handsome?"

I struggle to follow the change of subject. "He's not what I'd call conventionally handsome, but he's"—I remember August's words—"not *un*attractive."

Another laugh, just as sudden.

"What?" I say.

"If this William is your dream lover, surely he'd be devastatingly handsome and enthusiastically welcome you back."

"Apparently, I'm a realist even when I'm asleep."

She shakes her head. "I can see I won't convince you of anything today, so let's enjoy our tea while Del finishes his work. And let's instead discuss ways to handle your ghost in black, which I have a feeling is far less frightening to you than discussing William Thorne."

7

At just past six, Del calls for Archie, who apparently runs the local Uber equivalent—a guy you can ring up and get a lift from for a few quid. As we're waiting, I pull on my hiking shoes.

"Where're you off to at this hour?" Del says.

"It's not even six thirty."

"Those don't look like jogging shoes. You'd better not be heading into the moors by yourself."

When I say nothing, Del shoots Freya a look with, "You didn't warn her about the moors?"

Freya only sighs and shakes her head.

"Let me guess," I say. "Serial killers? The cabbie warned me about serial killers and sheep. I'm more worried about the sheep." I pause, narrowing my eyes. "I also seem to recall that when I was little, someone warned me about the dreaded moor hobgoblins."

Del looks at Freya.

"You had a penchant for sneaking out," Freya says. "Judith begged me to tell you local lore that wouldn't necessarily frighten you from the moors forever but . . ."

"Might make me less likely to sneak out on my own?"

"Yes. We've never had an actual serial killer in there, though."

Del opens his mouth, but she beats him to it. "There are stories about disappearances, of course, as with any wild place."

Del fixes her with a scowl. "Don't you say that every story is spun from a grain of truth?" He looks at me. "Girls go missing in our moors."

"Then it's a good thing I haven't been a girl in twenty years," I say.

Before he can reply, Freya says, "*People* have gone missing there. Hikers, day-trippers, suicides . . . It's not the Bermuda Triangle of North Yorkshire. Experienced hikers have accidents. Day-trippers wander too far from the paths. And some poor souls just want to end their lives in a place of peace and beauty. I will admit that this particular stretch does carry a legend of young women who vanished, their bodies never found. However, the last person to disappear was two years ago—a man who fell into the inexperienced-hiker category and who *was* found, alive."

"Alive and ranting about ghosts on the moors," Del says. "Ghosts of young women."

Now Freya's the one fixing him with a look. After a grumble, he says, "All right. He was dehydrated and suffering from exposure. But he *did* claim to see the ghost of a young woman."

"Which he recanted after he recovered, chalking it up to fevered hallucinations." She turns to me as a car heads up the road. "Once upon a time, people did disappear out there. But now, even in this isolated corner of the moors, you don't need to walk far to see the lights of a town. You know your way around the moors, and it's barely evening. Stick to the paths, and give yourself plenty of time to be back before dark."

"I will."

Archie's car pulls into the drive, and Freya introduces us. I get Archie's number in case I need a lift though the young man assures me Ronnie will get the convertible going. He also hints that if I need someone to care for the car after I leave, come September . . .

"You're volunteering to keep her safe and sound in your garage?" Del says.

The young man scratches his dark cheek, looking sheepish. "Well, no, I'd drive her, of course, when the weather's good, but I'd store her for free, and Ronnie could do more work while the lady's gone."

I thank him for the offer and promise to consider it. I will, too, if it gives Ronnie added encouragement to get the Austin-Healey running.

Once they're gone, I fully intend to head straight to the moors. I have my phone and my hiking shoes and my water bottle. It's not yet seven, meaning I have two hours of good light left. Yet as I'm crossing the lawn, I happen to walk through one of the good cell-service areas, and my dad calls. I don't dare walk and talk— I'm guaranteed to lose the connection—so I stop to chat for a few minutes. Which turn into an hour.

Neither Dad nor I have ever been called garrulous, but you'd never know it when we get together. Perhaps it's those ten years of separation. We're always trying to make up for lost time, mend that unwanted rift. Part, too, is that we're both historians.

Dad works in Toronto at the Royal Ontario Museum, which means we're accustomed to regular contact—daily phone calls, twice-weekly Dad-and-daughter coffee dates, Sunday dinners with his wife, and so on. I haven't spoken to him since the day before I left, so our quick check-in call turns into an hour-long intense discussion of the recent discovery of a new First Nations site off the coast of British Columbia.

I don't notice how long I'm on the phone. I just talk, and then I continue on with my plans, walking into the moors. I've been at Thorne Manor for two days without setting foot on the moors, and when I do, I can't believe it took so long. It's like renting a room beside a bakery and going two days before stepping inside.

People talk about their favorite place in the world. The place that, every time they return, makes them unreasonably happy. For some, it's oceans, for others, it's mountains or desert, an environment that speaks to their soul and puts a smile on their face and a spring in their step. The moors is that for me, and the fact it's taken two days speaks to just how conflicted I am about Thorne Manor and all it represents. There was a fear that I'd step into the moors again and find the magic gone.

The magic is not gone.

The moors . . . I always struggle to describe them. A windswept blanket of green and purple, paths that seem as if they go on forever, and then dip into a forested dale, or skirt a deep bog of peat. There are populated sections, of course, and plenty of farms and pastures, but this corner is open land where I can walk for miles and see nothing except, yes, sheep and, honestly, not many of those.

I wander, and I wander, lost in the moors and the memories it conjures. Then shadows snake over me, and I look up with a start. *I didn't see storms in the forecast.* But it's not a storm. It's nine p.m. There's a moment of alarm as I realize I'm farther from home than I expected. Then I see the setting sun, a watercolor splash of purple and yellow, and I spend another ten minutes snapping photos.

Oh my God, it's almost dark, and I need to get back now and . . . Ooh, look at the pretty sunset.

I should be ashamed of myself. I'm not. The setting sun is a marvel that I won't miss because there's nothing like a sunset on the moors. Also, it's been a very, very long time since I noticed the sun setting at all. I take those extra minutes to admire and document the sight. Then I'm off, walking briskly as the shadows lengthen.

I'll get back before actual night. That is, before the sun fully sets. I console myself with that as I cover the distance in long strides. I will admit to the briefest exhale of relief when I spot the distant roof of Thorne Manor. I fix my gaze on it and tell myself that the sun isn't quite down yet, and I don't need to turn on my phone flashlight, just keep walking—

Something touches my fingers.

I wheel, my hands flying up, phone flying out of one. As I see the phone fall, I mentally curse myself for my nerves. Clearly, my fingers brushed a bush or tall grass or . . .

Where I stand, nothing rises above ankle-height for fifty meters in any direction. Yet I can recall the distinct sensation of something cold touching my fingers.

Passing *through* my fingers.

Now I'm being silly. Spooking myself. I felt a night-chilled breeze. That's it. Nothing—

"Please," a voice whispers, right at my ear.

This time, I jump enough to stumble, my arms windmilling, and I catch a glimpse of a figure standing just behind me.

I veer to run, my hands clawing at the air as if for traction. Instead, my feet tangle, and I go down hard, cracking onto my knees and then tumbling onto my back, rising crablike on the heather to see—

Nothing.

There's nothing here except fast falling darkness, shadows swallowing me, leaving me squinting at empty moor.

Heart hammering, I start to rise when I catch sight of my dropped phone. I reach down, fingers closing on the cool metal.

"Please," a voice whispers at my ear.

I twist, phone rising like a sword, and she's less than five feet away, a feminine figure nearly lost in shadow. Her arms are wrapped around her chest, shoulders hunched, head down. She wears a dress that seems completely unsuitable for the environment—a blue gown with flounces and ribbons and crinolines. I can make out just enough of her face to know she's younger than me.

"The path," she whispers, as if she can barely find the words. "I can't find the path, and I'm so cold, and it's so dark."

I open my mouth to answer when I see she isn't looking at me. Her words are for herself, panic whispered under her breath.

"The path is here," I say, and I point, but she just keeps whispering to herself. I step toward her. I can see her better now, light hair and wide eyes, her figure small and pale and terrified.

I reach out, and my hand passes through her, my fingers chilling.

"The path," she whispers. "Should never have left the path."

I remember what Del said about women disappearing in the moors. This is no victim of foul play, just a woman who ventured into the moors and got lost. Now, she's close to safety, but the manor house must be dark, and she can't see it.

I hope she did see it. I hope she took those last hundred steps to safety.

I know better. Her ghost wouldn't be here if she'd found safety.

The house is close, though. Even if she collapsed here, someone should have found her. Someone—

"Oh!" she says, her head jerking up. I see her face then, a smile of relief crossing her features. "Hello! I was walking, and I lost my way."

She jogs my way, and I pause, wondering whether she finally sees me. She stops short, staring right at me.

No, staring at something *behind* me, her gaze fixed just off to my left.

"You!" she says. "You—"

Her hands fly to her mouth, and her eyes widen in disbelief. She lets out a muffled cry and then a shriek as she runs back into the moors.

I wheel. No one's behind me.

When I turn back, the woman is gone, the moors silent again. I stand there, frozen. Then I run for the house. I can see it ahead, the windows alight. Three more steps and—

A figure steps from behind the garage. I stop short. The garage is a good hundred feet away, but someone's there. It's a man with something gripped in both hands.

I douse my light fast. Then he pauses, his gaze scanning the moors, as if he spotted me.

Clouds cover the moon, but I can tell it's definitely a man. He clutches a sharp spade in front of his chest like a weapon. He's dressed in a sturdy wool shirt, trousers and an overcoat, and I need only to see the cut and the style and the materials to recognize clothing from a bygone time.

Another figure from the past.

Another ghost.

I shrink back. The man strides out, gripping the spade tight. Then he looks up at the house. I follow his gaze.

There's someone in the window.

It's the woman in black, that shimmering dark veil fluttering around her in the breeze through the open window.

I wrench my gaze back down to the man.

He's gone.

I look up at the woman. She's still there, illuminated by light, watching me. It's a wavering light, soft and unfocused and shifting the shadows around her. Then one arm reaches to her side, and the light goes out.

I can still see her shape, black on black, her veiled face fixed in my direction, her gloved fingers clutching the drapes.

Except there are no drapes in that room.

No candles, either.

I blink and look around, wondering whether I've somehow stepped into the past. Yet I can see the electric porch lights burning.

I glance up, and the woman releases the drape. It flutters, as if falling as she steps back, and then it's gone. No drape and no candle and no light in that dark window.

It's at least five minutes before I move. Five minutes of my heart hammering. Five minutes of my brain screaming for me to run, just run. Get to Del and Freya's house as fast as I can.

The light of their cottage shines in the distance, and that's where I should go. That's what any sane person would do. The alternative is to walk into this house. Which is *not* sane. Not sane at all.

Only there's one very good reason to go back inside.

Enigma.

I could tell myself she'd be fine. What's a ghost going to do to a cat?

Scare the life out of her. Stop her tiny heart with fear, left alone with something she doesn't understand.

I race to the front porch and yank open the door.

8

A s I run inside, I call for the kitten.

Silence answers.

I glance up the stairs. It's dark and still. I swallow and tiptoe into the kitchen, as if I hadn't already announced my presence by shouting for my cat. Still, I creep.

There's a light on here, and another in the kitchen, left to welcome me home. I slip through the dining room. Ahead I see Enigma's box.

A box . . . and no kitten.

I spin, scanning the kitchen, heart thudding. Then I hear a thready but distinct mew. Soft and yet clearly underlined with kitten annoyance. I'm in the house, and I called her, and she can't get to me, and she's not pleased.

The meow comes from upstairs.

I slowly turn in that direction. Then, I remember I didn't leave Enigma in the kitchen. I'm still uncomfortable giving her the run of the house—I'm not sure how kitten-proof it is. I put her in her bedroom box and shut the door.

I walk slowly to the foot of the stairs and peer up into darkness. Then I start up the stairs, taking one step at a time, wincing with each unavoidable creak. I reach the top and glance down the hall toward the bedroom my parents used to stay in, the one where I just saw the ghost in black. The door is open—I'd been poking around in there earlier. I need to pass that open door to get to my bedroom. To get to Enigma.

I creep toward it, and I tell myself I'll just keep going. *Don't look. Don't look.* Of course, I look. There she is, poised in the middle of the room. The veiled face rises, and I know those hidden eyes are staring right at me.

She takes a step in my direction. I tear down the hall to my room. As I pass the linen closet, something shimmers. I look to see what seems to be an arm reaching out. A small arm. A child's hand. I run faster.

My bedroom door is closed. I grab the knob, and my sweaty fingers slip. Ice touches my back. The ice of ghostly fingers, and then the knob turns, and I shove open my door and fall through. Even as my feet tangle, I keep my balance and spin. I catch one glimpse of the woman in black. Then I slam the door shut.

I stand there, still gripping the knob. When something touches my leg, I jump so fast I nearly step on Enigma. She meows— annoyance that I've been in the room for five seconds and haven't greeted her.

I blink hard. When I look at the door, it's firmly shut, and nothing comes through. Enigma hisses at it, and the hairs on my neck prickle.

The ghost is there. Poised on the other side. I know she is.

I reach for Enigma, and she fairly leaps into my arms. I cuddle her, and she purrs. Every few seconds, though, her gaze cuts to the door, eyes narrowing, telling me the ghost still lingers.

I move farther into the room. I pet and murmur to Enigma, reassuring her. The latter is ridiculous—I'm the one whose heart hammers, every stray creak making me jump. The room stays silent and still.

After a few minutes, I put Enigma back into her box. There's no way I'm opening my door before dawn. As I gaze at the window, I have to laugh at myself. I'm no Lara Croft, able to scale the wall with a cat under my arm. My eyes slide toward the garage, reminding me of the man I'd seen coming out of it. The *ghost* I'd seen.

As if on cue, a figure steps from the shadows. I draw back, heart in my throat, hand reaching to yank shut a curtain that isn't there.

Before I can take another step, though, I pause. The figure is still shrouded in dark as he walks from the garage, the moon caught behind him, casting shadows where there should be light. Yet I know it isn't the man with the spade. This one strides out, sure and confident. He's taller, dark haired, and when I take one careful step closer to the window, my hand is still extended for that missing curtain . . . and it brushes fabric.

I blink and see my fingers resting on thick dark velvet. Below, the garage . . . is no longer the garage. The stonework is solid and whole, no crumbling patches reinforced with cement. The boards that Uncle Stan painted red are bare wood, though already gray with age. The rolling garage door is gone, two big swinging ones in its place. Past the building stretches a stone fence that is rubble in my world.

The figure closes the stable doors and latches them. Then he steps into the moonlight, and when I see him, I only blink as my eyes confirm what my brain already knew.

It's William.

He's dressed in coarser garb—trousers and a rough shirt pushed up past his elbows. No jacket. Hobnail boots. Dirt streaks across one cheek and up one pale arm. Not the lord of the manor inspecting his fine steeds, but a true horseman, feeding his stock and laying hay and mucking out stalls.

He's put the horses to bed for the night, and now he's coming inside, moving fast and purposefully, his gaze fixed on the house. A shape darts from the shadows, and I surge forward, ready to warn him.

Of what? A ghost?

That's what I expect—the man with the spade. But it's only the calico cat—Pandora—dashing from the barn to fall in step with William.

When I move again, William notices the motion and looks up, frowning. Now, he shades his eyes, as if against the moonlight. My breath comes fast and shallow, half of me wanting to jump back out of sight, the other half praying I *will* be seen.

William stops short. His mouth tightens, his gaze locked on me. I lift a tentative hand in greeting . . . and he turns on his heel and marches back toward the stables.

I hurry from the room. I don't pause to wonder what I'm seeing, whether I've somehow fallen asleep. In that moment, I only see William, and I throw open the door and hurry from the room. Kittens mew from the master suite, but otherwise, the house is silent.

I creep to the stairs. In the dark, these look exactly as they do in my version of this house. Flip on a light, and I'd see the banister is still glossy brown, the stairs showing signs of wear only at the edge. Of course, I can't flip on a light. There's no switch, being decades before electricity. This may be a dream, but my mind still fills in all the era-appropriate details right down to a massive walnut hall stand carved with enough flourishes and finials to cover a complete dining room set. The doors are there, too, heavy doors leading to each side of the house, long since removed in my version but here to trap cold air in the foyer when the house is heated by fireplaces.

The front door is heavy enough that I need to tug it open with both hands. Outside, the gravel drive is cobblestone, looping past the house. Even the air smells different. I pick up the scent of spring bluebells from the moors, but the odor of horse is stronger still, mingling with hay and woodsmoke.

I jog around the side to the stables, dirt under my feet, the path as familiar as the smell. One door stands open, and when I step through it, I'm fifteen again, perched on a stall gate watching William work, the stable hands having long learned not to protest even when the young lord picked up a rake to muck out a stall.

Gas lanterns sputter, casting a wavering light through the night-dim stables. This might be the Thornes country house, but the stables are worthy of a duke's abode. From the outside, the building is nondescript. Inside, though, my breath catches, and I remember, as a girl, being furious at the modern disembowelment of such a beautiful space to make room for cars.

Underfoot is cobblestone, swept clear of hay, though the smell of it permeates the space. Even those cobblestones are arranged in whorl patterns. The true beauty, though, is the stalls. Each one is a work of art, wooden dividers with swooping lines, the doors carved and inlaid with wrought iron. The farrier's bench would bring a fortune today as a beautiful antique that people would proudly display in their homes, perhaps never realizing it'd once been used for shoeing horses.

The stables are also immaculate. I won't say I'd eat off the floor, but if I dropped a scone, I wouldn't hesitate to pick it up and wipe it off. Every grooming tool shines in its place. The horses shine, too, their coats glistening in the lantern light, eyes gleaming with health as they watch me pass.

One horse stamps and whinnies, but there's no sign of William. I pass stalls, counting six horses: four mares with spring foals, one gelding and a gorgeous black stallion who huffs at me, shaking his ebony mane.

"Go," a voice says behind me.

I wheel, and there stands William, his face unreadable, Pandora at his side, her cold glower saying everything his impassive stare does not.

Seeing him, any sense that this is a dream evaporates. I'm standing in front of him—seeing him, hearing him, smelling him, feeling the very heat of him, and in this moment, he is absolutely real. Denying that feels as foolish as looking on the black-veiled ghost and telling myself she's a figment of my imagination.

This is William, and he's real, and as long as he stands here, my heart will accept no other explanation.

"I—" I begin.

"I would like you to go." He enunciates each word with care and without inflection.

"It's me. Br—"

"I know who you are. I am asking you to leave, Bronwyn."

"I'm sorry," I blurt, and then continue before he can interrupt. "I promised I'd come back, and I didn't, and I'm sorry. I know I hurt you . . ."

Even as the words "I hurt you" leave my mouth, I know it's the wrong thing to say. His face goes cold for a split second before he laughs, and that laugh cuts icier than any glare.

"Hurt?" he says. "We were children. Did you honestly believe I expected you to keep your word? That I've been waiting for you?"

My cheeks heat. "Of course not. I just meant—"

"It's been twenty-three years, Bronwyn. The fact I even know your name is a shock. Apparently, my memory is better than I thought."

I flinch at that. "I—"

"I have lived more than half my life since I last saw you. A very full, very rich life, undimmed by any shadow cast by your sudden departure. We were children." He eases back, something in his face shifting, closing. "You aren't real anyway."

"Not real?"

Another shift, distancing himself from this conversation. "You're a phantasm. I've long accepted that."

"You think I'm a ghost?"

"Of course not," he snaps. "No sound mind believes in such nonsense."

"You said phantasm . . ." I say slowly.

"Phantasm, apparition, hallucination. Whatever you wish to call it. I was a lonely child, and so I conjured up a playmate. At fifteen, I was developing an interest in the female sex while too young to act on it. So I conjured you again. You fulfilled needs. I don't know why you're appearing now. Perhaps I have indeed been here too long, and I am in greater need of companionship than I realized. I do not, however, need you."

"I'm not a phantasm, William. Look at your cat. She sees me. I'm here."

His gaze meets mine, eyes ice cold. "Perhaps. But the answer remains the same. I do not need you."

I open my mouth. Nothing comes out.

"I am asking you to leave, Bronwyn." His voice has changed now, neither cold nor cruel, filled with nothing but a sincere wish. *Please leave.*

"If that's what you want," I say finally, drawing it out, searching his gaze for some sign of hesitation.

"Yes," he says. "Please."

I nod, and then I withdraw.

❦

I'M IN WILLIAM'S ROOM. I'M NOT LYING IN WAIT. HE GENUINELY wished me to leave, and I want to respect that. Yet nothing I do takes me home.

After two hours, his footsteps sound on the stairs. Panic explodes in me with the irrational urge to dive under the bed. I'm already humiliated enough. I remember that laugh when I made the mistake of saying I'd hurt him.

The fact I even know your name is a shock. Apparently, my memory is better than I thought.

I have lived more than half my life since I last saw you. A very full, very rich life, undimmed by any shadow cast by your sudden departure.

Even now, I cringe at those words. I didn't expect him to remember me. Certainly didn't expect my disappearance to cast any pall over his life. That's the last thing I'd want.

The door opens. He steps in, exhaling as he relaxes, shoulders rolling, hands reaching for the buttons of his shirt.

"William," I say.

He gives a start, his face gathering in obvious outrage.

I rise quickly, hands out to stop his words. "I was just warning you, before you—"

"I asked you to leave."

"Believe me, I'm trying. I'm *really* trying. I know you want me gone."

"I do."

"It'll happen. It has to, right? Maybe if I tap my heels three times . . . ?" I try for a smile, but he only frowns, and I realize I'm about a half-century too early for that joke. "I'm sorry. I'll just . . . I'll go wait in another room."

He steps aside as I pass, giving me a much wider berth than needed.

When I reach the door, he says, "Do you expect me to believe that?"

I turn. He has his arms crossed, face once again unreadable.

"Believe that I can't find the way back?" I say. "No, clearly, I've been lying in wait for two hours, hoping you'll run in and say you've made a terrible mistake, fall at my feet and declare undying love, thank your lucky stars that I didn't disappear into the ether again."

His face hardens. "You don't need to mock—"

"Don't I?" I say, my temper rising as I step toward him. "I came to the stables to apologize. That was all. I made a promise, and I broke it, and I wanted to say I'm sorry. You didn't need to be cruel, William."

"I—"

"I'm talking now. Yes, this is your house, but since I can't seem to leave it, I'm going to talk, and if you feel the need to flee"—I step aside and wave—"the door is there."

His mouth sets, and he steps back, arms crossing in answer.

I continue, "You say you believed I was a phantasm. Is it possible I believed—still cannot help believing—the same of you?"

"Me?" He sounds genuinely indignant. "That is ridiculous."

"Is it? I told you things of the future, which must have come to pass. Yet you never offered the same."

He sputters. "How would I—?"

"You could have left me a message. Hidden something for me to find in my time."

"How? Pry up a floorboard?"

"The point is that if you believe I'm not real, then it makes sense that I'd believe the same of you. That I might have"—my voice catches, in spite of myself—"been convinced of it by others."

His face darkens. "You told others about me?"

"My uncle died," I say. "He was . . ."

I stop myself before mentioning the circumstances. I've already heard William's opinion of ghosts and those who see them.

I continue, "In the aftermath, I made the mistake of confessing that I'd had . . . inexplicable experiences. My mother—"

"Your mother," he says with a scornful snort. "Of course."

"My mother and two . . ." I search for the word appropriate to his time, predating Freud and the birth of psychology. "Two doctors who treat diseases of the mind determined that I'd suffered a breakdown. I spent the rest of my summer in a hospital."

"They confined you to a lunatic asylum for telling them about me?" His voice rises, outrage mingling with horror.

"In my time, it's not an 'asylum.' It's a hospital where people go to rest and receive treatment. Humane treatment. Medication and therapy—talking, lots of talking."

He still doesn't look convinced. We're at a time when mental treatments were far from benign and reserved for those so affected they couldn't function in normal life.

"You were not mad," he huffs. "Anyone could see that. Yet you allowed them to convince you that you were?"

"I allowed them to convince me you weren't real," I say. "Which shouldn't be so shocking, considering you've apparently convinced yourself that I'm not real with no outside influence."

"How is that the same?" he snaps. "I had to invent some reason why you never returned. You chose not to return. You chose to let others convince you—"

"I didn't *choose* anything. I was fifteen, William. My uncle had just died, horribly and traumatically. My mother rushed to York-shire and found me babbling about time travel and a boy who lived in this house two hundred years ago. Naturally, she presumed I'd had a breakdown. The doctors agreed."

He shifts, uncomfortable now but still searching for a rebuttal.

"How do you think that felt? I wasn't a child, permitted imagi-nary playmates. I was old enough to know better, and yet somehow I didn't. In my mind, you were real, though I logically realized you couldn't be. They shamed me for what I saw. Now, you shame me for allowing that."

"I—"

"*No.*" I swipe a hand over my cheek, hot tears scorching it. "You say I chose not to return. Yes, yes, I did. Part of that wasn't a choice. My aunt stopped spending summers in Yorkshire after my uncle died. My mother certainly wasn't going to allow me back. But I could have returned when I was an adult. I chose not to. For twenty-three years, I chose not to because this house was all about you, and you were a figment of my imagination. A figment of my shame. And a figment of a wonderful dream I could never recap-ture. Yes, I stayed away. Because I believed you weren't real, and you just told me you thought the same of me, yet you have the gall to mock me for not believing in you?"

"I—"

"I hope you aren't real, William. I hope to God I'm asleep and dreaming right now because I don't see any trace of the boy I fell in love with. That boy might be hurt that I broke my promise—and yes, I know you aren't hurt, as you've made *abundantly* clear—but that boy would have given me the chance to explain. I'm sorry that I came here. I'm sorry I'm still here. I don't know why I crossed over or how to get back, but I'm going to go into another room and hope to wake from what I pray is simply a nightmare."

As I turn to leave, he grabs my upper arm. "Bronwyn."

I stop, but I don't turn around.

We stand there, saying nothing. His fingers rub my arm, and his voice lowers.

"Bronwyn. I'm . . ."

When he doesn't finish, I look to see his gaze on his hand, on his fingers stroking my arm. He pulls back, releasing me, and there's a jolt, a flash of darkness. And then I'm standing alone in my bedroom.

I stay there, standing, looking around at the dark room. After a moment, I stagger like a sleepwalker to the bed, my mind numb.

Enigma meows at my feet, and I scoop her up, hugging her close. Then I cry. I cry for everything I've lost. For Michael, for my mother, for my aunt and my uncle. And for William, for the boy I knew, real or fantasy.

I huddle on the bed, clutching a kitten, and I cry until I fall asleep.

9

I wake the next morning resolved. That's the best word to describe my emotional state. All that I'll allow it to be. Resolved.

Resolved to forget about William. Resolved to forget about the ghosts. Resolved not to allow either to scare me away from this house.

Resolved to sew drapes and strip wood and pick wildflowers and harvest berries and maybe even make jam from them. Resolved to *not* work on my paper because I've published enough in the last decade that I'm hardly concerned about missing a year in the publish-or-perish grind of academia. Resolved to spend my summer reading nothing that would ever make its way into a university syllabus and banish the words *guilty pleasure* from my vocabulary.

Resolved to let Freya know she has a standing invitation to tea. Resolved to get the convertible running even if that means tinkering with it myself. Resolved to walk for hours each day in the moors, and resolved to *not* lose a single pound doing it, no matter how many scones that takes. Resolved to blast my nineties classic rock and dance through the house whenever the mood strikes. Resolved to thoroughly spoil Enigma, enjoy her kittenhood, research whatever steps are needed to take her home with me and stop pretending that I might not actually do that.

I am resolved.

I begin by bouncing from bed so fast that Enigma squeaks her alarm. A few pats reassure her that all is well, and then I step off the throw rug and hear a board squeak underfoot where a board never squeaked before.

If you asked me which boards in this house squeaked, I'd have laughed and said, "All of them." I certainly didn't pay attention to which did. Yet I'd apparently cataloged that information in the soundtrack of my life within this room. When I step off the rug, bracing for the chill of the hardwood, the board squeaks under my heel.

I hesitate. Then I back up, weight into my heel, and feel the wood give.

The floorboard is loose.

I want to continue on. I want the resolve to continue on. Yet if I don't check, it'll pluck at the back of my mind, disrupting all attempts to enjoy a peaceful day.

I bend, slide my fingernails into a groove and tug. The board lifts as easily as if it were displaced yesterday. Underneath lies a yellowed piece of folded paper.

My fingers tremble as I pull out the note. On it are four words, the ink faded with time.

Bronwyn,
　　Your note.
　　　William.

I stand and stare down at the note. Stare and stare and stare until the letters swim before my eyes.

William is real.

I can come up with alternative explanations, but they all strain credibility at least as much as "A man left this note for me a hundred and seventy years ago because I stepped through time and asked him to."

William exists.

My fingers slide over the paper, so old it threatens to crackle under my fingers, and as I do, I back onto the bed, and I exhale in what starts as a sigh only to crystallize into a deep, shuddering sob, relief and grief, too. The crashing wave of relief that comes with acknowledging that my mind never betrayed me.

I've spent years chiding myself for my shame. A mental collapse is nothing to be ashamed of. The problem is that, deep down, I could never accept the diagnosis, and *that* is what shamed me most. My denials made me feel weak, lacking the strength to accept my breakdown and hold my head high.

Now I know why. Because I didn't suffer a mental break at fifteen. I didn't imagine a ghost. I've seen several here since, with Enigma's reaction proving they are real.

Now I have proof that William is real, too, and I don't know how to handle that. I should be elated, jumping back into his room to talk to him, finally talk to him. Yet I look at the note again, and I don't fail to notice the brevity.

I asked for proof. He gave me proof . . . and nothing more. There's no invitation to visit here. No hint that such an intrusion would even be tolerated.

Resolve. It can mean a determination to carry out a plan. It can also mean an ending. William has given me closure, nothing more. An answer thrown into the universe and then a door firmly shut. But perhaps, knowing how this ends—with me alone in this house at least a hundred years after his death—that abrupt conclusion is for the best.

I may have spoken in anger, but there was truth in my words, too. He's not the boy I knew. I'm not the girl he knew, either. Better that we settle our outstanding business even in a less than satisfactory way. Then we can both move on.

Which is what I must do. All that I can do if I'm to respect his wishes and stay away.

I gather wild strawberries. I make fresh jam for my scones, and I enjoy breakfast in the sitting room with a novel in my hand and a kitten on my lap. After breakfast, I walk the moors, and in the light of day, the ghosts from the night before seem impossible phantasms. Even if they aren't, the sun confines them to their place, and I tramp through the heather and eat a picnic lunch by a burbling stream and feel not a prickle on my neck.

I spend the afternoon helping Del and Ronnie with the car, and the engine actually turns over. Ronnie swears he'll have her running tomorrow; Del says he'll be lucky to get her going this month. The answer likely lies in the middle, which is enough for me.

Freya has gone off to the city, but she'll be by for tea tomorrow. So I have my afternoon snack with Enigma. Then the kitten wanders off, and I spend the next hour searching for a tiny feline I can hear but can't see. I find her in the old dumbwaiter, the curious kitten having squeezed through the unlatched hatch door, whereupon I lock her in my room and bicycle into town to buy a latch. A package of latches, actually. I recall what William said about her being a little adventurer, always getting stuck some-place. Apparently, she'd behaved so far because she was learning her new surroundings. Now that she's comfortable, she's resorted to type.

Does that make me think of William? Of course, it does. I won't for one second pretend I don't wish this had gone differently, that I don't yearn for a scenario where I could pop back to his time as I used to, talk to him as I used to. But he's made his feelings on the matter very clear, and I must honor them.

I install the latches and eat a late dinner, complete with two glasses of wine, which sounds so much more extravagant if I don't admit that for me, a "glass" is about three ounces. There have been too many evenings in the last decade where alcohol—and alcohol-induced oblivion—seemed like a fine idea, so I'm very careful with my intake.

When Enigma squeaks, I look up with a start, my gaze going

to the spot where I'd last seen her, curled on my legs. She's not there.

The sound comes again, from upstairs, and I follow it into the master bedroom where it seems to be coming from the other side of the balcony door.

The door that has been locked for twenty-three years.

I dash forward, certain Enigma has somehow found her way onto the parapet. Then she peeks from under the dresser and bats something across the floor. As it skitters over the wood, I think, *bug*, and whatever it is does indeed glitter like an iridescent beetle shell. It's a moonstone cufflink. Uncle Stan's, from a set I'd once bought him for Christmas.

My gaze goes from the dusty cufflink to that locked balcony door, and a shiver turns to uncontrollable trembling. Enigma chirps in alarm. I pick her up, and pet her and sit on the bed as I stare at that door and do the one thing I've avoided since I returned to Thorne Manor: remember why I left twenty-three years ago. The exact circumstances surrounding my departure.

That night, I'd fallen asleep on the sofa downstairs. Aunt Judith was staying with a sick friend, and I drifted off while reading, so Uncle Stan decided to leave me there.

I woke to . . .

I'm no longer certain what I woke to. In the hospital later, one young doctor experimented with hypnotism, and it seemed to have the reverse effect—instead of helping me untangle the chaos of that night, it snarled my memory even more.

I saw a woman. I know that only because I've been told that I said that. When I try to conjure her face, I'm not sure whether I'm actually remembering or creating the memory out of piecemeal bits related by others. I know that I woke to a woman standing over me, and I knew she was a ghost.

Screaming for Uncle Stan, I raced to the stairs. Then I remembered my friends making fun of a horror movie because a girl fled a killer by running upstairs when the front door was right there. So I stopped.

I wish to God I hadn't. That I hadn't, even in my terror, feared looking foolish. But I was fifteen, and there was no greater sin than being a silly, weak girl. So I ran out the front door.

Hearing me, Uncle Stan ran onto the parapet over the front door, the one I was forbidden to use because it was old and crumbling. Aunt Judith had long wanted that door sealed shut, but Uncle Stan had a chair out there where he liked to read his morning paper.

He shouted for me as I raced across the lawn. I wheeled to see him . . . and the ghost stepping out behind him. I shouted at him to turn around, and he did and . . .

I'll never know whether he actually saw her. As he spun, his foot snagged that damned chair. He stumbled, and he fell against the railing, and a horrible crack rang out as the railing broke and then—

I can tell myself I don't remember the rest. Of course, I do. If I could surrender one part of that night, *this* is the part I'd forget. I'll keep the memory of the horror that sent me tearing from the house. Just let me forget what happened next. Please let me forget.

I remember every second of it. Seeing my uncle fall. Hearing his yelp of surprise and then the thud of his body hitting the ground. Running over, screaming, to see him staring up, empty-eyed, his neck snapped.

I remember the rest, too. Kneeling in the night-damp grass and screaming until my voice was raw, until someone walking her dog in the village actually heard me. The villagers came, and they found me beside my uncle's body, ranting about a ghost.

Now I'm at Thorne Manor again and seeing ghosts again. I'm choosing to stay here, knowing the woman in black is probably the one who terrified me the last time. This might be the biggest mistake I've ever made, and yet, even knowing that, even knowing William is done with me, I choose to stay.

I'M BLESSED THAT NIGHT WITH DREAMLESS SLEEP. A GHOST-FREE, dream-free night. I wake, roll from bed, step off the rug . . . and the board creaks.

Remembering William's note, I hesitate, my toes rocking the board. Then I lift it before I can tell myself there's no need, that I've already retrieved his missive.

I tug up the board to see that folded piece of yellowed paper again.

I then open my nightstand drawer and confirm yesterday's note is exactly where I put it.

I reach down into the floor and unfold the note. It isn't the same one. It's longer, for one thing. I skim the perfect script.

> Bronwyn,
>   I would like to apologize for my behavior the night before last. I spoke in haste and in anger. I understand why you could not return.
>   William

I read the note twice, searching for a weather vane to tell me which way his mood blows. Does he regret that we didn't have more time to talk? Or is he simply realizing he was rude and correcting that while hoping I don't misinterpret it as an invitation to visit.

I fold the note abruptly, my fingernails creasing the edge with a zip of annoyance at myself for needing more. William apologized. That's enough. It must be.

I have another fulfilling day, the perfect combination of industry and sloth. Freya visits for tea. Naturally, she asks about my resident spooks.

Ghosts? No, I haven't seen a ghost in . . . Oh, it's just been so long.

Freya offers to discuss methods for dealing with the black-veiled ghost, should she return. I should take her up on this. Rejecting her offer is like rejecting insomnia remedies after one solid sleep. Yet I've had two excellent days in row, and I'm desperate not to jinx it. I'm enjoying the house and determined not to imagine anything that could make me leave it. I'm pretending I'm fine with how things ended with William . . . while subconsciously hoping I'll see him again, which requires staying at Thorne Manor.

Night two passes without incident, probably because, again, I keep myself so busy during the day that by sundown I'm in bed, where I remain until morning.

At dawn, I rise, and my feet hit that board, and it squeaks.

This time, I stop myself from looking. There won't be another note, no matter how much I might ache for one. I want a third good day, and I won't have that after I've lifted that board and found nothing.

Yes, deciding not to look is about as sensible as telling Freya I didn't need her ghost-banishing tips. It's whistling past the grave-yard. I'm happy, more than I've been in a very long time, and I'm bubble-wrapping that fragile happiness.

My resolve lasts all morning, mostly because I'm helping Ronnie in the garage. The Austin-Healey is running now, enough to get me to town and back, with only a small likelihood of stalling at the roadside. One wonderful thing about living out here is that if the car does die, I can walk home and call Ronnie to fetch it. You can't do that in Toronto.

Once Ronnie's gone, I clean the car, feeling like one of those sorority girls, dressed in shorts and a tank top, sudsing up for a charity car wash. Neither the tank nor the shorts are particularly flattering—I brought them for around the house—but no one's within a kilometer radius to see me.

I've never been car-proud. I don't even own one in Toronto. When the debt-noose tightened anew after Mom's death, my little Prius was the first thing I sold. Still, even I can't resist the fantasy of tooling around the countryside in a shiny antique convertible.

Yet scrubbing the tires and polishing the chrome gives me too much time to think . . . about one thing in particular. Finally, I throw down my polishing rag, stalk into the house and head straight to my bedroom, Enigma trotting after me. I stride into my room and pull up the board.

There is another note.

My heart thuds as I unfold it. What if he says something that undoes his apology? What if—?

Bronwyn,

I realize you may not wish to visit again after the other evening, but I would ~~appreciate~~ like another chance to speak to you.

William

I touch that crossed-off *appreciate*. Despite the yellowed paper and faded ink, there's a clear blotch before the strike, as if he hesitated there, pen dripping before he sliced through the word. Another blotch appears just before *like*, and I picture him sitting at his desk, pen poised, ready to strike it through as well, returning to the more formal *appreciate*.

I run my finger over the words, feeling the indent of them in the paper, and I don't see uncertainty or indecision. I see pride. Not "*Would* I like her to return?" but "Do I dare say it?"

Twenty-three years ago, I said I'd return, and I didn't. There is no way, in such a circumstance, that he could have shrugged and said, "Oh, well."

The wound may have healed, but the memory of it still stings his pride. It took effort to write *like*. It probably took effort to pen the note at all. He has taken a chance, and the next move is mine.

There's no question of what that move will be. This is a door I've been hovering at for three days. I close my eyes, as I used to, and I think of William, and even before I open them, I smell his room—sandalwood and smoke and stable—and I look to see . . .

An empty bedchamber. Which isn't at all surprising, given that it's the middle of the afternoon. As I hesitate, hooves pound over hard earth, the windows rattling with it.

I hurry to the window just as William passes astride the black stallion. He's bent forward, the horse flying at a gallop. As I lift my hand to get his attention, I see his face, all grim lines and thunder, and I hesitate. He whips past toward the moors, his expression saying he's in no mood for company.

Did he change his mind?

No. I won't fret and second-guess. Over the course of the day, something annoyed or frustrated him, and he's riding it off, as he always used to. I'll wait, and he'll return in a better mood.

I step into the hall, and the clatter of dishes below stops me.

Mrs. Shaw.

I could sneak past and wait in the stables, but her footsteps suggest she's zipping about, and I don't dare be spotted.

As I withdraw, I hear the kittens. I ease open the master bedroom door to see two tumbling kittens and no momma cat.

I'm about to retreat when a squeak alerts me to trouble. I glance in to see the black kitten hanging from the drapes. I hurry over and grab her, then extricate her claws from the fabric.

I return the kitten to her box . . . and one of her littermates promptly begins scaling Mount Drape only to find himself in the same predicament. I sigh, and instead of taking him down, I boost him up and let him find his grip again. He does and climbs a little farther before deciding to descend.

I spend the next while playing kitten tutor, watching all three of them climb and showing them how to find their grip when they lose it. I suspect William won't appreciate the lessons, but it's better than coming home to find a broken kitten on the floor.

After an hour, they decide they're ready for a more interesting climbing tree: me. I sit on the floor, adjusting my cell phone in my back pocket, and let them climb, wincing as the tiny claws dig in. Soon they tire and cuddle on my lap, purring, and I lie down to let all three curl up against me. When sleep comes, it claims all four of us.

10

"**B**ronwyn." The voice slides through my dream, and I chase it, abandoning a lovely fantasy of driving with the convertible top down. A hand strokes my hair, the touch gentle, the fingertips rough, callused when they brush my cheek. The scent of horse and hay wafts over me.

"Bronwyn."

My eyes flutter open to see William crouched beside me, his hand tucking hair away from my face. He pulls back and hunkers there, a smile tentatively touching his eyes, as if uncertain of its welcome.

"Come to steal my kittens?" he says.

I blink and rise, and three kittens squeak indignantly as they slide off me. I look at them and blink harder. Pandora appears, her tail flicking as she watches me.

"I think I already did," I say, "unintentionally."

"Hmm?"

"One of your kittens came through my bedroom a couple of days ago. I opened the door, and there she was. Then, the other day, I heard you talking about missing a kitten. I think it's her. She's a calico with white paws."

A pause, as if he's processing. Then a half smile as he looks at the cat. "Your missing baby has found a new home, Pandora."

"I'll bring her back," I say quickly. "I didn't mean to take her."

"You didn't take her, and you are quite welcome to keep her. She's a proper nuisance, that one. From the time she could toddle, even Pandora couldn't keep her in the box. Always poking about, getting herself into scrapes. She had a particular propensity for wandering in my room, usually in the dead of night, clawing her way onto my bed and demanding petting. I'm quite happy to be rid of her. I have homes for all the others. No one would take her."

His tone is light, jaunty even, but the lie shadows his eyes. There's a reason no one claimed Enigma from the litter—because he'd planned to keep her for himself.

"I'll return—" I begin.

"No," he says, firmer, and the shadow solidifies into resolve. "If you want her, she's yours."

I hesitate.

"Have you named her?" he asks.

"Enigma. Though that hardly fits since I now know where she came from."

His lips twitch in a smile. "And where is her box?"

"One's beside my bed, and one is in the kitchen."

"She has a name, and *two* boxes, one at your bedside. That answers my question, Bronwyn. You want her, and therefore, I would like you to have her. It's a fair trade for her mother, who I believe came from your side."

My brows rise.

He settles back. "There's a chest at the foot of my bed, one that I presume doesn't exist in your version of the room. Five years ago, I heard a squeak and opened it to find a calico kitten."

"Pandora," I say, smiling. "A fitting name."

"I thought so."

With that, silence falls, and it lies there, heavy between us. I'm searching for something to say when he asks, "How long have you been in here?"

"A while. I saw you ride out, but you didn't look happy. I trust that had nothing to do with me."

"Of course not. You'd said you were having trouble crossing, so I knew it might take a while. Also, you have your own obligations. I hardly expected . . ."

He slides me a sidelong glance and a rueful half smile. "No, that is a blatant lie, and I've resolved to be honest, should you return. I placed the note under the floorboard last night, and I know you've been receiving them because they disappear. But you weren't taking this one, and my patience wore out faster than I care to admit. In the span of an hour after lunch, I went from telling myself you were simply occupied to being utterly convinced you'd read and returned the note, proof that you'd given up on me."

"I wouldn't do that."

He nods, his gaze down, and silence settles between us again. I start to rise and realize I'm wrapped in a blanket. When I look down at it, William says, "Yes. I wrapped you. You seem to have crossed in a state of undress."

With some alarm, I peek under the blanket to see that I'm wearing exactly what I had been—shorts and a tank top.

I laugh. "I'm fully dressed."

"In your undergarments, perhaps."

"Nope, this is a twenty-first-century outfit, suitable for public display."

"Display is indeed the word," he murmurs under his breath. "And I say that while quietly lamenting the fact I wasn't born two centuries later if that is proper public costuming for ladies."

"I was thinking earlier that it's relatively demure," I say, "and not particularly flattering."

His brows rise. "Do mirrors not work in your world? I cannot quite imagine a more flattering outfit. Although, that shift you wore the other night would be strong competition."

He pauses, as if recalling it, and I do the same, thrown back into that moment of being in his bed, seeing him in his own state of undress.

"My apologies," he says, pulling back as my cheeks must flame bright scarlet at the memory. "That was inappropriate."

"Not at all," I say. "I'd forgotten that I used to change into dresses before I crossed over. I knew if anyone here saw me in shorts and a T-shirt, it'd be a dead giveaway that I didn't belong."

He chuckles. "Well, at the risk of being inappropriate again, I must admit that I would not have objected. Even those dresses, as demure as they are in your time, were quite . . . flattering."

I laugh. I'd never considered how he might react to my very un-Victorian summerwear. Which is probably a good thing because if I had thought of it, even at fifteen, I'd have been very tempted to "forget" to change out of my shorts and tanks just to get his reaction.

Even now, I do consider abandoning the blanket, but the thought only lasts a heartbeat. We're still on uneven ground, and I want him to be comfortable.

"I can offer you some hospitality," he says. "Mrs. Shaw has left for the day, and there's hot tea or a cold supper, whichever you'd prefer."

"Does the tea include Mrs. Shaw's scones?"

The corners of his eyes crinkle in a smile. "It does. Come, and we'll see whether we can find you something to wear."

As I walk with a blanket clutched around me, William explains that his mother passed nearly sixteen years ago. She'd been bedridden when I was here at fifteen, and while she'd recovered from that, she'd never truly regained her health.

After her death, he'd told Mrs. Shaw to do as she wished with his mother's dresses. With William's permission, the housekeeper had refitted them for members of the local minor gentry, women whose budget sensibilities overcame any aversion to secondhand finery. Lady Thorne's gowns were long gone, but since then, Mrs. Shaw had made a side business buying and reselling dresses, and

William let her store her stock in his mother's old bedroom. That's where he takes me—to two wardrobes bursting with finery.

It's like opening a door into another world, a Victorian Narnia through the wardrobe. One peek, and I become the girl who would crack open her mother's historical romances, too young to appreciate the actual romance part—much less the sex parts—but leafing through to devour the inevitable ball scene. It didn't matter if I'd read a hundred of them, all of a sameness. A young woman transformed into a society debutante, squeezed into a corset, layered with finery, adorned with jewels, her hair twisted into a masterpiece of soft curls and smooth sweeps. She'd step from the dressing room like Cinderella, whisked off in a coach-and-four to the ball, where she'd meet her dashing prince—or brooding earl or rakish lord—and dance the night away, belle of the ball, twirling effortlessly to the string quartet, slipping out to a convenient parapet for a clandestine kiss. Even my eight-year-old heart would pitter-patter at that kiss.

Now I'm opening a wardrobe to the core of that romantic fantasy. Dresses. So many dresses. It doesn't matter how many gowns I've seen in museums—these are a revelation. The smell of muslin and potpourri. The jewel colors and shimmering water-falls of fabric undimmed by age. My fingers stroke the silk bodice of a breathtaking gown. It's wine-red paisley on white, its long sleeves bedecked with enough ribbons to make my inner tween squeal.

"That one?"

William's voice jolts me, and I glance over only to be plunged straight into the heart of the fantasy. August called William "not unattractive." While he may not be conventionally handsome, his face is the ideal blend of the boy I knew and the man I'd like to know better, familiar and mysterious, every edge and curve making my fingers ache to reach out and touch. Freya teased that William had to be real because a fantasy lover would be perfect in every way. He *is* perfect, though. To me. As swoon-worthy as any man who ever stepped out of a novel.

And of course, even thinking that, my face heats, and I stammer a non-reply that has his brows knitting in confusion.

I force a laugh. "This dress is not exactly tea-time wear."

"As I am the only person here, I don't believe that's a concern." He glances down at his own outfit—the loose white shirt and coarse trousers better suited to a stable boy than a lord. "I will need to dress as well, and I shall choose my attire to complement yours."

"You don't need to change, and I'm too hungry to spend a half-hour lacing myself into that gown, as lovely as it is." I flip through and tug out a full-skirted green dress with short puffed sleeves. "This will be perfect."

As I shake it out, he says, "Do you remember when we planned to sneak you into a ball?"

I laugh. "I confessed my completely unrealistic fantasies, and while you warned me the reality would be a disappointment, you vowed to sneak me into one. Find me a dress and give me a mask and present me as your mystery companion for the evening." I shake my head. "We were very young, weren't we?"

"We were, indeed. I take it you no longer yearn for a ballgown and a coach-and-four?"

"Oh, no. I totally do. But I can just imagine what a disaster that would have been. Masked mystery companion works very well in romance novels. Reality is something else entirely." I turn, gown raised. "Now, if you will excuse me . . ."

He quarter-bows. "I will leave you to it as I change into something more appropriate."

I protest again, but he strides off with a wave of his hand and a cat at his heels. I watch him go as I grin like a schoolgirl. Then I take a deep breath and turn my attention to the task at hand.

I DO NOT WEAR THE GREEN DRESS. IT'S MADE FOR A WOMAN WITH A significantly smaller chest. Or, perhaps, a woman with a proper corset that would push that chest up into a veritable shelf of bosom. William might have found my mid-thigh shorts and tank top scandalous, but having half your boobs on display is perfectly acceptable in this time period. Victorians were an odd lot.

The dress I do wear still shows off more décolletage than I'm accustomed to, but the stays ensure I don't need to dig for a corset. Without, alas, I lack the ideal Victorian wasp waist, one a man could encompass with his hands. The thought makes me chuckle—no corset in the world could do that for me, not unless the man has the hands of an eight-foot giant.

While I might not be the romance heroine of my mother's novels, I'm not displeased by what I see in the mirror. It's a three-tiered blue-and-white confection of a dress, but actually quite simple for the time with a minimum of flounces and ribbons. It fits oddly until I remember this is the era of crinolines. I find one, and with it on, the dress drapes properly though it looks rather ridiculous for a casual tea at home.

In Lady Thorne's old dressing table, I find hairpins needing only a quick dusting. I arrange my hair in an artistically messy bun, curls dangling over my shoulders, and while I notice strands of white shot through the dark, it isn't as if William hasn't seen me makeup free and messy haired already. He knows exactly how old I am, being the same age himself with even more silver in *his* hair. Also, I'm dressing for tea with an old friend, not a ball with a potential lover. Or that's what I tell myself though I'd be lying if I said I wasn't hoping for at least a lingering look of approval.

While I might hope for it, I lack the confidence to swan out in my finery. I actually try to slip from the room and beat him downstairs so I can be pouring tea when he enters and, therefore, avoid seeing his reaction lest there be no reaction at all.

I ease into the hall . . . and his door opens. I freeze, wondering whether I can back inside and act as if I've forgotten something. It's too late, though. He's stepping out and seeing me and . . .

He stops. His gaze travels over me.

"Better than what I was wearing before?" I say lightly, hoping my voice stays steady.

He chuckles. "I would be lying if I said I vastly prefer your current attire. However, with this, at least, I will not feel as if I should avert my gaze."

"Good."

I walk into the light filtering through the hall window, and he hesitates again.

"You look," he begins; then, he falters, and I'm about to make some wry comment to save him from a forced compliment, but he continues, "beautiful, of course. That goes without saying. You were a pretty girl. You are a beautiful woman."

The way he says it makes my heart flip. He speaks as if remarking that the sunset is beautiful tonight. Fact not flattery. I'm *not* beautiful. I know that. But he sees beauty, and he states it as if I've surely heard it a thousand times.

Before I can respond, he says, "If I hesitated, it is only because I have not seen you like this. Your previous dresses were obviously of another time, as you were obviously of another time. You were . . . otherworldly. Like something from my nanny's fae tales. In that dress, though, you look as if you belong here, and that is . . ."

He trails, but his tone tells me that seeing me in this dress is as uncomfortable, in its way, as seeing me in shorts and a tank top, and I draw back, uncertain.

"Disappointing?" I say, forcing another smile. "No longer that otherworldly creature?"

"Not disappointing. Just . . ."

He looks at me with clear discomfiture.

"I can change my clothes," I say. "Or I could go and come again another time."

He snaps out of it. "Certainly not. Have I mentioned I've been in this wild place too long? Prone to moods and fancies, and I'll beg you to overlook them, please." He steps forward and loops his arm through mine. "I promised you food, and I should deliver, not gape at you like a schoolboy. Come. Your tea awaits."

11

Downstairs, William insists on fixing the tea while I wait in the parlor. I wander the room, taking in the decor. It's like when I found our old family home for sale on a real estate site, and I'd been fascinated, seeing my memories reimagined.

There's wallpaper, for one thing. Not subtly designed wallpaper, either, but a bright gold with a busy pattern. There are also pictures. And more pictures. And more pictures. Rather like a teen's room where they see each blank wall as a canvas that must be filled entirely. Large paintings in ornate frames circle the walls like soldiers, shoulder to shoulder in mismatched uniforms. Smaller portraits and paintings fill the spaces between and below. There's a piano, the top crowded with porcelain depicting Chinese pastoral scenes of the sort painted by artists who've never visited China. Burgundy velvet with gold paint seems the unifying feature of every piece of upholstery. My favorite, though, has to be the cabinet, every door on it painted with a scene from Greek mythology. It's a room of excess, and it is utterly, spectacularly Victorian.

I've barely done a visual sweep, though, before I call to William that I'm fetching something from upstairs, and when he comes in a few minutes later, he finds me clutching my cell phone.

He glances at it, brows rising in silent question as he pours tea. "Is that one of those calculating devices you brought before?"

"Nope. It'll do that, though." I flip to the calculator app and show him. He's so busy staring at it that I have to nudge my cup in place before he pours tea onto the table.

"The other device had buttons," he says. "How do you enter the numbers on that one?"

I tap the screen, and the keypad appears.

He shakes his head and lowers himself to his seat. "That is . . . I find myself wanting to say *magical* while realizing that will make me look like a cave dweller gaping at fire. You said the device isn't a calculator, though."

"It's a telephone."

Silence.

"That's—" I begin.

"Oh, I remember what a telephone is. I have made a tidy fortune recalling all the modern inventions we discussed and then judiciously choosing where to invest my money. That does not, however, look anything like your pictures of telephones. You keep that in your house?"

"In my pocket, mostly." I glance down at my dress. "Which I do not have, and I'd complain about Victorian tailors, but then I'd have to admit that things are no better in the twenty-first century. Dress designers simply don't comprehend the need for women to have pockets."

"That is a telephone that you carry in your pocket? Everywhere?"

"Pretty much. It's not just a phone, though. I can take pictures with it, read books on it, conduct my banking with it, send letters in the blink of an eye, even watch television. Did I explain about television?"

He gives me a hard look, and I can't hold back a laugh.

"Sorry," I say.

"You enjoy this far too much, rhyming off all the wonders of your world, contained in an object smaller than a cigar box."

I pick up my plate. "True, it is fun, but I actually brought it in hopes it'll help settle any doubts that I'm real."

"Ah, of course, because the best way to convince me that I'm not imagining you is to show me a device that cannot possibly exist outside the realm of fantasy."

"Er . . . Okay, you have a point. However, since you've just admitted that you've successfully invested based on my talk of the future, that alone should prove I'm not a product of your imagination." I pause. "Which also means that when you accused me of that the other day, you already knew perfectly well—"

"So, this magical device of yours." He extends a hand. "Let me see it and appropriately marvel at the wonders of your future world."

I pass the phone over.

As he taps the screen, he focuses so hard on keeping a neutral expression that I have to bite my lip to keep from laughing.

"Photos," he says. "I presume that means photographs?" He touches the button, indicating it for me, only to have it pop open. "These are all . . . ?" He taps one, and the screen fills with a picture of Enigma, posing wide eyed. He holds the phone out for Pandora, perched on the back of his seat. "We've found your missing baby, Pan. She's right here. Trapped in this tiny box."

The cat leans to sniff the phone and then glowers at me.

"Do you want me to take your picture?" I ask William.

"Not particularly."

"Too bad." I snatch the phone back and lift it. "Say cheese."

"Say *what*? No, do not take—"

I press the button and laugh. "Too late."

"Witch," he whispers, his eyes widening. "Do you know what you've done? Stolen my soul with a click of a button, trapping it forever . . . forever in . . ."

"Can't even get the rest out, can you? You did manage to say it with a straight face, though. Well, almost."

I press the button again, watching the screen as his voice sounds, saying. "Witch . . ."

William's brows jump.

I pass over the cell phone and show him how to hit Play. He watches the video clip I shot. Then he watches it again before turning to me with, "Witch."

I laugh and reach to take the phone back.

"Oh no," he says, whisking it away. "Now, I get to take your photograph."

I protest, but he insists, and I show him how to do it.

"Shall I pose with my scone?" I reach for the plate, only to find it empty. "Apparently, I've eaten the whole thing. Surprise, surprise. I am overly fond of scones as you can tell." I wave a self-deprecating hand at my figure.

He frowns and then nods. "Ah, yes. You do seem to have accumulated a remarkable quantity of crumbs on your bodice. Enough for nearly a full scone."

I smile at him. "Thank you."

His brows knit in fresh confusion. Then another nod. "I suppose it's ungentlemanly of me to notice the crumbs. It may also suggest I'm paying more attention to your décolletage than is seemly. Take another scone and pose for the photographer, please."

I do as he asks, and he snaps a couple. He checks them and takes more, testing angles. He snaps a few of Pandora, too, who gives me a fresh glower, as if this nonsense is clearly my fault.

William settles into his chair and flicks through the screen. "All of these are photographs? There must be hundreds."

"When it's that easy, we *do* take hundreds. Most are photos. The ones with a box symbol in the corner are videos."

I nibble my scone and sip tea as he flips through photos. Then I hear Michael's voice and stop cold.

"—first day of school, Professor Dale," Michael is saying.

"Put down the camera," my voice replies.

"Oh, no. The occasion must be documented. May I say you

look very fine today, Professor Dale. If my profs looked like you, I'd have been too distracted to ever get the grades for grad school."

I scramble up to take the phone back. William doesn't notice, his gaze fixed on the screen, expression unreadable.

On the video, my voice says, "I'll be late. We need to go."

"You're the prof. You're allowed to be late. We have a few minutes to spare, and I believe I am in need of a quick lesson in—"

I snatch the phone away, murmuring something unintelligible.

"That was . . ." William says.

"My husband."

He stiffens so fast that Pandora gives a start.

"He's passed," I say, adding that more quickly than I intend. I settle into my chair. "We met in graduate school. He died eight years ago. A cancerous tumor in his brain."

I look ruefully at the phone. "We can invent a tiny box that will shoot a million photographs, but there are some things we still can't do. Still can't fix."

"I'm sorry." A pause, stretching well past awkward. "I should have asked if you'd been—or were—married. Also, whether you have children."

I shake my head. "We wanted them, but we thought there was plenty of time. And then there wasn't."

Another long pause. "Your husband wasn't in that moving picture, but I saw a young dark-skinned man in several photographs with you. The voice seemed British but . . . something else, too."

"He was from Egypt. He studied in England before coming to Canada." *The first time we met was in an economics class. He said my name, and his accent reminded me of you. That's why I noticed him.*

I don't say that, of course. I just sit in that terrible, awkward silence.

"I'm glad you found someone," he says.

I tense, wondering whether there's an undercurrent of sarcasm there, a twist that alludes to the fact he did not, obviously, find anyone. He misinterprets that as doubting his sincerity and comes back with a firmer, "I am glad, Bronwyn."

He reaches for his tea and sips it. "As poor a light as this will cast on me, I must admit that as a callow youth wallowing in what he perceived to be lover's betrayal, there were times I took grim satisfaction in imagining you alone and lonely. I said I was not hurt by your leaving. I suspect I've never told a greater lie. When you left . . ." He sets his cup down. "When you left, I thought your trip had been cut short as you warned it might if your mother changed her mind about your visit. So I waited, certain you'd return the next year."

Guilt lashes through me. "I—"

He lifts his fingers. "I understand now. I'm not laying blame— you were caught in an impossible circumstance. I *was* hurt. I presumed you'd found a boy of your own time, and even that, while painful, would have been understandable. We were children caught in our own impossible circumstances. There wasn't a future for us. That did not, I fear, keep me from selfishly and cruelly hoping, at times, that you never found anyone to replace me. But now that you're here, I am genuinely glad you found love and genuinely sorry that you lost him."

I nod, my head lowered so he doesn't see the tears glistening. Then I say, softly, "And you?"

A pause. Then a laugh, a little harsh. "I was about to say I have not been so lucky, but then I realized that was entirely the wrong way to phrase it. The ladies of Fair Britannia have been lucky not to find themselves my bride. And I have been lucky not to find myself in a situation that would almost certainly make my life less satisfying than it is."

"So you never came close to marriage?"

"I did once though not of my own choosing. When I was twenty-three, it became clear that my mother was in a fatal decline. Her last wish was to see her children wed. So she found me a wife. She chose a very pleasant and pious girl, demure and quiet, devoted to works of charity. We would have . . ." He lets out a breath. "To say we would have been happy together would grossly overstate either of our expectations. I would have been comfortable with her, and I hoped that with motherhood, my bride would find the joy and satisfaction she would not with me."

"I'm sure she—"

"That isn't humility on my part, Bronwyn. I don't know the meaning of the word as you may recall. We would not have made one another happy. Our goal would have been a working partnership, which we might have achieved had not . . ."

He rubs his mouth. After a moment, he says, "My mother took an unexpected downturn. She lived to see her two children affianced but not wed. My own engagement failed. I decided my life was best suited to bachelorhood. A fitting partner would not have been unwelcome but . . ."

He shrugs and leans back in his chair. "As a horseman, while I have preferences in my mount, I enjoy riding enough to be flexible in my choices. There are, however, those who are not nearly as fond of the sport and, therefore, are much more particular to the point where they would rather forgo riding altogether than select an unsuitable steed. That would be my view on matrimony." He pauses and frowns. "Comparing women to horses is not the most flattering analogy, is it?"

"No, though, when you're talking about mounts and riding, it could take on a whole other connotation."

He seems to mentally replay what he just said, and his cheeks flame. "Oh my. That is not what I—" He sees my eyes glittering with amusement, and a laugh escapes him. "Not what I intended *at all*, though perhaps, outside of matrimony, my sensibilities regarding horses and women are not quite so diff . . ."

He trails off, those spots of color returning as he realizes what he's saying.

"You are more flexible when selecting women for companionship than you are for marriage," I say, really just to see him squirm. He does, and I burst out laughing.

He clears his throat. "I believe we ought to let that analogy die a quick and quiet death."

"Oh, but it's so much fun. And you squirm *adorably*. So terribly Victorian of you." I reach to refill our tea. "I'll release you from the conversation with a question about Cordelia. How is your sister?"

When he doesn't answer, I look up to see his expression and stop, tea spout poised over his cup.

"Oh, I'm sorry," I say quickly.

"It's all right. Cordelia and I had a falling out many years ago. I told her to leave, and she did, and I have not seen her since. I regret that, but . . ." He clears his throat. "Perhaps we could change the subject yet again?"

"Of course. I *am* sorry. I know you two were close and . . . That is not changing the subject at all. I . . . So . . . How is Mrs. Shaw?"

He laughs at that, a sudden one that startles me.

"Yes," he says. "That is where we are left. My family reduced to my elderly housekeeper."

"I'm sorry—"

"I understand how this might look, Bronwyn, but I assure you I am not a lonely and bitter old man, haunting the moors. You knew me perhaps better than anyone, and that alone proves that I was never one to seek the company of others. Society may call me a recluse, but I'm hardly a hermit in his cave. I participate fully in village life, and there is gentry out here, families I have maintained contact and friendship with. That may sound as if I doth protest too much, but I suspect you are one of the very few people who know me well enough to accept that I could be happy in this life."

I nod. "I do. I understand that, too. Before Michael—my husband—passed, he wanted me to marry again, have children. But once he was gone . . ." My hands flutter into my lap. "There are times when I think I should date, but part of me fears if I go looking, I'm bound for disappointment. I can't get that lucky a third time."

He pauses. "There was someone else? Someone you lost?"

I realize what I've said, and I want to withdraw, change the subject. But I steel myself and look up at him.

"Someone I left, and even if I didn't intend that, even if there was no future for us, it is still a lost love. It was wonderful and magical with a boy who was everything I dreamed of, and I honestly never thought I'd find that again."

William says nothing. His breathing has quickened, though, and he's watching me carefully, as if I might be talking about another boy.

"Michael wasn't you," I say. "I was glad of that—I wouldn't have wanted someone who reminded me too much of you. But he was his own kind of special, and when you've had that twice, it seems unwise to tempt fate by looking again. I have my work. I have my friends. I have my father and his family. I know that, to some people, it sounds as if I'm putting a good face on a bad situation, but I'm not. So, I just meant that I understand your choices."

He looks down at his hands, as if wishing for a teacup in them, something he could fidget with, focus his attention on.

"I didn't mean to make you uncomfortable," I say.

"No, of course. I'm not. I just did not expect that. About us."

"Which makes it uncomfortable. We were fifteen, William. Children, as you've said. It was more than half a lifetime ago. I'm grateful for what we had because it ensured I was never going to settle for less in a relationship. I just wanted you to understand that you did mean a great deal to me, and I certainly didn't leave because I wanted to."

"I know."

"Perhaps I should leave now, though, and come again another time."

"What?" He looks up sharply. "No. Please, don't. If you need to go, then of course, I understand, but in no way am I hinting that I'd like you to do so. We have tea to finish. Then, perhaps, if you have time, we could take a walk."

"A walk would be lovely, but I'd rather see your horses."

He laughs at that, relaxing. "Now you are trying to pay me a kindness. You do not need to feign interest in my hobbies, Bronwyn."

"I never do," I say. "I would like to see your horses. After I finish my scone."

He smiles, plucks another from the pile and drops it onto my plate. "There. Finish both, and I shall take you to see my horses. You will need the sustenance to endure my endlessly enthusiastic chatter about them."

12

After an hour with the horses, I return home. As much as I enjoyed the afternoon, I do need to care for Enigma. Also, an otherwise glorious visit could swiftly descend into the awkwardness of the guest who overstays her welcome. I return as easily as I arrived. It's as if, now that William has lowered the drawbridge, I can once again cross with ease.

I feed Enigma and give her the attention she requires to forgive my absence. My mind still lingers in that other world with William, and so, once she's content, I allow myself the luxury of dwelling in those memories. I draw an extravagant amount of hot water for the claw-foot tub, dig out the remains of Aunt Judith's lavender bubble bath and sink into the perfumed bubbles to replay the afternoon, as if I'm a fifteen-year-old after her first date.

It's only once I'm there, immersed in steaming, lavender-scented water that I remember doing the exact same thing when I *was* fifteen as my friendship with William turned into something more. I soak, and it all slips back. The first time I caught him watching me in a way that said he no longer saw a child. The first time our hands brushed on a walk, and his slid into mine. The first time he reached to help me hop off the pasture fence, and I ended up in his arms, his lips on mine.

We really did have the perfect relationship for fifteen-year-old me. A gentle descent into the world of romantic love. Which is not to say we never argued. A relationship where never a heated word is exchanged might seem idyllic, but it would have lacked the sense that I was involved with a fully rounded person, who came complete with his own passions and persuasions, ones he was willing to fight for.

I remember times when I'd storm off back to my world, or he'd stalk off to his barn, days passing before we spoke again, and there'd been a strange sense of satisfaction and accomplishment in those arguments. We discovered more about one another and navigated the deep waters of our differences, successfully returning to hand-holding walks in the moors and sweet kisses in the barn.

Our earliest point of contention was one that modern women would recognize in a heartbeat. William wanted to see me every day, and if he didn't, he grumbled and scowled. At first, that felt romantic, the boy who couldn't wait to see me again and sank into a fit of discontent when he couldn't. Soon, though, it became constricting, chafing, and I sensed the sinister shadow of control behind his fascination. When I had other engagements, I dreaded telling William, knowing I'd need to cajole him from his sulk.

That had quickly turned to resentment on my part. I had a life beyond my place in his, and I shouldn't have been made to feel guilty for that. It's a lesson I'm glad I learned young. I'm equally glad that I got that lesson with someone who, once I explained it to him, saw my point and stopped doing it. Today, he'd assured me that—while he loved my company—he understood I had other obligations.

As I remember that, I sink into the water, smiling. The girl I had been would lie in this tub, sighing at memories of stolen kisses and shy glances. The woman I've become sighs in equal pleasure at the memory of a man now deft at finding balance, letting me know my company is desired without making me feel guilty for leaving. The memory of a man who could be glad—

genuinely, it seemed—that I had found love with someone else. The memory of a man who heard me joke about obviously being too fond of scones and thought I was referring to an abundance of crumbs on my dress.

William is the best of the boy I knew, and yet he's become something more, too. Older, steadier, surer of himself and what he wants in life. The boy I knew had been swoon-worthy. The adult, though, is the most attractive, desirable, and sexiest man I have met in a very, very long time.

I allow myself the luxury of contemplating *that*, too—the hard lines of his face and the soft fall of his hair, and wanting to reach out and touch both. The way his muscles moved under his shirt. And what he'd felt like against me on the night I'd woken in his bed.

As delicious as the physical side is, there's more to desirability than that. There's the sound of his voice, the way he says my name, the low rumble of his laugh. There's the way he treats me, the way he looks at me, the way we tumbled back into comfortable conversation. Even our walk through the barn, seeing his eyes light up, listening to his passion as he discussed an intricacy of equine bloodlines I barely understood. All of that is, yes, sexy as hell.

I could pretend I'll be satisfied with friendship. I will be if I must. Given the choice between friendship and nothing, there is no choice at all. William is a man I want to know however I can. Yet I'd be lying if I said I didn't hope to read a little extra into those lingering glances and artless compliments. And so I let my mind linger, too, on possibilities, and when the bath runs cold, I simply drain a little and add more hot, extending my self-indulgence for as long as possible.

Before I first got into the tub, I'd placed a chair beside it for Enigma. She'd soon bored of batting bubbles with one dainty white paw, and when a meow or two didn't bring me out of the tub, she'd wandered off to pursue her own amusements. So I'm alone in the bathroom, sunk deep in the water, eyes closed, daydreaming of William, when something tickles my bare shoulder.

I brush it off without even opening my eyes. I have that kind of hair—tendrils are always escaping their bindings. When I sweep my fingers across my shoulder and don't find dangling hair, I only brush more violently, shivering at the thought of a creeping spider.

It's only when the tickle comes again that I remember another touch from the night I arrived.

My eyes spring open. I'm facing the window . . . which has gone completely dark. The sun has fallen, and I'm not safely in my room.

I want to laugh at that. What a foolish thought, as if I'm a girl in a fairy tale, warned she must be in her room from dusk to dawn.

I don't laugh. I can't.

I stay there, every muscle tense, barely daring to breathe as I listen.

Light flickers against the wall. I'd lit a candle for ambiance. Now, it's the only thing illuminating the room, a weak flame casting shadows on the wall.

I want to call for Enigma. I'm acutely aware of how ridiculous that is. Call a month-old kitten to protect me? No, not protect me. I want her to come chirping through the door, wondering why I'm still in the tub, her meows telling me there's nothing else here.

I haven't felt another touch. Maybe it *was* a bug. Maybe—

Cold breath tickles across the top of my head.

I swallow hard.

Beside me, shadows congeal into a dark shape. Darkness creeps alongside the tub, and I'm paralyzed here, submerged in lukewarm water, watching that shape until it comes into view.

The woman in black.

Every muscle bunches, ready to propel me from the tub and out of the bathroom. But I can't move. I can barely draw breath.

The woman steps to the front of the tub. Even so close in the flickering candlelight, I see only a black-gowned figure, nothing visible behind her veil but pale skin.

She reaches into the tub, and her fingers glide through the water, as if she's testing the temperature. They break the surface but make no ripples as they circle. Cold creeps out, ice crackling through the water.

I shiver, frozen as if that icy water traps me in place, watching her, unable to tear my gaze away.

And she's watching me. Even if I can't see her eyes, I feel her gaze. When I shiver, my teeth chattering, she withdraws her hand, and her head tilts, as if assessing.

"May I help you?" I ask.

The words sound so commonplace. Supercilious, even. There's a ghost in my bathroom, and I'm primly asking whether I might be of assistance, as if she's a stranger picking through my berry bushes.

That is not how I say the words, though. They come out high, stammered, barely intelligible.

She stops moving and stares at me.

"I-is there something you want?" I ask.

Her head drops. Was that a nod?

"How can I help?" I ask.

"Name . . ." she says, and there's more, but it sounds like a bad cell connection, and I don't catch more than syllables. Even those sound hollow, distant.

"Your name?" I say. "Who are you?"

A slow shake of her head. "Name me."

"Name you? I-I don't understand."

"Name . . . killer."

The hair on my neck rises. "Name your killer? You want—"

She stiffens, and I jump, water splashing. Her head swivels, looking over her shoulder.

She wheels back to me, so sharp that I jump again.

"—e's coming," she says, her voice still wavering. She says something else I don't catch, but the last word rings bell-clear.

"Run."

The woman vanishes, and I'm out of the tub, stumbling and slipping. I grab for a towel. My fingers graze the plush cotton, but when it slides from the chair, I don't pause to snatch it up. I race from the bathroom, water dripping.

Enigma's in the hall, fur bristling as she hisses. I scoop her up. As I'm rising, a shape moves by the linen closet door. A figure steps halfway through the wood. It's a child, a boy dressed in old-fashioned baggy knickers and a small embroidered jacket over a white blouse. He looks no more than seven or eight, his face out of focus.

He's coming.

Is this who she meant? The boy is still halfway through the door, his hands reaching. I'm moving too fast to stop in time. He grabs at me. The ice of his fingers pass through me, and I skid, one wet foot sliding. My back slams into the wall.

The boy steps through the door. His mouth works. No sound comes, though. Pale fingers grasp for me. Enigma yowls as she stares at him, her claws digging in. The boy stops, his shadowed face turning to mine.

"Run," he whispers, and then he backs up, disappearing into the closet.

I tear past and shove open my bedroom door, sliding and skidding through. I wheel and slam it shut. Then I lean against it, catching my breath, water dripping onto the hardwood floor.

After a moment, I set Enigma on the bed. I stay tensed, waiting, but when nothing happens, I head to the dresser.

As I'm passing the window, I catch sight of a figure. I draw back instinctively, realizing I'm naked. Yet when my mind replays what I saw, I go still, my breath coming fast.

A figure by the barn. A gray-haired man with a spade in his hands.

I snatch a nightshirt from my dresser and yank it on. When I return to the window, he's there . . . staring up at me.

It takes all my courage not to shrink back. I force myself to stay for a better look at him. Again, he's dressed in workman's clothes, not unlike what William wore to the barn. This clearly isn't an older version of William, though. The man is half a head shorter and rail thin. Like the boy in the knickerbockers, his face is only a shadowy oval, turned upward.

He watches me, and then he makes his way toward the moor, spade in hand. Despite his age, he moves with purpose, and within minutes, he's fading as he strides along the path.

The same path where I'd met the ghost of the woman who'd spotted someone near Thorne Manor and fled deeper into the moors, never knowing how close she'd come to freedom.

He's coming.

Run.

I'm sure I heard the "run" part. But the rest . . . ? It's like hearing a sound that your brain translates into words that make sense in context, but when you think back, you can't say for certain those were the correct words at all.

The man is gone, though, and any ghosts in the hallway are staying there. I back onto the bed and let Enigma cuddle on my lap. I don't know how long I stare at the window, stroking the kitten, before I'm finally calm enough to crawl under the sheets.

13

I sleep better than one might expect after that encounter. Perhaps because it hadn't been difficult to escape. The woman in black didn't try to hurt me. She didn't try to stop me from leaving. She'd *told* me to leave. Warned me, it seemed. So had the little boy. He could have leaped in front of me and sent me skidding the other way. Instead, he'd told me to run and retreated out of my path.

The man with the spade was another story. I definitely don't want to encounter him in a dark hall. Yet he seems to stay outside. He had another mission last night, and when I think of him striding into the moors with that spade, I shiver, remembering the woman who'd fled the other night, the ghost I'd seen out there, running for her life. There are conclusions I might draw, theories I might devise, but right now, I'm avoiding that.

These are not characters to be crammed into a play of my own imagining. There is a mystery here, one I want to solve, but I need more information. When Freya comes for tea today, I'll enlist her help.

After that, I'll see William as we arranged. By five, Mrs. Shaw will be gone, and I'll make sure Enigma is fed and tired and happy so I can enjoy my evening with William.

I rise from bed only to step on that loose board again. I tell myself I should check in case William has to cancel this evening. Really, I'm just indulging my inner schoolgirl, the equivalent of anxiously checking texts, hoping for some communication from a boy even when there's no actual need to communicate.

I pry up the board, and at first glance, I see nothing. At a pang of disappointment, I chastise myself. We aren't children. Not lovers, either. There's no reason to leave me notes.

I start to lower the board when I spot a small black bag in the shadows. When lifted, it clinks. I frown, jiggling the pouch. More clinking.

I back onto the bed. The bag is black velvet, fastened with a delicate silver cord. I untie that and upend the bag onto the bed, and gold flashes out, winking in the morning sun.

Gold coins.

I sputter a laugh. And I almost crawl back into bed because, clearly, I'm lost in a fantasy where I pull up floorboards to discover pirate treasure. It isn't seventeenth-century plunder, though. It's coins, a dozen gold sovereigns from the mid-nineteenth century. They're the "young head" Queen Victoria style with dates ranging from 1838 to 1850, worth a couple hundred pounds each, possibly more, in this mint condition.

As I set the bag down, it rustles. I reach in to find a note.

Bronwyn,

When you visited today, I tried to ascertain your financial situation. Despite my efforts to be crafty, you were, as always, cautious in your replies. I deduced, however, that you will struggle with the renovations to Thorne Manor.

I told you that I amassed a tidy fortune utilizing your information on the future. What I did not mention was how sorely I needed that windfall. On my father's death, my mother entrusted her finances to her brother, and after her passing, I discovered how badly he'd mismanaged it.

We were in danger of needing to sell the manor house when I recalled your jokes about using your knowledge as inside information. I invested what we had left on what you showed me of the future. Several of those speculations paid off immensely, and they continue to do so. Your gift of prescience allowed me to become the gentleman of leisure I am today.

Consider this the first well-earned return. Yes, the first. I know better than to fill a bag of gold coins for you. You are already going to balk at accepting this one. We'll speak more later. For now, I believe this is a reasonable amount that your conscience—and your pride—will accept.

I look forward to seeing you later today.

William

I stare down at the coins. Then I run my hand through them, hearing them clink, the cool metal sliding over my fingers.

As I reread the note, a few tears fall on those coins, but I wipe them away. I won't accept them, of course. I'm not starving, and it isn't as if the house is in ruins. I might not be able to fully restore it this summer, but I have enough to keep it livable. That may mean I'll be bringing a kettle to my school office rather than buying daily cappuccinos at the campus cafe, but that's a small price to pay for a summer house in the English countryside.

And just as I think that, my arm brushes the bag, and I hear another rustle. I reach in to find a smaller note, tucked in the corner.

By the time you read this, you will have already decided to give me back the coins. You certainly may, but I'll only return them to their spot, and if you don't fetch them, some future inhabitant will, because I will not take them out.

They are yours. Stop feeling guilty. Stop telling yourself you'll be fine without them, that the house doesn't really need new furnishings, et cetera, et cetera. You earned this money. I wish you to have it. I will be cross until you take it. I might even start withholding scones at tea.

Take the coins. Indulge yourself. More will come, and you will accept those, too. That is an order.

I read the note, and I laugh. Then I cry, tears spilling over my cheeks. Not since Michael died has anyone known me like this, and I've forgotten what it feels like.

I allow myself to cry until Enigma wakes, alarmed by my snuffles. I pet her and cuddle her. Then I finger the gold coins, smiling, my mind already racing ahead to what they can buy. Before I go, I tuck one coin into my pocket. Then I head downstairs for breakfast.

⚜

THAT MORNING, I FULFILL MY FANTASY OF TOOLING TO TOWN IN MY convertible. Off I go, the cherry-red paint and silver chrome gleaming, the top down despite the chill morning air. I feel like a fifties movie star, oversized sunglasses on, a kerchief barely containing the tangle of hair streaming behind me.

First to the grocer for staples and baking ingredients. Then a snack from the bakery. Chocolate biscuit and steaming tea in hand, I perch on the hood of my car and take advantage of internet service decent enough to suss out the value of a mint-condition Victorian sovereign gold coin. The answer is about three hundred pounds.

I have five thousand Canadian dollars scattered across my bed. That makes me eat faster and hurry back to find a secure hiding spot for my treasure. I keep that one coin in my pocket, though. I can't resist, occasionally taking it out and turning it over, entranced by the golden gleam and the fantasies of what it can buy.

In my imagination, my treasure has already been transformed into a refurbished parlor and a new refrigerator, the perfect mix of indulgence and practicality. Of course, perfect practicality would be using it to wipe out my remaining albatross of debt, but I have that under control. This will be for the house as William intended.

When tea time comes, that coin sits on the table, tucked under

Aunt Judith's newly polished silver tea service. Freya arrives with Del, who's come to work on the lawn and refuses all offers of tea.

We're barely finished slathering jam on our first scone before I pull out the coin and tell Freya all about yesterday's visit to Victorian Thorne Manor. Underneath my calm exterior, apparently, I'm fifteen again, bursting to share proof that William exists, proof that I have indeed crossed over.

I tell her the story, and I show her the coin and the photographs on my phone. I hadn't even remembered to check the photos until earlier this afternoon, and then I'd barely dared to peek, fearing they wouldn't be there. I know William is real—I'll no longer doubt and question—but I thought perhaps the slip in time would erase the photographs. Yet they're as clear as if I'd taken them yesterday . . . which I suppose I had.

This morning, I spent at least an hour trying to understand how the time stitch works. I can carry objects over it, as I did with my cell phone. I might be able to take Enigma. I definitely can't take a person, though—as children, I'd tried many times to grant William a peek into my world. The photographs and video remain on my phone, as clear as ever. The notes William left have aged. Yet he also said yesterday that when I removed the notes, they disappeared on his side. And that floorboard wasn't loose until he loosened it after talking to me.

Is there a version of William Thorne who lived his entire life without meeting me, and this is an alternative timeline? Or are our times indeed stitched together at this point, and I have always been part of his world?

Yes, there's a reason I'm not fond of time-travel stories. My historian brain crackles like fireworks at the thought of experiencing a world that now only exists in books. But the logical part of my mind runs in circles, getting forever twisted in the impossibilities and contradictions of it, looking for explanations where none can exist.

I need to stop thinking and accept. Questioning this is like turning away from a star-filled night, refusing to enjoy it before I understand the science of converting hydrogen to helium.

I tell Freya. I show her the coin. I play her the video. And she falls back into her chair, her smile gone, face unreadable.

"It's not a trick," I say quickly. "You can see the background in the pictures. It's this room. The windows are there and the—"

She lifts a hand, stopping me. She says nothing, though. My heart hammers. I've gone too far. It is a secret, my secret, and I've always known that, and the one time I dared share it, I wound up in a psychiatric ward, my world and my self-confidence shattered.

Hadn't I learned my lesson?

What on earth possessed me to tell Freya?

Hope.

Longing and need, too, the desperate desire to prove I didn't lose my mind twenty-three years ago. Which makes little sense when Freya isn't one of those who thought me mad in the first place. Yet logic doesn't matter when it comes to pierced pride and shattered self-confidence.

My mother is dead, and no one else cares why I spent time in a psychiatric ward. Except me.

I care. I deeply, deeply care, however much I want to rise above that and declare it a relic of my past.

It takes everything I have not to flee. I might, too, if it wasn't my house.

"May I see your phone again?" she asks.

I stiffly pass it over. She replays the video, and as she does, tears spring to her eyes. Then she laughs, a bubbling laugh of delight.

Her hands fly to her mouth as she shakes her head. Then she says, "I have never seen such a thing, never imagined such a thing."

"It *did* happen," I say. "I wouldn't fake—"

"Of course you wouldn't." She catches my expression, and her eyes round. "Oh, lass. You thought I didn't believe you? How couldn't I? The proof is right here in black and white." Another eruption of laughter. "No, in Technicolor as they used to say. You've captured . . ."

"A Victorian gentleman in his natural environment?" I say.

She chuckles. "It's one thing to be told about it, and I never doubted you at that. But I expected it would remain an act of faith. How could one hope for more?" She touches the phone, and William's voice comes as clear as if he were sitting beside us.

She smiles and looks at me. "Witchcraft, indeed."

I say nothing. I can't. Relief robs me of my voice, and yet there's trepidation, too. My sanity has been affirmed, my "fantasies" validated as reality. It's a dream I never dared voice, and now I fear if I say anything at all, it'll evaporate. I'll speak, and Freya will laugh again, this time in disbelief, admitting she thought I was indeed pulling her leg, and playing along, and I'm not really serious, am I?

She turns William's photograph into the light. "He is a Thorne, that is for certain. I've seen portraits. If he's unmarried at his age, it suggests he might have been the last Thorne to live here. The one who bequeathed the house to a distant cousin. There was a sister, as I recall, who flitted off for parts unknown. Not that her children could have inherited an entailed house anyway, but I believe there was an estrangement with the sister. Some scandal—"

She pulls back. "Listen to me, prattling on as if I'm a historian. As I said, there were many William Thornes, and this might very well have been any of them."

"No," I say. "I suspect you're right. William did have a sister, and he hasn't—hadn't—seen her in years. I also overheard his friend talking about a scandal. It seems, though, that whatever it is, William is using it as an excuse to avoid London."

Freya chuckles. "That makes sense. Some silly scandal he's cultivated to serve his purposes."

"It was certainly easy enough to do at the time," I say. "Say the wrong thing, sleep with the wrong woman, choose the wrong political side . . . A million tiny transgressions for society to feast on. I eavesdropped on the discussion, so I can't exactly ask him about it. That would be awkward, particularly when, from other things his friend said, I suspect it involved a lady."

"That would indeed be awkward," she says, her eyes twinkling. "He'll tell you when he's ready. When are you going to see him again?"

"Tonight," I say.

We chat about that before I move on to my ghostly encounters, first in the moors and later here in the house. For my ego's sake, there's no hint of my wild, skidding, dripping flight down the hall.

"So, four specters," she says. "The woman swathed in black, whom you've seen multiple times. The boy, who only appeared yesterday, but twice before that, you saw a flicker at the linen closet door, which may have been him. Then there's the woman in the moors and the man with the spade." She sucks in her bottom lip for a moment. "Have the ones in the house tried to hurt you?"

I shake my head. "I thought the woman was, the first time I saw her, but that was just me—if a ghost appears, I don't stick around to see whether she means me harm. Not after my uncle . . ." I swallow and then press on. "The only reason I didn't run faster last night was that I was stuck in the tub. In retrospect, though, all she's done is move toward me. The boy reached out, but once he got my attention, he backed away."

"All right, so we have four ghosts, though the woman in the moors seems to be more of a remnant."

"A spectral replay of a prior event." I pause. "Only hours before I saw her, Del mentioned young women going missing on the moors. My imagination may have conjured her."

"Did you think that at the time? Or only later, reflecting back?"

"Later," I admit. "At the time, she seemed real."

"So, let's stick with that."

I pour fresh tea for both of us. "*Have* young women gone missing there?"

"Young women, old women, young men, old men. It's always

the young women who capture the imagination, though. They're the ones who pass into folklore. The mother searching for her baby. The new bride waiting for her husband. Del's right that people tell stories of young women who went missing out there, which makes it seem as if they disappeared in droves. I've never really looked into it. I don't like bringing my work home." She smiles as she stirs sugar into her tea. "Back to the man with the spade. He seemed to be looking at you in the window, but he then continued on to the moors, yes?"

I nod. "Which could mean that he wasn't looking at me at all. He could be another remnant."

"Possibly. I get the sense, though, that you aren't eager to approach him and find out."

I remember that stern figure, spade clutched in his hand, and I shiver. "Not really."

"We'll skip him, then. The woman in black and the boy in knickerbockers are the two who are clearly interacting with you and do not appear to be threats. In fact, they seem to be warning you, possibly about the man with the spade."

"I know they told me to run. I *think* the woman said, 'He's coming,' but I'm not completely certain. She also said a few things I didn't catch. Something about names. She seemed to say, 'Name *me*,' which doesn't make sense. After that, she said 'name' and 'killer' with a word missing in the middle. I guessed she was asking me to find her killer, but that's when she got spooked by the other ghost and told me to run."

"Huh." Freya leans back, her eyes narrowing as she seems to consult her memory. "I've heard of folklore where people can't communicate with ghosts until they name them."

"Name them?"

"Identify them. It's a variation on folklore that says certain creatures—like vampires—need to be invited in. Ghosts need to be identified before they can speak."

"In other words, we haven't been properly introduced."

Freya chuckles. "Something like that. The woman and the boy

may be able to reveal themselves properly and communicate if you name them. But you have to get it right. The lore also says if you get it wrong, the connection breaks."

"Naturally," I mutter.

"As for naming her killer, that's similar lore. Name her killer, and you set her free. Ghosts on our plane are trapped by unfinished business. If you name her killer, she's free to pass over to the afterlife. Also, the lore says that if you encounter her killer's ghost, naming his crimes will rob him of his power."

"So, figure out who she is. Figure out who the boy is. Solve their murders. Then I'll have a spook-free house. No problem."

Freya smiles. "Just remember that, as unnerving as all this is, they've been trapped here for a very long time. They'll be patient. Wait and see what clues they give you before we start digging. We can't rush in and get this wrong. Now, let me tell you how best to communicate with ghosts . . ."

14

William and I arranged for me to arrive at five in the afternoon. At 4:45, I'm in my room, picnic basket in hand, mentally opening the gate between our worlds. It might not work right away, and I'd hate to be late. Or that makes a fine excuse for my eagerness.

The transition comes as smoothly as it used to. I stand in my room, thinking of William with my eyes closed, and when I open them, I'm in his room.

Alone in his room.

I circle twice in case I'm somehow missing his very large presence in a very small bedroom. Then I check my watch. It's 4:50. I'm early, and I can hardly expect he'll be as eager as I am for my visit.

I plunk down on the bedcovers to wait, basket on my lap, and mentally revisit the topics I want to discuss with him. Ghosts are nowhere on that list. The house hadn't been haunted when he lived in it, and so there's no need to mention it, which also avoids any discomfort of admitting I see ghosts when I know William is *not* a believer.

I'm compiling my list when the clock downstairs strikes four.

Four?

I must have missed a gong. My watch clearly says five, as does my cell phone. Five o'clock with no sign of William. That isn't like him.

Has he changed his mind about seeing me again?

I check his dresser for a note and find the paper he's been using to write to me with the pen and inkstand beside it. The inkstand is ivory, painted with green birds and flowers. A brass cap covers two inkwells, an opening for the pen in each. The pen itself lies on the blotting paper. It's a dip pen, long and slender, with a gorgeous mother-of-pearl handle and a grip that I'm certain is real gold.

Finding this on his dresser is as good a sign as any that William is a bachelor. Victorian bedrooms are not for writing in. With the mess a quill pen and inkpot can make, it was only good housekeeping to restrict it to a proper desk. I can already see splotches of ink on the gorgeous Persian carpet.

There's no note here, and I'm about to check the floorboard when I recall those four strikes of the clock and a thought hits, one that makes me wince. I slip into the hall and listen. The house is empty, Mrs. Shaw apparently gone, but I still creep down the stairs in case I'm mistaken. I find the clock. It's the same one that's in my house, a massive and ornate grandfather clock too unwieldy to move.

Sure enough, the face reads four.

I fetch the basket I left upstairs and check out the bedroom window, which I probably should have done sooner. The stable doors are open. I hurry down and through the back door. I take my time crossing the yard, so I can listen for the sound of unfamiliar voices. None come, but as I draw near, the ground vibrates with the thump of galloping hooves.

I turn as William rides from the moors. He doesn't see me at first—I'm in the shadow by the stable doors. He's wearing a loose-fitting white shirt, snug buff riding breeches and no jacket. He's riding hard, his head down, dark curls snapping, face all hard edges and determined lines. His eyes glint—a man on a mission, but still reveling in the excuse to push the horse faster as they fly over the ground. In passing, I notice that the coal-black stallion is a magnificent beast, particularly in motion, but my attention is far more captivated by the rider.

After a few seconds of admiring the view, I may fumble for my phone and snap a photo or two. I can't resist. As I'm lowering my phone, William notices me. His eyes widen, and he pulls the stallion—Balios—to a stop as he yanks out his pocket watch.

"You aren't late," I call as I walk over. "I forgot about daylight savings time. Or, as they call it in England, summer time."

His brows rise.

"We move our clocks forward every spring to take advantage of the longer days," I say while he motions Balios forward. "It started during World War I, about seventy years from now."

"Ah." He runs a hand through his hair, trying to tame it. "I was riding and lost track of time. I realized the hour and hurried back in hopes of washing up and dressing before you arrived." He swings off Balios. "If you'll allow me a few minutes to make myself presentable, I'll be as quick as I can."

"You look perfectly presentable now," I say. "If you insist on a moment to wash, I'll grant it, but there's no need to change." I lift the basket. "I brought a picnic snack, and what you're wearing is very suitable for dining out of doors."

"All right. Just let me walk and water Balios. He needs to cool down."

"I can do that for you." I smile. "I still remember how."

He agrees. The question, of course, is whether the *stallion* will allow it. There's a reason most people stick to mares and geldings as riding mounts. A stallion is headstrong and difficult, accustomed to leading rather than following. Or that is the common perception. The truth, as William would be quick to point out, is that, while wild horses generally have one stallion for a group of mares, the male often serves more as a stud and guardian with a mare in charge.

This doesn't mean a stallion is a docile creature, ready to be led by anyone. He requires a firm hand, a leader he trusts, as he would expect in a herd. Balios is very well trained, though, and when William hands him over with a few words and a pat, the stallion deigns to let me take him.

William promises the stallion a brushing after his cool down, but I recall enough of my lessons to give Balios that myself. I spend a few minutes with the curry comb and then the hard brush, cleaning the dirt and sweat from his hard ride. I'm finishing when William's voice cuts through the quiet stables.

"Trying to steal my horse now, too, I see."

He strides in with Pandora trotting at his heels. He has, despite my objections, changed, wearing a high-collared shirt, trousers and a dark waistcoat, the Victorian equivalent of casual wear, as formal as it looks to me. He carries a picnic basket even larger than my own.

"You didn't trust me to bring enough food?" I say. "Or didn't trust my cooking?"

"I trust both very well," he says, patting Balios's nose. "But apparently, we think far too much alike. I had asked Mrs. Shaw to prepare a cold supper, planning a surprise picnic of my own. Please tell me you haven't already picked out a spot to eat it. And if you have, perhaps pretend otherwise, allowing me some small advantage."

"I hadn't gotten that far."

"Excellent." He reaches for my basket. "I have the perfect spot in the moors, one I discovered a few years ago. It's a bit of a walk, though . . ."

"Then, it's a good thing I dressed for walking."

His gaze slides down my sundress.

"Did you want me to change into something from the closet?" I ask.

"Certainly not. However, since you mentioned the suitability of your outfit, it gave me the excuse to properly scrutinize it, which I was loath to do before now."

I sigh. "It's a sundress. A very proper sundress. It covers my knees, my shoulders and my"—I look down—"*most* of my bosom. Believe me, I have ones that show off much more, and none of them would be out of place on a city street."

"I was clearly born in the wrong century." Another look up and down my dress. "If you would be more comfortable in another of your dresses—a less 'proper' one—I wouldn't object."

"Somehow, I don't think my comfort is the issue. I'll stick with this one . . . or I'll spend the picnic talking to the side of your head as you politely avert your gaze."

His eyes glint. "I would only avert my gaze if it caused you discomfort. Since that doesn't seem to be the case . . ."

"Look all you want," I say. "Pay particular attention to my sandals, which scandalously expose my bare ankles."

"I noticed."

"Of course you did."

I shake my head and give Balios a final pat before we leave the barn.

15

William leads me to a spot that I can't believe I've never found before. That's my first reaction. Once I consider, though, I can see why I haven't. He only found it himself a few winters ago, and even then, it was Balios who discovered it.

It's a natural spring, bubbling over an outcropping of rocks, with a patch of moss below, so green and smooth that it seems like a picnic blanket spread by Mother Nature herself. The water explains why Balios found the place and also explains why we didn't. At the source, the spring runs fast and free into a small stream, but a little farther down, the stream feeds a bog that travelers avoid, which means they miss the jewel at the center.

When the bog thawed, William found a path through the rock on the other side. That rock acts as yet another natural barrier— why pick your way across ugly and jagged stone when there are so many lovely paths to follow?

I spread the blanket, and we settle in. Pandora had followed us part of the way, but when she discovered this wasn't a short jaunt, she returned to her kittens. We're alone with the cries of the plovers and the burble of the stream. The burble, too, of our conversation, which hasn't ceased since we left the stables.

My life dominates the conversation. Which is not what I'd intended, but as William points out, I heard all about his horses yesterday, and it's time for him to learn more about *my* career. He lives in a time when women don't attend university, much less teach at one. The first women's college *had* opened a few years ago, but it was geared toward producing governesses. Yet William is neither shocked nor even surprised that I hold a job unknown to women in his era. When we'd known each other at fifteen, our conversation taught him more than the technological advances to come. They gave him insight into the social advances, and being a Thorne—known for their progressive ideas—for William, women holding careers is hardly a sign of the apocalypse. In truth, a career like mine was nearly as much an impossibility for a man in his position, and it's an opportunity he'd have liked for himself.

As a historian, I know that when we pride ourselves on our "social advances," part of that arises from a misunderstanding of the past. Looking at England going into the nineteenth century and then coming out of it, you see that it advanced at least as much as it did during the twentieth century.

When William realized I'd married an African man, he may have been surprised, but he would also realize that was as natural a progression as women taking careers as university professors. England had its colonies, and while travel wasn't easy, colonial subjects did emigrate from Africa and Asia. Ronnie and Archie's family had been in Yorkshire for generations. That doesn't mean people of color enjoyed social equality in Victorian England, any more than women did.

William opens a jar of lemonade, and I prepare dinner from his basket, mine being more suitable for dessert. We dine on cold beef sandwiches, and cheese and pickled vegetables as we chatter like magpies. Or I chatter like a magpie. William might talk just as much, but the analogy doesn't work as well for his low rumble of a voice.

When we finish the meal, I present the dessert course, opening my basket to see his eyes light up.

"Cookies?" he says.

"Yes, chocolate chip, peanut butter . . . and peanut butter *with* chocolate chips." I lay three cookie stacks on a napkin.

With one big hand, he sweeps the top cookie off each stack and begins munching the chocolate chip one.

"You know I gave you the recipe for those," I say.

"And *you* know I have no easy access to chocolate or peanut spread," he says as he pours us each a glass of port. He's right, of course. The chocolate bar may have just been invented, but it won't be easily available until the factories in York open a couple decades from now. Peanuts have only recently become a commercial crop . . . in America. Peanut butter was an early twentieth-century invention, with both peanut butter and chocolate chip cookies arriving in the 1930s.

He continues, "You only provided the recipes to tease me. Even if I could obtain the ingredients, how would I explain the recipes to Mrs. Shaw?"

"Forget Mrs. Shaw. Bake them yourself."

He stops mid-bite and looks over as if I've suggested he dig his own well. No, that's unfair. William is perfectly capable of digging a well, and he would if the need arose. Baking cookies, though, is like asking him to paint a landscape when he's never lifted a brush.

Being a bachelor with only day staff, William can carve a ham or brew a pot of tea, but that would be the extent of his culinary skills. When I used to bring him cookies and say I made them myself, he thought that meant I hung around the kitchen and perhaps stirred the bowl once or twice under the cook's watchful eye. But when I explained we didn't have a cook, he'd been shocked. Being "in service" was one of the primary sources of income for the lower class, and that had led to a long discussion of the Industrial Revolution.

"I could possibly learn to bake," he says finally. "However, I fear I would never create anything as delicious as these. You have a gift."

I sputter a laugh. "You didn't see the batch that went into the trash. I got distracted and forgot to take them out of the oven."

"All of mine would have been like that." He takes another bite. "No, you'll simply need to continue supplying me with cookies as I am quite incapable of making them myself."

I smile and shake my head. He eats his cookie, paying more attention to the endeavor than it requires, and then picking crumbs from his shirt as he asks, with studied nonchalance, "You did say you were up for the entire summer, didn't you?"

"Until the first week of September, yes."

"Excellent."

"I'll drop cookies in your room each week while you're out riding Balios so I don't bother you."

"You may come, too," he says. "For short visits. Just long enough that I will not feel rude, taking your cookies without offering the pleasure of my company, however briefly."

I roll my eyes. He takes another trio of cookies from the stacks.

"I'm glad you like those," I say, "but if you gorge yourself on them, you won't be able to eat these."

I pull out a banana and an orange, and his eyes light almost as much as they did for the cookies. Oranges are a Christmas luxury, and while bananas are available, they don't become popular for another twenty-odd years, until Jules Verne included them in *Around the World in Eighty Days*.

He takes the fruit and says, "Anything more in that basket?"

I lift another couple of oranges. "There are more bananas, too, though I thought you'd keep them for later."

"I'll secret them away in my bedroom as I did when I was five." He opens a banana. "Did I ever tell you about the time Mrs. Shaw found two of these peels in my dresser drawer?"

I laugh. "No. What happened?"

"I mimicked utter bafflement. She decided they were an Irish curse and nearly fired our new Irish maid until my father stepped in and declared that the peels were clearly rotted vegetation I'd dragged in from the moors."

He takes a bite of banana. "So there's nothing else in that basket?"

"Are you hinting for me to bring you something?"

"Mmm, no. I just . . . I keep visualizing another item. A small black pouch." A sharp shake of his head. "Strange."

When I don't respond, he reaches for the basket. I whisk it out of his way. Then I pause before lifting the pouch, gold coins clinking.

"However did I know that was there?" he murmurs. "One would almost think I could predict it, knowing that despite my sternly worded letter, the person who brought that basket would still risk my wrath by returning my coins."

"Wrath?"

His lips purse. "Strident disapproval?"

"I just—"

"—wanted to be sure I really meant it. Wanted to be sure I understood that you are not wearing rags and cooking bone soup, creditors at the door, a debtor's prison in your future."

"There are no debtor's prisons in the future. And creditors don't knock at the door. They just call. And call. And call. At all hours of the day and night."

"Sounds terribly annoying. I believe I would prefer prison." He peels off a section of orange. "You are familiar with creditors, then?"

I realize I walked into that. "I had some trouble after Michael's death. Health care is free in Canada, but there are always . . ." My cheeks burn. "We have as many quack doctors and charlatans as you do, and I'm embarrassed that I fell for it."

"Someone you loved was dying at far too young an age. The charlatans offered hope where hope was desperately needed." He meets my gaze. "Falling prey to that isn't weakness, Bronwyn."

"But it was foolish, and yes, I've experienced the relentlessness of creditors firsthand, but I'm long past that. I own a condo—an apartment—in Toronto, which is not a cheap place to live."

"A large and lavish apartment."

"I'm on my own. I need neither large nor lavish. I just inherited a house in England, and I can afford to keep it. That puts me well above poverty, William. So far above it that I can't accept—"

"Charity?"

I squirm. "*Generosity*. I don't need—"

"And neither do I. My will bequeaths the manor to a second cousin I've only met once. My lifestyle is simple enough that the income from my horses covers it. That cousin will inherit both a grand manor and a tidy fortune."

"You're thirty-eight. A long way from—"

"I am not about to develop an opium habit, Bronwyn. Nor take up residence in a gambling hell. Nor marry some empty-headed chit who'll drain my coffers. Those are the only ways I can possibly die without thousands of those"—he points at the pouch —"going to a man who, while decent enough, has done nothing to deserve it. The advice you gave me all those years ago saved this house. It let me retire here to the lifestyle I dreamed of. You will allow me to repay you with a dozen pouches—a hundred if I wish."

"I don't need the money."

"And, again, neither do I. Indulge me, Bronwyn. Or, if you cannot, grant me indulgence. At least let me feel as if I have repaid my debt."

When I still hesitate, he says, "I meant what I wrote. If you do not take the pouches, I will keep adding to the stash, and some future homeowner will reap the benefits. He—or she—will almost certainly be a complete gadabout who will fritter it away while our poor house rots from neglect."

He's right, of course. There's also something about the way he says "our" house that melts my resolve. It is indeed ours, now that I have inherited it. His in his time, and mine in mine. Yet it's also a reminder of that divide, a gulf we cannot breach. It's "ours" in the sense that we both own it, but not "ours" in the sense that we share it. He cannot come into my world, and I don't know how long I can stay in his.

I shake off that melancholy thought. "I will use the money for our house."

"Fifty percent. Or, if you'd prefer to skip the negotiating process, I'll settle for seventy-five. Three-quarters spent on our house, one-quarter on yourself. Pay off your debts. Buy yourself frivolities."

"Like first-class airfare?" I smile. "I'll admit, while I can scarcely imagine paying that much for bigger seats and better service, after seven hours in economy, I'm tempted." I catch his look. "Yes, I know. I can cross an ocean in seven hours, and I'm complaining about legroom. Twenty-first-century problems."

"I was not going to comment. If I did, I would only say that if more *legroom* makes you happy, then you should have it. Everyone needs things that serve no greater purpose than to make them happy."

He reaches for another cookie and finds the napkin empty. A glance at me.

I sigh and take out the last three cookies, laying them on the napkin. He passes me a chocolate chip. I accept the offering, and he takes a bite from a peanut butter one, crumbs tumbling onto his shirt before he continues.

"What do you have in mind for the money?" he asks.

"I . . . I haven't thought about it."

"Liar," he says. "Which does not mean you wouldn't have returned the money if I allowed that, but your mind will have permitted some forays into fantasy, how you could use it if you kept it."

"Parlor furnishings," I say. "Aunt Judith had to sell them for the house upkeep after Uncle Stan's death. Also, the fridge leaks."

"That sounds dire." Another bite of his cookie. "Notice that I say that as if I fully understand what a *fridge* is."

I smile. "Sorry. Refrigerator. It's—"

"—an automatic icebox. One that runs on electricity, keeping food cold without the constant replenishing of ice. I just didn't know the term *fridge*. I remember every detail of every modern miracle you mentioned, Bronwyn. That is why you have a pouch of gold sovereigns in that basket. Now, while I'm certain a non-leaking icebox and a furnished parlor will bring some satisfaction to your life, not everything is about necessity. A home needs indulgence, too. What dreams do you have for our house? Completely nonessential flourishes and luxuries you would like to add?"

I try to demur—I live a life where every cappuccino comes with a prickle of guilt. But William pushes and suggests, and soon we're deep in a discussion of the necessities and frivolities I could add to the manor.

16

We talk about the house, and we drink the port, and by the time the sun is setting, we've abandoned all vestiges of formality, William lazing in the heather, me on my back gazing up at the sky.

"Did you become a ballet dancer?" he asks.

I laugh. "Do I look like a ballerina?"

His brow furrows. "I will admit, I've only attended the ballet twice, and merely because my fellows insisted. It is not a . . . high form of art, but I seem to recall it is different in your time. If you mean do you look like one of the ballet dancers I saw, I would certainly not mistake you for one of their ilk."

He's being very circumspect here, and I have to smile. During the Regency era, ballet gained a reputation as a place where men of the ton might select a new mistress. By Victorian times, while there were excellent troupes, the performances William likely saw would have been more slanted to the, ahem, male gaze.

"No," I say. "The life of a ballerina was never in my future. I'm far better suited to imbuing hapless undergrads with a passion for bygone worlds."

"Tell me you didn't entirely give up on dance."

"Never."

He tilts his head. "I'm not certain I believe that. You will need to demonstrate."

"Oddly, I feel no overwhelming need to prove it to you."

Silence.

I glance over at him. "I'm no longer five, William. You can't persuade me to dance by pretending not to believe I can do it. Just as you can't dare me to crawl into secret passages or jump from tree branches. Mere challenge is no longer the motivator it once was."

His lips twitch. "No?"

"No."

"You're right, then. You asked whether you looked like a ballerina, and I kindly pretended I did not know what you meant. The truth is . . . you are a bit . . . longer in the tooth than the average dancer."

I shoot up to sitting. "Hey!"

He arches a brow. "Am I incorrect?"

I glower at him. "You and I are the same age."

"Yes, but it is different for a horse breeder than a ballerina. Also different for a man—"

"Finish that sentence at your peril, sir."

His lips twitch again. "Also different for a man—"

I pitch a pebble at him. It bounces off his shoulder.

He picks it up and lifts that brow again. "You seem to be lacking strength if this is the best you can do. I would understand if you have given up dance. A pity, really, but with age—"

"Nope."

"Nope?"

"It's not going to work. Give it up."

He eyes me. "What if I asked nicely?"

"Don't strain yourself."

A low chuckle. He clears his throat. "Bronwyn Dale, I would be delighted if you would honor me with a demonstration of your inestimable dance skills."

"Mmm, better, but I'm comfortable right here."

"You aren't making this easy."

"It could be, dear William, that I'm not eager to leave this agreeable spot and perform for you."

A moment of silence. "Challenge failed. Flattery failed. All I have left, I fear, is bribery. I know better than to offer money, and we seem to be all out of cookies. I may have a sugar cube or two in my pocket for Balios. Would that work?"

"You will find, I believe, that women are not as susceptible to sugar cubes."

"Sadly. Life would be so much easier if they were. Hmm. Well, since I am asking you to do something for me, I should offer the same in return. I would like you to dance for me. What could I do for you?"

A hundred jokes should jump to mind. Instead, my wine-sodden mind throws up an image of that first night I crossed over. In a blink, I'm there, in his bed, his skin against mine, the searing heat of him, the deliciously masculine smell of him, his groan at my ear as I press against—

I yank myself back only to see William watching me. His eyes glint bright blue, and his wolfish grin insists he knows exactly what I was thinking.

"Whatever could I give you in return?" he muses. "I feel as if you have some idea."

I pull myself together under the cover of an airy smile. "Why, yes, I think there is something you could do for me. The question is whether you'd agree. I'm not certain you would. It's rather . . . strenuous."

That grin glitters as bright as his eyes. "I'm certain I could manage whatever you have in mind."

"It would take time, too. Time and effort and energy. A great expenditure of energy."

"I have plenty of that. Time, too. All the time in the world. You only need ask."

I fold my legs demurely behind me and lean forward, meeting

his gaze. "I would like you to take me for a very long . . . very exciting . . . very exhilarating . . . ride."

I expect a laugh—a burst of laughter—as I ask for a horseback ride. Instead, I get a deep and throaty rumble, his eyes flashing in delighted surprise.

That's when I replay my words and realize I left out a key word in my request.

"*Horseback* ride," I blurt, cheeks flaming. "A ride on the horses. Into the moors. That's what I meant."

"Of course it is," he says, and that grin threatens to swallow me whole.

"It *is*. I meant a horse ride."

"Naturally." He leans back. "Whatever else *could* you mean? That is the only way to ride. Well, we could take a coach-and-four, but that would hardly be as exhilarating, and you specified exhilarating."

"Stop."

His eyes meet mine, brows rising. "Stop what? Is there another type of ride you could have meant? There must be since you felt the urgent need to clarify."

"Stop."

"I will admit, you often have me at a disadvantage with your talk of fridges and phones. Again, you seem to be implying a meaning to a word that I don't understand. Pray tell, what else, in your world, could riding refer to? Asking me for a long, exciting, exhilarating—"

I leap to my feet. "So, you wanted to see me dance?"

"I feel as if you are changing the subject."

I kick off my shoes.

"Ah," he says. "Whatever this other ride is, it requires the removal of footwear, does it?"

I meet his gaze. "Not necessarily," I say, as boldly as I can, and he laughs then, his head thrown back, laugh echoing through the silence.

"Indeed," he says. "Well, while I do not understand what you meant at all, I said I'd happily exchange services with you. You dance for me, and I will give you a—"

"Horseback ride."

He purses his lips. "I'm not certain it could be done on horseback."

I meet his gaze again. "Then you, sir, lack a proper imagination."

The laugh bursts from him, definitely surprise now. Very, very pleased surprise.

Before he can come back with a rejoinder, I say, "I'm going to dance, and you owe me nothing for it."

"I would quite happily owe you—"

"A kiss," I say. "If you insist on repaying me, I will take a kiss. On the cheek."

"May I choose the cheek?"

"Yes." I point to the left side of my face. "This one." I point to the right. "Or that one. Others require at least a second date."

Another laugh, and before he can respond, I start dancing.

I've had a little more alcohol than usual, which doesn't fully— or even mostly—account for the warmth coursing through me. I'm fully relaxed, fully comfortable, fully myself and confident in a way I haven't been since Michael.

There is a cliché—embroidered on far too many pillows— about dancing like no one is watching. I appreciate the difference between doing ballet with a class or alone in my living room where I don't need to worry about pleasing anyone except myself. There's something better, though—dancing in front of someone who makes me feel the same as when I'm alone. Someone who wants to watch me and doesn't care a fig whether I do it right, just wants to see me lose myself in the moment.

Earlier, I watched William riding without him knowing I was there, and I reveled in the sheer joy of *his* joy, of watching him fully in his element. Now, that same look lights his face as I dance in the moonlight, and I close my eyes to slits to indulge in the very selfish pleasure of watching him when he doesn't know I am, seeing him admiring me.

The look on his face makes me feel things I'm not sure I'm ready to feel, quite certain I don't *dare* feel given all the impossibilities of our situation. So, I won't dwell on those impossibilities. I'll dance, and I'll be happy.

I dance to the music of the wind and the turtledoves, heather soft beneath my bare feet, the earthy smell of it enveloping me. When I pirouette, I let my eyes close, just for a moment, and when they open, William is gone from his spot on the ground.

There's a split second of panic as I'm certain I've twirled straight into my own time. And then he's there, in front of me, standing with his face lost in shadow as the moon rises behind him.

I slow, and he reaches for my hands, and I'm about to tease him. Then I see his expression, and any frothy quip dies in my throat. He takes my hands and stares as if I'm some fae creature he found dancing in the moors. His fingers tighten around mine, firm but cautious in case I panic and flee.

My breath catches as his fingers slide up my arm, setting goosebumps rising. His gaze never leaves mine, his eyes dark with an expression I can't quite read, longing and desire and something almost like fear.

His lips part, but no words come. His breathing sounds quickened and shallow, as if he's holding himself very still. Only his fingers move, the tips barely touching my skin as they glide up my arm, pausing to brush hair off my shoulder, a lock rubbed between his fingers before they're on my cheek, stroking, butterfly soft.

"I missed you," he says, his voice so low I barely hear it even in the silence. "I missed you so . . ."

His voice catches then, and he moves toward me, lips pressing against my forehead, one hand still on mine, the other sliding through my hair.

He pulls back and looks down, and I want to say something.

The moment I think that, I recoil. I do *not* want to say anything. I don't *dare* say anything. I'm afraid that, if I do, it'll be a lighthearted quip to break a mood that has my heart skipping so fast I can barely breathe.

I want to break this moment. Shatter it. Cast it off.

I want to kiss him. Kiss him until he forgets what he was saying, and I forget what I want to say. Kiss him and unbutton his shirt and push him onto the heather and shatter the mood that way. Lose ourselves in pleasure, and when it ends, we'll have forgotten there were words to be said, and I'll be safe.

His fingers caress my cheek, tilting my face to his.

"Are you afraid?" he whispers.

"No," I say, and that's all I want to say, all I *plan* to say. Instead, I hear my voice again, whispering, "I'm terrified."

His face moves down, so close his breath tickles my lips.

"So am I," he whispers, and he kisses me.

I'm ready for a kiss from the man whose bed I woke in. A man with a firm, confident touch. Instead, I get a kiss from the boy I knew. That kiss casts me back in time. Not to the first one, which however sweet, had been best suited for romantic comedy. Neither of us had kissed anyone before, and it was like driving a car for the first time. After years of watching others do it, I'd thought I'd known how, and then I sat in the driver's seat and . . . well, my overwhelming memory is a tornado of panic amid squees of delight. "Oh my God, he's kissing me! Ack, is this right? It doesn't feel right!"

We'd gotten the hang of it, of course, that first awkward kiss only igniting a mutual determination to practice until we did. Tonight's kiss reminds me of the ones after we got it right, but before William relaxed enough to trust in that.

The kiss is tender with a hint of uncertainty, his hands framing my face, his touch light. That kiss waits for undeniable proof that it's welcome. When I give it, I get a kiss of exploration, firmer but still gentle, William relaxing, his hands sliding down my back as mine encircle his neck. The kiss deepens, his body pressing against mine, my fingers entwining in his hair. Hunger licks through me, his tongue finding mine, his kiss hard and hungry, only to pull back, holding himself in check.

I feed into that hunger, letting him know it's not unwelcome. I don't challenge his slowing pace, though. This is too delicious to rush—the tease of it, a flare of passion and then pulling back, finding a gentler pace only to surge again, even the calm tingling with anticipation. It's like floating on a sun-dappled ocean, waiting for the next crashing wave. Then, he breaks the pattern with a deep, crushing kiss that leaves me gasping and him chuckling raggedly.

When I close my eyes and tilt my face back to his, ready to resume, his fingers glide along the curve of my jaw. I peek, and his lips curve in a smile that crinkles the corners of his eyes.

"Thank you," he says, "for not letting me frighten you off. When you first arrived, I was angry, and you could easily have walked away."

"I think I did."

The smile deepens. "True, but you didn't go far."

"Because I couldn't cross back. I was stuck."

"You aren't making this conversation easy, are you?"

"I could pretend that I laid in wait and then lied about being stuck so I could keep trying to explain after you asked me to leave. But that makes me sound like a creepy obsessive ex-girlfriend. You know the sort. Sneaks into your bed. Steals your kitten. Bakes you cookies. They make movies about exes like that. They never have a happy ending."

He laughs softly and runs his thumb over my cheek. "Well, I'm hoping our story does. I also want you to know that, whatever ending we do find, I will never expect you to stay. I will be here, though. I'm not going anywhere. I wasn't before you arrived, and I'm certainly not now. I'm here. I will always be here. You need only to step across and find me, and that's all I'll ever ask of you. That you come back for as long as you want to, and you let me know if that changes."

"I will. I promise."

I rise on my tiptoes, my lips brushing his. As my eyes close, movement flashes over his shoulder, and I give a start. His arms tighten around me. Something moves in the darkness. My gaze swings to it as I say, "What's—"

His arms fall away, and I tumble backward.

17

I hit the ground flat on my back, and I stare up in astonishment at William. He isn't there. And my brain snaps to that conclusion a heartbeat before it processes the fact that I'm staring at empty space. I fell because William vanished, leaving me supported by nothing but air.

I sit, wincing as pain throbs through my back. I roll my shoulders and struggle to inhale, finally managing a sharp, searing breath. A few slower, experimental breaths. Nothing seems broken. The wind's just been knocked out of me.

I blink, corralling my thoughts. I was kissing William . . . No, I was just resuming the kiss, our lips brushing, when I saw something over his shoulder.

A figure moving behind him.

My heart stutters, and I leap to my feet with, "William?"

Of course he doesn't answer. I'm alone in the moors, our picnic baskets gone, too, telling me that while everything else might look the same, I've fallen out of time. Fallen out of *his* time, back into my own.

Someone was walking up behind him.

I spin, as if there's a door I can yank open, a way to fly back and warn him, protect him. There's only one way in, though. I know from experience that I can fall *back* to my time in other places, especially if I'm startled, but that's a one-way exit. The entrance is at least an hour's jog away, and William is alone in the moors with someone creeping up behind him.

Was someone creeping up behind him?

I struggle to recall what I saw. Movement. A shape moving behind William. Not approaching him. Certainly not rushing at him. Just moving behind him.

I'd heard nothing, and I should have. If a person approached, they'd have needed to slog through swamp or scramble over rocks.

So, basically, I spooked myself. I've been seeing ghosts, and I spotted a flicker in the darkness. Instead of just jumping backward, startled, like a normal person, I'd jumped clear through time, landing here.

Landing here . . . in the middle of the moors, alone, at night.

I shiver. Well, it could be worse. At least the moors are the same in both time periods. I'll need to be careful not to let William take me on any long walks that could have me time-jumping into the middle of a modern highway.

I also take comfort in the fact that I jumped midsentence when I'd obviously been startled by something, and there's no way William will think he said or did anything to send me fleeing across the centuries.

I look around into the dark, empty moors.

Very dark. Very empty.

Better empty than haunted, right?

I square my shoulders. It can't be much past nine p.m. Hardly the witching hour. And I know where I am, roughly speaking. Just turn on my cell phone flashlight . . .

My hand slides to my hip where it finds nothing resembling a pocket. Because I'm wearing a sundress. I'd put the phone into the picnic basket . . . which is in the nineteenth century.

I sigh. At least if I don't return, William has technology that could make him the Bill Gates of his time. Or get him hanged for witchcraft.

A three-quarter moon is rising in a cloudless sky. I probably wouldn't have bothered with the flashlight anyway. I know the direction of the house and the basic route. While we're down in a dale here, all I need to do is climb one of the nearby hills, and I'll see lights in the distance. This is the twenty-first century—the moors may be big enough to get lost in, but there are plenty of villages lighting up the night sky. Even if I need to walk a few miles, it's not as if I'll starve after that huge picnic dinner. Just to be sure, though, I drink my fill of spring water. There, I'll be fine for at least a day or two before I die of dehydration.

I set out across the rocks. I make it ten determined paces before my foot slips, wedging between rocks, pain shooting up my ankle. I mutter an oath and give my foot a shake.

The moon may be bright, but it's not midday. I need to take this slower. At the thought, my heart thuds, a little voice in me shrieking, "Slower? You're lost in the moors at night. Move!"

I'm not lost, and it's only late evening. I'll be fine. As long as I don't run pell-mell over the rocks and twist my ankle.

I watch where I'm putting my feet. They're bare, which helps with grip, but also means I feel every sharp edge. Step by step, I move, focused on my route, only to look up, expecting to see the path . . . and realize I've barely traveled twenty feet with another hundred to go.

Deep breaths. I *am* fine. It's just frustrating, that's all.

When a wide boulder blocks my path, I start around it to see the ground covered in small and jagged stones. My toes curl at the prospect. Over the boulder it is, then. That isn't as difficult as it sounds. The rock is long and low, mid-thigh level. I can't hop onto it gracefully, but I can clamber up. I'm doing that when a voice whispers at my ear.

I jump, and my knee slams into the rock. Pain shoots down my leg. When I tentatively touch the spot, blood smears my fingertips.

Another whisper. This time, I wheel, hands raised as if against an attacker. No one's there. I know no one is. As the pain subsides to a dull throb, the hairs on my neck rise. I rub them down.

Another look around as I struggle to recapture what I heard.

Was it a voice? Or am I as nervous as a spooked cat, unable to shake that awareness that I am alone in a place far less welcoming by night? A place where people disappear.

That last thought snaps the spell, and I give my head an angry shake. Now I'm being foolish. There's a light breeze out tonight. It whispered past my ear, and I cracked my kneecap jumping at it.

Calm down. There is no one within two miles, for better or worse. Just take it slow and steady.

I grip the boulder and heave myself onto it, wincing as my knee bends, fresh blood trickling. Once on top of the rock, I push to my feet and—

A figure flashes in front of me. *Right* in front of me, materializing less than a handspan away.

My arms windmill as I fall back, and somehow I manage not to fall backward off the boulder and dash my brains out on the rocks below. I catch my balance and overcompensate, toppling forward, instead, my mangled knee slamming into rock again, my howl of agony ringing across the moors. I huddle there, catching my breath, blinking past the pain until I can lift my head, and when I do, the figure has vanished.

Rage courses through me. Blind fury as I realize how close I came to smashing my skull or breaking my neck or any of a hundred things that could have left me there, unconscious or immobile, in the middle of the moor where my joke about dying of dehydration wouldn't have been a joke at all.

"What do you want?" I bellow into the emptiness.

Silence returns, the night as calm and still as it'd been moments ago.

"You want something from me?" I say. "Then talk to me. Kill

me, and all you'll get is another ghost on your turf. A very angry, very vindictive ghost."

A whisper at my ear again.

I spin, scowling at empty air. "I can't hear you, and I'm not convinced you want me to. It's so much more fun to scare the life out of me."

Another whisper, more urgent now, and some of my fury seeps away. That tone says the ghost is trying to communicate. I remember Freya's advice for communicating with spirits, passed down from her grandmother with the Sight. There were objects and ingredients I could use, but obviously I have none of them here. The biggest piece of advice, though, required nothing at all. Be firm, and be kind. Do not let them order you about, but remember their difficult situation. Listen and offer support and a reasonable amount of help.

My voice softens as I say, "I'm not ignoring you. I just don't understand what you're trying to say."

The air ripples. That's the only way I can describe it. A frisson of energy whipping around me. Angry energy. Frustrated energy.

Then a figure materializes ten feet away. It's a woman. Or I presume that from the half-opaque shape. She seems wrapped in a burial shroud, which makes no sense for the region, not unless I've somehow encountered a ghost from Roman Britain. There's a tiny corner of my historian's brain that cartwheels in excitement at the thought. There were Romans in the moorland, and the remains of an old road connect what would have been two forts in the area. But this is not a burial shroud. It's just a sheet, inexpertly wrapped around her. It covers her head, leaving her face hidden. I struggle to make out even her size as her figure blurs each time I focus on it. I can tell the ghost is female, and that's all.

When I move closer, she backs up. I take another step. She retreats again.

"Are you telling me to stay away?" I say. "Or leading me somewhere?"

She lifts one shroud-draped arm and points in the direction I just came. I hesitate, torn between curiosity and the exhaustion of not wanting to retrace my steps. I tune out my throbbing knee and begin the slow process of picking my way over the stones again, following the woman until I'm only a few feet from the stream where William and I had our picnic. That's when I realize where she's leading me. Into the bog.

18

I shake my head. "I can't go there."

That ripple of energy again, tension slicing through the air.

"I'm sorry, but I could barely get through the bog in daylight. If what you want me to see is on the other side, where the ground's dry, I can try—"

She jabs her covered hand, the air so electric it sets my every nerve on edge.

She doesn't want me to see something on the other side. She wants me to walk into the wetlands. Out onto wet ground at night, when I can't see where I'm going.

Fresh anger darts through me. "Do you really think I'm going to fall for that?"

She jabs again, the air sizzling with her own anger.

"No," I say, recalling Freya's advice to be firm. "You nearly killed me on that rock, so I don't trust you. I'm not wandering into the bog at your beckoning."

I turn around. She bursts up right in front of me. I don't startle this time. I only glare and stride right through her.

Her whisper sounds at my ear, and this time, I catch the words, " . . . think you're the first . . ."

"First what?" I say, turning on her.

She's gone. I continue walking. I plant each foot firmly, every muscle tense, ready for her to pop up again. Instead, she only whispers at my ear.

" . . . warn you . . ."

"You're trying to warn me?" I say without stopping. "The only person endangering me right now is you."

" . . . listen . . . ," she hisses.

"I am listening. I'm just not hearing anything worth listening to."

The air ignites, a lash of bitter cold, gale-force strong. I stumble but keep my footing and press on.

" . . . warn you . . . him . . ."

"You're trying to warn me about *him*. Can you tell me who *he* is?"

A whisper that I can't make out. I do catch enough to understand that I should already know who she means. In my mind, I see the man with the spade.

"Okay, I'm warned," I say. "But I'm not going into the bog. Now, please leave me alone."

A whirlwind of air so cold it burns my eyes. My breath hangs in frozen condensation, and I brace myself for another blast. None comes. I start forward again, step by careful step, ready for the sudden gust that will knock me off my feet.

It never comes.

She has done what I asked. She's left me alone.

I cross the rocks and come out onto flat, soft moor, my toes reveling in the sponge of heather underfoot. The smell of it wafts up, and somewhere in the distance, a cow lows, and a dove coos, and I realize how quiet it'd been before. Too quiet even for the moors at night, every beast going silent as the ghost appeared.

I round a corner to see a white shape moving across the field. I yelp and fall back . . . and a sheep turns to bleat at my foolishness before clearing out of my way.

"Sorry!" I call, my voice echoing in the night.

I find the path easily enough, and then I'm off, circling the bog as I make my way home. I relax, my strides lengthening, step confident, swing around a corner and nearly collide with the ghost.

I draw back, my lip curling in a snarl. Then, I see that it's the woman from my first night out here. I've all but run into her, poised on the path, her breath coming in sharp, shallow bursts.

"P-please," she says. "Please stop."

I wave my hand inches from her indistinct face. She only swivels, gaze tripping over the stunted trees all around us.

"I know you're there," she says. "I saw you."

She keeps looking.

"I hear you breathing," she says. "You *want* me to hear you."

She turns in a full circle, hands clenched but lowered, as if ready to defend herself but having no idea how. Her face is blurred enough that she could be anywhere from eighteen to thirty. I can make out dark eyes and light hair, sweat sodden after her flight. Her blue dress is torn, the crinolines askew.

"Stop this," she says, trembling as she struggles to steady her voice. "Please. I don't know what you want. I don't know why you're doing this. I don't care. Stop it, and let me leave, and I'll never come back, and I won't tell anyone what you did. Just let me—"

A scream as she pitches forward, as if struck from behind. Blood sprays as she drops face first to the ground . . . and disappears.

I stand there, stock still. When a gasp sounds, I jump, only to realize it comes from my own throat. I've been holding my breath, and now it bursts forth.

I stare at the spot, waiting for the scene to resume so I can see what happened to her.

I *know* what happened to her.

It's a long time before I can gather my wits enough to leave, and when I do, it's at a jog, my lungs burning, panic welling up. I tear down one path and then turn onto another, and a man steps around the next bend. I jerk back, but it's too late. He's looking right at me. It's the man with the spade. Except he isn't carrying the spade. He's carrying a body. A figure lies draped over his arms. A figure wrapped in a bedsheet.

The man keeps coming, moving straight for me. I scramble off the path, but there are no trees here to hide behind. It's open moor, and all I can do is run. I take three steps and look back over my shoulder to see the man still walking along the path, his face set in the same grim expression, gaze fixed straight ahead. He walks with the slow, measured pace of a pallbearer in a funeral procession.

"Hello?" I say, my voice creaking.

His stride doesn't even hitch. I ease toward him, ready to turn and run at any sign he hears me. But he isn't there, at least not in the sense that the other ghost was, where I could interact with her. This is one of those "spectral replays," like the woman I just encountered on the path. I take a deep breath, realizing I'm safe, and as my panic subsides, curiosity slips into its place.

I keep going until I'm jogging alongside him. Then I swing into his path. I see his face more clearly than the others, the lines and sags of an old man's face. Weather-roughened skin, red across his cheeks and forehead like windburn. Sunken brown eyes, still bright but emotionless, as if he's retreated somewhere inside himself.

As he walks toward me, I back up, so I can keep examining him. He's lean but strong, as I noticed before, his back straight, shoulders narrow and arms hidden beneath his coarse shirt, yet he carries his burden easily.

His burden . . .

A figure wrapped in a sheet. The same sheet that shrouded the ghost I'd seen tonight, the one who tried to lure me into the bog. Her face and hair are covered, but I've no doubt it's the ghost I saw. One hand has fallen partially free of the shroud, pale fingers bouncing with each step. I catch a glimpse of blue.

A blue dress beneath the shroud.

This is the ghost that challenged me on the rocks. It's also the woman I just saw, fleeing her unknown assailant.

Maybe I should have connected them sooner, but they'd seemed two separate people. A frightened woman lost in the moors and a vengeful spirit enraged by her inability to communicate. Two very different situations, showing two very different sides of the same woman.

If I'd been lost in the moors, alone, and then stalked by a killer, I'd be terrified and tearful, too. Then, if hundreds of years later, my ghost met someone she could communicate with, and that person couldn't hear me? Refused to follow me? I'd be just as furious as the shrouded spirit.

I'm still backing up, committing the figures to memory, when the man turns. It looks as if he's leaving the path, but then I see a narrow one to the side. I hurry after them. Another ten paces, though, and he does indeed abandon the path, heading deeper into the moors. I take two steps, and mud squelches around my bare feet.

The bog.

I've circled around and come back on the opposite side of the bog.

The bog where the shrouded ghost tried to lead me.

The bog where this man is now taking her body.

An image flashes, the man looking up at the house, at that window. Looking to see whether anyone noticed him slipping into the moor, spade in hand.

That's what the shrouded ghost had been trying to show me. Her burial place.

I hurry after the man, but in the back of my mind, self-preservation beats a drum tattoo of, "No, no, no." There'd been a very good reason why I refused to follow the woman into the bog. The same reason William's picnic spot remained untouched. The same reason he took us the long way over the rocks. The wetlands are dangerous even in daylight. At night? I'm risking my life with every footstep.

Still, I press on until one foot strikes the wrong spot, instantly sinking to mid-calf. Panic seizes me, and I scrabble for firmer ground. My leg pops free, and I stumble. My other foot slides on the damp earth. I flail, and then down I go, and the ground seems to rise up, sucking me in. More flailing, more panic, until I manage to drag myself from the muck.

I sit on the ground, heart pounding, as I catch my breath. Then I crawl to ground firm enough to stand on. When I'm upright, I look out to see the dark figure of the man, surefootedly picking a path into the bog. I strain to watch him, noting the direction he went. Finally, he's gone.

Gone to bury his dead.

19

It's nearly midnight by the time I get to the manor house. Muddied and exhausted, I tramp across the yard. As the front door slaps shut behind me, Enigma squeaks from upstairs and tumbles down the stairs so fast I use my last iota of energy scrambling to catch her. Then I sit on the steps, kitten on my lap, stare into darkness and catch my breath.

Memories of the man fade, my heart slows, and I'm reminded that the moors aren't the only place I see ghosts. It's past dark. I should take Enigma and flee to my room. But I don't, because tonight, I *want* to see the ghosts. I want to talk to them.

I make my way upstairs, straining ears and eyes, but there's no sign of the woman in black. I'm turning when I catch movement at the linen closet door. A flash of a white-sleeved arm, lace at the wrist.

"Hello?" I say, gripping Enigma tight.

There's nothing there now, but I know I saw it, as if the ghost of that boy in knickerbockers had started to come through . . . and then retreated.

I steel myself and walk toward the door.

"Are you there?" I say. "I'd like to speak to you if you are."

I think I catch a whisper. I hesitate. Then I throw open the closet door to see . . . nothing but shelves, empty except for a single change of bed linens and two extra sets of towels. My gaze slides to the side where a hatch leads to a cubby, one of the myriad odd nooks and crannies found in old houses. This one, though, has a panel on it that leads to the secret passage. William discovered the passage in his version of Thorne Manor, and I recall my childish delight on finding it still existed in mine.

The passage is an oversized gap between walls, constructed when the house was originally built. It runs from the linen closet to the master bedroom. As to its original purpose, William and I had envisioned a hiding place for a highwayman's treasure. Or a family escape route in case angry villagers descended with pitchforks. Or a horrible prison for an insane relative.

By the age of fifteen, we were old enough to discern the true purpose. In William's house, there was no linen closet—the passage ran from a guest room cubby to the master suite. In other words, it allowed the first lord to sneak from his bedroom to a guest's. By William's time, the passage had been forgotten. One end led into his mother's room, blocked by a massive wardrobe, an heirloom that had stood there since before her marriage.

Now the hatch to the cubby is locked. I yank on the padlock and twist it, but it only squeaks at my efforts, that squeak sounding like mocking laughter. I prod the base of the latch, hoping for wood rotted enough to snap. It's solid, though. Either I'll need to find the key or break down the door.

I step back out of the linen closet, nearly tripping over Enigma, who's joyfully exploring this new place. I'm turning when I see my bedroom door.

My bedroom.

William's bedroom.

William.

William, who doesn't know I'm all right, who last saw me disappear in the moors at night.

I run to my room and yank up the floorboard. Underneath is a letter. I snatch it out.

Bronwyn,

I am endeavoring, with very limited success, not to worry about you. Admittedly, part of that is the fear that I spoke too soon of any future, however tentative, between us.

Rationally, I know something startled you, and you fell back into your time as you have before. I also reassure myself that you are quite capable of finding your way home through our moors. Still, I am worried, and so if you receive this note, I would appreciate if you would remove it from its place, signaling that you have returned safely.

I would like to say that I will not lie awake waiting, but I doubt I will find much rest before I am certain you have returned. I shall lie abed with a book and endeavor not to check the floorboard every five minutes.

Here he signed it, only to stroke that out and add more.

In my concern for your welfare, I closed the note rather abruptly. I should add that I very much enjoyed our picnic, and I hope we may repeat the adventure soon . . . preferably with a less abrupt conclusion.

William

I quickly change out of my filthy clothing. Then I stand in the center of the room and close my eyes and concentrate on seeing him. Air flutters past, a warm shimmer, the opposite of what I felt with the shrouded ghost. When I open my eyes, I'm in William's room. He's on the bed, and I start to warn him it's me. Then I see a book, toppled from his hand, and his head lolling to one side, eyes closed. He's fast asleep.

I pick up the novel. *The Tenant of Wildfell Hall.* While the cover proclaims the author as Acton Bell, it's actually Anne Brontë, the youngest of the famous sisters.

"Interesting choice," I murmur, too softly to wake him. I'll need to ask him about the book—the tale of a woman exiled to a bleak mansion . . . in the Yorkshire moors.

As I tuck the novel onto his nightstand, I glance at him. Victorian men's nightwear is familiar to anyone who has seen *A Christmas Carol*, with Ebenezer Scrooge in his long nightshirt. As with most things, William eschews tradition in favor of comfort, and I certainly can't argue with that. Like the last time, he's naked, one leg under the sheets, twisted enough to preserve a modicum of modesty while leaving plenty on display to be admired. And admire I do.

When I see my cell phone on the bed table, I'm tempted—sorely tempted—to take a picture. Or two. Or three. That, however, would be wrong, given that he's unable to consent. I sigh with regret and console myself with mental snapshots instead, walking closer for a better view, taking in the flow of his muscular body, the cut of his jaw, the pulse at his throat, those full lips parted in sibilant whispers of breath, black lashes on pale skin, the curl of hair against the nape of his neck.

I stand beside him, and it takes all my willpower not to reach out and touch that curl, run a finger down his bicep, brush a kiss on his cheek . . . on his shoulder, on his stomach.

Another sigh, stifled before I wake him.

I *want* to wake him, of course. In the most selfish pit of my stomach, I long to brush a kiss over his bare shoulder, whisper at his ear. See those blue eyes open. See his lips curve in a smile when he realizes it's me. See his arms reach and move into them and feel myself tugged into that bed with him.

I ache to crawl into that bed, slide in on the other side and press against him. Kiss and touch him, run my fingers over his sleep-hot skin and see his eyes flutter open.

I'm well aware, though, that the fantasy is just that. I imagine his eyes opening and him smiling and pulling me to him. The truth is that, woken from a deep sleep by someone leaning over him, he's liable to leap up, striking with both fists, and honestly, I wouldn't blame him.

Also, while I'm keeping my distance and allowing myself no more than the fantasies of kissing and touching and caressing him, even watching him sleep crosses a line. My only excuse is that I didn't intend this intrusion. I expected him to be awake, and now that he isn't, I should leave.

So I tear myself from his sleeping form, and I walk to his

dresser, where his paper and pen wait. Then I dip the carved gold nib pen into the inkwell and begin a note.

Dear William,

It took me a while to get back to the manor house, but I returned safely. On reading your note, I crossed over, but it seems I arrived too late. You'd fallen asleep, and I didn't wish to wake you.

I pause there, blotting the pen before I lift it, poised over the paper as I think. Should I leave it at that or . . . go a step farther?

Do I *dare* go a step farther?

I take a deep breath and add a new paragraph.

I will admit, though, that I did consider waking you. I could not help remembering that night when I inadvertently woke in your bed. I have never properly explained that, and I should. I want you to know that I did not intrude intentionally. I woke in what I thought was a dream.

However, I will also admit that I have revisited that "dream" often, and on seeing you asleep in bed tonight, it took a great deal of willpower not to crawl in beside you, which would—regrettably—be wrong. Tempting. Powerfully tempting, but wrong . . .

I pause before adding the closing. Thus far, he's only ended his with his name, and perhaps I should stick to that. It's safest to stick to that. But I've already taken a step onto unsteady ground with that last paragraph, and so I might as well push through. I sign it.

Yours,

Bronwyn

I reread the closing, and I have to chuckle. It's hardly a declaration of undying love. But it still feels as if I've risked a forthrightness he might not be ready for. William may be open-minded and unconventional for his time, but he's still a product of that time when men take the steps in a relationship. Women may choose to follow, but stay a step behind, letting their partner lead the courtship dance.

I could rewrite the note. There's plenty of paper. Write it again and take this version with me where he'll never see it.

I don't. If he's taken aback by my boldness, then we have an issue to work through. I'm no blushing maiden, eager to hand the relationship reins to him. This will make it clear, as it needs to be.

I tuck the note inside his novel, leaving it sticking out enough that he can't miss it in the morning. I watch him for one final moment, resisting the urge to give him a goodnight kiss, and then I return home.

20

I sleep in the next morning, too exhausted for dawn's light to wake me. When I do rouse, I go straight for the floorboard. Under it is another note . . . and another black velvet pouch that jingles when I lift it. I toss the pouch aside and pounce on the note instead.

Dearest Bronwyn,

I am pleased to hear you returned home safely. I am not nearly so pleased by your note, however.

My stomach drops as I force myself to read on.

Exactly how do you expect me to go about my daily chores now that you have placed that image in my mind? It was quite bad enough that I retain vivid memories of that first night, the most pleasant and stimulating dream I can recall. Now, you tell me that you were in my room last night, considering a repeat performance.

At least you did not provide me with details, or I would get absolutely nothing done today.

There were details, were there not? You didn't simply stand by my bed, and think it looked terribly comfortable and dream of crawling in and sleeping beside me. That would be dreadfully disappointing.

Reading between the lines of your note, I feel there were details more to my liking, ones you thankfully omitted. When I say, "thankfully," note that I also mean, "regrettably." My busy schedule thanks you for not providing details. The rest of me is fraught with regret, my imagination forced to fill in those details, and now it is eight in the morning, and Mrs. Shaw has already knocked to be sure I am not ill as I lie abed thinking of your note.

I must rise and head to the stable. Speaking of regrettable situations, I will be away for most of the day. Would you have the evening free for me? I should have asked yesterday, but our parting was sudden.

If you cannot visit this evening, I will ask that you cross over and leave me a note while I am gone. Also, if you were inclined to share more of your thoughts from last night, I would not complain.

I will see you this evening, I hope. Seven o'clock my time would be perfect. I shall be away until shortly before then.

Yours,

William

I may have read the letter three times, grinning the entire time. Then I pen one of my own. In it, I assure him that I'll be there at seven his time. I also give details of what I envisioned last night. Details, admittedly, more worthy of a sensual romance than a hot sex scene. There's no need to rush to the latter. I dwell on the lead-up, on what I imagined doing as I stood over him, the kisses and the caresses, where I wanted to kiss, where I wanted to caress.

When I reread the letter, my cheeks burn. I tapered off before anything explicit, but yearning leaps from the page. I don't discard it, though. He asked for details, and I delivered.

I fold the note and close my eyes, thinking of William. Then I'm in his room. His empty room, as expected. I tuck the note into his book, in hopes that if Mrs. Shaw cleans his chambers, she won't move it.

I return to my time and scoop up Enigma, who has been

watching the proceedings with confusion . . . and growingly urgent cries for breakfast. We go down and dine on our respective morning meals, and I curl up in the sitting room, reading and luxuriating in a lazy morning.

It's not until I go up to dress—nearly noon—that I remember the pouch. While it feels mildly mercenary, it's a decadent pleasure to be sitting cross legged on my bed, running gold coins through my fingers, imagining all the ways I'll use it, both sensible and indulgent, as William demanded.

Speaking of imaginings . . .

After I'm finished playing with my gold like a comic-book miser, I lean over the bed to peek under the floorboards. There's a new note. As I snatch it up, I grin.

Of course, the moment I realize I'm grinning with anticipation, my smile freezes. What if my note was too much? What if—

Dearest Bronwyn,

I suppose I have only myself to blame for that. I fairly pleaded for details, and so what did I expect you to provide? Nothing, if I am being quite honest. Perhaps, at most, a teasing note that rapped my knuckles for my impudence. Instead, I received . . .

I did mention that I need to run errands today, did I not? Very, very important errands that cannot be impeded by me sitting on the edge of my bed, reading your letter repeatedly, allowing my imagination to fill in the visual details, like that moving picture you showed me, now playing in my mind, of you standing over me in bed, touching me, kissing me, sliding in beside . . .

Blast you, woman. I have work to do, and now all I can think about is that letter and, worse, imagine if I had been here when you delivered it, if I had returned only a few minutes sooner and caught you tucking it into my book. I could have taken it out and read it, insisting that you remain while I did so, and then having you there with me when I finished reading . . .

I have plans, I will have you know. Plans for my day, and plans for our evening together, and none of them involve me enjoying the contents

of your letter for the next few hours while hoping you might return.
Now, I am torn between proceeding with my plans and begging you to
come as soon as you read this, so you might show me exactly what you
had in mind last night.

No, as irresistible as that thought is, I will resist its siren call. My
plans are very precise and important, and I will regret it later if I alter
them.

I will see you at seven. And if, on seeing you, I bring up your letter,
please do rap my knuckles and remind me that such fancies can—and
must—wait.

Yours,
William

My grin returns, wider than before, and I dance my way
downstairs. A memory surges of me pirouetting through the
house, voluntarily doing the dishes and dancing as I put them
away, Aunt Judith in the doorway saying, "Met a boy from the
village, did you?"

I had visited a boy, indeed. That was the day William kissed
me in the barn, and I don't think I stopped dancing all summer.
Or not until . . .

I banish the rest. At the thought of ghosts, though, I'm
reminded of the secret passage and my determination to get
through that door. I return to the closet and try the lock half-heartedly, as if it might somehow come free now after a few tugs last
night.

It doesn't, and with that, I leave it alone. Last night, I'd been
spooked, desperately needing answers, and I'm not sure how I
expected that passage to answer them. A whim, really.

I'll check it out, of course. At some point. But I have chores of
my own to accomplish before I meet William. So I leave the door
and dance off on my cloud of euphoria to tackle neglected
housework.

At 6:45 William's time, I stand in the middle of my bedroom, watching the bedside clock. I've bathed, primped, even shaved. Not that I'm expecting anything tonight . . .

Oh, who am I kidding? I might not be *expecting* anything, but I'm certainly hoping for an ending to my evening that has me very glad I performed all necessary ablutions.

At 6:50, I make a test run, which just means that I try crossing over early in case it fails and I need to try harder. It doesn't fail. The air buzzes with that warm electrical charge, and before I can even open my eyes, hands slide around my waist, and lips press against mine. I start with a tiny—I hope—yelp of surprise.

William chuckles and tightens his arms around me in a quick embrace and quicker second kiss before stepping back.

"Hello," he says.

I lift to brush my lips across his with my "Hello," and his eyes gleam with pleasure.

"I got the time right?" I say.

"You did." He lifts his hand from my waist to trace his finger down my cheek. "I will also admit I may have been anxiously waiting here for a while, worried that my last note may have been"—he purses his lips—"a little forward."

I laugh. "I was worried about the same with mine."

"It wasn't too much?"

"Was mine?"

His lips curve in a grin, eyes dancing. "Certainly not, as I think my note made clear."

"It did. However, I also noticed that, while you waxed appreciative on my epistolary efforts, you did not return them in kind. It was most disappointing."

His lips lower to my ear, whisper tickling as he says, "I certainly can, having had more than enough time to consider the matter. Shall I tell you how I would have responded, had you carried through with your inclinations and climbed into my bed?"

Heat rushes through me, and I shiver, knees weakening. Yes, that's terribly cliché of me, but my knees literally do weaken, and if he hadn't been holding me up, I might have swooned at his feet. Or, possibly, jumped him, which wouldn't be nearly so period appropriate.

I look up into his face. "I would love for you to tell me. The only thing I'd like more is for you to demonstrate."

His breath catches, and his grip on me tightens, eyes clouding with desire so sharp my knees really do give way, just a little.

"You did warn me about this," I manage. "Should I rap my own knuckles?"

He laughs, soft and hoarse, and he straightens. "I believe so. I really do have plans for this evening, and they do not begin this way."

"Do they *end* this way?"

A chuckle, ragged and knee weakening. "A gentleman does not divulge his intentions. And I fear that if I do, I will divulge them in great detail, upon which we will decide not to leave this bedroom." He takes a deep breath, steps back and waves me to the door. "Our evening begins down the hall. Follow me if you please."

William leads me to the master suite. As he grips the doorknob, I say, "You're taking me from one bedroom to another? Well, the bed *is* much larger in here. Or, perhaps, we're going to begin in one and move to another, make our way through all the rooms. Intriguing. Potentially exhausting, but if you're up to it . . ."

He casts a look over his shoulder.

I rap my knuckles. "Sorry."

"Indeed. There will be none of that." He pushes open the door. "At least, for the next few hours."

"Hours?"

His mock-scowl makes me grin. He steps back to usher me through. Teasing has never been my style, but he so obviously appreciates it—while so obviously trying *not* to appreciate it—that my inner coquette has been unleashed. I'm about to tease again when I see the dress, laid across the bed, and I stop, gaping.

Victorian dresses are often ornate or overdone. This one is simplistic perfection. Copper satin shimmers like fresh-minted pennies. The only ornamentation is the short puffed sleeves with black lace oversleeves. Sophisticated and stylish and utterly gorgeous.

I glance at William, expecting to see his lips tweaked in a very satisfied smile. Instead, he's running a finger over his chin, watching me apprehensively.

"It is . . ." He clears his throat and straightens. "We never discussed your fantasy of attending a ball beyond the basic concept. I know the dress is a large part of that, but as for exactly what sort of dress you imagine . . ." Another throat clearing. "I am hoping this one is . . . vaguely suitable."

"Vaguely suitable?" I throw my arms around his neck and give my most girlish squeal, making him chuckle in relief.

I back away and run a hand over the dress, the satin whispering beneath my fingers. Before I can speak, he hurries on with, "I am not taking you to a ball. I would if there were any I knew of in the area. I shall take you another time, but for now, I have brought the ball to you."

"A ball for two?"

He pulls at his collar. "Yes, that's hardly a proper affair, and not at all what you imagined—"

I press my lips to his, stoppering his words. Then, I pull back with, "Tonight I'd prefer a ball for two. Thank you."

A flush creeps up his face as he tugs again at his collar. Then he glances down at his own clothing. "This is not my attire for the evening, of course. I will be changing shortly, after the—"

The front door knocker sounds. I stiffen, but he only turns to the hall with a soft curse. "She's early."

Another rap, harder now. He glances at me, looking flustered. "You are a widow."

"Uh, yes, I believe we've established—"

"A widow I knew as a childhood friend."

"Also correct but—"

"I must answer the door before she decides I am not at home. Put on that dress, please."

I glance at the gown, but he's pointing at the blue-and-white dress I wore the other day, now draped over a chair.

"I thought—" I begin, looking at the copper ballgown.

"That dress." Another point at the other dress, and he's gone.

I quickly change into the blue-and-white dress. I'm still pulling it on when footsteps sound on the stairs. Two sets of them. I grab my sundress and stuff it under the bed. A rap comes at the door.

"Lady Dale? Are you presentable?"

"I am," I say . . . and it's only as the door opens that I realize I'm still wearing my sandals . . . and my leather-band watch. I slide the latter off, palming it as William walks in, followed by a plump teenage girl, dressed in a simple gown and bonnet and carrying a basket. When she sees me, she stops short, and I frantically assess as best I can without a mirror. My hair is in a messy bun, suitable enough for the time.

She stops staring and curtseys. I incline my head, and before I can speak, William says, "This is Mary, from the village. She's come to help you prepare for the evening since your own maid could not accompany you on the trip."

"Thank you," I murmur.

"As I mentioned, Mary, Lady Dale is a childhood friend. I had the pleasure of reuniting with her recently, and she has graciously accepted my invitation to visit. She's also indulging my very awkward attempt to provide a proper evening's entertainment, complete with dancing."

"Yes, my lord," she says. "I understand."

"You also understand that I expect discretion. While Lady Dale is indeed a widow, this is still not an entirely appropriate visit, one she makes as a concession to my eccentricities." His look darkens with warning. "I would not wish to later hear gossip that might give Lady Dale cause to regret her kindness."

The girl only gives a very adolescent hint of an eye roll. "Yes, my lord. You do overthink the matter if you want my opinion. You could dance with her in the village square, and no tongues would wag."

"Perhaps, but I have chosen a more discreet path, and I thank you for understanding that. Now, I am off to prepare myself for the evening. I will expect Lady Dale downstairs at"—he checks his watch—"quarter past eight."

Mary promises I'll be ready, and William withdraws, shutting the door behind him. A soft mew from the hall. I remember this is the room where the kittens sleep, but when I look, their box has been moved.

I turn to Mary, who seems to be waiting for a proper greeting. I give one and thankfully resist the urge to offer a handshake. She's looking at me again with that odd expression, the one that has me glancing in the mirror to confirm that nothing betrays my time-traveler status.

"Is everything all right?" I ask. "I know this is an unusual situation, but Lord Thorne really does prefer to stay at home, and I did not think an unescorted visit would be terribly scandalous." I smile. "I am a widow, after all."

"You are . . . not what I expected, my lady. That is all."

My brows rise.

"You are older than I thought you would be," she says. "You must be nearly thirty."

I laugh. I have to. She says it with such forthrightness, only coloring slightly as I laugh.

"I meant no offense, my lady," she adds.

"None taken," I say. "I am actually flattered if you think I'm only nearing thirty. I believe Lord Thorne mentioned we were childhood friends?"

Her cheeks redden. "Oh, yes. He did. I should have thought . . ." Her gaze sweeps over me appraisingly. "You do not look his age. It must be very fine air in the Americas. Lord Thorne told me you lived there for a time with your late husband."

"I did," I say. "Long enough that I acclimated to American life, so you will need to excuse my accent and any odd turns of phrase or manners."

She nods. "That's what Lord Thorne told me."

He's been clever. It's no mistake that he's chosen such a young girl to help me, one who will have little experience with either Americans or women of nobility.

"I will also admit something terribly scandalous," I say, voice dropping to a conspiratorial whisper. "I did not leave my lady's maid at home. I do not actually have one. We didn't keep one in America, and I do plan to hire one here, but I haven't quite found the time. So you will need to forgive me if I have forgotten the finer points of being dressed for an English ball."

Her eyes widen. "I'll be no help there, ma'am. I've never even seen one myself."

I wink at her. "Well, then it's a good thing Lord Thorne hasn't attended one in a while, either. We'll muddle through, and I suspect he'll be none the wiser as long as my dress isn't backward."

She laughs at that and lifts her basket. "We'll have no trouble with the dress. I'm a seamstress by trade. That's what I'm mostly here for—to be sure the dress fits properly. I've also brought a hair iron and pins and a bit of face paint. I've never been to a ball, but I do dress my sisters for the village dances."

"Excellent. Then let us begin with the dress."

Her gaze moves to another article of clothing, this one on a side table. The corset.

I sigh. "Yes, I nearly forgot that. Tried to, at least."

That makes her laugh, and she assures me she won't tighten the stays more than necessary.

"We aren't in London," she says. "I hear they lace them so tight there that ladies faint at balls. I don't know why they just don't make the dresses larger. Fortunately, Lord Thorne chose one with a generous cut."

I'm about to make a joke about that when I look at Mary—who is larger than me—and hold my tongue. On a conscious level, I know that I shouldn't fret about my weight. I'm healthy and active. When I feel the need to joke about my extra twenty—or thirty—pounds, I'm succumbing to cultural pressure when the truth is that I'm happy and comfortable and haven't actively tried to lose weight since I met Michael. This is how I'm built, and I need to quit the self-effacing comments. At best, they're a sign of low self-esteem. At worst, they seem like a cry for validation.

I tuck my sandals away quickly enough that if Mary notices, she dismisses them as some strange American fashion. My under-garments are a larger issue. I play shy and get her to turn away until I can stuff my bra away and yank a chemise over my under-wear. I should have drawers on, but there aren't any here, and again, I can only hope she presumes that, under the chemise, I'm wearing a short pair, another American fashion.

I slide into the corset, and Mary tightens it just enough that I can look into the mirror and be very pleased with a modest smoothing of my figure and rounding of my breasts. Next should come the under-petticoat, followed by the crinolines and the over-petticoat, but we're missing both petticoats, and I'm not unhappy about that.

The dress fits like a dream, though Mary still tut-tuts and fusses with it, pinning to achieve a tighter bodice. The neckline plunges lower than I like, and I tug it up when she's not looking. Otherwise, the fabric flows over me, hugging and accentuating my curves in a waterfall of shimmering copper.

As Mary pins and stitches the dress, she prattles nonstop, encouraged by my questions about village life. While I don't ask about William specifically, she takes pains to let me know how generous and kind he is.

"Like all the Thornes," she says as she sews. "We've been lucky in High Thornesbury. Lord Thorne may have his strange ways, and outsiders may whisper, but we are pleased to have a lord who stays close, especially when he is such a fine gentleman."

She pulls the thread tight. "I know you have lived abroad, ma'am, so you may not have heard the whispers. You will, though. My ma says society ladies gossip even more than we village folk. Pay it no heed. The lord has his ways, and that makes people invent vicious stories. Everyone in the village knows there's no truth to them."

I could ask for details, and I have no doubt she'd tell me everything. However, I am almost certain the scandal involves a woman . . . possibly more than one. Whatever William's eccentricities, he's popular with the ladies, as August made clear when I overheard their discussion. William might have his "strange ways," but that combination of outer roughness and inner kindness would mean he'd have no shortage of willing paramours.

William's past affairs are his own business, and I'm glad he wasn't lonely in that regard. Yet with a romantic evening ahead of us, this isn't the time I want details of his past, any more than he'd like me reminiscing tonight about my life with Michael.

I'll hear the stories later, and I'd rather get them from William himself. I'm glad, though, that he has the village's support. If they believed the worst of him, his isolation would be so much less bearable.

I insist on applying my own makeup. As much as I enjoyed having someone dress me and alter my gown, I'm not quite so keen on a nineteenth-century teenager putting on my makeup. I do that, and Mary watches with great interest, asking questions about my American techniques.

Next comes hair, and I'm happy to return to the role of princess-for-a-day, letting Mary take over. She *oohs* and *aahs* over my hair, the thickness of it, the natural curl. I've always thought my hair was my best feature, and I've refused to cut it short as I grow older. I've also refused to dye it. My friends see that as bravery, which always makes me laugh. No, it's as much vanity as leaving it long or refusing to flat-iron it. I like the curls, and I like the threads of white weaving through it, and I don't care if neither is fashionable.

Mary brushes my hair until it gleams. Then she parts it in the center and twists it into a chignon at the back with tendrils hanging around my face. Each of those tendrils gets individual attention with tongs heated in the fireplace and a spritz of sugar water to hold the curl in place. William left a gorgeous copper comb for my hair, and Mary marvels over it before attaching it to the chignon.

It is only then that Mary allows me to walk to the mirror. I look at my reflection and . . .

I've confessed my Victorian ball fantasies to William. Even when I was fifteen, they were only fantasies. Deep down, I'd always been certain that if I ever got the chance to dress for a ball, it would be like putting on a witch or a ballerina costume for Halloween. In my mind, I'd be magically transformed, but when I looked in the mirror, I'd see only a game of dress-up.

Today, I expect to see Bronwyn Dale, twenty-first-century history professor playing at nineteenth-century lady. But the woman looking back from the mirror has stepped from the pages of a Victorian novel.

The woman in that mirror belongs here, in this place, in this time. All these years I've spent traveling to William's world, I've never really felt as if I belonged. Now, I do. In that mirror is Lady Dale, widowed childhood friend of Lord Thorne, dressed to accompany him to the ball in a gown of copper and black, hair tumbling over her back, cheeks pink with carmine, brown eyes sparkling with no need of cosmetics.

Mary hurries over and tugs my dress and adjusts my curls though I see nothing wrong with either. I let her fuss. Then the clock strikes the quarter-hour, and my head shoots up.

"William," I murmur.

I realize I've called him by his first name, and my cheeks heat, but Mary only giggles and hurries to the door. She opens it with a sweep of her hand, motioning me through.

❧ 22 ❧

I step into the hall and make my way toward the stairs. The dress reminds me of my wedding gown, the weight of the fabric, the swoosh of it across the floor. My steps slow to a dignified pace in case I trip over the hem.

I reach the top of the stairs, and William is below. I can see only the cuffs of his black trousers and his shoes as he waits. I take a deep breath and begin my descent, one gloved hand on the railing, my gaze on his shoes . . . and then his legs . . . and then his evening jacket as it comes into view. When I see his face, I stop. I must, or I'll pitch down the stairs, my traitorous knees giving way. William grins, his face lighting like a boy's, and I'm suddenly lightheaded, gripping the railing.

Concern flashes across his features, dissipating with relief when I smile. Still clutching the railing, I descend the last few steps as the glow in his face washes over me, making me feel like every heroine in every romance novel, seeing her would-be lover's face light up at the sight of her dressed for the ball.

On the last step, he takes my hand, raising it as he leads me toward him, his gaze traveling over me.

"You look . . ." He doesn't finish. His gaze darts back up the stairs, and I glance over to see Mary peeking down. At a stern look from him, she retreats.

"Let me try that again," he says, his voice lower. He takes my other hand, lifting it, looking me over from toe to head in a slow sweep that says more than words could. He leans toward my ear and whispers, "You are the most beautiful thing I have ever seen."

My throat closes, and before I can respond, he pulls something from his pocket and murmurs, "This will be gilding the lily, but . . ."

He lifts a necklace, and my breath catches. It's a huge sapphire, ringed with diamonds, the central stone suspended in a scroll-work of diamond-studded threads. Below the sapphire, still more diamonds hang, arranged in flowers. And because, clearly, that wasn't nearly enough diamonds, the entire chain is comprised of, yes, diamonds. It is a thing of dreams, the sort of piece that would have even me pressed to the museum glass, heart beating, mind strumming with fantasies of feeling those cool jewels slide around my neck.

"That's . . . that's . . ."

His lips twitch. "A pretty bauble?"

My mouth works, and all I can manage is a squeaked, "It's incredible."

"Then it has found the perfect setting." He lifts it to my neck. "May I?"

I nod wordlessly.

"It was my grandmother's." He steps behind me to lower it over my head. "Now, it is yours, and not merely for the evening." He bends and tucks hair behind my ear as he whispers. "Yes, you will need to become accustomed to extravagant and presumptuous gifts from me, Bronwyn, and it shall become very awkward —and tiresome—if you protest each one."

I say nothing. I'm frozen there as the jewels slide around my neck, just as cool as I'd imagined. His warm fingers fasten the clasp and then linger on the nape of my neck, making me shiver before he steps in front of me again.

"Gilding the lily, as I said." His gaze drops to the sapphire and diamonds nestled between my breasts. "Or gilding the lilies, I should say."

I laugh softly, and his gaze lingers far longer than necessary. When I rap his knuckles, his brows arch.

"I said nothing," he protests.

"You don't need to."

His lips curve in a wolfish smile. "Are you certain? I could tell you what I was thinking. You need only ask."

His gaze returns to the jewel. Another rap on his hand, and he chuckles.

"I was merely admiring the stone." His hand slides up my bodice, thumb barely grazing the side of my breast, sending a shiver through me. "And thinking what a truly lovely setting I've found for it. One that your dress shows to magnificent perfection."

"Do you think?" I murmur. "The neckline seems a little . . . off. I will admit, I adjusted it after Mary finished."

The wolfish grin again. "Did you?"

"Hmm, yes. She had it more like . . ." I touch the bodice, and he reaches to stop me before I impede his scenery, but I tug it down, instead, to where Mary had it, and his eyes widen.

"Is this appropriate?" I ask, frowning innocently. "It seems to be how the dress is designed, but I do feel rather exposed. One quick move, and I'm liable to pop—"

His fingers fly to my lips, and I grin under them, fluttering my lashes at him.

"Should I readjust it, my lord? Back to how I had it before?"

I reach to do that, but he stops me with a growl, and I laugh. He slides his thumb over the side of my breast again, this growl thickening with frustration.

I look up at him through my lashes. "If you're enjoying that view so much, perhaps I should lift my skirt and allow you to see . . ." I lower my voice to a hushed whisper. "My ankles."

He laughs, a burst of it that has him shaking his head. "As

lovely as your ankles are, the current view is far more stimulating." He pauses. "Though I must admit, I might be more tempted
if you offered me another view of your calves. They are remarkably shapely, ushering along thoughts of where they lead and—"

I rap his knuckles.

Before he can speak, chamber music starts, and I jump.

"Is that a—?" I begin to ask whether it's a gramophone, but
we're at least a decade before de Martinville's work inspired
Edison's and Bell's mad race to invent the phonograph. I turn in
confusion toward the music, which seems to come from deeper in
the house.

"One cannot have a ball without dancing," William says. "Nor
dancing without music. That was one of my tasks for the day—
hiring a trio. I have, of course, paid well for their discretion."

At that, he seems to remember another temporary employee
and leans into the stairwell to call, "Mary?"

She pops her head out. "M'lord."

"You may leave now. Your services were appreciated."

"Yes, they were," I say as she comes down the stairs. "Thank
you very much."

She glances toward the music. "Must—*ought* I to leave,
m'lord? The lady may need help with her undressing."

"I am certain I—" He clears his throat. "I am certain *she* can
manage."

"Is it proper, though, m'lord?" Mary says as I bite back a smile.
"She hasn't come with her maid, and it seems as if I shouldn't
leave her alone without a chaperone."

"There's no need to concern yourself on that point," William
says. "Lady Dale is quite accustomed to men. She is a widow."

I choke on a laugh as William's eyes widen. "That is not—I
meant only that she is accustomed to dealing with men. She is not
an inexp—naive maiden who fears telling a man his attentions are
unwanted. She is quite safe with me, unchaperoned."

"He is correct," I say. "I am past the age where I require a
chaperone to safeguard my virtue. I can protect it myself, and I

know Lord Thorne enough to trust his behavior for the evening however unorthodox the situation."

Mary casts a longing glance toward the music.

William sighs. "There is a cold buffet in the next room. You may help yourself to a plate and enjoy the music for two dances. Then . . ." A dark look. "You are gone."

She curtseys, says, "Yes, m'lord," and scampers off.

William sighs again, deeply, as he turns to me. "Not quite what I had in mind, but it will only be two dances."

"Perfectly reasonable." I take his arm, and we walk through the parlor to the formal dining room, which is currently devoid of furniture, save a long table with the aforementioned cold buffet, a pitcher of lemonade and a bottle of port. The musicians are there, too—a violist, a cornetist and a pianist using the family piano.

"If you are hungry . . ." William says.

"Not yet." I look at the open room. "This is the dance floor, I take it?"

"It could be," he says. "However, it is a lovely evening, and if you are so inclined . . ."

He leads me to the back door and opens it. The rear yard is awash in light, candelabras burning around the freshly cut lawn. The windows are all open, and music wafts into the night.

I smile over at him. "Yes, please."

He offers his arm again, and we sweep out to the lawn as the music swells, as if we're stepping onto a grand dance floor, some well-dressed butler announcing, "Lord William Thorne and Lady Bronwyn Dale."

I smile at the thought as my gown whispers over the grass. William leads me to the center of the lawn, candlelight dancing in the twilight. He takes both my hands, holding me in front of him, and the music slides into a waltz and . . .

And I freeze.

"I don't know how—" I begin, eyes widening in panic.

"Follow my lead," he says. Then he bends to whisper. "And remember that there is no one here to see you but me, and I am too moonstruck to notice if you cut loose and dance a fisherman's jig."

I laugh. "I believe I can avoid that."

"Then, we are prepared." He lifts my hands and begins the dance. It's slow and measured. I might have panicked, realizing I don't know the steps to a Victorian waltz, but I am, after all, a dancer. I pick it up within a few refrains, and soon we're swirling over the grass.

When we whirl past the doorway, I see Mary there, her face glowing as she watches, transfixed, and my heart trips a few beats. The look on her face is the same that must be on mine every time I watch this scene in a movie, the heroine and her lover gliding over the floor, me swooning in my seat, envying her, *being* her, if only for a moment. Dreaming of being swept across the floor by a dashing man who looks at me the way he looks at the heroine. The way William is looking at me.

When we twirl past again, I smile at Mary, but she doesn't notice, her gaze turned inward to her own dreams, her own fantasies, and I send up a wish that someday this will be her, dancing in a village hall with a young man who watches her as if the world has fallen away and it is only the two of them, pirouetting through a dream.

The music picks up speed to something I don't recognize, and William leads me through that, and even before it ends, Mary slips away as she promised. Then we are truly alone in our universe, the musicians hidden in the dining room, only their music wafting out.

We dance, and we dance, and it's glorious. It's moment upon moment that my heart snapshots, tucking each away in memory. The smell of the fresh-cut grass mingled with the sweet smoke of the beeswax candles and the faint perfume of William's after-shave lotion. The music, soft enough that I can still catch William's whispers in my ear, still hear his breath when he draws me close. I am entranced by the candlelight and the star-speckled sky, and with him, mostly with him, the twinkle of his eyes, the curve of his lips, the bounce of an unruly curl that will not stay in place no matter how many times he discreetly tucks it back.

We dance until my feet ache, and I don't care. He doesn't slow, and so neither do I. Dance follows dance until we reach a rather energetic one, and when we come out of it, he's winded and red cheeked. So am I, but I hide it better and use the excuse to tease, "Shall we adjourn for the cold supper, m'lord? I seem to have quite exhausted you."

When he looks up, his eyes glint. "I would not say I am entirely exhausted. However, yes, I fear that if I continue, I might very well collapse before long. Yet I do hate to end the dancing and disappoint you."

"I would be far more disappointed if you pushed yourself to the limits of exhaustion." I take his arm. "You may lead me in for supper, m'lord, and we'll consider the dancing at an end."

W illiam takes me inside. At a nod, the musicians pack, having obviously been warned that such a dismissal would come. By the time we've filled our plates, they're gone. When I glance in that direction, William murmurs, "Should I have asked them to play while we eat? I can summon them back."

"As much as I enjoyed the music, I feel we have reached the private portion of our evening."

"Agreed."

He pours me a glass of port, and we head outside to a spot where he's arranged two chairs and a small table. Before I can sit, I say, "Actually, we could have both music and privacy."

I lift my skirts and hurry into the house, returning with my cell phone. I waggle it as I walk out.

"That plays music?" Before I can answer, William shakes his head. "Of course it does. It is the miracle box. The only thing it cannot do is bake you scones."

"No, but I could order them delivered to the house." I glance at the manor. "Well, a hundred-and-seventy years in the future, which would do me no good, so I'll settle for playing music."

I hit the icon. Pearl Jam screams forth, and William jumps. I hit Stop.

"That man seems to be in some degree of pain," he says.

"Ha ha. It's the music of my youth. Very fine music, I might add. Not, however, thematically appropriate."

I zip through my playlists and launch a blues one with the volume turned down to background music, allowing us to converse. We talk of dance parties past, amusing stories from ones he's attended, and then the sort from my youth, awkward high-school tales. We talk, and we laugh, and we eat, and we drink. When a favorite song comes on and I've had two glasses of port, my feet begin to move, fingers tapping the tabletop.

He puts out a hand to lead me back to the dance floor, but I demur with, "As I said, I don't want to wear you out. Not yet."

A wicked flash of a grin. He seems about to say something suggestive and then stops, his grin easing down to a smile. "Would you dance for me, then? If you are not overly tired."

"I believe I could manage that, though it would require a change of song."

He passes over my phone. I flip through my playlists.

"Another piece of modern music," I say. "Not as pained as the last. A favorite dance tune for when I'm alone. It isn't quite classical ballet, though."

"As I said, you could dance a fisherman's jig, and I'd be thoroughly enthralled."

"Tempting, but no. We'll try this."

I hit Play. Sia's "Move Your Body" begins. His head tilts in consideration, listening and nodding as I move onto the lawn. I slough off my shoes, the grass tickling my feet and swishing as I walk to the middle of the cleared area.

The tempo is just right, not too fast for classical dance, but with a beat that I can throw myself into, skirts gathered in front, draping gracefully in the back as I twirl and kick, the weight of the dress falling away, tiredness forgotten, inhibitions forgotten, too, dancing as if I'm in my living room.

When the song finishes, I open my eyes, and William is there, an arm's length away. He steps closer, hands going to my upper arms as he leans in, his eyes dark, voice low and thick as he says, "The song is correct. Your body *is* poetry."

My cheeks heat, and I duck my gaze, suddenly feeling like my teen self, caught dancing through the barn when I thought he was busy with the horses.

His fingers slide up to my shoulders, his voice still a murmur. "Your body is the music that has echoed through my dreams since I was fifteen, Bronwyn. I heard it, and I could never stop hearing it. I tried to pretend I'd forgotten you. I forgot not a single particle of you. Not the sound of your voice, not the music of your laugh, not the whisper of your sighs. I remember the way you smelled when I'd bury my face against your neck. You left a sweater behind once, on a cool morning. When you asked me about it later, I said I hadn't seen it. I lied. I could not part with it any more than I could part with the bracelet you gave me. I still have the sweater, and it cannot possibly still smell of you, but when I open the drawer, I swear that it does. When you left, I was hurt, and I was afraid, terrified something had happened to you."

"I—"

He presses a finger to my lips. "But I knew it hadn't. I felt that, somehow, if you were gone forever, I would know it. Whatever stopped you from returning, I knew it was not your fault. Yes, I blamed you when you first returned, but that was wounded pride and a desperate cry for truth, for you to tell me what I already knew—that you did not leave me by choice. If I truly believed you had, I would never have kept that bracelet or that sweater."

I open my mouth to speak, but he presses his lips to mine, stopping any apologies. When he pulls back, he stays so close his breath tickles my lips.

"I have not forgotten an inch of you," he says. "You grew up with me even when you were gone. I would dream of you, at eighteen, nineteen, what you would look like, feel like, sound like. At twenty-five, I would walk into a ball and immediately find the one woman who looked as I imagined you would. I would only watch her, never approaching, never asking her to dance, knowing *that* would shatter the illusion. She would speak, and it would not be your voice, your words, your laugh. She would embrace me, and it would not be your touch, your smell, your body. I admired from afar and chose other partners, ones I could not possibly mistake for you, leaving you to haunt my dreams."

His fingers trace along the collar of my gown, sliding it toward one shoulder, lips lowering to trace kisses along the bare skin, making me shiver.

"That night you came to my bed, it was no surprise at all. Yet another dream of you. A gloriously vivid vision, achingly perfect. The curve of your neck . . ." He kisses down my throat. "The swell of your breasts . . ."

His fingers trace over the tops of them, sliding toward my shoulder, pushing the dress down and kissing the exposed skin as I arch, sighing. His hands move to the back of my bodice, deftly unfastening the hooks and laces, and the top of the dress billows down, the corset barely containing my breasts. He chuckles at that and bends to slide his tongue along the edge of the fabric and then under it, finding a nipple, tongue sliding over it as I gasp. His hands move to my hips, and he teases my corseted breasts.

I writhe and groan, and his hands knead my hips. Then they tug down the dress, letting it pool at my feet. He releases the crinolines next and moves closer until the hardness of him brushes my stomach, and it takes all my willpower to stay where I am, to not press against him.

I hover there, barely able to draw breath as I strain for him. He runs his fingertips over my breasts and releases them from the fabric. His breath catches, and he nuzzles along my neck, still standing just far enough away that I can feel only the tease of him brushing my belly.

His hands slide over my hips, sheathed in my chemise, cushioning between my skin and the corset. He finds the hem of the chemise and tugs it up. When his fingers slip under to bare skin, he stops short.

"Yes," I murmur. "There was something missing from the attire you so helpfully provided. No drawers. I made Mary turn her back while I put on the chemise and prayed she didn't realize I was missing something."

His fingers trace along the hem of my chemise, skimming over bare skin.

"I *am* wearing underwear," I say. "They just . . . change a bit over the next hundred and seventy years."

Those warm fingers creep up my hip, pushing the chemise along with them. When they find the fabric of my panties, they stop and toy with it, experimenting and then sliding down again, William's breath catching as he realizes how little fabric is there. Not exactly a thong, but very different from mid-thigh Victorian drawers.

Both hands glide up my hips now, pushing the fabric of the chemise with them. He groans and presses, ever so gently, against my stomach before stopping himself and stepping back, my shift still raised, his hands still on my hips. He looks down and makes a noise in his throat, and his hands slide to my rear, fingers digging in as he presses against me, hard and urgent.

"I was very clearly born in the wrong century," he says. "And I am half-inclined to put out the candles and wish for clouds to obscure my view before I fall on you like a lust-sick boy."

I ease out of his grasp and take a slow step back. "Perhaps I should give you a moment to recover. I could dance for you again."

Another step back, and his gaze travels over me, my breasts overflowing the corset top, the chemise falling to cover my hips and panties.

"Like this?" I say. Then, I tuck the chemise up under the corset, my legs and black panties bare. "Or like this?"

He groans, a long, drawn-out rough sound that sends fresh heat coursing through me.

"Would you like me to dance for you, William?" I say.

"I am not certain I dare answer," he says, his voice so thick I can barely make out words. "I fear if you do, I really shall fall upon you, rutting in the grass."

My gaze sweeps over him, still fully dressed. "Like that? I hardly think so." I step toward him. "First, you would need to remove this." I unbutton his black evening jacket and push it off his shoulders.

He reaches for me, but I take his hands and place them at his sides.

"Uh-uh," I say. "You got to undress me without distraction. Allow me the same privilege."

I remove the stickpin from his cravat and pierce it through the fabric of my corset, between my breasts. His gaze moves there, lingering, breathing hard before pulling away with a shudder that sends an accompanying shiver through me.

I look up and meet his eyes, deep wells of desire that weaken my knees and counsel me to glance away before *he's* not the one throwing his companion to the ground like a lust-sick youth. And that thought does not help one bit, making it three long seconds before I can breathe again.

I don't, however, break eye contact. I steel myself, and I keep looking into his eyes as I unfasten his cravat and let it fall. The white waistcoat follows. Then I unfasten his shirt, one button at a time, fingers sliding down the revealed skin, gaze forced on his, refusing to enjoy the sight of my progress until I've finished the task and tugged his shirt from his trousers. Then, I let myself look, gaze tracking over his bare chest, the black hair and pale, muscled skin below.

I push his shirt over his shoulders and look my fill, sighing with a whispered, "You are glorious."

He chuckles, a deep sound that's half growl as my fingers trail over his chest, tracing each rib, each muscle on his abdomen before rising to lightly brush his nipples. He inhales at that, and his hands start to rise to take hold of me, but he stops himself, arms dropping to his sides, giving himself over to my explorations. I taste him then, my tongue tripping along his collarbone and across his chest to his nipples, flicking over them, making him groan, his hips moving just enough to brush hard against my stomach.

I bend, tongue continuing down through the curled hair that arrows toward his groin. When I reach the top of his trousers, I'm on my knees, teasing my tongue over his waistband.

I pull back, still kneeling. His hand moves to my shoulder, gripping as if to pull me up, but I remove it and say, "I just want a better look."

He groans, hands fisting at his sides. I unfasten his trousers and tug them down. He helpfully steps out, and he's dressed only in his silk drawers. Well, presumably, he's also wearing socks, but that's certainly not where my gaze is going, considering what's right in front of my face, urgently tenting his drawers.

I lean in and tickle my tongue over the silk, feeling the heat and the throb of him, and enjoying the strained "Bronwyn" I provoke.

There's lust and pleasure in it, but warning, too, a warning that we may be reaching a point of no return. Or a point of no return for *one* of us . . . which while pleasurable for the other, isn't quite as satisfying.

One last lick, and then I push to my feet, cup my hands around his face and sigh. That's all I can do—deeply sigh in the pleasure of seeing him, poised there, trembling with desire, his eyes burning with need, my own body flaming in response.

I let my hands slide down his chest and over his hips, and then I step back.

"Would you still like me to dance?" I ask.

His gaze devours me, hungry and hot, and my own flame burns so bright I'm not sure I *can* dance, not sure I can do anything but slide back onto the grass and say, "Yes." *Yes, please.*

But that's what he says. *Yes.* And so I turn the music back to "Move Your Body," and I dance for him. I dance in the corset, breasts peeking over it, pendant leaping, my hands lifting the chemise as I spin. I dance as I shed the panties, letting the chemise hide what lies beneath. Dance as I unlace the corset and let it drop with my back to him, as I adjust the chemise over my breasts, chuckling at his grunt of displeasure when I turn, still covered.

I pirouette as I never have before, a perfect spin, one leg raised, hands lifting the chemise over my head and casting it aside, and I dance naked for him, no more than a step or two before he's there, pulling me against him, our bodies moving together in half-clutch, half-dance, and I feel him against me, realize he's naked.

I lift up onto him as he spins me, and I come down on him, his eyes flying wide, lips parting in one moment of surprise before his hands drop to my hips, and then we're on the ground, and he's over me, with me, in me, and it truly is the most perfect sensation ever, waves of pleasure rocking through us both almost before we hit the ground.

The pleasure seems never ending, and even after he must have spent himself, he continues until my gasps and shudders slow, and I collapse into the grass.

His hands go in my hair then as he looks down at me, our bodies still entwined.

"I love you," he says. "That may not be what you're ready to hear, but I need you to know it. I love you. I have always loved you. I will always love you. I cannot do anything *but* love you, Bronwyn Dale."

"I—"

His fingers move to my lips. "You don't need to say it. I need you to know it. I do not need you to respond in kind."

I take his fingers, move them aside, and look into his eyes. "I loved you when we were children together. I loved you when you were growing into a man. I loved you—desperately, agonizingly, achingly loved you—when everyone told me you were not real. It tore me apart. You might say I didn't need a hospital's care, that there was nothing wrong with me. But there was. The boy I loved wasn't real, and I didn't want to live in a world where he'd never been. I lost something there, some part of my heart and my soul vital for living, and there was a time when I didn't want to continue."

His breath catches, pain flooding his eyes.

Before he can speak, I say, "I pushed on, and yes, I found happiness and healing, but part of me was always yours, could never be anyone's but yours. You have said that you won't expect me to stay in your world, and you have no idea how much that means to me. But just because you'll never expect it doesn't mean I will never consider it. I cannot promise to stay forever, but I can promise I will never leave forever. Not again. No matter what."

He leans down, and he kisses me, gentle and sweet, until the hunger licks through us again, and then he lifts me up and carries me into the house.

24

Once in William's bed, we take our time, that initial overwhelming surge of need sated. This is a long, slow exploration, getting to know each other's bodies and showing our full appreciation for them, culminating in passionate lovemaking that has us both dropping into deep slumber.

I wake from that slumber to kisses on my shoulder, fingers stroking my thighs, and it's that first night all over again, sleepy caresses and slow kisses and bodies entwining, only this time, ending as it should have, as it has in my fantasies.

More sleep, and then I'm the one who rouses, the one who touches and kisses as lightly as I can, not wanting to wake him, just wanting to luxuriate in the smell and feel of him, in having him there and knowing he'll stay, that this is not a dream, not a single night's passion. We have made our commitment, and I have no idea where that will lead, but I've found something I spent two decades aching for, and so I can't help touching, kissing, reassuring myself he's there and he's mine.

When he responds, moving against me, burying his head in the crook of my neck, I go still. He lifts his head, one sleepy eye half-open.

"No?" he murmurs.

"I just didn't mean to wake you."

A drowsy half smile. "I believe I was only half-sleeping, waiting for the excuse." His arms go around me, pulling me to him with a light kiss. "Go on back to sleep. I will exercise patience at least until morning."

I slide my hands down his hips. "I wasn't saying no. I just didn't want you to think I'd woken you for more. It has been a strenuous night, and you probably need your—"

His mouth comes to mine, and he pulls me on top of him.

AFTER THAT, WILLIAM FALLS INTO EXHAUSTED, SATIATED SLEEP. AND I lie there, wide eyed, my body having clearly mistaken that for wake-up sex and telling me it's time to rise. After lying there for at least twenty minutes, envying his deep and even breathing, I roll over to see what time it is.

Of course, there's no bedside clock. No cell phone, either. I remember I left mine out on the lawn . . . in the grass . . . gathering dew. I sigh, push up and pad to the door. When I open it, Pandora is right there, and I falter. I don't know what I expect—that she'll attack me for being the cause of that closed door? She just sits and watches me circle past. Then she follows me down the stairs.

I step out the back door and realize I'm naked. Normally, I'm a whole lot more aware of that—even going braless can be uncomfortable. But it isn't until I step out and get blasted by cold pre-dawn air that my euphoria parts enough for me to realize I'm not wearing anything.

I bolt for our pile of clothing, which causes plenty of uncomfortable bouncing. I pass my ballgown—I'm definitely not "throwing" that on. I see my chemise, and I start for that, but then I spot something more appealing: William's shirt. I jog over and snatch that and my panties. Both are dew-damp, but I pull them on anyway. Then I grab my phone.

By the time I'm back inside, I'm wide awake. I spot the cold spread still in the dining room and recall that William mentioned giving Mrs. Shaw the day off. If I return to bed right now, I'll only disturb him with my tossing and turning. So I head into the kitchen to poke about and come up with ideas for breakfast.

That, as it turns out, is unnecessary. It's the mid-nineteenth century. No housekeeper would leave her middle-aged bachelor lord to fend for himself come morning. He might starve.

Breakfast has been prepared with a cold plate in the icebox and a pastry tray on the counter. That does not, however, mean I leave the kitchen. I'm a historian, and this is an actual Victorian kitchen, the pages of my dry textbooks come to life. I might know that iceboxes were used as refrigerators and were usually made of wood, the fancier ones like this with a spigot for draining the melted ice. I might even have viewed such appliances in museums. Yet seeing one in use is an entirely different thing. While Pandora watches from her perch by the stove, I poke and prod about like a kid in the best hands-on museum display ever.

After about thirty minutes of exploring, my eyelids begin to flag, and yawns punctuate every third breath. I head upstairs, cell phone in hand, cat at my heels. When I walk into the bedroom, William is still sound asleep, sprawled naked on the cover, and I pause to admire the sight, feeling the weight of the cell phone and again wishing I could capture the moment . . . when I remember that I can.

Last night, I'd spoken of seeing him in bed and longing to photograph him, and he'd said I was free to do so whenever I wished. So I take photos, lots of them, all from suggestively discreet angles. He'll hardly be concerned about naked pics emerging online, but it's more fun finding the artful shots that will, later, only spark my imagination to fill in what's missing.

Partway through my photo session, Pandora realizes I'm not about to do anything interesting and hops onto the bed, curling around William's feet, which means I need to take more photos. I admire the pictures and admire the live version and imagine what it will be like to wake beside it, feel him reach for me, kiss me . . .

I hesitate at that last image, breathing in through my mouth and realizing I'm in desperate need of a toothbrush. In fact, some overall freshening up wouldn't be a bad idea. Nineteenth-century makeup sits heavy and smeared on my face. My hair has gone from sexy sleep tousled to witch's wild snarl. And, yes, I can enjoy the satisfaction of knowing William would not give a damn, but since I'm up anyway, there's no reason not to take five minutes to primp before returning to bed.

I use the water pitcher and basin for a quick wash with bracingly cold water. Then into the master bedroom for a hairbrush and a mirror. I also find the small purse I'd brought yesterday with my travel toothbrush and paste. There's a lot of misinformation on Victorian levels of hygiene. It varied, of course, mostly by social class. It's hard to bathe regularly when your only option is to boil water and crouch in the family washtub with a precious bar of lye soap in hand.

William has no such concerns. Mrs. Shaw would prepare a bath for him whenever he wanted it, and mucking stables meant he wanted it more often than the average noble. Dental care is another thing. There are toothbrushes made from boar's bristles. Also, tooth powder often made of ingredients we wouldn't put in our mouths today. Even with these tools available, the average person wasn't brushing twice a day. They may not even own a toothbrush and powder tin.

I remember when William and I were about four, and I brought my toothbrush over so I could brush after our picnic. I won't say I was that kind of kid, but I did go through phases, and I'd been on an "I must brush after every meal" kick, probably after seeing the shining white teeth of a prima ballerina.

Bringing the brush led to a discussion and to William realizing his teeth weren't quite as clean as mine. I hope I didn't point this out, but I might very well have—at that age, children are bluntly honest. He'd resolved to pay more attention to his, and that resolve never wavered, leaving him with twenty-first-century dentition . . . which may also explain part of his popularity with the ladies.

There will not, however, be a spare toothbrush around, so I brought my own. After that, I need my bra. I don't, obviously, plan to wear it to bed, but I wouldn't mind keeping his shirt on once we wake, and that'll be more comfortable with a bra. William might prefer me without it, but after last night, my breasts are tender, and a little padding between me and his starched shirt would be appreciated.

When I open the drawer where I'd stuffed my bra, a heavy picture frame shifts within. I pull it out to see a young couple. They aren't smiling—at this time, photography required the subject to stand still forever. The man is in his early twenties, light haired and very handsome. Despite his unsmiling countenance, his eyes radiate an easygoing joviality. The young woman sits in a chair and wears an expression of barely contained impatience. I can't blame her for that. It's probably discomfort, too, given that her corset has indeed reduced her waist to the fabled handspan. She's pretty and dark haired with light eyes that flash despite the limitations of the sepia-toned photo. There's something familiar about her, and I'm trying to figure out why when I feel paper on the back of the frame. I flip it around to see an engagement announcement for the forthcoming nuptials of August Courtenay and Cordelia Thorne.

August . . . presumably, the same August I heard downstairs the other day. William's old friend. And his fiancé is William's little sister.

My fingers brush Cordelia's face, and I have to smile, her expression reminding me so much of her brother. I feel a pang, too, for having never known her as more than the distant figure of a little girl searching for her brother. Always looking for William, always wanting to be with him, driving him to the point of affectionate exasperation.

They'd been so close. What could have driven them apart? The scandal? That's my guess. Either it involved her—and she hadn't appreciated her older brother interfering—or it involved *him*— and he hadn't appreciated *her* defending him. Those seem most likely, given what I know of William and also what I see in this photo, the stubborn lift to Cordelia's chin, that flash of pride in her eyes, the mirror of her brother's.

If it was pride that drove them apart, can that be reconciled? That isn't a conversation for today, but it will come, and I can use this photograph to launch it.

I saw your sister's engagement photo in a drawer . . .

I'm sliding the frame back when I see another photograph, tucked beneath a pile of handkerchiefs. As I reach for it, something crashes downstairs. I look around for Pandora, but she'd returned downstairs. Another bang. Is she trapped somewhere? William did say Enigma was her doppelgänger, always getting into trouble and tight places.

I hurry down the stairs. As I round the corner, Pandora streaks past, ears flat, and zooms upstairs.

She seemed to come from the kitchen. Did she get into our breakfast? I sigh and march to check it out. Then a figure darkens the doorway, and I stumble back with a stifled yelp.

It's a man. A man who is not William. Yet he bears a face I know . . . because I was looking at it only moments ago.

He isn't quite the same young man—he's my age now. Still strikingly handsome with an angular face, blond hair and hazel eyes. His clothing is immaculate. William dresses well, but his fashion choices are those of a man with money and complete trust in his tailor, little interest in going the extra mile to stand out from the crowd. This man makes that extra effort from the cut of his cloak to the gleam of his riding boots.

"August?" I say.

Those hazel eyes blink at me. Then his lips curve in a grin. "I see William hasn't been nearly as lonely as I feared, locked away in these moors."

I drop in a slight curtsy. "Lord Courtenay, is it? I'm afraid that I don't quite know how to address you. I'm Bronwyn Dale."

As his brows furrow, that grin fades into utter confusion.

"My accent," I say with a chuckle. "Yes, I'm American. I'm a friend of William's, though I suppose that's obvious, given the hour."

He's still staring. He blinks. And then he laughs, a musical alto as he shakes his head, his face glowing with open delight.

"You are the *girl*," he says.

I fix a smile. "I'm certain plenty of girls have passed through William's life, but alas, I would not be one he's spoken of."

His eyes only gleam brighter. "True. He's never uttered a word about you, which has always been the problem."

"I . . . Uh, let me go wake William for you."

August swings into my path. "You're the girl who broke his heart. The girl who wasn't there."

When my mouth opens, he cuts me short with, "I recognize you. It took a moment, but once you spoke, that accent was unmistakable. I saw you that summer. How old were we? Sixteen? No, fifteen. That was the year I lost my"—he clears his throat —"my watch while walking in the moors."

I stifle a snort.

He only continues, "We were fifteen, and my family had come up from London. I was enjoying the attentions of a lovely local lass. This young lady had a very fetching sister, yet I could not convince William to meet her. In fact, I could barely convince him to meet *me*. He seemed utterly preoccupied with his bloody horses. I became concerned for his welfare."

He lowers his voice, conspiratorially. "Dreadfully jealous, to be honest, but *concerned* flatters me better. I snuck around and spotted him with a girl, which seemed to explain the problem. Except this girl was . . ." He frowns. "At first, I half believed her a fae from his beloved moors. Such an odd manner of dress, light and airy gowns that barely reached her knees, more fancy under-garments than dresses. When I got close, I realized she had a strange way of speaking, not only her accent but her words, her patterns of speech. She spoke a lot like you."

"A fellow American? I must tease William about that. His first love was an American girl."

August chuckles. "I'm sure that excuse works far better on those who did not spend two years in the Americas. Your accent is not from there. Back to my story, though."

"It is a lovely one."

"Isn't it? Terribly romantic with a tragic ending that appears to have taken a distinctly optimistic turn. I mentioned the girl to William, pretending that a villager spotted them together. He outright denied it. Blamed it on wild imaginations. Yet he still had very little time for me, very little indeed, and when he did, he was distracted. Distracted and happier than I've ever seen him. After that, though, he changed."

When I flinch, August's good humor softens. "William was fine. He was never the jolliest of boys, and other things happened later to—" He clears his throat again. "The point is that you are the girl, and if I were to put forth a long-held theory of mine, I believe you are from . . ." He leans in, eyes twinkling. "The future."

I laugh. "That is quite a story. Sadly, though, it is untrue."

"You're not that girl? Or not from the future?"

"Neither."

He eases back against the wall, all studied nonchalance. "You do realize what you're wearing, don't you?"

I look down. "William's shirt, which is not what I would typically wear to greet guests, but you were quite unannounced."

"So, you are from our world, and yet have been standing here dressed like that, nary a thought of the potential impropriety?"

I look down at my attire and inwardly wince. While I'm fully covered, being spotted in a shirt that falls mid-thigh would have sent a proper Victorian lady shrieking for cover.

I hide my reaction and straighten, chin up. "Perhaps I do not care about the impropriety. Perhaps my . . . past or even my current circumstances are such that I'm quite accustomed to greeting men dressed in scandalous attire."

"I couldn't even drag William into brothels when we were young. He's certainly not hiring companionship now."

"I didn't say it was a career."

"So, you are naming yourself a loose woman?"

"I would take no insult at the term."

He barks a laugh. "I see that. Quick-witted and caring not a whit for your reputation. I can see why you captured his heart."

"Have I? That would be lovely. I only hope there's some corner of it left after this terrible American girl broke it. Now, having pointed out my attire, which understandably offends you—"

"Not at all. You wear that shirt *much* better than William does."

"Perhaps you could help me find a blanket or other covering?"

"I see nothing at hand. Terribly sorry. Now, while we wait for William to wake, tell me about the future."

I glance about, but unlike in my world, there's no cozy wool blanket at hand, and I am actually covered, so I decide not to worry about it.

"You wish to know the future?" I say.

His eyes gleam. "I do."

"Well, in the very near future, I foresee you dealing with an angry friend, one who does not appreciate surprise guests."

August waves his hand. "He'll get over it. I *know* you're from the future, though. I figured that out years ago when William started making very prescient investments . . . and shared his predictions with his oldest and dearest friend. That knowledge could only come from someone who'd seen into the future . . . or known someone who lived there."

"Perhaps he has a time machine, as H. G. Wells—"

I cut myself short, as I remember the book—and the very concept—won't be around for another forty years.

Before I can say something else, footfalls thunder down the stairs, and William flies around the corner . . . stark naked.

August covers his gaze, shuddering. "Really, William? No one needs to see that so early in the morning."

I'm about to joke that I'm okay with it when I see William's expression, fists balled at his sides as if he hasn't quite decided they aren't needed.

"What are you—?" William begins.

"Wait," August says as he disappears into the kitchen. "Let me find you something to wear before we continue this conversation."

He returns with a blanket.

"I thought you didn't know where to find one," I say, my brows arching.

I'm joking, but William's gaze slides down my outfit. The look he turns on August is positively murderous.

"You held my guest in conversation while refusing to help her cover herself—"

"I forgot where the blankets were kept," August protests.

William's look only darkens as he wraps the large blanket around both of us. "I don't know why you're here, August, but I would strongly suggest you depart and hope I am in a better mood when you return. Lady Dale is my guest. You surprised her in a state of undress and allowed her to remain that way as you ogled—"

"He wasn't ogling," I say. "He caught me off-guard, and I forgot what I was wearing. Then we got wrapped up in a discussion. He seems to have mistaken me for a girl he glimpsed with you one summer, a girl he thinks comes . . ." I glance at August. "What did you say? From the future? It's a very fine story. You ought to write it down."

I'm trying to defuse the situation while warning William, but if anything, his face goes darker still.

"You spied on me?" William says. "You told me a villager had spotted me with a girl."

"I lied," August says. "I spied because I was concerned for your well-being. This is obviously the same girl, now grown to a woman, and I do believe she's from the future, having fed you the information you used to secure your fortune and also increase mine."

"Yes."

William's word hangs there, and we both look at him, waiting for the rest.

"Yes," he says. "You are correct in all of it. Now, leave us to enjoy our morning in peace."

August turns to me. "See how easy that was."

"I believe you know where to find the door," William says.

August's smile fades as he goes serious. "I wish I could go, William. But I'm here on a matter of rather urgent business. I do apologize for disturbing your day with Lady . . ."

"It's Bronwyn," I say. "No lady attached."

"And you may call me August. I apologize to you as well, Bronwyn, for catching you unawares and teasing about not knowing where to find a blanket." He looks at William. "Bronwyn is correct that we became engrossed in our conversation. A battle of wits, which she was winning, and I was too intent on the game to be a gentleman and fetch her a blanket. I am sorry for that, too."

"That apology goes to her, not to me," William says.

August apologizes, and I brush it off with, "We were distracted by a very entertaining argument."

"August is always entertaining," William murmurs.

"That's not the adjective you usually use," August says. "Now, if I may join you for breakfast, I can explain our business problem."

"You two do that," I say. "I need to pop home. I'll return later today, William."

He catches my arm before I can go. Then he hesitates, grip loosening.

"Why don't you join us for breakfast?" August says. "I would very much appreciate the opportunity to better display my manners and my wit. I shall occupy no more of William's time than necessary."

"If you're sure—"

"Excellent. I shall set out Mrs. Shaw's lovely cold breakfast and brew coffee. Please tell me you have coffee, William?"

"In the cupboard from your last visit," William says.

"Do they drink coffee in the future, Bronwyn?"

"They have entire shops devoted to coffee, one on almost every street corner."

He sighs. "Heaven."

William shakes his head and ushers me upstairs.

25

A t the top of the stairs, William pulls me into a kiss that leaves me gasping. One gulp of air, and then another kiss, deeper still, the blanket falling as he pulls me against him.

"Good morning to you, too," I say when we finally part.

He chuckles, but there's an uneasy edge to it.

"It really was a mistake, William. I heard a crash in the kitchen, and Pandora came running up, so I thought she knocked something over. Your shirt covers me, so I wasn't thinking how inappropriate it is in your time, and August and I really did get caught up in our conversation—"

He cuts me off with a kiss. "I'm not the least bit concerned about him seeing your bare legs, Bronwyn. While I'm annoyed that he didn't help you find a blanket, I do not suspect you of flirting with him. As for August, the man flirts like others breathe —he scarcely realizes he's doing it. If he did, it was not intentional."

"Are you all right, then? You seem a little off-kilter."

"Oh, I'm fine. I certainly did not wake to find your side of the bed empty and fly up in a panic, worried you'd changed your mind."

I hug him. "I most definitely have not."

He looks down at me. "At the risk of sounding like a fretful boy, I realize I may have said things last night that were more than you wanted to hear just yet."

"I believe I reciprocated them."

"I also know I was very . . . physical in my affections, affording you little sleep."

"And it was glorious." I put my arms around his neck. "You did and said nothing last night that I am not *thrilled* about. Now, how about we get dressed, go downstairs and have breakfast, and then we will separate for the minimum amount of time before I return in hopes of compensating for the fact that our first morning together has been rudely interrupted."

⚜

THE COFFEE IS . . . WELL, LET'S JUST SAY IT'S BETTER THAN SOME overpriced espresso chains, which isn't saying much. Coffee in Victorian times was relatively new, and with no modern machines, it's made almost like tea with ground coffee being steeped in cloth bags. Also, it's not exactly quality coffee to begin with.

When August asks me how it tastes, I try to demur, but August seizes on that with the fervor of a true aficionado. Coffee in the future is better? Tell him about it. Where is it from? How is it made? He's genuinely fascinated, and by the time we're done with the conversation, I'm promising to bring better coffee. More importantly, we're both relaxed and comfortable, devouring the repast he's laid out.

"So this business problem . . ." William says.

When August glances at me, William says, "Bronwyn is no society maiden who expects frivolous conversation over breakfast until we can retire to our manly business discussions."

"Certainly not," I say. "And in truth, I suspect many of those maidens—and matrons—would be happy to hear such conversation if it wasn't deemed too 'complicated and coarse' for their untutored and delicate ears."

August laughs and says, "You sound like . . ." He wipes a hand over his mouth and cuts a slice of ham. "All right, then, the problem is with a shipment. William and I have shared interest in a shipping company that docks in Whitby, and one of the ships was supposed to depart last night, but the new harbormaster is causing trouble."

"He wants a bribe," William says. "Which he's not getting. Bribery is for thieves and smugglers, and to suggest we are either . . ." He stabs his ham and mutters expletives under his breath.

"Agreed," August says. "I was hoping you'd come to the wharf and tell him that yourself. I'm better at charming, and you are better at scowling. This particular problem requires scowls."

I take a strawberry from the bowl. "Then, William is your man. I will busy myself at home for the afternoon."

August assures William they'll settle the matter as quickly as possible.

"I have hopes of returning to London by morning," August says. "I have made a promise to someone who expects me to keep it." He glances at me. "My son. He'll be driving poor Margaret to distraction."

"Ah," I say with a smile. "Yes, your wife will appreciate your prompt return."

They both go still, and before I can speak, August says, his voice strained, "No, Margaret is his governess. My wife left us."

William winces as I hurry on, with some desperation. "How old is your son?"

"Two. Nearly three."

"Do you have any pictures?" I ask.

"Portraits? Not with me, I fear."

"Of course. Sorry. I'm forgetting my time period."

A faint smile. "Ah, so in the future, parents carry pictures of their children?"

"Photographs, yes."

"On tiny devices that can hold hundreds, perhaps thousands," William says. "Be happy August doesn't have one of those, or we'd be here all day. Here's Edmund eating an apple. Here's Edmund playing with his dog. Here's Edmund sleeping."

I chuckle. "People do exactly that. Wait . . . your son's name is Edmund? Isn't that your middle name, William?"

"He's named after a relative," William says. "Not me."

"Yes," August says. "I named him after my great-grandfather's brother, whom I never knew, rather than the childhood friend who loathes the idea of being anyone's namesake." August lowers his voice and whispers. "It's a great responsibility, you know."

"Ah. Well, I'm sure your great-grandfather's brother was a lovely man."

"Undoubtedly. As for *my* Edmund, perhaps you can convince his favorite uncle to come to London for a visit? Bring you along, show off the sights of our grand city?"

Uncle?

Wait. Yes, of course. August was engaged to Cordelia. William's sister left years ago, and so did August's wife . . . because they're the same person. That's why William winced at the reminder.

I'm spared from a reply by William grumbling that there's no need for him to go to London when August will bring Edmund to the summer house next month.

"And how about you, Bronwyn?" August says. "Do you have children?"

I shake my head. "My husband passed away before we reached that stage, unfortunately."

"Ah. Then you must have them with William."

William and I sputter in unison, but August waves us off. "Not immediately, of course. After you're married. That part's important. Or so they tell me. Give it a year or so. Edmund would be delighted with a baby cousin."

William glowers at him. "Are you *trying* to frighten Bronwyn off?"

August leans toward me. "He will make an excellent father. Wait until you see him with Edmund. He's a natural parent."

William stands abruptly. "And you are a terrible one, dawdling over breakfast and delaying your return to your son."

"Is that a hint to drop this conversation?" August looks at me. "That sounded like a hint, didn't it?"

I smile and shake my head. "You two go. I'll tidy up here and see you on your return, William."

William turns to August. "Please note the use of my name and the lack of yours. You will say your farewells to Bronwyn before we leave and not inveigle your way into dinner."

August's brows shoot up. "Inveigle? Me?" He glances over. "What is for dinner, out of curiosity?"

I shoo them off and tidy quickly so I can get home to Enigma.

☙❧

I'VE BEEN AWAY FROM ENIGMA TOO LONG, AND I FEEL TERRIBLE ABOUT it. Worst of all is the guilt that comes from knowing I haven't even thought of her for nearly twelve hours. I made sure she had everything she needed before I left, and I'd played with her yesterday until she collapsed from exhaustion, but I'm still racked with guilt.

I made a commitment to this kitten, and I can't leave her alone for that long while I'm off gallivanting with my new lover. Yet I'm not sure how to resolve the issue. After I return and shower her with affection, I test popping back *with* her. I sit on the floor and hold her . . . and end up in William's bedroom empty-handed. I try from the spot where, in William's world, there stands the chest where Pandora came through. I end up sitting on that chest, with no kitten.

My failure sparks a larger problem. William said he's committed to making this work, while understanding I have my own life here. That would make sense if I worked down the road and could pop back to the twenty-first century each morning, returning to him in the evening. But my job is across an ocean. Changing to a local university isn't like switching jobs in retail. Even if I *could* get a position, the commute alone would be hell.

So stay with him, a little voice whispers. *Find a way to take Enigma, and stay there. Surrender the rest.*

Give up my modern life to live in his world. It seems like such a romantic sacrifice. It's not. It's the death knell of a relationship.

One of Michael's cousins met a girl in the United States and took her home to Cairo where she knew nothing and no one. They lasted two years, separating amid a maelstrom of blame, she being desperately unhappy away from her family and he being hurt that he wasn't enough. I've seen other variations on that story—girl abandons her home or her family or her career goals for a man and ends up miserable and resentful.

My career is important to me. My *world* is important to me. I could live here for a year or two in perfect bliss, holed up in Thorne Manor, William occupied with his horses while I managed the household. Then I'd get restless, hemmed in by the isolation and the restrictions of his world, missing my father, my stepmother, my friends.

So what is the answer if he can't come to my world and I can't stay in his? The very question steals my breath, and all I can do is remind myself that we have all summer to figure this out, and we *will* figure it out.

I had plans for housework and errands, but guilt over Enigma keeps me from them. So I spend all my time with her, and she responds the way a child would, saddled with a guilt-stricken parent who returned from a work trip. She's happy with the play and the cuddles for about an hour, and then she's had enough of me and wanders off for some kitty alone-time.

After lunch, I strip woodwork. There are few things in home renovation as satisfying as removing paint, watching long strips slough off in ribbons, revealing the gorgeous wood beneath. I'm busy with that when a clatter sounds, and I realize I haven't see Enigma since before lunch. I drop my scraper and leap up as if I've left a baby in the bathtub.

"Enigma?" I call.

No answer. I race up the stairs, shouting her name like a crazy woman. I skid into my bedroom, heart thudding. Her box is empty. So is my bed. There's a kitten-sized divot in the comforter.

"Enigma?" I call as I hurry down the hall.

Silence.

"Enigma!" I call, adding a "Here, kitty, kitty, kitty!" because obviously it's the universal language for feline summoning. And maybe it is—no sooner do I croon that magic phrase than I hear an answering meow.

I'm in the master bedroom, and the sound comes from the walls. *Inside* the walls. I freeze in confusion. Then I remember the secret passage.

Back in the hall, I throw open the linen closet door to see the padlock. It's still affixed. So how did Enigma get in there?

I return to where I heard the kitten, but she's very clearly inside that wall. She must have found another way.

I run to the garage for the pry bar.

🦋 26 🦋

I pry off the old lock. The panel comes away with an explosion of dust that sets me coughing and sputtering. I duck into the passage, where I can stand. It's so narrow I need to move sideways. I cringe as my shirt slides over the filthy wall, and the stink of bat guano warns me not to shine the flashlight up.

It's been over thirty years since I last did this. At fifteen, William and I had been far more interested in sneaking into the moors for kisses than creeping through dirt-crusted walls to spook the maids. Still, I'll admit to a thrill as I ease along the passage.

There's the scrap of carpet I dragged in as a child after William got a splinter and I'd been too young to realize the carpet wouldn't be in *his* version of the passage. Here's the spot where the passage widens, and William brought two old pillows for us to sit on. The pillows are still there—or the moldering scraps of them, the rest having spent the centuries lining baby mouse nests.

As I move, my flashlight shines on marks carved into the wall, and a forgotten memory bursts back. I see William, at five, carving our names into the wood with a pocket knife. He starts to put a plus between them, and my hand clamps on his.

"What's that?" I ask, my heart tripping.

He frowns at me. "The algebraic sign for addition. Because we're here together. William *and* Bronwyn."

"Where I come from, if you put a plus between a boy's name and a girl's name, it means they're boyfriend and girlfriend."

His head tilts in thought, and my heart trips faster, certain he's going to say, "Eww" or make a face, because that's what boys do.

"So you're not my girlfriend?" he asks.

My cheeks heat. "I could be. If you asked."

"I just did."

"Not like that. You need to say, 'Bronwyn Dale, will you be my girlfriend?'"

He grumbles, and there are such echoes of the adult William in that grumble. But he says the words, and I accept, and he puts a plus between our names. Then, in a surge of boldness, I take the penknife and add, "4ever." He squints at it, sounding it out, and then nods, satisfied.

Now, I'm staring at those names on a wall, tears spilling over my cheeks. Happy tears for a promise kept, and sad ones for time lost.

Was time lost? I'm not certain it was. I feel horrible for any pain I inflicted on William, but the truth is . . .

Would I have had it any other way if that meant Michael never came into my life? No. As much as I love William—have always loved him—I would not have wanted to miss out on Michael. If I'd known William was real, that place in my heart would have been full, and I would have never paid attention that first time Michael said my name, and my life would be poorer for it. I'm a better person for knowing him, loving him, and I'll never wish that away.

I touch the "4ever" and send out a fervent hope that it's a prediction come true. William and I were "forever" in our way, and now we can be that in every way.

I'm staring at the names when Enigma's annoyed meow

reminds me that I'm not here to traipse down memory lane. I have a kitten to rescue.

I turn a corner, which is not easy, given how narrow the passage is. When I shine the flashlight, I see no sign of Enigma. She should be easy to spot with her bright orange and white fur. She's not there, though, which means I need to duck past the window.

This is why secret passages work so much better in basements. Up here, they're restricted to the flow of the building. This particular one sticks to the interior walls for most of the way, but here it passes along the outside, past a small, deep-set high window in what is now the bathroom. Easy enough for a child to pass. Not so easy at my age.

I wonder whether that window was added later, and I imagine the renovators cursing at such a thick wall, even thicker than was the norm for the period, wondering why this blasted one had well over a foot-wide gap. I chuckle at the thought and squeeze under the window. Then I'm rounding the next corner, shining the light . . .

There's no sign of Enigma.

That isn't possible. This is the last leg of the passage with the door that once led into the master bedroom. That door has been boarded up for two hundred years. Where could Enigma . . . ?

That's when I see the hole in the floor, and I remember the very first time William and I came this far along the passage. We'd been four or five, William clutching a candle to lead the way. He'd been pointing out that boarded-up door ahead . . . when I'd seen a gaping hole right in front of him. I'd leaped forward and yanked him back, the candle sputtering to the bottom.

The next time we visited, we laid boards over the hole for safety. One of those boards now lies askew, the others gone. Crashed through the hole.

I remember the clatter from earlier.

The board crashing through . . . with my kitten on it.

I race forward, calling her name, and drop to my knees at the edge. The flashlight beam ricochets off the walls as my hands tremble. All I see are two rotted and broken boards lying atop a pile of rags at the bottom. I swing the beam over them.

"Enigma? Where are—?"

A mew answers but from underneath me. An orange tail flicks, no more than a couple feet below. Putting the flashlight aside, I stretch out on my stomach. Then, I ease my head and shoulders over the hole. And there she is, sitting on a thin plank of framework just under the hole. She must have caught herself while falling and scrambled up there. Now, she looks at me, completely unperturbed by her predicament. Trusting that I'll rescue her.

I take a deep breath and try not to panic. I also try not to calculate how far she'll fall, though my treacherous brain still throws back, *At least fifteen feet*. Another deep breath, and I remind myself of the pile of rags below, which would cushion her fall.

Pile of rags? Why would there be . . . ? I shine the light down and freeze, staring at what looks like—

Enigma mews. I lean as far as I dare so she can see me.

"I'm going to get you out of there," I say. "Let me grab a ladder and—"

She jumps. Before I can freak out, she's clinging to my shirt. And then I do freak out, her weight jolting me so hard I start to fall. I frantically grab for the side of the hole while my other hand grabs the kitten hanging by her claws from my shirt. Enigma settles in against me, as unconcerned as ever.

I get a handhold and then cradle her as I shimmy backward over the rough passage floor, ignoring the jab of splinters. Finally, I'm as secure as I can get, and I pull up from the hole, lifting Enigma with me. It's a dangerous and tricky move, and when I'm finally sitting there, holding her in my lap, I shake from both nerves and exertion. The ungrateful feline chirps and attempts to inflict a second heart attack by scrambling up my shirt, out of my grip. Before I can grab her, she hops off my shoulder and trots back down the passage.

As I twist, she disappears through a gap in the boards that I wouldn't have thought big enough for a mouse. Then she turns and pokes one paw through, as if waving for me to join her. I grab the remaining plank covering the hole. The wood is soft in my hands, rotting. As I shove the board in to jam the mouse hole shut, Enigma yowls her disapproval.

I return to the linen closet and make the rounds of every room adjoining the passage, turning on all the lights. Then, I return to the passage and walk through in the dark, looking for stray light to indicate holes. I don't find any.

When I turn the final corner, I stay at the end, not daring to get near the hole in the dark. That's when I remember what I saw down that hole.

I turn on my flashlight, return to the hole, kneel and shine the light down. The heap still looks like rags. Rags that weren't there when William and I were children, exploring in his time.

Back then, William and I made up endless stories about this hole. One day, we'd pulled back the boards and lowered a candle . . . to see nothing except the candle that we'd dropped when we first discovered the hole. It was empty then. It's not empty now.

I'm shining my light when a small silver circle reflects back. I twist the light and squint until I can make out a silver button on a dark shape that takes form as a boot.

As I hold the light at arm's length, something materializes under the pile of not-rags. White against the dark floor. Two white, jointed sticks, digging into the dirt.

The bones of two small fingers.

I pull back, breath seizing. I sit on my haunches, arms wrapped around my knees, so close to the edge that when I inhale a deep, ragged breath, I rock and then nearly fall as I scramble back. I crouch there, inhaling and exhaling. I want to tell myself I saw wrong, dash out and padlock the door, never to return.

How long has that door been locked?

Not long enough to blame whoever put a body in the hole. The clothing is too rotted, and that door wasn't locked when I was little.

I look back in the hole, and there's no mistake. Fingers protrude from under cloth. A booted leg rests at an unnatural angle. More white peeks out where cloth has rotted away.

I'm certain of what I see, and as I look at it, I remember a figure stepping from the linen closet door. The reason I'd first tried to open the passage. The boy in knickerbockers kept appearing through that door. I knew it meant something. Now, I stare down at what looks like the body of a child, broken at the bottom of the hole.

I shine the light down, but I can't make out what the skeletal remains are wearing.

You'll find out soon enough when you report this to the authorities and they remove the poor child's bones from your wall.

I shift the light, trying to see better.

You are reporting it, aren't you?

I should be running for my phone right now. There's a body in the walls of my house. I must report it immediately.

Yet I'm crouching here, and I'm thinking of the boy in the knickerbockers. Of the veiled woman telling me to name her killer. Or name *their* killer? This boy didn't tumble down the hole to a horrible, accidental death. If so, someone would have found the cubby open and gone looking. He didn't fall through those boards like Enigma. The broken wood is on *top* of him.

That hole was open when he fell . . . and then someone put the boards back in place.

Freya thinks naming their killer will set them free. If I move his remains, would that change? His ghost is bound *here*, and it might have nothing to do with his bones being in the wall, but if I move them, and I can no longer communicate with him, I stand less chance of finding his killer.

Two nights ago, I tried to speak to the boy. I'd seen him hesitantly step from the linen closet door. I'd heard his whisper. But

I'd drawn the line at summoning him when he didn't appear on his own.

Now I need to try.

27

When Freya came to tea the day before last, she gave me ways to contact the dead. Some require ingredients and rituals. The simplest way, though, is to open myself up to them by stilling my mind and pulling them through to me, the same way I pull myself through to William's world.

I start at the top of the hole. I form the boy's image in my mind, coaxing him from his world, telling him I need to talk to him. I can help him. I pour everything I have into the invocation, and I might as well be trying to call him on my cell phone for all the good it does.

I repeat the process outside the linen closet door. Still nothing.

Finally, I sigh and head for the stairs. I'll gather ingredients for a proper séance and . . .

"He doesn't mean any harm by it," a young woman's voice trills from below. "He's actually very fond of you. But he's terribly shy and a little awkward."

I freeze. There's someone downstairs. Inside my *house*.

Has Freya brought a friend to visit, and when I didn't hear the knocker, they walked in?

The voice that answers, though, is much younger than Freya's.

"He does not seem shy at all. He seems disinterested."

"Perhaps *shy* is not the correct word. William is not timid, but he is overly fond of his own company."

William? I freeze.

The second woman replies, "When August arrived, William was happy enough to speak to *him*. They're in the barn now, chattering away . . . after I requested William's company on a walk, and he said he must tend to his horses."

"And he is doing exactly that, is he not? Even August cannot pull him away from that task. August has been his friend since they were children. William is comfortable with him. As he will be with you once he gets to know you better."

"How can he do that when he barely speaks to me?"

"The answer, I believe, is to try *less*. Our young Lord Thorne hates to be chased, but he does love a challenge. Pay him no heed. Better yet, make it clear you are having fun without him. That will catch his attention. I propose you and I take that walk without him. Then over dinner, we shall regale him with stories of the adventure we had."

"The adventure we had *without* him?" The second woman's voice lightens in a soft laugh.

"Precisely."

Two figures appear in the front doorway. They're opaque, spotlighted only for a blink as the door opens, framing them. Two women, their arms linked companionably, both seen only from the back. One with fair hair. The other dark. A glimpse of Victorian dresses, too faint to make out details. The door shuts, and the women are gone.

Instead of conjuring ghosts, I've called forth a sliver of the past. Except I have no idea why . . . or what it means.

I run down and throw open the door. The women are gone. Or so I think until I catch a shimmer of them heading for the moor. I jog after them. Something moves to my side, and I spin to see the faint outline of another figure. A fair-haired man, as opaque as the women. He calls after them, and I recognize his voice. It's August.

There's a teasing exchange between him and the women, and the light-haired one lays a hand on his arm.

Then all three disappear, and I'm left standing in the yard, staring at the empty moors.

§

I'D BEEN TRYING TO SUMMON THE BOY, AND INSTEAD, I GOT AUGUST and two women, one of them dark haired. Was that Cordelia? I know from her photograph that she was a brunette like her brother.

So I'd seen Cordelia talking about William with another woman. A woman who was trying to catch William's eye. A friend of Cordelia and August's? Brought to Thorne Manor as a potential wife for William after his engagement ended and his sister married? But why show *me* that conversation?

That's what I'll need to figure out. In less than an hour, though, I'm supposed to meet William again. Bookmark this place and return to it tomorrow when I can speak to Freya.

§

WILLIAM ISN'T HOME YET. HE'D EXPECTED TO BE BACK BY FIVE, SO that's when I arrive, but his room is empty, and a quick trip to the barn reveals Balios's stall is also vacant. I grab some straw and weave a very lopsided heart, which I leave in William's room to let him know where I am. It's been a long time since I've let myself be silly with anyone, and the sensation bubbles through me like gloriously cheap champagne.

It's also been a long time since I dressed to catch a man's eye. I took care with my lingerie choices yesterday. Today, I've gone further. A little less Victorian-friendly, shall we say.

My sundress is also a deliberate choice. At our picnic, William had hinted about me wearing one of the more scandalous choices from my closet. It is, of course, only scandalous by his standards, but it's the shortest one I have, falling to mid-thigh, with a scoop-neck bodice aided by a push-up bra. The sundress fabric is airy light, hugging and sliding against my thighs as I walk.

I'll fully admit how much I'm anticipating William's reaction to my outfit. I've abandoned my sandals, and I'm working bare-foot as I tidy the stables, and that too, I know will catch his eye.

The smaller stable door bangs open with enough force to give me a start.

His boots slap against the dirt as if at a hard run. He swerves into the stall section, sees me and stops short, his shoulders falling in a hard exhale.

"You're here," he says.

The dim lighting casts him into shadow, a tall figure with dark hair tumbling over his forehead, his jacket askew, broad shoulders quaking as he pants. Sweat trickles down the open neck of his shirt where he's torn off his cravat.

"Is everything okay?" I say, stepping toward him. "Where's Bal—?"

I don't even get the word out before he's catching me up in a crushing kiss. There's need and desperation in that kiss, and I'm swept up in it, kissing him back. When we part for breath, I manage to croak. "Balios?"

His brows knit, as if he doesn't recognize the word. Then, breath ragged, he says, "Out front." He kisses me again, brief and hungry, like a near-drowned man gasping for oxygen between words. "Finished late in Whitby." Another kiss. "Bloody harbor-master." Kiss. "Rode back as fast as I could." The next kiss falls on my neck, hard enough to leave a mark before he murmurs, "Ran upstairs but . . ."

A shiver, and I know the rest. He'd been late returning, rode hard to get here, leaving Balios out front as he raced up the stairs only to find his room empty.

I open my mouth to say I left a message there, but he stops my words with a desperate kiss, pressing himself into me with a groan. Another shiver, as if he can't relax even now, the grip of that panic so tight.

I remember his light words this morning, joking about how he *hadn't* leaped out of bed, certain I'd fled in the night. I remember the other day, watching him ride off in a frustrated temper when he thought I wasn't coming. There is no logical reason for him to panic today when he's barely an hour late. But this isn't about logic.

I hear August's voice again.

You're the girl. The one who broke his heart.

We need to talk about this, deal with it. Right now, though, he needs something else.

As those kisses pour out his fear and worry, rough kisses turn into rough clutches. Before I know it, I'm lying in a pile of hay, my skirt around my waist, William fumbling with his trousers.

He grabs my hips and then pauses, eyes going wide in a flash of consternation, as if he realizes he hasn't taken a moment to be sure I agree to what he's doing. I wrap my fingers in his hair and arch myself against him in answer, and he heaves a shuddering sigh of relief as he thrusts into me.

⚜

YESTERDAY, EVEN DEEP IN THE NIGHT, WILLIAM NEVER DRIFTED OFF after sex. He's the boy I remember, who liked touch, sometimes embracing or cuddling, but mostly just physical contact. Even when we were both deep in our books on a sunny afternoon, he'd have his hip against mine or his head on my shoulder, whatever form of touching could not be misconstrued as a prelude to something inappropriate for a fifteen-year-old Victorian girl.

Last night, that restriction gone, I got all the caresses and kisses and touches, even after the sex was over. Hands on my hips, fingers stroking my sides, teasing kisses along my shoulders and neck, his body still entwined with mine as he got his fill of less ardent, but no less passionate exploration. It was quiet contemplation, drowsy and gentle, a shared reverie of skin against skin that only gradually lifted to include words, murmurs and soft conversation before we slid into sleep.

Today, though, when we finish, he stays over me, his entire body rigid. When he lifts his head, guilt shadows his eyes.

"That is not what I intended at all," he says.

I chuckle. "It was fine."

He shakes his head. "No, that was unacceptable." He pulls up just enough to look me in the eye. He can't hold my gaze, though, and shakes his head. "I planned to come back and sweep you off your feet with a romantic evening. Instead, I fall on you in the stable, ravage you like a selfish boor."

"That wasn't ravaging," I say as I prop onto my elbows. "I said yes."

He flushes. "I know. I would never— I mean that it was not the sort of lovemaking I intended, and I apologize."

"I enjoyed it perfectly well, and we have all night for you to show me something different." I duck to meet his gaze. "I'm not a blushing maiden, William. If I don't want something, I'll stop you, and I know you *will* stop."

He nods.

"I left a message in your room," I say. "To tell you where I was."

He reddens again. "Instead of looking, I behaved like a raging idiot. I keep behaving like one. This is not the side I want to show you, Bronwyn. Not at all. I'm ashamed of myself, and I am so—"

I kiss away the apology. "Don't. Please. Twenty-three years ago, I left without a word. I wish to God I could undo that, William, but I can't."

His mouth opens, consternation filling his eyes again. Before any denial comes, he shuts his mouth and meets my eyes. "I do not blame you. What's happening with me now . . ." He glances away. "I do not know what this is, but I will deal with it. I don't want you to indulge my fears."

"I'm not," I say. "I'm acknowledging your right to them. I left you. Not after a fight. Not after anything that could have been construed as an excuse for parting. I disappeared, and you had no way of knowing why. That won't happen again. I'm no longer a child who can be convinced you aren't real. Yet that won't stop you from worrying. What if something does happen? What if I'm sick or injured . . . or worse? What if I can't get to you? What if we argue, and I don't come back, and you can do nothing about that?"

"Yes." That's all he says, and I know what it means.

Yes to all of that.

I put my arms around his neck. "The last is the worst, isn't it? That you can do nothing about it. In a normal world, you could always come to *me* for answers. But if I leave, you have no recourse but sending letters that I cannot even return."

"Yes," he says, the word thick now, a faint tremor running through him. "Yes." He kisses me, and it's desperate again, deep and hungry and filled with longing and fear, but before it goes beyond a kiss, he pulls back and runs one thumb over my cheek.

"When we were young, I used to panic every time we argued and you left," he says. "I never admitted that. I felt foolish even then. Afraid and powerless. Even at fifteen, those were unfamiliar emotions for me, and I didn't know what to do with them. I still don't. Yet no matter how often I drove myself into a frenzy of worry, thinking I'd driven you off forever, that never stopped me from losing my temper and arguing with you again and telling you to go, just like . . ."

Just like I did with Cordelia.

I am afraid I'll do that again, and you'll do what she did. Take me at my word, fly off in a rage and never return.

This is what he means. I see it in the spark of grief that flits over his face as he realizes what he's saying.

William drove his sister away. Combine his temper with hers, his stubbornness with hers, and therein lay the recipe for personal tragedy.

I must remember what happened with Cordelia and how that affects him.

Thinking of her brings a harsher slap of awareness. William is alone. He might have joked about that on our first meeting when I was reduced to asking about his aged housekeeper, but it hadn't really penetrated. He's truly alone. His father passed when he was ten, his mother when he was a young man, and then his only sibling left. Even by modern standards, they'd been a close-knit, loving family, the kind I envied. Which was even rarer for William's time and class.

Now they were gone. All of them. One pair of grandparents had been dead when I returned at fifteen, the others estranged before he was born. His only remaining relative is that distant cousin who'll inherit the estate, the one he's only met a time or two.

For a man raised in such love, that isolation would be devastating, and it makes our situation even more difficult. I could disappear in a blink. Like his father. Like his mother. Like his sister.

I cup William's face in my hands. "I will never argue, stomp off and not return. I didn't do that when I was three or five or fifteen, so I'm not going to do it now. You never told me to leave. We walked away from each other. We knew when an argument was getting too heated, when we might lose our tempers and say things we didn't mean, and we parted, you going your way and me going mine. I always knew, though, that you couldn't reach out to mend it, so I returned. So long as I have the ability to return, I will do so. If you tell me to leave, I'll come back later. If you really and truly want me gone, I will, of course, honor your wishes, but you always have that floorboard space to tell me differently."

"I will never want that, Bronwyn."

"But if it ever did happen—for either of us—we respect one another enough to end things properly. I will not walk away and make it forever, and you will not tell me to go and mean forever."

He nods, and when he kisses me again, it's softer, still rich with longing and desire, but that edge of fear slipping away with the tension in his body. His hands slip under me, pulling me against him. A pause, and I have to chuckle at that, already understanding the language of his lovemaking, this pause a polite request to continue in the direction he's heading. I slide my nails down his back, pulling him against me, and he chuckles and continues on course.

28

"Can I ask you about August and Cordelia?" I murmur as we lie there afterward on the stable floor. "I stepped onto treacherous ground a few times at breakfast, and I'd like to not do it again."

I brace for William to tense, but he only knits his brows, as if in confusion.

"I saw their engagement announcement in your mother's room. I can understand why August is so hurt by her leaving, especially when they had a child."

His brows only knit more. Then I jump as he gives a short laugh. "Cordelia is not Edmund's mother."

My cheeks heat. "Ah, so he was born, as they say in your time, on the wrong side of the sheets. August's child that Cordelia took on to raise as their own." I pause. "Or is he adopted?"

As I talk, William waves one hand, clearly telling me that he can explain. I'm too caught up in the puzzle.

"August was engaged to my sister," William says. "He did not marry her. She left before the wedding. Edmund's mother—and August's wife—is another woman entirely. Rosalind."

"But August said you're his son's uncle . . . Ah, that's an honorific."

"It is. I'm the boy's godfather. There was no marriage between our families."

"I'm sorry."

I catch the look on William's face and say, "Or, perhaps not. You weren't thrilled with the prospect of your dearest friend as your brother-in-law?"

William settles onto his side, pulling me against him. "August would have made a fine brother-in-law. A fine husband for my sister, though? Let's just say I was not in favor of the match. He was far too fond of the ladies, and they were too fond of him. Even my fiancé used to make eyes at him when she thought no one was looking."

"Ouch."

He shrugs. "With August around, one became quite accustomed to not being the center of female attention. He swore that he would be a faithful husband, and he was when he finally did marry though I'm not certain the same would have applied with Cordelia. That was marriage for duty. Rosalind was love."

"*Two* women have left him?"

William makes a face, and it reminds me of the one he made at breakfast when August snapped about his wife's abandonment.

"Rosalind did not leave," he says, "though please don't say that to August. He is the most good-natured of men . . . but that is the one topic certain to ignite his temper. I have spent two years trying to convince him Rosalind would never abandon him and Edmund. He will hear none of it. I fear if I continue to pursue the subject, it will prove the breaking point for a friendship I thought unbreakable."

"I'm sorry," I say and kiss his lips. "That's not fair. He must have loved her very much, though."

"Too much if such a thing is possible."

"What happened?"

He flips onto his back and sighs.

"You don't need to tell—" I begin, but he pulls me onto him and says, "That sigh is grief for my friend and for his wife, not annoyance at telling the tale. August is the son of an earl. Third son. The family has a summer home near York that makes Thorne Manor look like servant's quarters. Rosalind adored it. She loved to walk, and she loved to ride, and the moors gave her plenty of opportunity for both."

"A young woman who loved the moors and horses? I'm surprised you didn't marry her yourself."

A look passes behind his eyes, and I stiffen, then force it back with a soft, "I'm sorry. She chose August, I presume."

"What?" He blinks at me, startled. Then a short laugh. "No, not at all. I enjoyed Rosalind's companionship, but she was not to my tastes otherwise. In another life, *she'd* have been my younger sister, instead of—"

He clears his throat. "No, there was nothing between us. If I looked uncomfortable at your jest, it's because August . . . When I say he loved her too much, what I really mean is he was unhealthily jealous of her love. He spent his youth changing women as often as he changes clothing. But then he met the girl he truly wanted, and he could not believe *every* man didn't want her. Worse, he could not quite believe *she* wanted *him*."

"Ah. That's . . ." I connect his explanation to his pained expression earlier. "He was even jealous of *you*?"

"Yes. For absolutely no reason, let me assure you. Not only did I never harbor such feelings for Rosalind, she never had eyes for anyone but August. So back to my tale. They were at the family estate for the summer. One night, after they'd gone to bed, she rode out. She did that sometimes. That is, she used to before August began following her, thinking she was cuckolding him. She'd stopped, for his sake, and I'm not sure why she went that night, but the next day, her horse was found drowned at the base of a cliff overlooking the sea."

"Oh!" I gasp.

"He'd stumbled and gone over. Rosalind loved to ride along that clifftop and . . ."

"The horse lost his footing, and they were both drowned."

"Yet the lack of Rosalind's body convinced August that she'd run away. Which is ludicrous. Ran away and abandoned her horse, which then ran off a cliff in despair?" He snorts. "It's madness, and I do not know why he will not accept the very obvious fact that his wife is dead."

"Because it hurts too much," I murmur. "He'd rather hate her than mourn her. Easier to think she's run off with some unsuitable man, and she'll return one day, begging forgiveness."

He shifts, uncomfortable. "Like a young man who decided to hate a girl because she didn't come back through time for him? Almost ran her off when she did?"

"It's not the same," I say softly. "August's self-delusion is unhealthy and self-destructive. I'm glad you're here for him, though."

"Well, I am glad I wasn't here that night. They'd visited here that very day, and we'd departed together as I needed to return to London. Otherwise, I fear August would have thought Rosalind was coming to visit me, particularly after late-night revelers claim they saw her heading this way."

I frown. "But we're ten miles from the ocean."

"Yes, and one ought not to doubt the word of three men, drunk on youth and gin." He rolls his eyes. "It makes for a fine scandal, though. My dearest friend's wife came for a secret assignation, and I murdered her and tossed her body into the sea."

"What? People think . . . ?" My mind spins. "You said scandal. That day I overheard you with August, there was some mention of a scandal."

His brows rise. "And you didn't ask me about it?"

"I thought it involved a lady. I was going to ask, but it didn't quite seem the time to bring up past relationships."

He chuckles. "Well, I admire your discretion, and I appreciate your faith in me, that you suspected only something so relatively benign. The scandal does involve women, but not, alas, a deliciously forbidden affair."

"I was thinking duel." I pause. "Wait, women? Plural?"

"I killed my sister, too, don't you know?" he says, and his tone is light, but anger and pain simmers behind his blue eyes. "Murdered my sister and my best friend's wife. Oh, and I also killed you."

"Wait? What?"

"You and I were seen at least once by local villagers. The young lord, spotted in the company of a mysterious girl, who was never seen again after that summer. At the time, no one thought much of it. But after Cordelia left, people remembered . . . and added you to my death toll."

"The locals—?"

"No, the villagers—bless them—defend me, sometimes with fisticuffs, I fear. It's others, taking their stories and twisting them. The locals also know that Cordelia left of her own accord. One of their own drove her to the train station. They also know that I was not here the night Rosalind died. I was in a coach bound for London, with witnesses."

I open my mouth, but words won't come. I know rumors can be vicious, but this is ridiculous. Accusing a man of murdering his sister . . . when witnesses saw her leave? Of murdering his friend's wife . . . when witnesses place him a hundred miles away? Of killing a mysterious girl seen with him once or twice?

"I'm sorry," I say, finally. "People can be nasty and horrible and downright stupid."

He shrugs. "They like a good story, and I was not particularly popular in some society circles. Too successful at business. Too successful"—he clears his throat—"in other ways."

I smile. "With the ladies as you'd say. I'm still sorry, though." I pause. I see an opening here, and I take a moment to evaluate his mood. He's calm, relaxed, relieved at having revealed his "scandal" and getting nothing but outrage on his behalf.

I could ruin that mood with my question, but I'm going to gamble and decide that this is, instead, the perfect time to pose it with care.

"As much as I'd love to dismiss the impact of the rumors," I say, "I know at the very least, they're inconvenient. It would help if Cordelia returned. She hasn't, though?"

He shakes his head. "No. I wish she would, and not merely for the sake of the rumors. I would like to know where she is and if she's well. If she has children, they can still inherit my fortune even if the property is entailed."

"Have you ever . . . tried to find her?"

I ask very carefully, ready for him to tense, but he says, "I have. Soon after she left, I regretted the haste of my actions and hired a man to search for her. He found clues, but he never caught up with her. I expected she would eventually come home."

And she did not. At least he knows she got somewhere safe and began her own life. She eluded William's private detective, not ready to come home, but after all these years, surely that must have changed.

Cordelia doted on her big brother, and she's out there, and if I can reunite them, I will. For now, I'm reassured to know he wants to make contact. One day, I'll bring his sister home to him.

29

William puts Balios to bed with extra brushing in apology for his failure earlier. While he's doing that, I return home to visit with Enigma. Then I come back, and we assemble a meal from the kitchen and take it up to the library to eat.

Yes, William has a library, and I'm very displeased that it took me this long to realize it. Had I only asked where he'd put the kittens the other day, I'd have discovered this wondrous addition to Thorne Manor in a converted guest bedroom. I remember William's tales of the library at his family's London home. It'd seemed the very model of a Victorian library, complete with rolling ladders and overstuffed chairs flanking two fireplaces, the entirety decorated with oddities from distant lands.

Here, William has a space probably a quarter the size . . . and possibly holding every book from that London house. Each wall-sized bookcase is so jam-packed that my inner librarian is torn between giddy delight at the sheer quantity and shuddering horror at the complete lack of organization. Yet this is a library for personal reading, not public display, and as such, it's the perfect little book-stuffed nook. There's one comfortable chair, parked in the middle of the room, facing the fireplace, with a reading lamp beside it. A pile of cushions on the floor suggests that not all reading is conducted in that chair, and tonight, we make use of those pillows, William shoving the chair unceremoniously aside so we can lounge on the thick Turkish carpet, propped up on pillows.

Dinner is a casual combination of tea and supper, a hodge-podge of whatever looked best from the overflowing cold repast Mrs. Shaw left, supplemented by cookies and fruit I brought. We graze from a floor buffet as we read. It's a library, and so we're reading, stretched out before a roaring fire, bare legs entwined, clothing . . . somewhere. Let's just say that it's a good thing all the food could be served cold, because we hadn't gotten to it quite as soon as expected.

We're reading our respective books as we did at fifteen on those afternoons when it was too wet to walk, and we just wanted to be together. I've missed this, enjoying my book while listening to the soft rustle of William's own pages turning, the faintest snort of a laugh or grunt of displeasure as his story unfolds. Sometimes, Michael would pull out a professional journal while I read my novels, but he radiated energy even while sitting still, and it wouldn't be long before I'd suggest a walk or a bike ride. I loved all the things we *did* do together—reading just wasn't one of them.

One advantage to an actual Victorian library is that it's filled with novels lost to the annals of time. The classics survive, but even William's current read—*The Tenant of Wildfell Hall*—isn't found alongside *Jane Eyre* and *Wuthering Heights* in modern book-stores. Some of the books we consider Victorian classics weren't even widely read in their day. On William's shelves, I find novels I've never heard of, which he assures me were "all the rage" in their time.

I'm enrapt in a book he suggested when a line about a "fair-haired lady in a blue gown" reminds me of the ghost in the moors. An image sparks, that of the light-haired woman in my vision of the pair heading out to the moors. I'd thought the dark-haired woman must be Cordelia, but she wasn't August's wife, which casts the entire conversation into another light.

William said Rosalind loved walking on the moors. Was she the dark-haired woman? Not necessarily. Standing behind them, I couldn't tell which woman had said which lines, and it'd been the light-haired woman who'd laid her fingers on August's arm.

Let's say then that Rosalind was the light-haired woman, and the dark-haired one had been her companion, brought to Thorne Manor to meet William. That works. Yet it doesn't answer the question of *why* I saw them.

My gaze returns to my book, to the line about the fair-haired woman in a blue gown. I picture the ghost I saw fleeing in the moors. She'd had light hair, and while I didn't get a good look at her face, what I did see suggested she'd been a young woman. She'd been at least six inches shorter than me and had a slight figure, wearing a dirt-streaked blue dress decorated with flounces and ribbons.

I picture the fair-haired woman walking out my front door. She's a handspan shorter than the other woman and much smaller in build. She's wearing a shawl over her shoulders, but I catch a glimpse of a skirt. The figures had been opaque, making her dress color indistinct, but it'd been heavily flounced and ribboned.

I remember what William said about Rosalind.

She loved to walk, and she loved to ride, and the moors gave her plenty of opportunity for both.

Cold fingers trail down my spine.

No, that can't be right. The vision doesn't fit with the circumstances of Rosalind's disappearance. She'd gone riding at night, not walking into the midday moors with a friend.

They'd visited here that very day, and we'd departed together, as I needed to return to London.

So Rosalind and August visit William earlier that day. She brings a companion to try catching the bachelor lord's eye. The two women walk into the moors together. Late that night she returns to the moors—had she seen something?—and meets her death.

Rosalind had been staying at the family's country estate, which means she'd likely be riding an unfamiliar horse. What if something in the moors spooked it, and it threw her? What if her *killer* spooked it, and it threw her? The horse panics and bolts, later tumbling off a cliff on its mad gallop home.

"William?" I say.

His gaze rises above his novel with a "Hmm?"

"May I ask you a silly question?"

"Please do. I'm at a rather bleak part of this novel, and a silly question would be a welcome diversion."

"You wouldn't have a picture or portrait of Rosalind here?"

His brows shoot up. "A picture of my friend's dead wife?"

"I said it was a silly question, and it's really just a segue to an even sillier notion." I inwardly apologize to him for the lie I'm about to spin. "There's a legend in High Thornesbury about a woman's ghost that's said to be seen in the moors. I'm wondering whether it arises from the old rumors that Rosalind died near here."

As soon as I see his stricken expression, I curse myself for my insensitivity. For him, this isn't ancient history. It's the recent death of a friend.

I hurry on with, "She's a full-figured brunette. I don't suppose that described Rosalind."

He relaxes and chuckles. "No, it most certainly does not. Rosalind was light haired. As for full-figured? I used to tease that she was terrible advertising for her bakery, looking as if she never sampled her own wares."

"Rosalind was a baker? I thought August was the son of an earl."

"He is, and Rosalind had the lineage to match, but her family name didn't put food on the table. She caused quite the scandal by opening a bakery in London. That's where August met her. He went in to buy sweets for a paramour and walked out forgetting both the sweets and the paramour." William chuckles. "Rosalind led him on a merry chase, but when she finally capitulated, she came with a dowry she'd earned herself."

I remember at breakfast, when I'd made a comment about women and business, August said I sounded like someone. He meant Rosalind.

An ache wells inside me. William isn't the only one who'd have found a kindred spirit in August's wife.

That's when I realize that William has just described the woman in my vision. And the ghost on the moors. Light haired. Slight of build. Rosalind.

My gut clenches.

William doesn't notice my expression—he's on his feet and heading for a bottle of brandy perched precariously on a shelf.

"I'm sorry for bringing up the ghost," I say. "That was insensitive of me."

"Not at all," he says. "I am amused to think they're still talking of ghosts on the moors even in your day. I thought they'd be past that nonsense." He stops, then turns, wincing. "And *that* was insensitive, wasn't it? Obviously, they still believe in ghosts, given your own experience."

His expression is kind, no hint of mockery. This is my chance. Seize the moment and confide—

"I would have thought people would be more enlightened," he says as he pours brandy into two tumblers. "It is bad enough that they believe in ghosts themselves, but to have convinced a child that she was seeing them? Irresponsible."

"I'm the one who thought I saw ghosts, William," I say quietly. "And I wasn't a child."

He turns, wincing again as he brings the brandy over. "I know. I've put my foot down my throat, and now I keep shoving it in deeper. I only meant that I do not blame you one whit for thinking me a ghost. You'd suffered the loss of your uncle, and you were young, and at that age, I half believed in fairies." He smiles and hands me a glass.

I take it and drink a bigger mouthful than I should, gasping as it burns.

He chuckles. "That's stronger than the port. I should have warned you."

He settles in beside me and boosts me onto his lap, and I'm grateful for it, so he doesn't see the disappointment that made me chug my drink. As he nudges my hair aside to kiss my neck, I'm actually glad I didn't tell him about the ghosts. Would I really unburden my secret by telling him that his friend has been trapped on the moors for two hundred years?

I sip the brandy and let it burn away a lick of shame. Someday, I'll tell him. First, though, I need to set Rosalind free.

His lips move up the side of my neck. "I'll wager I know who that ghost on the moor really is." He whispers in my ear. "You."

I give a start. "What?"

He sets his chin on my shoulder. "Those old stories about my mysterious girl of the moors. A voluptuous beauty with sable hair."

"Sable?" When I twist to look at him, my smile is genuine. "That is positively poetic of you, Lord Thorne. I might, er, point out, though, that I suspect you've never seen an actual sable."

When his brows knit, I say, "They're dark brown."

His gaze rises to my medium-brown hair. "Well, that is embarrassing. That's what I get for relying on a word I've only encountered in novels. It's a good thing I never shared the poems I wrote for you. Sable featured prominently."

I slide off his lap. "You wrote me poems?"

"Calling them such may elevate them to a status they did not deserve. They are the terribly earnest odes of a fifteen-year-old boy. There's a reason you never saw them."

I open my mouth to ask whether he still has them. Then my gaze flicks to the fire, which is likely where they ended up after I left.

I smile. "Well, I do wish I could have read them."

"Don't say that, or I may dig them up from whichever book I

stuck them into and force you to read about your sable hair and chestnut eyes, rich chocolate with hints of warm honey. Yes, I freely mixed my metaphors. Also, I might have been hungry."

"The poems are here?" I leap to my feet. "In one of these books?"

"Did I not dissuade you with the threat of atrocious food metaphors? There is also one poem devoted entirely to the sound of your laugh. And, before you decide that's terribly sweet and romantic, there were at least two odes to your breasts."

I sputter a laugh.

"I was fifteen," he says.

"And so you would not compose odes to them now?"

His gaze drops to the body parts in question. "I believe I could compose epic poems to them now."

I grin. "I may hold you to that. For now, though, I want to find these poems." I glance at the massive stacks of books. "Any hints?"

"I believe you'll find one in a copy of Shakespeare's sonnets, as great an insult to the bard as ever there was."

I laugh and dive into my treasure hunt while he reclines on his pillows, calling out clues as he watches me scamper around his library in search of the poems a fifteen-year-old boy once wrote me.

⚜

I'M ASLEEP ON THE LIBRARY FLOOR, CURLED UP IN WILLIAM'S embrace, my dreams dancing with the music of those poems. Yes, they weren't exactly Shakespearean sonnets. To me, though, they're the most perfect odes ever written to young love. After I devoured them, he composed a new one, performance art that still sings through my veins, passion in word and touch and kiss.

When the whisper first comes, it weaves through my dream, a discordant thread that I block. It grows louder, a woman's voice, whispering words that I try to bat away like annoying insects at my ear.

Fool.

Beware.

Danger.

Then . . .

Run.

My eyes fly open to see the pale oval of a woman's face, lips parting in a "Run" that is not the worried urging of the woman in black. This is a sneer spat from a twisted visage. One glimpse of a face that slams me in the gut, a flash of remembered horror from a night twenty-three years ago.

Run.

I jolt upright, heart slamming against my ribs, hands flailing against the specter. But she's no longer there, her face leaving only the faintest impression, a wisp of smoke I can't catch, an image I can't form again in my mind.

When I jump up, William gives a start. As I crouch there, staring, he scrambles, arms going around me and pulling me to him.

"Did you hear something?" he asks, and his words make the hair on my neck rise.

Yes, yes, I did.

Heard something. Saw something. Let me tell you about it. Please let me tell you about it.

He peers around the room. "The kittens don't usually wander from their box, but Pandora can make the most terrible noises. Is that what you heard?"

I swallow hard, keeping my face turned from his.

This is not the time to unburden yourself, not if you fear that the ghost is a woman he knew.

I run my hands over my face. "No, it was just a nightmare."

He pulls me onto his lap, holding me tight, asking whether I want to talk about it. I only shake my head and insist it was nothing.

"Shall we move to a proper bed?" he asks. "That might help you sleep."

The clock strikes five.

"I should probably go home," I say. "Spend a little time with Enigma and return for breakfast."

He tenses, but only for a second before kissing me. "If you're certain you'll be all right . . ."

"I dreamed that she was hurt," I lie. "I'll feel better seeing her before I return for breakfast with you." I pause. "What time do you expect Mrs. Shaw?"

"I stopped by the village yesterday to tell her I won't require her for a few days. She insisted on coming up briefly to prepare meals, but she won't arrive until late morning. By then, I fear I'll also be gone. I must return to Whitby on business. I'll be back by evening. Is that all right?"

"That's perfect. Thank you."

⊗🌱⊗

BY THE TIME I GET HOME, THE SUN IS JUST RISING, AND ENIGMA IS UP, ready to play "pounce on Bronwyn's toes under the covers." So I'm not going back to sleep, which is fine—I have too much on my mind.

First comes kitten-playtime. Then I dress and head downstairs to prepare a hot breakfast for William.

As I cook, I send off a quick e-mail to Freya. I have questions about Rosalind that I might be able to answer with a trip to the village library and archives. Freya has already offered to take me there if I want to know more about William, and this is a fine excuse to accept her offer . . . along with the chance to talk to someone about the ghosts.

Did I actually see a ghost in William's library? I'd been certain of it, but the rising sun tugs doubt in its wake. I've never seen a ghost in his time period. I'd been seized with certainty that it was the same specter who sent me screaming from sleep the night my uncle died, yet I've had no experiences like that since I returned. The woman in black and the boy in the knickerbockers both told me to run, but in warning. The one last night had been pure threat.

Run or else.

The thought of the boy reminds me of the bones in the walls. I push that guilt aside. I need to figure everything out before I report his body.

Is he connected to Rosalind's death? It seems that he should be, but I'm not sure how. There's no boy . . .

An image flashes. August in the dining room, his eyes glowing with pride as he talks of his son. I give a convulsive shiver.

Please do not let that be the answer.

I could check. Pop over to William's side after he's gone, slip into the passageway and see whether the body is there. If it isn't, then it could be August's son, due to perish in a few years, and I can make sure that never happens.

I'll investigate that this afternoon once both William and Mrs. Shaw are gone. For now, I set the boy aside to focus on Rosalind. She is the woman in the moors. I'm sure she is.

Is she also the woman in black?

Another image flashes. Another hidden face. The woman in the shroud.

Is that also Rosalind? I'd been sure the woman in the moors was the same as the one in the shroud, and it does still fit. The strong-willed woman William described could easily be the angry ghost I encountered, frustrated at my inability to understand and help her.

If is it Rosalind, though, then there is one more question I must ask William.

30

We'd agreed that I'd return at eight for breakfast, and I arrive twenty minutes early to find William in the barn. That gives me time to sneak in with my basket of food. I narrowly avoid discovery as he comes charging into the house to change for breakfast. He stops in the entry and inhales, as if catching the scent of food, but after a quick "Bronwyn?" he dashes up the stairs, and Pandora comes in to watch me set the table, accepting scraps of honeyed ham and bacon.

I've cooked a full "American" breakfast. Bacon, ham, eggs, pancakes, hash browns and toast, bringing it all in an insulated bag. I also brought proper coffee, plus orange juice.

The juice proves to be the highlight of the meal along with the maple syrup for the pancakes. He tears through the food with such appetite that I almost wonder whether I brought enough. When I comment, he only remarks that he needs to get rid of it all before Mrs. Shaw returns.

We're nearing the end of the meal when I lift my empty fork, hoping I look as if a thought just struck me. "Speaking of Mrs. Shaw, I was thinking yesterday that I seem to recall another employee of yours. Or perhaps a day laborer? I only remember that he was rather fearsome."

William's brows lift.

I describe the man with the spade, fudging the age by saying that he looked old to me, but of course, when we're young, anyone over forty seems elderly. I barely finish my rehearsed description when William nods and cuts a slice of ham. "That would be Harold. I don't believe I ever thought of him as fearsome, but I suppose he could seem a dour sort."

"Harold?"

"Our head groom. Mrs. Shaw's husband."

My gut twists.

"Are you sure?" I say as lightly as I can. "I thought I'd have remembered if she had a husband."

I describe the man in more detail.

William nods. "That was certainly him. He tended to fade into the background beside his wife, content for her to speak while he tended to his chores. He was an excellent groom. I'm not fond of sharing my stable, but Harold is sorely missed."

"Is he . . . retired?"

"He passed a year ago. That's when I suggested Mrs. Shaw move to the village. Harold liked to be near his stables, but I knew she'd enjoy the company of her grandchildren more."

Harold Shaw died last year. Meaning he was still alive when Rosalind disappeared.

⚜

I RETURN TO FIND AN EMAIL FROM FREYA, INVITING ME TO COME down at any time, and we'll visit the library together. At one o'clock, I'm in the parlor of her picture-perfect cottage. It's tiny, maybe a quarter the size of Thorne Manor, and guilt stabs me at first, thinking of myself knocking around in that huge house, having it all to myself. But one glance around Del and Freya's cottage tells me that the size is a choice. It's impeccably refinished and furnished, suggesting no lack of retirement funds.

This cottage tells the story of a couple happy to live in each other's pockets, and that turns the guilt to envy. I could have this with William. We'd pursue our own interests outside the home, yet when we were there, we'd be happiest in close proximity, doing our own thing, like reading together last night.

I can have that. I only need to give up everything else in my life for it. Give it all up . . . only to resent him later.

No, that will never happen. It can't. Yes, I grieve for what could be, but would I rather not have William at all? What we do have will be wonderful. Just not conventional. Not without challenges. The first of those challenges is ridding Thorne Manor of ghosts, which I'm tackling now. Free the ghosts so I may live there in peace, knowing they're also at peace.

I bring Freya up to speed. When I finish, she reaches for her tea, missing the cup entirely.

"I feel horrible about the boy," I say. "There are bones in my walls, and I'm just . . . leaving them there."

"Rightly so," she says. "Folklore would indeed suggest that moving his bones could disrupt your ability to communicate with him and, more importantly, to help him. Once you call in the police, we'll lose access to his remains."

When I shift in discomfort, she lays a soft hand on mine.

"He will not be there forever, Bronwyn. I know it is difficult, staying in a home that has a boy's remains in the walls."

I give a soft laugh. "Yes, it should be, shouldn't it? The truth is, I've barely thought of that. It feels no different than having his ghost there."

"He is fine for a little longer. He will be finer still if we identify his killer."

That *we* lifts some of the responsibility from my shoulders. We're in this together, and I appreciate that more than she knows.

Freya continues, "I sincerely hope it isn't that poor man's son. I cannot imagine the tragedy that would have been. To lose a wife *and* a son while he's still so young."

"If it is August's son, what happens if I interfere?" I ask. "If I have William bar up that passage so Edmund doesn't die in it?"

"The butterfly effect? Do a good deed in the past and change the world in unexpected ways?" She shrugs. "We have no idea what it will do, but I'm sure that will not stop you from preventing his death."

She's right, of course. If I can save young Edmund, I'll do it.

"We can also look up the boy in the archives," Freya says. "That might give us answers. What was his father's name again?"

"August Courtenay. He was the younger son of an earl."

She goes still. "Courtenay? And his wife's name? The baker?"

"Rosalind."

She lets out a gasp of delight and springs to her feet, gasping again as she massages her hip and chuckles about forgetting not to do that. Before I can speak, she's across the room at a bookshelf. She returns with a box and pulls out a very old journal. When she lays it on the table, she grins, looking like the girl she must have been.

I touch the journal's cover and then carefully open it to find a handwritten recipe book. The name inscribed is Rosalind Hastings, with the Hastings crossed out and replaced with Courtenay.

I stare up at Freya. "This is . . . hers?"

That grin again. "One of my fondest treasures." She sits in her chair. "Rosalind Hastings was a cousin of mine. Many generations past and several times removed. She was something of a family legend. Lady Rosalind, who defied tradition and refused perfectly good marriages to make a living as a baker . . . And there, she not only made her fortune but found an earl's son to marry. Her bakery is still in London today."

"What?"

"She sold it, of course, when she married, but it still bears her name. It does not, however, have this." She taps the book. "This went back into the family. I grew up hearing stories of Rosalind from my grandmother. The one with the Sight. She ran her own business and looked on Rosalind as a role model. She gave me this book when I began baking. When I was young, I adored the story of Rosalind. Thrilling, romantic and, ultimately, tragic. As I grew older, the tragedy stuck with me more. Newly married with an infant son, gone riding at night and tumbled off a cliff." She looks at me. "Which we now realize might not have been what happened at all."

I nod and gather the teacups. Time to go to town and search for answers.

❧

WHEN I TOLD FREYA ABOUT THE MAN WITH THE SPADE, I DIDN'T mention that now I know his name. Mrs. Shaw is Del's ancestor. I presume Harold Shaw is, too. That means telling Freya that her husband's ancestor may have murdered hers, which is just . . . really, really awkward.

My first step, though, is looking up young Edmund Courtenay. I find nothing except proof of his existence—a birthdate and confirmation that his parents were The Honorable August Courtenay and Rosalind Courtenay, nee Hastings. I'd need to do a full records search to get a date of death, and that isn't available at the High Thornesbury archives. I'm both disappointed and relieved. Disappointed because I hoped to find that Edmund Courtenay died a very old man. Relieved because it gives me an excuse not to look up *my* William's death date. I desperately don't want that information. It isn't just fear that I'll see a date sooner than I expect, but the grim reminder that, in my world—*this* world—William is dead. Long dead and turned to dust.

Freya had spoken of August's tragedies, hoping he didn't lose both wife and son. That'd given me pause, thinking, *But his son is alive. August was just talking about him.* To Freya, though, they're both dead even if they lived to be a hundred. A tragedy that has not yet come in William's world is ancient history in mine.

As unsettling as that is, my focus is on a tragedy that has already passed in William's world, and that one I do find in the archives. The death of Rosalind Courtenay. The information I find matches William's account to the last detail.

According to an article from the time, Rosalind was known to ride at night, but had not done so since her pregnancy. She rose to "tend to" her ten-month-old son, which I presume is a euphemism for breast-feeding him, a practice less common than wet nurses in her time and social class. At two a.m., a trio of "carousing youths" spotted her riding out of High Thornesbury, heading up the hill to Thorne Manor. The next day, her horse was found drowned in the ocean ten miles away. Police dismissed the claim of the drunken young men and presumed she'd gone to ride by the ocean, instead, where she'd fallen with her steed. The article also notes that the current resident of Thorne Manor, Lord William Thorne, had entertained the Honorable August Courtenay and his wife earlier in the day, but was already in London when the youths claimed to have seen Rosalind heading to his home. Since Lord Thorne lived alone, this further supported the police's belief that Rosalind had not gone to Thorne Manor. Yet if I am correct, she had. Something drew her back to the manor and the moors, where Harold Shaw followed and killed her.

I hoped for a photograph, and not surprisingly, there isn't one. That article, however, does contain a line that sends a chill through me. When the young men were trying to prove they saw Rosalind, they claimed she was riding a dark horse—which she was—and that the horse dwarfed her small figure, clad in a gown of blue, her blond hair streaming out behind her.

Small figure. Blond hair. Blue gown.

That fits the ghost in the moors. It all fits.

I continue my search but only find references to Rosalind's story in local history books, the sort self-published by someone with an eye for tourism rather than truth. One claims Rosalind is seen riding along the cliff every year, dressed in white, calling for her lost child. Another names William as her killer, the "mad lord of the moors" who slaughtered his entire family, starting with his father . . . who actually died in India on business. When Freya sees what I'm reading, she clicks the browser shut.

"That filth will do nothing but give you nightmares, lass," she says. "If you want the real legend of William Thorne, we'll grab a pint in the pub. The owner knows all the old tales—the true versions."

When I hesitate, she lays a hand on my shoulder. "It would do you good to meet a few people, Bronwyn. Your neighbors wish to respect your privacy, but they're curious. They remember your aunt, and they remember you, and they'd like to say hello."

I flush. "And I've been rudely ignoring them, dashing into town on errands and then dashing home again."

"They understand you've been busy, but stopping by the pub would be a nice gesture. I'm meeting Del for a pint, so I was going to ask you to drop me there anyway."

"Let's get that drink, then. I'm done here."

❧ 31 ❧

The locals joke that the pub—the Hart and Hound—was the first building built in High Thornesbury, the village growing up around it. The Hart and Hound is actually the oldest building in town . . . but it'd started life as a church. The transformation apparently came in the nineteenth century, by which time it had undergone so many changes of use that it was no longer scandalous to house a tavern in a former house of worship. It dates from the fifteenth century, and few traces of its first incarnation remain, the steeple having long since been removed, leaving a rectangular stone building with narrow arched windows.

Those windows don't let in much light, but the cool darkness is a welcome respite from the strong late-spring sun, and we slip inside to find the place empty save for an elderly man at the end of the bar, speaking to a woman behind it.

The woman looks up and steps out to greet us. I barely catch a glimpse of her—tall and slender with a graying blond braid—and then she's enveloping me in a hug, whispering, "It's so good to see you, lass."

I stammer an appropriately vague response, and she laughs, holding me at arm's length.

"You have no idea who I am, do you?" she says.

I stammer more, my cheeks heating.

She leans in for another quick hug, and that's when the smell hits. Her perfume, a floral scent, mingled with the yeasty odor of beer.

"You're—" I begin. "You found me. That night. When my uncle . . ."

"Aye, lass. Out walking my dog, I was, and I heard you crying."

"Screaming, you mean," I say with a wry twist of a smile.

She gives me a searching look. "No, lass. You were just crying. Crying like your heart would break, bent over your poor . . ." She pats my back. "Enough of that. As for not remembering me, your aunt didn't bring you in here. We'd done no more than pass in the street, like a hundred others who stopped to say hello. We remember you far better than you remember us."

She says it kindly, but I flinch, both at *why* they remember me and the reminder that I have been ignoring the locals, using their businesses only for what I needed, as I would in Toronto.

When I apologize, she cuts me off. "You have your hands full with that old house, and everyone who *has* met you says you are as sweet and kind as they remember. Whatever happened up there that night didn't change you, and I'm glad of it."

Oh, but it did. I'm just really good at hiding it.

"We're all so pleased to see you hale and hearty, coming back to us a proper professor, no less. Like your daddy." She swings back behind the bar. "Now look at me talking when I should be serving. What'll you have, lass? And Frey?"

As we place our orders, Freya whispers, "You can ask her about that night if you'd like."

The woman—Daisy—brings our drinks, and I ask about her family instead. We chat for a while before I broach the subject with, "About that night. I-I'm afraid I don't remember much."

"A blessing," she says.

"I just . . . I know what happened afterward . . . I went to a hospital and spent some time there."

Her face hardens, and she flicks a tea towel hard over her shoulder. "I know."

"They helped me forget things, which was useful at the time, I guess, but now I'd like to remember. That night, did I say anything about what drove me outside?"

"The ghost, you mean?"

I try not to flinch.

"You saw a ghost," she says, her voice firm. "Nothing wrong in that. The fault lies with those who made it seem wrong."

"Did I give details? Describe what I saw? What she said?"

"Nowt, lass. Only that she said terrible things and drove you from the house, and then she went after your poor uncle."

After that, conversation drifts. Two men come in, heavy boots tromping mud in their wake. Day laborers, Freya whispers. Daisy serves them and returns to us, and Freya steers the conversation to Thorne Manor, asking whether Daisy knows any good stories for me.

Daisy laughs. "Stories about the Thornes? You'll need to start me somewhere, or I'll be talking all night. We could begin with the first William Thorne, who used to promise a copper to any child who could do a trick that made him laugh. *Everything* made him laugh, and soon High Thornesbury had an entire generation of little circus performers . . . with pockets full of coppers."

I smile, and I'm about to ask for another story when one of the day laborers calls, "Tell her about the mad lord of the moors."

Daisy stiffens as does the old man at the end of the bar. Ignoring the laborers, she says, "Then there was the first lord's wife, who—"

A mug slaps the bar right beside me as one of the day laborers slides into that seat. He's about my age with thinning hair, and he seems to mistake my breasts for eyes, his gaze settling there as he talks.

"Did I hear you're the new owner of Thorne Manor, lass?" he asks.

"Yes," I say, the word brittle.

"Well, then ask our lovely bar mistress about the mad lord, the one who murdered all those girls. Might make you decide to spend your nights elsewhere." He grins, clearly ready to suggest *where* else I could spend them.

Daisy starts to interject, but he continues, leaning in close enough for me to smell tobacco and wet sheep as he whispers, "He murdered his own bride on their wedding night. They say you can still see the blood at night when the moon hits it."

"No, not his wife. 'Twas a lover," his friend says as he ambles over. "Two lovers. A girl he met in the moors—a comely milkmaid —and his best friend's wife, who he was—" He makes a rude gesture.

"Don't forget the sister," the first man says. "Two lovers and a sister, which makes you wonder just how close he was with his sister." His brows waggle suggestively.

"Enough!" The old man at the end of the bar clangs his mug down. "Perhaps they have no love for the old families where you're from, but while you are here, you will respect ours."

Daisy waves for the old man to sit down and says to me, "There are stories about that particular lord, but they're just stories. Entertaining tales to tell over a pint . . . if you aren't in High Thornesbury. Lord Thorne's sister took off for London— with witnesses who saw her off—and his friend's wife plunged over a cliff while he was in London, again with witnesses."

The day laborers grumble and glower. As they wander back to their table, Daisy leans over and whispers, "Those two have been causing trouble all week. You might call and tell Del to come by a little later today. They're usually gone by six."

Freya's mouth sets in annoyance, but she aims it at the two men and then thanks Daisy, saying they will indeed come by later. That's when I realize what Daisy means. I think of Del as a man, but yes, once he speaks, he sounds female, and these two are certain to make something of it.

We finish our pints, and then I drive Freya to a neighbor's, where Del is working on fence repair, and I head home to prepare for my evening with William.

❧❧❧

WILLIAM HAD ASKED ME TO CHECK THE FLOORBOARD BEFORE I CAME over, in case he wouldn't be back in time. I'm not quite sure the logic behind that works, but I do as he requested and find a note . . . one with three simple words: close your eyes.

I laugh and pocket it as I bustle about, getting ready. Enigma sits on the dresser, watching me with a look that so obviously says, "You're going away again, aren't you?"

I've spent the last hour racing through the house with a length of fluffy yarn trailing after me, and I'll pop back this evening for cuddles, but I still feel guilty enough that I almost forget to shut my eyes as I cross. I remember at the last second and put my hands over them for good measure.

The smell of a hearth fire tells me I've crossed, but before I can open my eyes, William's hands go over mine. Then he chuckles, and as he says, "There you are," I'm about to reply when I hear a very familiar kitten mew. His hands slide away, and when I open my eyes, he's scooping up a tiny calico kitten, who purrs against his hand before shooting me a haughty look, as if to say, "See? *Someone* loves me."

"Enigma?" I say. "You crossed over!"

Another look, one that clearly implies that she could have crossed over any time she liked. A *mrrup* from the doorway as Pandora trots in. Seeing her missing kitten, her eyes narrow, and Enigma leaps back into my arms, as if to say, "I'm ready to go now."

I chuckle and lower her to the floor where her mother sniffs her over as Enigma now shoots me a pained look.

"I suspect she hasn't crossed back before because she's happier where she was," William says.

"The center of attention?"

He smiles. "Oh, she was always the center of her mother's attention, to her eternal dismay."

Pandora lifts Enigma by the scruff of her neck, the kitten mewling at the indignity.

"Uh-uh, Pan," William says, taking Enigma away. "This one has flown the nest, and she will be staying with her new person." He hands the kitten to me, and Enigma snuggles in, sneaking looks at her mother.

I'm turning to William when I notice a chair where his dresser should be.

"You redecorated?" I ask.

He curses and slaps a hand to my eyes again. "Bloody cats disrupt everything. Let us try this again."

He turns me around, takes his hand away and waves a flourish around his bedroom. Which is . . . no longer a bedroom. The bed is gone as is his dresser and washbasin. Where his dresser once stood by the fireplace, there are now two chairs, one over-stuffed horsehair, the other looking as if it's been pulled in from the parlor. The red velvet and gold paint chaise longue from the parlor now sits under one window. A writing desk has replaced the bed, and there's a bookshelf beside the desk that has definitely been requisitioned from his library, books still haphazardly stacked in it. He's also relocated the terrestrial globe, the elephant's footstool and the stained-glass floor lamp.

"It's a bit rough." He makes a face. "More than a bit, actually. A muddle of what I could acquire at short notice plus pieces temporarily relocated to give you a sense of my intentions."

"But . . . your bedroom . . ."

"I'm taking my mother's old chambers as I should have decades ago. This one . . ." He shrugs, his cheeks coloring. "This was my connection to you. Part of me always hoped you'd come back and feared I needed to be in this room if you did. Now, I can relocate to a larger room with a bed more suitable for two while giving this one to you."

"To me . . . ?"

"As an office." He walks to the desk. "This isn't the final piece. I know a desk is important—or, I should say, I know it is important to others. I usually do my paperwork by the fire." He points to the chairs. "If it wouldn't bother you, I'd do it here, alongside you. This chair"—he points to the one from the parlor —"is as temporary as the desk. Simply to show you what I have in mind. I will have both a chair and desk built to your specifications."

My first reaction is joy, utter delight at the thought of him making space for me in his life, space that recognizes my career. But then I realize what I'm looking at. A place for me to do my job . . . in his world.

He said that he'd never expect me to live here permanently. Now, I realize that was no more genuine than when he'd said those words as a boy, clearly hoping I'd leap in with the offer to abandon my home and family for him.

When William turns, he is the boy who gave me his first romantic gift—a fancy pen and inkwell, engraved with my name —with a hopeful smile fluttering on his lips, his eyes glittering with expectation, praying he's done the right thing and I will throw my arms around his neck in joy.

I did exactly that then. This time, he sees my expression, and his smile fades. He rubs a hand over his face, beard shadow *skitching* beneath callused fingers.

"I am moving too quickly," he says. "Presuming too much."

"I . . ." I swallow and set Enigma down. Then I step toward him. "I want to be with you, William. Desperately. But there isn't a permanent place for me in your world."

Horror dawns on his face. "You think . . ." He looks around and curses. "Of course you do. You think this is me rearranging my home to welcome you permanently. A place for you to work, pursuing your passions like August giving Rosalind a pretty kitchen to bake his bread, as if that would be sufficient substitute for her livelihood."

He looks at me. "No, Bronwyn. A thousand times, no. You are a historian who studies my world. I don't even know how you'd pursue such a profession while living *in* that world. This isn't meant to replace your career. It's for you to pursue it here when the opportunity affords itself. You said you hope to spend your summers at Thorne Manor, pursing research. I simply thought if that is what you choose . . ." He waves around the room. "I would like to give you a place to do that here, *when* it is convenient for you to do so. Even when you are in Yorkshire, I do not expect you to spend every minute here. I just wanted to accommodate you when you do visit."

I exhale. "Thank you." Another deep breath, and the fear passes, and I can look around the room with fresh eyes. Then, I really do grin and throw my arms around his neck. "It's perfect. Thank you."

He holds me at arm's length. "I said I wouldn't ask or expect you to give up your life to be with me. Let me amend that, lest it seem as if I'm hoping you will. I will not allow you to give it up. I have seen how resentments can fester, bitterness eating away love, and we will not make that mistake. I would quite happily live in your world if that was a choice. Right now, it is not. So we will work out a solution to our rather unique problem, but it will never be one that sees you surrendering your life to share mine. Agreed?"

I entwine my hands in his hair and answer with my kiss.

I can't sleep, and there's no reason for it. No ghost whispers in my ear. My kitten is here, purring at the foot of the bed, finally allowed in after enthusiastic lovemaking that left me satiated and exhausted enough that I *should* be sound asleep. William certainly is. He's dead to the world, a still-life portrait of a beautiful man in repose.

As perfect as his body is, tonight I'm watching his face by the glow of the almost-guttered fire. He looks so happy that my heart lifts. He is as happy as I am, in love, and my head swims with possibilities, possibilities we discussed into the night.

We'll make this work. If Enigma can cross freely, then I can truly make a home on his side when I'm in Yorkshire. And I'll be in Yorkshire whenever possible. Summer term, from May through August. Thanksgiving week in October. Nearly a month over the holidays at Christmas. Reading week in February. I'll stay in my version of Thorne Manor when William is busy, and I'll become part of the community. When he's here, I will be, too. That will be our life together, and I couldn't be happier.

So why am I awake? Something gnaws at my gut, and I want to dismiss it as my worrywart ways, as Michael called them. I could never receive good news without a tiny part of me tensing for trouble.

Something's not right.

Something doesn't fit.

About the ghosts? When I ask the question, a ping in my brain says yes. The theory I've concocted doesn't quite work.

I rise and pad across the room to Lady Thorne's dressing table, again without knowing why. Then, as my fingers touch the cool wood, I remember the engagement notice inside for August and Cordelia.

I slide open the drawer. At the creak, Enigma wakes with a mew and dashes over. I freeze, but William keeps sleeping.

As I lift Cordelia and August's announcement, I see the other picture frame beneath it, the one I'd noticed before August's arrival pulled me away. The photo is upside down with the newspaper clipping stuck to the back. It's another engagement announcement, this one for the impending nuptials of Elizabeth (Eliza) Stanbury . . . and William Thorne.

This is William's engagement announcement.

I chide myself for a dart of jealousy. I did more than get engaged after I left William. I married—very happily. While I'm very glad he isn't married now, I can hardly be jealous of an engagement that never even reached the wedding ceremony.

I read the full announcement. Then, I cautiously turn over the frame, bracing, and rebuking myself again. Can't be jealous of his engagement, and certainly can't be jealous of his fiancé, a girl he didn't love.

Eliza Stanbury isn't my competition. She never was. After that flicker of jealousy, I flinch on her behalf, thinking of what she might have endured after a broken engagement. I feel pity and outrage, too, at the thought of a young woman forced to marry a man who didn't love her, didn't want her, and could say nothing more than that he'd hoped she'd find satisfaction as a mother because he couldn't provide it as a husband.

Eliza is no longer the young woman I'll see in this photo. She'll be middle-aged, like me, married and likely a mother. Yet I still brace for envy, knowing I'll compare myself to this fresh-faced girl and see every deepening line in my own face the next time I look in the mirror. But that's my problem, and I still want to see her. I want to see *him* even more—my William at twenty-three, midway between the boy I knew and the man sleeping across the room.

I reach for my phone to take a photograph of this picture, the substitute for a memory I missed. I turn the frame over, and my gaze shoots to the top. As in the photo of August and Cordelia, William stands slightly behind a chair. His face is rigid and unreadable. Resolute. He may not be thrilled with the marriage to come, but he wants to please his mother, and his lack of enthusiasm for the match has nothing to do with his intended bride.

I touch the line of his jaw, and the curl of his hair, and I smile. It's William exactly as I'd have imagined him at this age, hardening into the man he'd become, but still clinging to the softer boy I remember.

As my gaze slides to Eliza, I struggle to keep that smile in place even as my insides twist. Then I see her face, and a fist hits me square in the gut, air knocked out of me as I jerk back.

It's the woman from the moors.

The woman who died in the moors.

Not Rosalind Courtenay. Eliza Stanbury. William's fiancé.

***

I WANDER BLINDLY BACK TO WILLIAM'S OLD ROOM, ENIGMA AT MY heels, and then, somehow, I'm on my own bedroom floor, still clutching the photograph, as if by looking at it long enough, I'll realize my mistake.

I must be wrong. The woman in the moors has to be Rosalind. It fits.

No, I can *make* it fit. Use the shaky testimony of three drunken youths to tie Rosalind to Thorne Manor and the moors, so she becomes the woman I saw, when it makes far more logical sense that she died with her horse, plunging off the cliff.

The most basic description of Rosalind matches the woman in the moors—light haired and slight of build. But Eliza Stanbury is also light haired and slender.

Then there is her face.

I've never seen a clear image of the moors woman's face, but I've seen enough to leave an impression in my mind. That's why I wanted a photograph of Rosalind. Now, it's a photo that confirms instead that the woman in the moors is Eliza Stanbury.

I struggle to remember William's exact words about his fiancé. I can't because there weren't any. He only said that no marriage came of the engagement. I'd seen pain in his eyes, and I hadn't prodded.

She's dead, William. How did you fail to mention that?

Excuses bubble up, frantic excuses to explain away his omission.

Weak excuses, every last one of them.

He didn't just "not get around" to telling me his fiancé died in the moors. He deliberately omitted that information when it should have naturally arisen.

He murdered his own bride on their wedding night. They say you can still see the blood at night when the moon hits it.

I balk at the memory of the day laborer's words, yet cradled in this twisted legend is a grain of truth.

William's fiancé died, and people thought he did it. When he first told the story of his scandal, I'd been outraged. How could such a ridiculous story arise when there was clear proof to the contrary?

Every story begins with a grain of truth.

That scandal wouldn't have begun unless there was one crime against which he had no clear defense. Not that he killed Eliza, of course. Harold Shaw did. But that's where the story started—the mysterious disappearance of William Thorne's bride-to-be. Then other disappearances piled on later, sticking to him because they suggested a pattern that made the story so much more delicious. Not merely the killer of his bride-to-be, but the killer of three additional women who'd been part of his life.

Yet one fact remains. William deliberately omitted Eliza from his tale, and I need to know why.

As I rise from the floor, Enigma yowls outside my bedroom door. In my fugue state, I hadn't even noticed she'd crossed back with me, and now I absently open the door for her . . . and there's the shrouded ghost.

I fall back with a yelp. Enigma leaps onto me, and her claws dig in as I scoop her up.

The ghost stays where she is. Eliza Stanbury wrapped in her death-shroud. William's fiancé, murdered by Harold Shaw, carried into the moors, buried and forgotten. Pain and pity washes away my shock.

"I'm sorry, Eliza," I say. "I know what happened to you, and I'm sorry."

She only stands there, her shrouded face turned toward me, her figure wavering and indistinct.

"I will find you," I say. "I'll bury you properly and make sure others know what happened."

She lifts a beckoning hand and begins to walk away. I know I'm meant to follow, but I hesitate, cuddling Enigma, our hearts both slamming in our chests.

Eliza turns to me. "Come," she whispers.

"Just tell—"

"See."

Each word is laborious, as if communication saps her energy. She wants me to see something because she cannot explain it in words.

I grab sweatpants, a shirt and sneakers from my room. Then I shut the door on Enigma. The kitten yowls with fury, and I whisper apologies while I hurry after Eliza.

As I step through the door, another figure materializes to my left. It's the woman in black. She moves into my path. Two ghosts, both covered. I'd presume the woman in black was also the shrouded ghost. She is not. The shrouded ghost reaches out. Her fingers brush the woman's veil, and the woman in black fades.

"Soon," Eliza whispers as the other ghost disappears.

I follow Eliza down the hall. There's a shimmer by the linen closet. The boy begins to step out. He's halfway through, shadowed face looking my way. Then he retreats.

"Who are they?" I ask Eliza.

"His others," she whispers.

"His other victims?" I say.

"Wait. Understand."

It's still dark outside. Four a.m. when I check my phone. The moon is bright enough to light my path, and I follow Eliza into the garage. She pauses by the tools and points at a shovel, and my stomach drops.

"You want me to find your body," I say. "I will, but it's still night and—"

The air electrifies in a flashbulb of frustration. She finally has the chance for peace, and I'm complaining about darkness and hard work.

I tuck my cell phone into my pocket and then pick up the shovel and follow Eliza into the moors. When she tries to veer off path, I firmly refuse. I will help *without* dangerous shortcuts.

Finally, we must leave the path to head into the bog. I pick my way through the night-dark wetland until I reach the spot she indicates. Then I dig.

Unearthing a corpse always seems so much easier in the movies. Of course, in the movies, it's usually done by a fit young man, not a thirty-eight-year-old history professor who hasn't lifted a dumbbell since grad school ... and even then, only to keep her fiancé company.

The wet ground means it's easy to break the surface. It also means the earth is as heavy as lead. Soon, I'm drenched in sweat. I'm about to take a third break when my shovel strikes down with a dull thump.

I kneel, cell phone propped to shine on the spot as I scoop dirt by hand. One nail breaks. Then another. I keep going. Soon I have uncovered fabric. Beneath that fabric lies the hard mummified flesh of a corpse buried in a bog.

The sheet is blackened with age, and it's stiff around Eliza's body, but it's clearly the same one that shrouds her ghost. I keep clearing until I see blackened flesh. It's the hand I saw when Harold had been carrying Eliza, that hand fallen partially loose from its bindings. Now, it's almost entirely freed.

Eliza whispers behind me, and I give a start, having almost forgotten she's there. What must it be like, seeing her blackened corpse uncovered?

"I'm sorry," I murmur. "I don't mean to disturb—"

"Truth," she says. "Only truth."

All that matters is the truth. I nod. I keep clearing, and she whispers, "The ring."

I look down at the blackened hand. There's no sign of a ring on those wizened fingers, but they're still partly covered by the sheet. I prod it back even as my brain warns I'm disturbing a crime scene. I only need to move it a little, though, before I see a gold ring inlaid with a huge sapphire and flanked by diamonds.

My fingers move to my throat, to touch a necklace that's not there. Yet I can still picture it. Sapphires and diamonds, the setting a perfect match to this ring.

William must have given the ring to Eliza. It's part of a set. My stomach twists at the thought, but once again, I chide myself for my jealousy. He gave his grandmother's ring to his fiancé, probably on their engagement. He might also have planned to give her the necklace on their wedding day. If I'm uncomfortable receiving a gift meant for his future bride, I can broach the subject with him later. This is about Eliza.

"The ring," she says.

I nod. "This proves who you are. It'll help."

"My grandmother's ring."

I turn to look at her. *My* grandmother? She must mean it would have been her grandmother by marriage.

I nod. "I'm sorry, El . . ."

I trail off. Freya speculated that once I named the ghosts, they'd come clear and could communicate clearly. Yet I've been calling this ghost Eliza, and she can still barely utter a word.

Is that because I need to say her full name? If so, wouldn't she have *told* me that?

Name me.

A shiver runs down my spine. I open my mouth to say her full name, and then I stop, remembering Freya's other theory—that I might only ever have one chance.

I'm sure, though, aren't I? Certain this is Eliza?

No. No, I'm not.

I look down at the ring.

My grandmother's ring.

My heart pounds as I claw dirt from the body, exposing the shroud. Near the head, a piece has fallen away, showing hair beneath it. One dark curl of hair. The world tilts and fades, and I see two women walking out my front door, arm in arm.

I look up at the ghost. I can't judge her height or size—she wavers too much for that. But this shroud beneath my fingers doesn't cover a short, slender woman. She's tall and sturdy . . . like the dark-haired figure in the vision. Like the dark-haired young woman in a photograph, sitting beside August.

"Cordelia," I whisper. "I name you Cordelia Thorne."

The shrouded ghost sighs and sinks with relief, the steel melting from her spine. As it does, she shimmers, and her shroud falls free. Beneath it is the young woman from her engagement portrait, wearing a pale blue dress with delicate white flowers.

Her eyes glisten, bright blue eyes, so like her brother's. Her chin dips, and her voice is tear-choked as she says, "Thank you."

"I'm going to figure this out. I know he killed you. I know someone killed Eliza, too, and I'm not sure—"

"Him. It was all him," she says, her voice coming clear. "He killed us. Teddy, Eliza, me and . . ." Her eyes glisten with fresh tears. "That is why I appeared to you. To show you. To warn you."

I don't tell Cordelia that her killer is long dead. She must not realize how long it's been. Instead, I say, "Teddy?" as the name tickles a memory.

She nods. "The boy in the knickerbockers, you called him. He was the first. I have told myself it was an accident, but I fear . . ." An audible swallow. "I fear that even after all he has done, I still love him too much to accept the truth."

Those moths gnaw at my insides. I force myself to remain

calm. "Yes, I understand he was part of your household. You knew him a long time and doubtless had formed an attachment."

Her brow furrows.

"I've seen him," I say. "A ghostly image of him. Harold Shaw. Your head groom."

She stares at me. "Harold? Harold didn't murder us." She meets my eyes. "It was my brother."

"W-William?" I say.

Cordelia moves toward me, her hands outstretched. "I'm so sorry. When I was a child, I saw you with him. I did not understand how that was possible. I still don't quite understand. Time . . . shifts. I am there, and I see you with him, and then I am here, and he is not."

She rubs her eyes. "That doesn't matter. What matters is that he can hurt you, as he hurt us."

I shake my head. "You've made a mistake."

My voice doesn't waver. It's no timid plea for her to be wrong. She is. I know that in my gut. Of course, when I think that, my brain kicks in, like a debate team captain throwing out challenges.

Can you be sure? You've only known him a few days.

That's a poor attempt, laughable, even. I've only known the man of thirty-eight for a few days. I knew the child for years. I knew the adolescent for a summer.

In the course of a lifetime, a summer is a fleeting moment, yet even these last few days are worth months of casual acquaintance, building on an already solid foundation.

I *know* William Thorne.

You may feel as if you do, but can one person ever really know another?

Yes, they can. After years of marriage, Michael could still surprise me, but it was trivial things, like discovering he didn't care for mango. No fundamental revelation of character surprised me. I knew him at that level. And I know William the same way.

You wouldn't be the first woman to say that and be proven wrong. Does that make you better than them? Smarter? Wiser?

This one makes me flinch. I had a colleague, a woman I considered a friend, who'd discovered her husband had been stalking his former intern. My friend had steadfastly denied it, breaking down in tears, pleading with me for help. But I knew her husband, and I'd endured his attentions myself. So when his wife defended him, I judged her. I would never make this mistake. I would never be so blind to my lover's faults or so quick to defend him.

Is that what I'm doing here?

My gut says William is innocent.

My brain agrees, but warns me to tread with care.

And my heart? My heart is the timidest of all, retreating behind a stone wall of "Please let him be innocent," hastily erected fortifications in case I'm wrong.

Cordelia isn't falsely accusing her brother. There's pain in her voice and in her eyes, deep and agonizing pain. She thinks her beloved brother murdered her, and she has suffered nearly two centuries under the weight of that horrible conviction.

"It wasn't William," I say. "I saw Harold carry your body here to bury you."

Fresh pain. "Harold loved my brother. We all did. William is difficult, and he is hard, but that only makes the prize all the sweeter. When he smiles, the skies open overhead, and the sun shines only on you."

That is indeed the allure of falling for a difficult man. It's the siren's call of a million literary bad boys. They're a challenge. Winning them is so much better than gaining the heart of a sweet boy who turns his smile on everyone.

Except William is no literary bad boy. When August compared him to Heathcliff, William scoffed. Rightly so. Heathcliff was an egocentric, obsessive sociopath who would destroy his supposed true love rather than see her happy without him. There's no evil in William. He's hard and difficult, but the villagers adore him, and he earned their love through genuine goodness.

"I saw—" I begin.

"You saw Harold with my corpse. You saw a loyal family pet helping his master. William killed me in a rage, and Harold cleaned it up for him. Buried me and let William tell the world I'd walked away. That we'd argued, and I left."

Cordelia and I had a falling out many years ago. I have not seen her since. I regret that, but . . . Perhaps we could change the subject?

I want to ask Cordelia how she died, but first I must speak to William. Hear his story, untainted by her version of events.

Am I saying I think she might be right?

No, I'm not. Yet there may be a tragic grain of truth here. Not that William put his hands around Cordelia's neck and strangled the life from her, but that they argued, and something happened, and she accidentally died.

"You doubt me," she says.

"I don't doubt that you think William—"

Her frustration lashes like an electric whip. When I stagger back, her eyes widen in horror, and she hurries toward me.

"I am sorry," she says. "I don't know how I do that. It isn't intentional. But I need you to understand. I have two deaths on my conscience, and I cannot bear a third."

"Two deaths," I say. "Teddy and Eliza. You believe William killed them as well."

"You do not understand my brother, Bronwyn. You please him now, and so you see only the best of him. You are a plaything, an amusement, a trifling."

I must flinch, because she surges toward me again, saying, "I'm sorry. That sounds cruel, but if I must be cruel to save you, then I will. Teddy adored William, and my brother enjoyed the attention . . . until he did not. He tired of Teddy, and Teddy did not tire of him. So William claimed that Teddy went for a walk alone in the moors and never returned. Then there was Eliza. At first, William thought her sufficiently dull and plodding, no threat to his freedom. He would marry her and live the life of a country lord with his horses and his mistresses and a dutiful wife to manage his household. But Eliza pursued William like a lovesick boy intent on winning a shy maiden. She stole what he values most—his privacy. Like Teddy, she would not leave him be. I tried to reason with her. The day she died, I took her walking in the moors to give him time without her, but we became separated—I'm convinced William had a hand in that. She was lost in the moors, just like Teddy. She was never found again, just like Teddy. William killed her, just like—"

Her gaze rises over my shoulder, and her blue eyes harden.

"No," she spits. "No, you will not."

She stamps one foot, glowering into the predawn moor. I turn, following her gaze, and there is Harold, the head groom. He stands ten feet away, spade gripped in both hands, gaze fixed on her.

"No!" She lunges at him, but stops short, as if afraid to go closer. "Have you not done enough?"

He doesn't move. Just stands there, empty gaze fixed on Cordelia. Then he raises the spade and slams the pointed tip into the earth, and she screams.

She screams . . . and disappears.

I wheel on Harold. "She's right. Haven't you done enough?"

"No." His voice comes like the rasp of a file on metal. "I have not."

He lifts the spade from the earth and walks away, fading as he goes.

☙❧

THERE'S NO POINT IN LINGERING. THE GHOSTS ARE GONE. I MAKE note of my surroundings so I can find Cordelia's body. Then I return to the house.

Once back, I gather the items Freya suggested for summoning ghosts. I work quickly—it'll be dawn soon, and I'll lose my chance if I tarry.

I sit cross legged on the floor outside the linen closet. I leave

Enigma in my room—I don't want her frightened if I succeed. *When* I succeed. I'm determined to do so.

For two hours, I attempt to summon the spirits of the woman and the boy. I even use Teddy's name. It does no good.

I'm about to give up when I hear the softest sound of a boy crying. I throw open the linen closet door, but the noise seems to come through an open window. I hurry down the stairs and out the front door, following the soft crying around the side of the house, and there is the boy. He's wearing the same outfit as his ghost—the baggy knickers and white shirt. He sits beside the house, his head on his knees.

I hurry over and bend in front of him.

"Teddy?"

He doesn't lift his head. Doesn't pause his quiet sobs.

"Teddy?" Another voice says behind me. It's an older boy's voice, high and musical.

I turn to see a fair-haired boy of about twelve jogging toward us. He bends beside Teddy and puts a hand on his knee. Teddy looks up, swiping away the tears, his face a mask of mortification.

"I—I wasn't—" Teddy begins.

"It's the hay, isn't it?" the boy says. "It always makes my eyes water. I swear William knows it, and that's why he works so much in that blasted barn, hoping if the hay bothers me enough, I'll leave him alone."

The older boy smiles, but Teddy only drops his head. "He doesn't want you to leave. He likes you, August. You're his friend."

"So are you," August says. "But William and I are of an age, and there are things we can do that you cannot. Like riding into Whitby for the day. William could have been kinder when he said you couldn't join us. I've already told him that, and he feels badly."

August lowers his voice conspiratorially. "Bad enough, I suspect, to bring you a treat." He shifts on his haunches. "When William is brusque, do not take it to heart. If I did, our friendship would have died ages ago. He gets so caught up with his blasted horses that he snaps at any distraction—you, me, even Cordie."

August pushes to his feet. "Speaking of little Cordelia . . ."

He shades his eyes, looking around.

"Harold!" August calls, and I see the groom rounding the back of the house. "Have you seen Cordelia? William and I are going to Whitby, and Teddy here is in need of a playmate."

Harold nods. "I believe she's playing in her room. I can take the lad up."

August's hand moves to Teddy's shoulder, as if he's ready to say no, he'll take the boy to Cordelia. Before he answers, though, the figures fade, and I'm left alone at the side of the house.

I turn toward the old stables, and I see myself inside, leaning into a stall while William brushes an ancient pony. It's the summer I was fifteen, and I hadn't been visiting for long. This is the only pony in the herd, and all the other horses are at pasture.

"He's too old to be with the others," William explains. "I let him out when they come in, but he's happiest right here. There's a run he can use to get some sun." A pat on the pony's withers. "That's all he wants at his age—a bit of sun, a bit of attention and an apple or two, mashed up so he can eat it."

"How old is he?"

"Thirty-three."

I whistle. "That's *ancient*. I remember you used to have a pony, but this isn't him."

"No, this one belonged to . . ." A half-shrug. "A boy I knew. Theodore. His family has a summer home on the other side of the village. Teddy was three years younger than me, so he mostly played with Cordie, but he liked to follow me around."

"Just like Cordelia?" I said, smiling.

"Exactly like Cordelia. Between the two of them, I scarcely had a moment to myself all summer. When I was twelve, I resolved to be firmer. I enjoyed riding with him, but there are limits to how long a twelve-year-old wishes to play with a nine-year-old. As it turned out . . ." His hands tightened on the brush. "He only wanted a little of my time, and I was a selfish brute."

I moved beside him. We hadn't shared that first kiss yet, so my fingers only hovered over his arm, not daring to touch more than the folds of fabric. "What happened?"

William swallowed. Then he said, his voice low, "He wanted to play in the moors. I said I was busy, and when he pressed, I became . . . brusque. So he went alone. I did not realize that, of course. If I had, I would have gone after him. He didn't know the moors the way Cordie and I did. I should have paid more attention. I did not and . . ."

A sharp intake of breath as he set aside the brush and turned to me. "We searched for days. All they found was his coat by the bog."

I gasped, hand flying to my mouth.

"Yes," he said darkly before turning back to the pony. "He was alone out there, and it was my fault."

I argued with him, and I could tell others had done the same, but that would never change how he felt, never abolish the guilt.

"This was his pony." William's lips quirked in a strained smile. "Teddy was a terrible rider, but he did love this old beast. After he passed, his parents planned to put the pony down. I offered to take him. He has a place here for as long as he lives."

He reaches over to pat the pony's piebald neck. "I am also far more tolerant of Cordelia's demands on my time, as you might imagine. As Mother reminds me, Cordie will be grown and married soon enough, and then she'll want little to do with her older brother. I should enjoy her adoration while it lasts. And I do. I have learned my lesson."

I stand there, at the side of the house, staring at the barn. Then I run inside and up the stairs to the secret passage.

WILLIAM THOUGHT TEDDY HAD BEEN LOST IN THE MOORS, BUT I know exactly where he is, and I think I know what happened to him. Harold took him upstairs to see Cordelia, but he never got to her room. Harold showed him something guaranteed to catch a young boy's attention: a secret passage.

I'm in the passage, shining my flashlight down the hole, and seeing nothing more than I did before. I want to get a better look at what the small body is wearing, to confirm that it's the knicker-bockers Teddy wore in the vision.

I need a stronger light. In the garage, there's a corded trouble light Ronnie used to see under my car. I'll get that and an extension cord.

Before I go, I try one last time, leaning into the hole as far as I dare.

My flashlight beam catches on those boot buttons again. I strain to remember Teddy's boots in the vision. Had he—?

Something hits me between the shoulder blades, sharp and fast and hard. My hands shoot out, dropping the flashlight as I instinctively grab for the edge. My fingers slide over wood, and then I'm clawing, madly clawing as I fall headfirst down the shaft.

34

I slam into the bottom. Pain explodes through me, and my first thought is: I am dead. I've hit the stone foundation headfirst, and I am dead.

I'm lying on my side, pain coursing through my head, my shoulder, my hip. I managed to twist as I fell, and I'm not sure what part hit first. Everything hurts, but I can move. I am alive.

I try to push up on one arm and—pain rips through it. Fresh panic sparks. I've fallen fifteen feet onto stone. I've broken my neck or snapped my spine, something that means I can't rise. I'll never rise again. I'm trapped here in the walls of Thorne Manor, paralyzed—

My arm quivers and screams with pain, but my foot strikes the wall with a dull thud. I focus on moving my foot, and it hits the wall with another thud. I fall back to the floor, exhaling in relief.

In the event of spinal injury, do not move the victim. I've read that countless times, yet I have no idea why it's so dangerous to move. Books never explain that part, and I barely passed high school biology.

But if I don't move, I'll be trapped here, pinned between these walls, my damned phone left in the kitchen—

Take a deep breath . . .

Pain sears through me as I inhale.

I pause and focus. Is it sharp pain, as if a lung is pierced? Another careful breath. No. It's the duller pain of injured muscles.

Relax and focus.

Do not panic.

Do not go into shock.

Is it possible to go into shock from a fall? Again, I have no idea. Just one more thing to worry about, one more specter looming over me.

Specter . . .

Had an intruder snuck up behind me? That makes more sense than "a ghost pushed me," but I would have heard footsteps. I would have felt the heat of living flesh through my thin shirt.

Does it matter who pushed me? Not right now.

I need to stand. If my spine is injured, surely my body will send a warning shot of pain to tell me to stay still.

I'll take it slow. Put my hand down, brace myself and lift—

A twinge of pain as my wrist snaps back, my hand half-resting on a rounded stone. I brush that aside, and it clatters across the ground, a hollow sound that prickles the hair on my neck. Beneath me, I feel more rocks and sticks, and I reach down to touch one. My fingers run over a sharp broken end and down the smooth sides.

I go still, my heart pounding. I tentatively find the "stone" again and run my hands along to discover it's the bulbous end of a bone. An arm bone shorter than my forearm.

The bone of a half-grown child.

I hunt for my flashlight, flinching each time I touch bone. When my hand slides over a smooth globe, my breath hitches. My fingers find the eye sockets, the missing jaw, extinguishing any doubt of what it is.

I reverently set the skull aside and keep feeling for my flashlight. I find it lying atop half-rotted fabric. When I flick the switch, nothing happens. I smack it against my hand . . . and it blinks on.

The beam illuminates bones and clothing. The remains of a nine-year-old boy.

Hands trembling, I force myself to examine the bones, searching for some sign of how Teddy died. There's a depression in the skull, and several of the vertebrae have separated. The last might mean nothing—no tissue connects them, and my fall could have jolted them apart. That skull depression isn't as damning as it seems, either. It could indicate a blow to the head, or it could simply be from the fall. Either way, Teddy didn't die slowly, trapped in here, alone and afraid. I can banish that horror from my mind. His body was dumped here.

Harold led Teddy upstairs, murdered him and dumped his body in the hole.

Why? I have no idea, and it doesn't matter. No one will stand trial for this murder. I already suspect Harold of Eliza and Cordelia's deaths. What do all three have in common? They interfered with Harold's favorite, his young master. They pestered William and would not leave him be, and while no sane person would kill for that, it's a motive if I need one.

There is another suspect, though . . .

In my mind, I replay the visions, seeing August watch Cordelia and Eliza go into the moors, seeing him seem to tell Harold that he'd take Teddy to Cordelia.

I shake off the thought. Right now, none of this matters. Teddy may not have died trapped between these walls, but I'm trapped here now. While Freya is coming for tea tomorrow, she knows I can step between worlds. If she finds an empty house, she'll presume I'm with William. If I never return, she'll think I stayed with him.

I'm not the only one trapped, either. I locked Enigma in my room. I do keep a water bowl upstairs, but it was empty this morning, and I forgot to refill it.

How long will she live without water?

How long will I?

Stop. Just stop.

I squeeze my eyes shut, and when I push to my feet, I forget to take it slow. Pain rips through me, but by that point, I'm upright, and if I've damaged anything, it's too late. Yes, everything hurts, but everything works, and that's the important part.

I shine the flashlight around. I'm trapped between the inner and outer wall. I'm also between two upright studs, about eight feet apart. A sliver of space so narrow I can't turn sideways.

Deep breaths. The pain in my ribs is subsiding, and I *can* breathe. Good enough.

It doesn't take long to explore my narrow space. There's a solid stone wall on the outside, thick beams on each end and the interior wall in front of me. Above is the hole I fell through . . . fifteen feet over my head.

I eye the interior wall. If there's a chance of breaking through, this is the spot.

I slam my shoulder into it . . . and hiss in pain, the sound echoing through the empty space. I kick with everything I have, but there isn't room to draw my leg back more than a few inches. I slam my fists into the wall, and I don't even dent it.

I need a tool, and there's only one here. My stomach clenches as I pick up a thigh bone, and I stop several times, unable to do it. But then I remember Enigma, trapped in my room. I swing the bone against the wall . . . and it snaps in two, and I stand there, holding the broken pieces, realizing I've desecrated Teddy's remains, and I slump to the floor, hot tears streaming down my face.

I scream, then. I scream because I am *not* alone. A spirit pushed me into that hole, and it's here, watching me, gloating, and I curse and scream at them until my throat is raw.

"Show yourself!" I shout for the dozenth time, my voice a raspy whisper.

A cry answers. Not a human one. Enigma hears me shouting and banging and calls back a yowl of fear. Then a bang, as if she's thrown herself against the door. Another bang, and fresh tears come as I whisper for her not to worry about me. Just be calm. Please be calm.

The yowling stops, and I exhale in relief. Then I square my shoulders.

"Show yourself," I say. "I know you're here. You pushed me down that hole."

The air ripples beside me, and I jump. I shine the flashlight to see nothing but blackness. Then I make out a form. Black on black, only half materialized.

"No," the word comes soft.

"No?" I look where her eyes should be, behind the shimmering black that shrouds her. "So, you didn't push me?"

"Never."

This is not Cordelia. So, who could it be? The answer comes in a heartbeat.

"You have reason to want to harm me, though," I say.

"I could. Yet I do not."

I stand tall and say, "I name you Eliza. Lady Elizabeth Stanbury."

The figure shimmers, and the blackness enshrouding her falls away until I see the young woman from the engagement photograph, slight and fair, dressed in the blue dress she'd worn, fleeing her killer on the moors.

I open my mouth to ask what happened to her. Before I can, she cocks her head, gaze shifting as if listening to something I can't hear. Then she smiles. "The kitten. Of course. Clever kitten." She turns to me. "Go to him. Save him."

She pushes me. Reaches out and gives me a hard shove that topples me backward, staring in disbelief as I slam down onto the ground, pain knifing through me, the flashlight flying from my hand. When I lift my head, everything's dark.

She tricked me. Damn it—I knew better. Eliza was William's fiancé. She'd loved him, and she had every reason to hate me, every reason to push me down that hole.

I reach for the flashlight, but only touch down on bone. I rock forward, tears filling my eyes as I howl in rage and despair.

When my voice breaks, I still hear my howl, echoing as if through the entire house. It stretches longer than an echo should. Higher pitched, too. And it's coming from the other side of the wall.

"Enigma?" I croak.

That isn't possible. I know I left her locked in my room.

Thunder rolls through the house, and I back against the stone wall.

"Bronwyn?" The thunder becomes running footfalls.

I know that voice. I know my name in that voice, as little sense as it makes to hear it in my world.

"Enigma!" William says. "I cannot hear her with your yowling." The kitten stops as he says, "Bronwyn!"

I bang on the wall. "I'm here. I fell down the hole in the passage."

"Hold on. I'll get an ax."

I say no, just get a rope, and I'll climb out, but he's already gone. Then I call again, to tell him where to find an ax in my garage, because that's where he must be—in my time somehow. He's already gone, though, and so I sink to the ground, and when I do, a smell rises, one that wasn't there before.

The smell of death.

I reach out one tentative hand toward the femur I dropped. My hand touches bone, but it isn't the smooth knob from before.

It's darker than it was earlier, and when I look up, I see the hole is covered.

William didn't cross over. *I* did.

I remember Eliza's words.

The kitten. Of course. Clever kitten.

Go to him.

Hearing me screaming, Enigma had crossed through the stitch to get William's help. The problem, of course, was that I was still on my side. Eliza solved that with her shove, literally pushing me through time.

It only takes a few minutes for William to find an ax, and then he makes sure I'm well away as he chops through the wall. As soon as the hole is big enough, he rips it larger, calling, "Bronwyn!" as if I might be gone.

I stagger forward, and then he's halfway into the wall himself, his arms going around me as I fall against him, sobbing.

35

Villiam and I sit on the floor in his parlor. I huddle against him, his arms locked around me until I can breathe again, think again, move again. When I attempt the last, I gasp in pain.

"The fall," he whispers.

He kneels beside me, feeling my arms and my chest. He has me breathe as he examines my ribs, and then he tests my limbs. I could tell him they're all fine, but I want a few minutes to bask in his anxious ministrations.

How long has it been since anyone cared when I hurt myself? Since I could stub my toe or wrench my shoulder and have someone cluck over me, offering painkillers and bandages. It's such a simple thing, a childish thing, but it's meaningful in a way I never realized until it was gone, one of the thousand things I lost when Michael died.

So, I accept William's coddling and his promises of cold compresses and hot tea, and I only draw the line when he insists on bringing the doctor.

"How would you explain me?" I begin.

"I don't care. I'll pay the physician enough that he won't, either."

I shake my head. "No offense to Victorian medicine, but I'll visit a doctor in my world. For now, you've treated enough horses to diagnose a broken rib or sprained ankle, and I have neither. There's something more pressing we need to discuss."

I pause. Then I throw my arms around his neck, hugging him tight, my face buried against his shoulder as I compose myself for what will come next.

Cordelia thinks that William murdered her. Murdered Teddy and Eliza. She came to protect me, warn me against him. Yet here I am, hugging him as if none of that ever happened.

Because she is wrong. Mistaken. My task here is to set Cordelia straight. Lift the burden she's suffered under for nearly two centuries, believing her brother killed her.

With William silently following, I return to the kitchen, take a lantern from a shelf, and shine it through the hole in the wall. I motion for him to look inside. He does. Then he stands there, perfectly still, as the grandfather clock ticks into the silence. When he withdraws, he staggers, and I steady him.

"Teddy," he whispers. "The clothing. There's enough . . ."

"I'm sorry," I say.

"He was here the whole time. In the walls of . . ."

He shudders convulsively, and I guide him to a chair. He drops into it with a thump, and then tugs me to him. I ease onto his lap, and his arms go around me as deep, shuddering sighs roll through him.

After a minute, he says, "No one checked there. No one thought . . . They didn't know about the passage, and I didn't consider . . . I'd never shown it to him. I was past that age by the time we met. He must have found it, fallen down the hole and broken his neck."

I give him a moment and then ask gently, "May I ask about the day he disappeared? I'm sorry if I sound like a police constable. I'm trying to figure things out and—"

"You don't need to explain, Bronwyn. You may ask anything of me."

"That day, August was over, and you two were planning to ride into the town."

A flash of confusion, as if wondering how I know, and then a nod, accepting that I do.

"We were riding to Whitby," he says. "August's family was staying with us for a few days, and we'd planned a trip to town. Knowing August was here, Teddy had his father, Lord Wakefield, drop him by. We couldn't possibly take him all the way to Whitby, and I was annoyed at Teddy for inserting himself into my weekend with August. I was . . . sharper than I should have been."

"August tried to smooth things over."

"As usual. Poor August. He's spent his life mediating between me and the world. Yes, August told me I'd been overly sharp. Then he went to console Teddy and explain the situation in a gentler manner."

"He suggested Teddy play with Cordelia."

William nods. "Harold said Cordie was in her room. He sent Teddy up, but the boy evidently no longer wished to play with a girl two years his junior. Cordelia said he never knocked on her door. We thought he'd come back down and gone into the moors. That's what he wanted us to do when I snapped at him. His coat was gone, so we presumed . . ." He swallows. "He must have found the passage instead."

I walk to the wall, step through and shine the lantern around. William stands at the entrance while I finish my examination.

"The hole is covered," I say, lifting the lantern overhead. "If Teddy opened it and tumbled in, it would still be open."

"It was closed the last time I was in there, though that was before Teddy disappeared." He frowns in thought. "I believe I was about ten. I spooked Cordie by scratching on the walls, and she was so frightened, I never did it again. The hole was definitely covered."

"It's still covered now," I say. "It broke in my timeline. Also, you found his coat by the bog, right? That isn't possible if he fell through and died."

"You think someone . . . ?"

William sways, looking ill. Then he straightens, pushes into the tight gap and bends before the bones. I pass him the lantern. He examines the boy's body with deft, sure hands, and I remember the fifteen-year-old boy who'd pored over medical books, both equine and human, half practicality and half personal interest. In another time period, when a lord's role was not so clearly defined, he'd have become a doctor or, more likely, a veterinarian. He never had that chance, but he knows what he's doing now.

After he's done examining the remains, he backs out of the wall. "With the tissue gone, it's impossible to tell what killed him. It seems to have been the fall, though. He landed on his face, striking his forehead and breaking his neck. Yet it seems, given the boards over the hole, that the fall wasn't accidental. Someone pushed him and then planted his coat in the moors."

"He was murdered." I pause. "Like someone else who apparently was lost in the moors." I look up at him. "Tell me about Eliza."

A spasm crosses his face, and I reach to grip his forearm. "I know the story, but I need to hear it from you, William. I'm sorry." I take a deep breath. "So Eliza went into the moors . . ."

A moment's hesitation. Then he lowers himself onto a chair near the stove. "Yes, she went into the moors with Cordelia. They became separated, and we launched a search. We did not find her. At the time, I thought she'd fled an unwelcome marriage. I was not the most ardent of suitors. To be blunt, it was like mating a stallion with a mare. A business arrangement. I tried to be kind to Eliza, but I had no interest in wooing her. She . . ."

He glances my way. "I wanted what I had with you—someone who could be not only my marital partner, but a true partner, a friend and a lover. Eliza was not you. There would be no friendship between us. Nor, to be indelicate, did I fancy her as a lover. I would do my duty and father children, but I expected I'd slake my appetites elsewhere as discreetly as possible. I realize that shows me in the worst possible light, my only excuse being that I was young and a selfish cad."

"You believed that Eliza realized you would never love her, so she snuck off through the moors? Caught a train to some new life?"

"I hear the incredulity in your voice, Bronwyn, but I seem to recall we share an affinity for popular novels where such things happen with alarming frequency. I do not know what happened to Eliza, but yes, I have long realized she never left the moors. That she perished."

"Like Teddy."

He flinches and nods, his gaze down.

"And your sister? Did she disappear into the moors, too?"

His head jerks up, brows creasing. "Cordelia? No. My sister left."

"Tell me more about that. Specifics, please."

He sighs, running a hand through his hair as he settles back. "Yet another story that shines an unflattering light on me, I'm afraid. Cordelia and I argued. A terrible row during which I told her to leave. She said she didn't have any money. I emptied my safe—a small fortune—slammed it down in front of her and rode off into the moors. She took the money along with her things."

"And someone saw her depart?"

"Half the village spotted our coach speeding away. Harold took her to the rail station himself."

I pause. Then I steel myself and say, "Do you remember when I asked whether you thought I was a ghost? Your reaction suggested—very strongly—that you don't believe in them."

"I don't. Tales for so-called spiritualists who bilk the grieving with ridiculous table tapping. August and I have argued on this point. He's quite enraptured by the idea of spiritualism, but I have no patience with it. The dead are buried and . . ."

He slows as his gaze turns to me. I don't speak. I can't. I'm holding myself too tight, fingers digging into my knees, every muscle tensed.

He knows what's coming. I see it in his face, dawning realization that this is no idle change of subject.

"I see ghosts," I say flatly. "No table-tapping. No ectoplasm or spirit slates. I've studied Victorian spiritualism, and you are correct. Fakery, all of it. Preying on the grief stricken. But I have seen ghosts in this house. That's why my mother took me away and had me committed. It wasn't about you. I encountered a ghost, and my uncle came to my aid, and"—I swallow—"he died falling from the balcony."

William reaches for my hands. As he grips them, they tremble.

"Since I've been back . . ." I inhale. "There is a boy. He's about eight or nine. I never see his face, but he has dark hair with a cowlick, and he's dressed in knickerbockers."

Color drains from William's face.

"That's Teddy, isn't it?" I say.

He nods.

I glance at the hole in the wall. Then I pull a stool over to sit before him. "Did August know about the passage?"

William's gaze narrows, and I brace myself for what's to come. I'm about to accuse his best friend of murder. Multiple murders.

I'd been so convinced Harold was the killer. But August fits better.

August.

My stomach twists just thinking about it. The man I met is charming and affable, and I genuinely like him. Yet I can't help but remember how cold he went when talking about Rosalind. I remember, too, what William said about him loving her too much. Obsessive love, jealous love, convinced his wife was unfaithful, unwilling to share Rosalind even with the career she obviously loved. A man determined to convince the world that his wife didn't die, that she merely ran away.

Their marriage disintegrating, August decided to rid himself of his wife, and for him, the answer was murder because he'd done it before. Done it and gotten away with it.

Years earlier, William had sent Cordelia away. Where would she go? To her fiancé. To August. Not for shelter, but to break off their engagement before she began a new life with her small fortune, the chance for a strong-willed young woman to be independent. August's ego and jealousy couldn't handle that, and he realized how easy it would be to kill her when William already expected her gone. Then August recruited Harold to bury her in the moors.

And Eliza? I remember her touching August's arm. Flirting with him right in front of his fiancé. William said Eliza had a crush on August. Had it been more than a crush? August certainly had a reputation for that. They have an affair, and Eliza threatens to expose it if he doesn't marry her. But marrying her would destroy both his reputation and his friendship with William, so he killed her.

As for Teddy, August seemed so gentle and kind with the boy, and I'd love to think that was his true face, but this would be another manifestation of his jealousy. He was jealous of William's attention, resenting the boy who threatened their time together, perhaps telling Harold he'd take Teddy up to see Cordelia and then showing him the passage instead.

Now, when I ask whether August knew about the passage, William's expression says he knows exactly what I'm thinking, and he's fighting not to snap back in anger at my outrageous insinuation.

"I could say that you are mistaken," he begins. "That I know August, and he is the last man who would do such a thing. But that is not a defense, so I will argue instead with logic. Yes, August knew about the passage, but when Teddy disappeared, he was with me. After he spoke to Teddy, we departed for Whitby posthaste. We didn't even learn of Teddy's disappearance until we returned that evening."

"August was also there the day Eliza disappeared. I saw her

go into the moors with Cordelia. He came out of the stables, where he'd been with you. He went after them."

"Yes, he did. He attempted to join their walk in hopes I'd come along, which would please Eliza. Yet Cordelia sent August back before they even reached the path. He was with me until my sister returned hours later after losing Eliza, and he stayed at my side as we searched."

I consider, and then I say, "Who took Teddy upstairs that day to see Cordelia?"

"Harold. And yes, I am certain of that."

I pause. Then I say, "I've seen Harold carry a body into the moors."

His head jerks up, eyes blank with confusion.

"I saw him bury a body out there," I say. "Then, I was led to it. That's what happened this morning. I was led into the moors to find the body of a young woman."

"Eliza." Pain shadows his eyes.

"I'm sorry." I lay my hand on his knee, and he takes it, our fingers entwining. After a moment, I say, "I'm sorry about Eliza, but I'm even more sorry that it wasn't *her* body I found."

His gaze lifts to mine, a line creasing between his thick brows.

I shift uneasily, the distance between us suddenly vast and awkward. I don't want to tell him like this. I want to climb onto his lap and hug him before I confess that his beloved sister is long dead. Yet that feels wrong, as if I'm inserting myself into a hole in his life. *She is gone, but you still have me.*

I inch forward until our knees touch. Then I clasp his hand tighter, his fingers warm in mine.

"I found Cordelia, William."

He rocks back so suddenly our knees bash, and I have to catch myself before I fall.

"No. That isn't—" William shakes his head. "I'm sorry if you found another poor girl out there. That must have been terrible. But Cordelia left. Harold took . . ."

The words trail off. Three beats of silence follow. Then his eyes meet mine again, dawning horror in them.

"Harold took her to the rail station," he says, his voice barely audible.

I don't speak. I can't. I just wait. I hold his hand in mine, and I watch him, and my heart breaks as I see him putting the pieces together.

"You say you saw Harold . . ." He swallows. "You saw him with a young woman's body. Carrying her into the moors."

"Yes."

"You found . . ." His eyes close, and he shudders.

"I found the body that Harold buried," I say softly. "He carried her wrapped in a shroud, and that is what I found. Her body in a shroud."

He shakes his head. "The private detective I hired . . . He was lying to me, wasn't he? Giving me scraps and promising more if I kept paying his fees."

I nod. "It was Cordelia I found, William. This was on her finger." I lift the ring I took from Cordelia's body, and the jewels catch the midday light. "Is it hers?"

"Yes. It's part of a set. I got the necklace for my future wife. She got the ring." He trails off, as if remembering *where* I found this family ring.

"Cordelia . . ." he whispers.

In the silence, his hand grips mine.

"You fought with your sister," I murmur, "and you told her to leave. You gave her money. You rode into the moors to get away from her, and when you returned, Cordelia and her things were gone, and Harold . . ."

"He was coming back from driving her to the rail station. Except that wasn't where he took her, was it?"

He shudders, and again, it takes every bit of strength not to go to him. I just keep holding his hand as his thumb strokes mine.

I know now what his fight with Cordelia was about. I've felt the answer prickling at the edges of my mind.

There is a third solution to this puzzle, and it's the only one that truly fits.

Did it make any sense that William sent Cordelia away after a simple argument? Didn't tell her to get out of his sight temporarily but gave her enough money to leave forever?

Earlier, this had poked at my mind, whispering there was something wrong with William's story, a whisper amplified by Cordelia accusing him of her murder. A whisper that wondered whether they'd fought, and there'd been a shove, a slip, some unintentional blow in the heat of the fight, and Cordelia died.

Yet there is another explanation. One I didn't see until now. And the more I think about it, the more certain I am, with horrible clarity, that I finally have the answer. The terrifying, tragic answer.

"You fought," I say softly, "with Cordelia."

He says nothing, just keeps staring into the past. He's lost there in a place I can't reach him. A place he's never entirely left.

"Can you tell me more about it? Please?"

His gaze lifts to mine, such dread and grief and sadness in his gaze.

"You need to tell me what it was about," I say. "I think you realize why."

He nods, the movement barely perceptible. Then he says, his voice a whisper, "I would never have let her leave if I thought she truly had . . ." He swallows.

"She killed Eliza, didn't she?" I struggle to keep talking, to wrap my head around this new theory. "Cordelia led Eliza into the heart of the moors and left her there to die. That's what you fought about. You'd found proof and confronted Cordelia with it."

He shakes his head. "Not Eliza. August."

"August?" I frown.

"Harold caught Cordelia taking rat poison from the stables. He warned me she had it. Warned me she was planning something, and it was not killing rats. I thought he'd lost his mind. And yet . . ."

He pauses. "And yet, I did not relieve him of his post, which proves that I was grappling with fears and doubts myself. The next day, Cordelia brought lemonade to the barn, a cold drink for August, teasing me that I could fetch my own. My suspicion sparked immediately. While bringing her fiancé a drink may seem a small and ordinary kindness, it was not the sort of thing my sister ever did. She was . . . ill-accustomed to considering the needs of others. Still, though, I told myself I was being foolish. I took the glass myself. As I lifted it to my lips, she knocked it from my hands. I quickly sent August away on some pretext. Once he was gone, I confronted her. She denied it, obviously, told me I'd gone mad. Then I demanded the truth about Eliza. I always suspected Cordelia lied when she said Eliza wandered off. Not that she'd hurt her intentionally, but that she'd played a trick. Snuck away to give Eliza a fright."

William continues. "That's all I thought it was. My sister's sense of humor could be cruel, and I suspected she'd played a trick that had gone horribly awry. I even felt sorry for Cordelia, saddled with that guilt. But after August . . ."

He takes a moment before continuing. "My accusation caught Cordelia off guard, and she accused me of wanting Eliza gone myself. She didn't admit to anything, but the way she said it told me the truth. That she was responsible for Eliza's disappearance. And that it wasn't an accident."

My stomach clenches, and in my memory, I see a girl chasing after her brother. I remember William's face when he spoke of Cordelia, exasperation mingled with affection. Seeing that, I'd longed for a sibling myself, an older sister to trail after, a little brother to dodge and spoil. Now, I see a very different look on William's face—a pain so deep it takes my breath away, and I steel myself for what comes next. What must come next.

I rise, take a deep breath and say, "Cordelia Thorne, I accuse you in the deaths of—"

An invisible hand grips my arm. I twist to pull away, but a jolt of electrical shock hits me. I dimly hear William shout, "Cordelia!"

and then I'm yanked through time and pushed hard, landing on the sitting room floor in my own world.

I leap to my feet and spin to face Cordelia.

"Cordelia Thorne—"

"No! Please." She lunges toward me but stops short, her hands hovering in front of my mouth, as if fighting the urge to physically silence me.

Tears shimmer in her blue eyes. "Please, listen to me. Just listen. He's tricking you. Accusing me of his crimes. If you name me their killer, Eliza and Teddy will never be free. This is their only chance. Please."

"I believe William."

Her ghost pulses, anger sparking, but she reins it in with a deep breath. "You love him. I understand that. I did, too. Deeply and completely. But I'm the one who confronted *him* with *his* crimes. That's why he killed me."

"And Teddy? Harold sent him up to see you. You said Teddy never knocked, but he did, didn't he?"

"No, he did not. Harold . . ."

She trails off, and I can see her mind whirring.

"Harold murdered him?" I say helpfully. "But if that's true, then William didn't kill Teddy, did he? *You* led Teddy into that passage, Cordelia. You pushed him down that hole, and closed it up and planted his coat in the moors—"

"A mistake," she blurts. "Yes, that was my fault. I showed Teddy the hole, and he leaned in too far. He died, and I panicked and put his coat by the bog."

"Maybe," I say. "Or maybe you pushed him, playing a cruel prank. You didn't expect him to die, but he did. So you planted his coat to hide your crime. No one suspected a thing, and Teddy was gone, no longer stealing William's time. Then, when you were older, you remembered how easy it'd been, and you set your sights on Eliza. You talked her into walking in the moors, and you told August not to follow. Then you abandoned her there."

"I did not. We became separated—"

"You abandoned her, hoping she'd become lost and die. An 'accidental' death, like Teddy's. Except Eliza found her way back, and you chased her in again and murdered her."

"I did not—"

"You murdered her. You have killed—or tried to kill—everyone who came between you and William."

"No!"

The word slices through the room, and Cordelia's face twists in rage. And with that look, a memory slams back, and I know I've seen this face before. On the ghost who woke me twenty-three years ago.

The ghost who woke me that night, the one responsible for my uncle's death, the one responsible for my stay in a mental hospital.

Cordelia Thorne.

36

Recognition punches me in the gut, and I double over, gasping. I look up to see Cordelia in her rage, and the memory flashes fresh and new, released from whatever bonds held it.

That night twenty-three years ago, I woke to Cordelia's face, twisted with hate and fury, spitting at me to leave William alone or she would destroy me. I hadn't recognized her at the time. When I'd caught glimpses of her in his time, she'd been a girl of ten, and this was a young woman more than twice that age. I'd looked at her face and seen William's bright blue eyes, only twisted in unimaginable hate, and it had terrified me.

I'd run from Cordelia, and my uncle had died, and my battered mind remembered the connection to William even when I'd forgotten it, twisting that into a subconscious certainty that my visits to William had caused my uncle's death. I'd broken some cosmic law, and my uncle had paid the price.

That wasn't what happened at all. I'd enraged a little girl by stealing her brother's attention, and centuries later, as a ghost, she'd seen me passing through time to visit him, figured it out and tried to stop me.

Now she's come for me again to turn me against her brother.

Only, I've uncovered her secrets, which means I can banish her forever, and she can't allow that.

"You killed Eliza," I say. "You killed Teddy, and you killed my uncle. Cordelia Thorne, I accuse—"

The air sizzles between us, and Cordelia disappears. I say the words anyway. When nothing happens, I begin to make my way upstairs, every muscle tensed for her to reappear.

I crest the top of the steps. As I do, something flickers by the linen closet.

I stop. Then I say, "Theodore Wakefield, I name you, and I name your killer as Cordelia Thorne. You are free—"

Teddy bursts from the closet door so fast I fall back. He stands there as clear as when I saw him outside with August, wearing the same clothing but streaked with dirt. He rushes at me. I stagger back, but he only catches my hand. I feel his touch as a faint chill, like being seized by a cold breeze. He tugs me toward my room.

"Quickly," he says. "You must go quickly."

I stumble after him through the door into my room.

He wheels and grabs both my hands, cold enveloping them.

"Now go!" he says. "Back to William."

He shoves me, and I tumble through time, landing in a room that, for a moment, is unfamiliar, as I stare at a writing desk.

My new office.

William's old bedroom.

No sooner do I think that than William roars downstairs. "Where is she?"

A voice responds, female and urgent, but pitched too low for me to catch more than the sound. I remember his last word as I disappeared.

Cordelia.

He'd seen her. As she was pulling me through, he'd caught a glimpse of her, and now she's with him.

"Either you tell me what you've done with Bronwyn—" he begins.

Cordelia cuts him short with protests that I'm fine. She swears I am, but he keeps asking, panic lacing his voice, the panic that something has happened to me, and he can do nothing about it because I'm no longer in his world.

I could be dead, and he won't even know it unless she tells him.

His worst fear come true.

As I scramble to my feet, Cordelia begins to tell him that she took me away so she could speak to me alone and set the record straight. But I wouldn't listen, and so now she's appealing to him.

"You killed me," she says. "You made a mistake. You thought I was a murderer, and you killed me for it. I understand why, but now you must listen—"

"I did not kill you." His voice has changed. Tension still raises it an octave, but he's fighting for calm. Threats haven't worked, so he's trying something new. I slow my steps as I listen.

He continues, "I sent you away. I gave you money and told you to get out of my life, and I have regretted that ever since. But I did not kill you."

Cordelia's gone quiet, drinking in his words like water in the desert. He regrets sending her away. He did not kill her. It is exactly what she longs to hear.

I stand poised on the steps, listening. This is what I need. Let him calm her so I can name her crimes.

William continues, "I thought you were alive, out there somewhere. Harold said he'd taken you to the rail station with your trunk, and I believed him. Others saw him driving the coach through the village."

"Because you paid him to do so. Constructing your alibi."

"I rode off after our fight. You saw me go."

"You must have come back."

"Must have?" He pauses, as if assessing. "You do honestly believe I killed you . . . because you didn't see who did."

"I went to the stable. I planned to ride after you, but you struck me from behind. I never awoke."

"You saw me ride off, Cordelia. I know you did. You were in the yard, and I all but rode you down."

"You pretended to ride off in a temper so you could circle back and kill me."

"*Silently* circle back? My saddle has enough metal to ensure anyone walking in the moors hears me coming."

I begin making my way downstairs, step by step.

Keep her calm, William. Please.

"I-I do not know how you came back silently," she says, "but you managed it. You returned and struck me over the head."

"That was Harold. When I came home hours later, you were gone, and he was returning in the coach. He said he had taken you to the rail station, and I believed him."

"Why would that old man kill me?" she says. "I was his mistress, and I did not ill-treat him."

"He saw you take the rat poison. He must have heard me accuse you of trying to poison August, and he decided I was wrong to send you into the world where you could hurt others."

Was that Harold's motive? Perhaps partly. But I think it was more about protecting William. Cordelia would never have left her brother. She still hasn't. She will forever try to come between him and anyone he cares for.

I will not say that. William has extended a kindness Cordelia doesn't deserve, and I understand why. What good does it do to rage? There is no punishment he can inflict on her. William only wants her gone. Gone from this place. Gone from our lives. If kindness will achieve that, then I'll swallow my gall and let her have this small mercy.

I take another two silent steps.

"You did not kill me?" Cordelia says.

"I could not, no matter what you had done."

A sigh and a rustle of fabric, then sobbing, as if she's collapsed against him.

"You can be at peace now, Cordie. That's what I want. For you to be at peace."

"I will be," she says. "*We* will be. Together."

A ragged, choking breath.

William. Gasping. Choking.

My feet tangle as I race down the steps, shouting, "Cordelia Thorne, I name you as the killer of Theodore Wakefield and Elizabeth Stanbury."

A thud from the other room, and I imagine William falling to the floor, getting his breath, as Cordelia disappears. Then another thump. A crash, and I realize that's not what I'm hearing at all. It's William, fighting for his life as his sister tries to kill him.

I run faster. "Cordelia Thorne! I name you as the killer of Theodore Wakefield! Cordelia Thorne! I name you as the killer of Elizabeth Stanbury!" The words come out in a rush as I tear through the parlor.

I fly into the kitchen, and that's where I find them. Cordelia holds William's face between her hands. Her body shimmers and glows, that glow snaking around William as he gasps, his eyes bulging.

I launch myself at them. I grab at Cordelia, but it's like seizing air, and my fingers pass right through to William. His hand slams into me as he fights to breathe, and I reel back as that glow pulses between them.

She's drawing his breath from him. Draining his life.

I grab to pull William away, but whatever she's doing, it has him as immovable as if he's been cast in cement.

"Cordelia Thorne! I name you as the killer of Theodore Wakefield and Elizabeth Stanbury and, my uncle, Stanley Dale!"

Cordelia staggers back, that glow fading, William catching a mouthful of air, like a swimmer surfacing.

"Cordelia Thorne," I step between them. "I name you as the killer of Theodore Wakefield and Elizabeth Stanbury and Stanley Dale."

She spins on her brother. "William . . ." she says, her voice breathy.

"I know what you've done, Cordelia," he says. "When I sent

you away, I wanted you gone from my life. I was a coward. I knew you were a danger to others, and I allowed you to live because I could not bring myself to turn you in to the authorities. I certainly couldn't do what Harold did. I said that I regretted you leaving. I meant that I regretted *allowing* you to leave."

"No . . ." she whispers.

"I knew what you were, and I knew what you'd done, and I let you go because I still loved you. I regret *that*."

"No . . ."

"I finally understand what you wanted. You had a fantasy of us growing old together. An endless childhood. Your brother looking after you forever, the two of us in this house, all my attention for you in a way it never was when you were a child. I am sorry for that."

He pauses. "No, I am sorry you *felt* deprived, but I know that I was kind to you, and I did find time for you. It simply wasn't enough. There was a hole that you needed filled, and I couldn't do it. I still cannot."

He steps forward. "Even if you take me, you will not have me. My ghost will remain, waiting for Bronwyn, so I may watch over her. If you kill her, I'll end my life and join her. Either way, you will not have me. What you *can* have is peace and a place in my memory still touched with the love I bore for my sister. Let us go, and you leave me with that."

Her figure wavers, and I think that's done it. She finally understands, and she'll take that and leave. But then she blazes back, brighter than ever, her face set as she says, "No."

"Yes," says a soft voice behind us.

I look over to see Eliza with Teddy beside her, holding her hand.

"Banish her, please," Eliza says. "You've freed us. Now, banish her."

Cordelia snarls and lunges at Eliza, who does not move.

"You can't harm us now," Eliza says. "For over a hundred years, you've terrorized us. Now, we have been named, and you can do us no harm. Your sins are named, too, and you have no reason and no *right* to stay here. So you will not."

She turns to me. "Banish her."

"I-I'm not sure how."

"Just say the words. Only the living can do it."

I take a deep breath. "Cordelia Thorne, I banish you from this house and from our lives. I wish you peace, but I want you gone."

"No!" Cordelia says, tears evaporating as she snarls.

She keeps snarling, beyond protests, just cursing and snarling like a wild beast. I say the words again and again and again . . . as she fades. Even when she's gone, her howling rage echoes through the room, and I stand there, paralyzed and tense, waiting for her to return.

"She's gone," Eliza murmurs. "May she indeed find peace whether she deserves it or not."

She turns and points at the ring. "Take that."

I shake my head. She grips my hand and, again, I faintly feel her touch, like a warm breeze brushing my skin. She propels my hand to the ring and presses it overtop.

"Yours," she says. "You earned it. As you have earned . . ."

Her gaze turns to William, standing there, silently waiting, tensed to fight again. She walks to him, still gripping Teddy's hand, and she looks up into his unseeing face.

"At least now I know it was not my fault I could not win you," she says. "Your heart was already taken."

"You've earned him," she says to me. One last smile for William. "Now be sure you earn her in return."

Teddy turns my way and gives a shy wave, and then they fade until William and I are alone in the room.

William stands there, confused and tense.

"Cordelia is gone," I say.

After a moment, he puts his hands around my waist, and we collapse into the chair. We sit there, holding each other as the hall clock ticks.

"I'm sorry," I say. "For what Cordelia did to you."

"I believe that's my line," he says with a wan smile.

I shake my head. "What you went through all these years is far worse."

He's quiet. Then he says, "I won't say it was worse, but yes, I've spent thirteen years tormented by thoughts of what I unleashed on the world. I could not bring her to justice, and I have regretted that ever since. Knowing now that she was never out there, never hurt anyone else . . ." He kisses my forehead. "It will be easier. So much easier."

I take his face in my hands, and I kiss him. I pour all my fear and my pain into that kiss. Fear for how close I came to losing him and pain for what he's suffered, that shadow cast over his life.

William says he was happy to stay here in self-imposed exile. I don't doubt that given the choice, he'd have spent most of his life at Thorne Manor. But how much of it *was* a choice? How many times had he gone to London, heard whispers of how he murdered his fiancé, and been reminded of the person he suspected had really killed her? Reminded of the fact that his sister was out there in the world, possibly doing the same to others?

"I am desperately sorry for everything you've been through," I say. "And I wish I could have been there to go through it with you. When I saw Cordelia today . . . I told you that my mother took me away after a breakdown here when I saw a ghost. It was Cordelia. She tried to drive me away then, and my uncle . . ." I swallow.

"Your uncle died," he says softly.

I nod. "Cordelia told me to stay away from you. After my breakdown, I blocked her exact threat, but some part of my mind remembered and kept me . . ."

"Kept you away from our house. Kept you away from me." His lips press to mine, and when he pulls back, he stays there, looking into my eyes. "Cordelia did everything in her power to keep you from me, but now she's gone, and no one is ever going to keep me from you again."

"She did everything in her power to *take* me from you. To take away everyone you cared for, everyone who loved you. I might not be able to make up for all that, William, but I'm certainly going to try." I take his face in my hands. "I will not leave. I promise you that. Whatever it takes, I will always find my way back to you."

"And I will always be here for you to find."

He lifts me, and carries me upstairs and lowers me onto the bed, already bending to kiss me and . . .

The room fades. It doesn't disappear as it always has. It's a gradual transition. I see him bending for that kiss, and I strain up to meet it, and his bedroom disappears, and another appears, superimposed over it. The last thing I see is William's eyes going wide as he sees me fading.

"Bron—"

That's all he manages. And then he's gone.

◈

WHEN I LAND ON THE MASTER SUITE BED, I'M NOT CONCERNED. I RUN to my own room, close my eyes and try to return. Nothing happens. I *feel* nothing happening, like ramming my head into a solid wall where before there had been a curtain.

I solved the mystery. I freed the ghosts and banished the killer and lifted the shadow from William's life. I accomplished my task, and so the way has closed.

The stitch has broken, and I'm on the wrong side.

37

I can't get back to William. I've tried, and I've tried, and I've tried. A month has passed, and the only thing that's changed is that I spend *less* than half my waking hours trying to return.

The ghosts are gone. Eliza Stanbury no longer walks my halls. Teddy Wakefield no longer slips from my closet.

Some shameful corner of my soul wishes I'd never set their spirits free. Wishes I'd left them in limbo if it meant that passage stayed open. Yet even that's pointless. If I hadn't stopped Cordelia, she'd have killed me and then taken her brother.

I don't allow myself to think that William is dead and gone in my time. He's alive in his, and that's what matters. He pens me notes, an avalanche at first, whereupon we devised a code for communication. To ask a question, he places two coins in a box. If I take both, the answer is yes. One, it is no. We've tried more complicated systems, but they fail, so we're left with this. I can only remove or leave what he offers.

He knows I'm desperately trying to return. So he writes, and he leaves me pouches of coins, and we pretend this is temporary. When autumn comes, he knows I must return to school, and so he'll wait. For how long? I don't know.

Yes, actually, I do.

I've found the records of his death. I had to for my own peace of mind. William Thorne the Fifth dies at ninety-three, an astounding age for the time. He dies unmarried with no heirs save a second cousin who inherits his estate.

So yes, William waits for me, and I long to tell him not to, but I can't. I'm not certain it would matter anyway. He hadn't planned any other life before I arrived. He has his manor house and his horses, and he'll be, if not happy, at least content.

I am not content.

I've tried every way to get back. I've curled myself into that bedroom floorboard space as if I can pull forth whatever magic it retains. I've stood in that wall gap where I returned the last time. Teddy Wakefield has been buried. So, too, has Cordelia, and if the villagers wonder how I found them, they only whisper about the new lady of the manor putting the spirits to rest, and they're pleased with me for it. It provides them with fresh stories and legends, which are always welcome.

I spend my days lost in a pit of rage and grief and despair. I devote what energy I have to caring for Enigma. Otherwise, I half-heartedly tread water just enough to keep my head above the surface. Eat just enough. Bathe just enough. Leave the house just enough. Even that's mostly for Del and Freya so they won't make good on their threats to summon the doctor. And it's for William, too. He lives for another forty-five years. I need to keep taking his notes from under that floorboard for just as long if I can.

Five weeks after the stitch broke, I wake, pivot straight for the floorboard . . . and vomit all over my bedside carpet.

I'm sick half the day, and then it clears, and I declare it food poisoning only to wake vomiting the next morning. Freya comes early and catches me with my head in the toilet, Enigma helpfully leading her to me. Over my protests, Freya summons the doctor.

"Could you be pregnant?" That's the first thing the young woman asks, and I laugh because I remember being her age and hearing those words at every doctor's appointment.

My throat's been sore for a week now.
Could you be pregnant?
I twisted my foot, and it's throbbing and tender.
Could you be pregnant?
There's this odd rash on my arm . . .
Could you be pregnant?

Michael and I had made a joke of it. That's what happens when you're a woman in her twenties—you're a walking pair of ovaries waiting to be seeded.

I haven't been asked that question in years. Now, though, when I start to laugh at it, I stop.

Could you be pregnant?

Oh.

I HAVE SPENT FIVE WEEKS IN THIS PIT, AND IT TAKES ONLY TWO LINES on a small white stick to make me leap—no, *vault* out of it. This body I'm neglecting is no longer mine alone to abuse. It houses the beginnings of a child.

William's child.

Five weeks ago, I fell into William's bed with no thoughts of protection from pregnancy or disease. He would have presumed I was a sensible and responsible adult, who'd taken care of that with my twenty-first-century medical magic. I didn't, and I've never, in my life, been so thrilled about making a mistake.

After Michael's death, I wanted his child even more than ever. I longed to discover he'd secretly bequeathed me that gift in a test tube somewhere. Of course, he hadn't because he would have considered that wrong and selfish, leaving me with a child when he wasn't there to help raise them.

Now, I carry William's baby, and I don't care whether I'll be a single parent. I'm joyful the way I thought nothing on earth could make me again. When our child is born, I'll find a way to let William know. I can give him that, and I can give him the gift of a daughter or son who'll be loved as fiercely as any parent ever loved a child. And I'll keep trying to cross over—I'll never stop trying.

I soldier through the morning sickness, and I mend my body and my mind. I commit myself to making a place here, not only in this house but in the community. Our child will spend their summers here, and I suspect High Thornesbury will be more their home than my Toronto neighborhood. So, I lay the foundation for both of us as I take a role in village life, volunteering at the library and visiting the pub for stories and gossip and non-alcoholic refreshments.

I have a standing pub date every Thursday late in the evening when Freya holds her "witching hour," regaling locals and visitors with folklore tales. That particular Thursday, I'm volunteering at the library until nearly eight, but there's enough of a gap before the pub night that I motor home for a late dinner.

I'm heading for the house in twilight when I catch a glimpse of a distant figure. It's Harold Shaw with his spade. I've spotted him many times since that last day, and I presume I'm still seeing a vision from the past—like Eliza in the moors—rather than his ghost. But that evening, he stands leaning on his spade, very clearly watching me. We make eye contact, and he turns into the yard and motions for me to follow.

When I catch up, he's digging in the wild edge of the property. His spade, of course, does nothing—his ghost simply goes through the motions. When he turns to look at me, I understand, and I hurry back to the garage and grab my own spade. I take care not to strain myself. I have a fetus the size of a rice grain inside me—I doubt I can injure it lifting shovels of dirt. The ground is soft, the digging easy. I'm still careful.

"Is it Eliza?" I ask as I scoop up another shovelful.

Harold says nothing. Doesn't seem to hear me. Just stares down at the spot, watching me dig. When my spade hits something with a hollow thump, he nods in satisfaction. I clear the object. It's a box, and at first, I think it's a casket, but then I see a trunk.

I bend and clear the dirt with my hands. There's a huge brass latch, and I struggle to undo it. Then I brace myself for what's inside as I yank it open and—

A trunk full of clothing.

I lift out a beautiful gown of green velvet. Something slides from it. A box. I pry that open to find antique jewels. I set the box aside and keep emptying the trunk. Clothing. It's all Victorian women's clothing until I reach the bottom and find a bag filled with gold bullion and bills.

I told her to leave. She said she didn't have any money. I emptied my safe—a small fortune—slammed it down in front of her and rode off into the moors. She took the money along with her things.

I look up at Harold. "This is Cordelia's. You buried it here."

His chin inclines in the barest nod.

"You didn't take the money or the jewels. Is that what you wanted to show me?"

A barely perceptible shake of his head, those eyes fixed on me. Waiting for me to figure it out.

"I name you Harold Shaw."

He nods, but says nothing.

"I'm not sure what you want," I say with some exasperation. "I'm not going to name you as her killer."

His gaze meets mine, and I feel the message there.

"You want me to? But you ended her life to protect William, and I'm not sentencing you to . . ."

I trail off. If I name his crime, do I sentence him to anything? I presumed I would, but what if it only releases him?

"You need me to accuse you," I say. "To name you as her killer so you can be free."

A nod.

"Thank you for showing me this," I say, nodding down at the trunk. "Thank you for not taking anything from it. Thank you, too, for doing what William could not, what would have destroyed him. He knows what you did, and he forgives you, and he is grateful. I am even more grateful."

His face stays stiff, but relief passes behind his eyes. The relief of a man who committed a horrible crime for all the right reasons but has never reconciled that.

I straighten. "I name you, Harold Shaw, as the man who took the life of Cordelia Thorne to protect the lives of others."

A soft sigh, the first sound I've ever heard from him. And with it, he fades into the night. I stand there, watching him go, and I sigh myself, an exhale of relief. It's done. Now, it's truly done.

I bend to the trunk. Museum-quality clothing, exquisite jewels and a small fortune in gold and pristine bills.

"Well, our child will want for little, William," I murmur. "Thank you, Harold."

I take the money bag, put the jewels in it, close the trunk and head for the house.

As I near the house, something flickers in my bedroom window, and my chest seizes. I hurry forward, and in that window, the drapes move, and I run faster, only to see an empty and open window, the new sheers fluttering in the summer breeze.

I take a deep breath and head to the garage where I return the shovel to its place and wash my hands. I should take the money and jewels inside, but I'm already late for Freya's pub talk. So I put them into the car trunk for now.

I put the top down on the car and drive out into the gorgeous summer night. I'm ripping past the house when . . . the front door opens.

I catch the movement out of the corner of my eye and hit the brakes. There, stepping from my front door . . .

My entire body seizes, as if convulsing. I don't breathe. I can't breathe.

William.

It's William, wearing his cutaway morning coat, with Pandora at his feet.

He raises a hand in greeting, and I want to hit the gas. Hit the gas and speed away as fast as I can, because I cannot be seeing this. I have not fallen back through time—I'm in my car, on my paved drive, looking over my ripped-up lawn, gardening project in progress. This is my world, and William is in it, and that's the cruelest trick my eyes could play on me.

Unless . . . I remember that movement in the window, thinking it was a ghost.

You want your William back? Here he is. Yes, the records indicate he died at ninety-three, but you changed history, Bronwyn. The butterfly effect. He died at thirty-eight, and you may have him now, a spirit in your world.

I'm frozen there, staring. William strides out as Pandora disappears back through the open door.

He keeps walking until he's twenty feet away. Then he eyes the car, his face creasing in a smile as he says, "That does not look like a horse."

And I cry. I burst into tears because I know this is not real. He can't be here, and I don't *want* him to be if he's a ghost, and so I pray it's my mind, snapping at last, showing me the thing I want most in the world.

When I burst out crying, he breaks into a jog, reaches into the car and wraps his arms around me. Solid, warm arms. My hands fly to his chest, and his brows rise at that. Then he realizes I'm pressing my hands to his heart, which beats strong beneath them.

"Not a ghost," he says.

I cry again, a huge wracking sob of a cry as I melt against him and he lifts me out of the car. He lowers me onto the hood, his arms still around me.

"How?" I manage.

"I have no idea. I was in your new office, and then the room changed entirely. It was most disconcerting." A hint of a smile.

"Then I realized it was your bedroom, which was a far more pleasant surprise. I went to the window and saw you returning from a walk. I came down the stairs, and I had a devil of a time unlocking the front door. By the time I did, you were speeding off in this beast."

He eyes the convertible warily.

"It's a car," I say.

"I imagined that. I believe, however, I will stick with horses." He squints at the garage. "Are there still stalls in there?"

I start crying again. I can't help it. I cry, and I hug him, and he holds me and kisses the top of my head.

"No matter," he says. "I'll simply need to build a new barn."

"You may want to start with a nursery," I say.

He gives me a blank look until I set his hand on my belly, and his eyes go wide.

I laugh. "Good news, I hope?"

"Of course," he sputters. "The best news."

He hugs me then, tight, before suddenly backing away in horror, looking down as if he might have crushed our child.

"I'm not *that* pregnant," I say.

He hugs me again, looser, breathing in my ear. "A baby. I can scarcely believe it."

"August did say we should start soon."

He laughs. "And so we did. Well, then, there's only one thing to be done. We must postpone plans for both a nursery and a new barn as we have a wedding to plan before your belly begins to show."

"William Thorne," I say. "That is the most romantic proposal I have ever heard."

"You're a widow," he says. "It's really more of a practical arrangement."

I sock him in the arm. When a sound comes from the house, we look to see Pandora holding Enigma in her mouth, meowing around the kitten.

"She's telling you she found her kitten," I say. "And you all can go home now."

"*She* can if she likes. She can go, and then she can return. The way is open now, for all of us."

"That would be . . ." My voice catches. "Amazing. But . . ."

"What if it's not? That is the question, isn't it? Perhaps we should stay here and not tempt fate."

That isn't an option. I know that. I couldn't stay in his world forever because I had a life here, and William can't stay here forever because he has a life there.

"The kittens all have homes," he says, as if reading my mind.

"Mrs. Shaw—" I begin.

"—is overdue for her retirement."

"Your horses . . ."

He's pensive for a moment before shrugging. "If given a choice between you and them, there is no question. They will find good homes, and I will buy new ones. If you doubt that we can pass freely between our times, we will stay here in yours."

Yet even that does not resolve the problem. More than once, I've fallen through time by accident, pulled back here when I didn't intend to cross. If William stays and we ignore the time stitch, I'll spend my life dreading the moment when he falls back into his own time . . . stranding me in mine with our child. Or, worse, *without* our child.

William lifts my face to his. "I believe the way is open. My gut tells me that it is. But we do not know how I crossed, and so perhaps it is unwise to take a chance."

I glance out at the property, and I imagine a figure holding a spade. A figure who's no longer there and never will be again.

I look up at William. "Just before you arrived, Harold showed me where he buried Cordelia's chest, and I realized he wanted me to name him in her death. To set him free. I did so, and that's when I saw something in the window. That's when you crossed over."

"The spirits all finally at rest, the stitch opened for us both. Permanently."

"I hope so. Perhaps we ought not to tempt fate, but . . ." I look up at him, heart slamming against my ribs. "I believe we must, or I'll go mad, waking every morning, fearing you've fallen back into your own time where I cannot follow."

He nods gravely and says, "Yes." Nothing more. Just "Yes."

We stand there, frozen in place. Then he scoops me up over his arms.

"Do we dare?" he asks.

My breath catches, and I want to refuse. I'm afraid, and I don't want to risk it.

I lift my chin and look up at him. "Yes, Lord Thorne. I dare."

"Then let us madly tempt fate together."

He carries me into the house and up the stairs. Once in my bedroom, he kicks the door shut behind him, to the protests of two cats. Then he gently tosses me on the bed and lowers himself over me, his face poised above mine.

"Now?" he whispers.

I nod, and I close my eyes as he closes his, bending to kiss me, lips touching mine as I imagine his room and—

I fall.

I literally fall, hitting the floor hard, William landing on top of me.

"Oww . . ." I say.

He lifts his head and peers about my new office, the two of us lying on the floor.

"Forgot there's no longer a bed here, didn't you?" I say.

"Damnably inconvenient."

I grin up at him. "Shall we return to the timeline *with* the bed?"

"I believe so."

He kisses me again, and I picture my own room and—

I land in my room—under the bed—William on top of me, crushing me.

"Bloody hell," he grunts as he wriggles out.

I laugh. It's all I can do, throw back my head and laugh as he tugs me from under the bed and lifts me onto it, and then I stop laughing as his lips press to mine, firm and warm and solid. His arms go around me, and mine around him, and the world stays where it should be, the two of us locked together in time at last.

THANK YOU FOR READING!

I hope you enjoyed Bronwyn and William's story. If you'd like to know what happened after **A Stitch in Time**, I have at least two more stories for you.

The first is a holiday novella, out now. **Ballgowns & Butterflies** is part of "Under a Winter Sky," an anthology of four winter-holiday novellas. My story features Bronwyn and William's first Christmas together.

The second is a companion novel featuring Rosalind and August. As you may have guessed, Rosalind didn't ride off a cliff or abandon her husband and infant son. Tentatively titled **A Twist of Fate**, this fall 2021 release tells the story of what happened to Rosalind when she disappeared…and what happens when she finally gets back to her family.

ABOUT THE AUTHOR

Kelley Armstrong believes experience is the best teacher, though she's been told this shouldn't apply to writing her murder scenes. To craft her books, she has studied aikido, archery and fencing. She sucks at all of them. She has also crawled through very shallow cave systems and climbed half a mountain before chickening out. She is however an expert coffee drinker and a true connoisseur of chocolate-chip cookies.

Visit her online:
www.KelleyArmstrong.com
mail@kelleyarmstrong.com

 facebook.com/KelleyArmstrongAuthor
twitter.com/KelleyArmstrong
instagram.com/KelleyArmstrongAuthor

CPSIA information can be obtained
at www.ICGtesting.com
Printed in the USA
BVHW031523090321
602112BV00005B/216